RIDERS OF THE LONG ROAD

Riders
of the Long Road

STEPHEN BRANSFORD

Doubleday & Company, Inc.
Garden City, New York
1984

FOR
Wesley John Bransford
&
Betty Ellen Penfield

Library of Congress Cataloging in Publication Data
Bransford, Stephen, 1949–
Riders of the long road.
I. Title.
PS3552.R326R5   1984   813'.54
Library of Congress Catalog Card Number 84–7984
ISBN 0-385-19399-8

"I believe the Devil and women will get all my preachers."

Francis Asbury, *Journal*

Contents

Contents

Prologue

ROOTS
OF BITTERNESS
1771

"SILAS!"

Emily's scream pierced Jonathan's slumber. He lurched upward in the chair, eyes fluttering open. Who was Silas? he wondered. And why had his mother called his name?

From the adjoining room came the rustle of the Negroes as they scurried about her sickbed. Their sudden activities threw darting shadows from the candlelit bedroom across the floor of the library where he sat. He stood to his feet, holding his breath, listening. The anguish of his mother's sudden cry had started his heart pounding against his chest. Outside, a flash of lightning illuminated the rain-wet cracks of the tall window shutters. Thunder rattled them an instant later.

"Em'ly . . . dear, dear, Em'ly."

Jonathan heard Chayta, the house slave, crooning to his mother.

"It's so dark," Emily complained.

But the boy could see candlelight flickering in her room. Why did she say it was dark? Here was another in a series of strange symptoms that clanged like warning bells of something dreadfully wrong. Jonathan had seen his mother through many illnesses in his twelve years, but through all of them, she had always been able to compose herself. She had been able to comfort his fears by her own quiet confidence. But not this time. She seemed to be sinking deeper and deeper into the fever, in a way that made him feel small and helpless.

Days ago he had seen a sudden change in her. She had become abruptly preoccupied with sad thoughts and memories, which she recited tearfully to Jonathan as he sat upon her bed. That had never been her way. She had always shown a sunny disposition, cheering those who came to bring her cheer. But now, suddenly, she began to talk in bitter tones, speaking of friends who had dealt treacherously with her long ago, of her painful childhood as an overlooked middle daughter in a family where being a son was the only thing that mattered. She talked of pets that had died, of the Captain's long absences—things Jonathan did not want to hear. During these dark utterances he began to excuse himself from the room. He felt dirtied by what he had already heard, and deeply agitated.

The gulf between mother and son widened further when, to his painful dismay, she became intolerant of his frequent requests for her involvement in games, books and discussions of interest to him. She sharply bid him leave her alone. Such things in the past had always pleased her during her long hours of convalescence. He painfully asked himself: What had he done to cause her to raise her voice at him now?

More recently she had succumbed to spells of unresponsiveness. These were most alarming and difficult to understand. He could see that her eyes were open, seemingly alert yet not reacting to whatever was in the room, including her own son. When she spoke from these trancelike states, her voice had a frightening quality. To Jonathan, it no longer sounded like his mother crying out, but rather as if a stranger had entered her body and spoke through her lips.

With these thoughts in mind, he hurried across the library, the heels of his buckled pumps clicking on the hardwood until he came to a halt just short of the bedroom doorway. The mounting dread in his eyes remained hidden behind the reflection of candle flames upon his spectacles.

"Where am I going?!" His mother sobbed from inside the room, then she moaned, "He's not here . . . where is Silas?"

Silas! The name rang in the boy's head again like a tolling bell. Curiosity won a battle against an urge to run away, and he moved forward into the bedroom. The house slaves had taken positions faithfully about Emily's bed. Chayta bent soothingly over her brow, Macaijah, Chayta's son, waited nearby with a tray of damp towels, while the graying old butler, Andrew, knelt on the near side of the bed, stroking Emily's hand.

His mother's eyes were open, unnaturally wide, staring upward. ". . . so dark . . ." she continued to murmur, "dark . . . dark . . ."

"Mother," Jonathan's tremulous voice broke in. Her head tilted slightly in response. He moved toward her, calling hopefully again, "Mother?"

"Silas!" she suddenly cried, eyes glistening with fever. She elevated her frail torso on the bed, her complexion glowing with an unnatural flush. "Silas, you have come!"

Jonathan was stunned. He halted mid-room. "Momma, it's me, Jonathan! I am not—" He could not finish.

This blue-eyed boy with the wavy blond hair, like most children, had experienced recurring nightmares of being lost, or chased, or suffocatingly trapped. But he had awakened from these dreams and experienced the great relief of finding his mother in her bed, ready and willing to hug away the night terror. But on this night *she* was the terror he felt. She stared weirdly at him without a trace of recognition, and called him Silas, a name he had never before heard.

Chayta, the wizened old Negro, moved quickly to his side. "It's the fever, sweet-hon," she entreated, her fingers nervously smoothing the lace of his gentleman-boy blouse. "She don' know what she see."

Emily stared blankly at her son as she slowly slipped back onto her pillow, depleted by the expended effort, the rapture-glow fading on her face.

Why did his mother not know him? Why, instead, did she call him Silas? Jonathan teetered momentarily. He felt torn up by the roots, losing his sense of up and down, as if he were being tossed through the air like a garden weed. He forced himself forward once again, pleading softly, "Momma?"

This time, at the sound of his voice, her eyes narrowed slightly. They began to focus, then gradually to moisten with tears from some deep inner well.

"Jonathan," she whispered, reaching for him.

His face contorted with relief and fear and need, and he rushed to her, crushing his head against her frail bosom, just as he had done so often when she was healthy. Clinging tightly there, the boy buried his cries close to his mother's heart, his fears poured from him in waves of relief. But the relief, so divinely felt, was short-lived. Her arms weakened and fell limply to her side. His cries grew hesitant as he sensed her slipping away again. He pulled her to him, tugging at her arms, trying to revive the response he needed from her. The boy continued pulling at her for a full minute, until his fears overwhelmed and choked him to silence.

From her gaping mouth, the sharp odor of bilious breath arose to fill his nostrils, nearly gagging him with its putrid stench. His stomach knotted and groaned. How could this be happening to his mother? Was it just an awful dream? Slowly, numbly, he began to let go of her.

In the year of Our Lord 1771, nearly every twelve-year-old boy in the American colonies knew what death was about, having seen it once or twice, but not Jonathan Barratt. His twelve years had been lived with his mother in the luxury of Bath, a settlement of wealthy residents, far from the harshness of colonial life.

The town of Bath had been built around a natural hot springs, which bubbled out of a hillside in the Appalachian foothills west of the confluence of the Potomac and Shenandoah rivers. The springs had been discovered by the young George Washington while surveying for Lord Fairfax in 1750. Washington recognized the health-giving merits of the waters and brought the location to the attention of Lord Fairfax. Subsequently, Fairfax, who owned some five million acres in northern Virginia, made personal use of the springs for bathing and for the treatment of his own ailments, but in 1756 he granted the site to the Virginia colony. He hoped that the springs would attract the civilizing influence of the wealthy class to this wilderness, and thereby increase the value of his lands. His hopes were realized.

Once it was made public, talk of the healing waters traveled rapidly up and down the Atlantic seaboard, especially through the circles of high society. On the emerging American continent, most of the inhabitants of the land were poor settlers, and to them, survival skills were all the luxury they could afford. They snorted at talk of a hot springs resort as if it were immoral. Since only the rich had the means to properly develop and enjoy the sensual comforts of the springs, Bath became their exclusive domain. With the cooperation of the colonial government, a group of investors laid plans for the building of a great and expensive inn at the springs. Finances were easily found for the popular project, and soon it was done.

The privileged few came from as far away as Boston, Philadelphia, and Baltimore to stay seasonally at the Bath House Inn, to dally about its healing spa, taste its fine wines, delicately prepared meals, and to enjoy its musical theater in the fresh blue mountain air. Soon a good number of the visitors began to build seasonal and permanent residences there. By 1761, when Boston sea captain Nelson Barratt decided to build a home for his wife and son in Bath, a population of over two hundred well-heeled patrons already occupied the haven year-round.

Captain Barratt sought out the hot springs because early in the third year of marriage, his young wife, Emily, had become prone to chronic fevers, a condition which came upon her unexpectedly following the birth of her first and only child. All of the current torturous, and therefore supposedly beneficial, medical practices were employed on her behalf—bloodletting, purges, and exotic herbal gruels—but nothing proved effective against her body's tendency to let the disease ravage her. Returning from a West Indies voyage, the Captain put into Baltimore to deliver cargo, and while in port took the two-day journey westward to inspect the springs of Bath. The entire settlement impressed him as a place where Emily could find the best available care for her condition during his long absences at sea, and immediately he arranged to buy a choice plot of land on the valley floor below the Inn. In all, he garnered nearly fifteen hundred acres.

Until that time, none of the residents of Bath had sought to buy the rich valley farmland which surrounded the town. Their interest had only been in the springs themselves, which bubbled from the hillside above the valley floor. They built their resort homes and shops specifically to be near the springs, and were thus arranged on either side of a single cobblestoned street which ran for three hundred yards up a gentle grade, ending beneath the wide veranda of the Bath House Inn. The hot springs and natural mud fumaroles housed within its earthen basement, were contained conveniently there by a series of rock-lined bathing tubs.

The shops and homes along Bath's main street were built close together like colonial town houses found in Philadelphia or Baltimore. This building style was totally uncharacteristic of this region, but was adopted not only to be close to the springs but also because the residents did not wish to waste their expensive leisure time caring for large grounds and cumbersome houses. Most of the buildings were constructed of quarried limestone and milled timber, materials found in abundance nearby. Cherry, oak, and hemlock trees bent their branches of blessing over the street, while in trim garden boxes tulips and roses bloomed by the doorways, splashing the happy scene with vivid color. Small alleyways ran between the buildings, providing tiled walkways that led to a series of elegant floral and herbal gardens running the full length of the street behind the buildings.

Within two years of his initial visit, Captain Barratt had completed a great Georgian mansion in Bath, the first of its kind, located to one side of the junction of the Martinsburg road and Bath's picturesque main street. The main entrance to the house looked westward, over those fifteen hundred acres of rich Barratt valley lands, while to the south Bath's main street could be seen sloping upward to the Bath House Inn.

Spectacularly, the mountain behind the town of Bath was topped with a perpendicular granite escarpment which looked over the small valley like a huge protecting sentry. Northward, through a notch in the valley wall, the Appalachian ridges and valleys could be seen descending, in a series of smoke-blue layers, toward the distant Potomac River. Any visitor to Bath in those days was impressed by the sheltering nature of this resort community. Even the foothills seemed to favor it with their surrounding arms.

But Jonathan's shelter had been even more complete than that which wealth and nature could supply. During his sea captain father's long and frequent voyages, his mother poured her abundant energies into her only son. Whatever neglect or frustration she may have felt from her marriage to this absent captain, she more than made up for in attentions to Jonathan, providing for him a haven from peers, menial chores, boredom, unpleasantness, and the common frictions that produced earthiness and survivability in other children. As a result, Jonathan felt things other boys his age did not feel. They had had such sensitivities dulled by obligatory lessons in manliness and the disappointments of life.

Each time young Jonathan grew brave enough to attempt play with the children of Bath, they soon discovered that this odd boy could be made to cry by simple name calling, which was a delightful weakness to exploit. The gentleman-boy could be startled easily, hurt easily, repulsed by crude playground rhymes and demonstrations of cruelty to insects and small animals. In a matter of a dozen minutes of play, Jonathan would become the butt of every physical, verbal, and singsong gibe, of which children are the most cruel practitioners.

His only weapon, the one which worked wonderfully well with his mother and other adults, was to employ the voice of reason with his tormentors. But reason won no respect from children. It invited only more unreasonable responses. Perhaps it reminded the others of the natural spontaneity they no longer allowed in themselves, and made them the more determined to eliminate it from this "crybaby."

The most sensible way out for Jonathan, then, was retreat. He withdrew from the streets and playgrounds of Bath to the Barratt mansion and the haven his mother had created for him there. He could easily engage his mother in the endless pursuit of games and books and conversations, which continued to nurture and protect him—and thus put off the day of reckoning when he would endure the rites of passage in the ugliness of life. A process that was to begin with the death of his mother.

Most colonial children Jonathan's age had already known the numbing effect of seeing family members die, especially young brothers or sisters, for large families commonly lost one or two, to a variety of unexpected causes. Some simply ceased to breathe in the night as if carelessly brushed by the Death Angel's wing. Others screamed against their fevered discomforts, red-faced, spending their tender lungs until their crying thinned to a whisper and the futile, silent coughing, after days or weeks, finally failed to expel the smothering fluids. They were found in their beds, bluish and still in the morning.

Some children fell into meandering streams, some tumbled from haymows, others toddled beneath the flashing hooves of whip-driven horses. Some merely stood, as curious children do, behind rank mules as they were being backed from their stalls.

Families would gather to lay their stiffened bodies to rest in the ground behind log houses, bathed in tears and lovingly tucked with embroidered linen, there to wait for Resurrection Day in small oaken boxes. Scripture was read. Mothers clutched sodden handkerchiefs and resolved bravely to bear more children. Mothers often died in childbirth.

Uncles died, and cousins too, from working long past fatigue with rust-poor tools until they accidently severed fingers. Days later they could only watch helplessly as fiery tracks moved up their forearm, igniting an inner hell which burned them down slowly, organ by organ, in a stew of toxic poisons. They died bloated and discolored but cradled by wives, sons, and daughters who cleaned, caressed, and cared for them to their last breath.

Death came to neighbors and total strangers in duels, hunting accidents, at the hands of savages or outlaws, in public executions, by consumption, cholera, or "fever years."

So it was that most colonial twelve-year-old children had seen death enough to know how to meet it. They knew at least how to grieve with their loved ones, to touch the waxen face of the corpse and to sense in that touch the profound absence of the spirit. They knew how to say goodbye and to bury. Eventually the trembling, timid questions also ceased, and the children went back to play. When death was well met, childhood hardened into something less fanciful, less sensitive, but perhaps more fitting for life in colonial times.

But Jonathan Barratt of Bath had not taken that course. He was yet uninitiated, still ready to run and thrash like a well-hooked trout and throw himself against the unbreakable cord of death, which, he would soon learn, holds every living thing.

Jonathan raised up from his futile embrace to look at his mother's face. Her gray, blistered lips cruelly reminded him of other days, of the warm kisses she had once bestowed upon him. Her eyes were sunken in their sockets like an old woman's. Her head trembled from side to side and her lips formed whispered dream-words he could not understand. She was lost to the world again, and to him.

Chayta also watched, her hands resting on his shoulders. Then, on some mysterious inspiration, she bent forward, placing her ear close to Emily's moving lips. The wizened Negro began to repeat the faint words as she heard them: ". . . in . . . the . . . Bible . . ." She raised up thoughtfully and repeated in a puzzled tone: " 'in the Bible' . . . that's what she says."

She turned and sat on the bed, pulling Jonathan before her. She reached for a towel from the tray Macaijah held.

"Jonathan," she said, "maybe Em'ly likes us to read to her now. For her comfort." As she spoke she deftly wiped Jonathan's nose and cleaned the lenses of his spectacles.

Macaijah watched this with a look of veiled disgust. He was fourteen, two years older than Jonathan, and it was his opinion that his mother treated Emily's son with too much gentleness and partiality. To him it looked ridiculous for a boy of Jonathan's size to have his nose wiped. But being a slave boy, he never spoke such things; they just smoldered unnoticed in his eyes. He and Jonathan had been well-matched playmates in their younger years, but recently, as Macaijah's body had taken a sudden spurt of growth, he found the young master of the house far too timid and physically soft for his own outdoor, rough-and-tumble interests, and to avoid him he found many ways to be occupied away from the house.

Chayta set Jonathan's spectacles once again on his nose.

"You go bring us the Bible from the bookshelf now," she said. "Macaijah, help him with the ladder. Hurry now." She pushed Jonathan toward the door.

Macaijah waited near the door with his hands folded and eyes averted until Jonathan passed through, then the slave boy followed him out.

Chayta turned quickly to Andrew. "Watch the door," she whispered sternly. "Keep the boys out."

"What be?" he asked.

"Outside," she urged. "Quick!"

Andrew made his way to the door, looking constantly back over his shoulder with a puzzled expression as he went. But he did as she asked.

Chayta leaned close to Emily, stroking her forehead with a damp towel. "Emily," she pleaded in a low voice, "please don't talk about Silas no more. That was long ago. He's gone outa your life for good, now leave it be."

"Silas?" Emily called weakly.

"No, Em'ly." Chayta took her strongly by the jaw and turned her head so she could see into her fevered eyes. "Silas is gone, Em'ly dear. Don't speak of him no more."

Andrew peeked around the doorway in time to see Emily, staring back at Chayta uncomprehendingly, whispering, "No more?"

In the library Macaijah steadied a stepladder for Jonathan. The boy climbed the ladder and removed a large leather-bound Bible from a high shelf. Climbing shakily down again, he lost his grip and the volume dropped with a thump onto a richly inlaid secretary below the ladder. Dust sprang up around it.

He climbed the rest of the way down and then moved to the secretary. He studied the cover of the book for a moment. He had seen it on only one or two other occasions when his mother had, for the purpose of a moral lesson, used it in tutoring him. Emily had called it "the Book of Books." It looked impressive, he thought, with its fine leather cover and gilt-edged pages. He wondered at what wisdom such a book might contain.

Macaijah handed him a feather broom.

He unclasped the ornate latch that held the covers together and with the feather broom cleaned the dust from the gold-gilt pages. Using both hands, the boy opened it. Its pages fell open to a place where a letter and a clump of wildflowers had been pressed for safekeeping.

It seemed such an insignificant thing; the boy found a letter. He passed it by at first, like a bothersome scrap, a thing of no concern to him, especially not at this troubled moment. But in time the words written in that letter would drive him on a quest he would never have otherwise chosen.

He pushed the letter and flowers onto the opposite page and beneath them found a scripture passage that was underlined in ink. This was something good to read, he reasoned. His mother, no doubt, had drawn these lines beneath the passage, pulling the pen carefully and slowly across the page as he had seen her do with other books. These must be important words.

He promptly took up the open Bible at that very page and carried it to his mother's bedroom. Macaijah followed.

His mother lay now in a broken sweat, trembling, whispering as before. Jonathan came forward to stand beside her bed, holding the large book in his arms. The old Negro woman nodded that he should proceed. Jonathan straightened himself and began to read as his mother had had him do on so many happier occasions, from other books. They had loved to sit for hours in the Barratt library, reading, Emily reading passages to him, then the boy reading to his mother. At those times, he read proudly, with a strong, confident voice. But now his voice trembled like an unnerved schoolboy's.

" 'The earth which'—"

He stopped to swallow an ache in his throat.

" 'The earth which drinketh in the rain which cometh oft upon it, and bringeth forth he . . . herbs . . . meet for them by whom it is dressed, re . . . ceiveth blessing from God. But that which beareth thorns and briers is rejected'—"

"Rejected!" Emily cried suddenly.

Jonathan's head jerked up, startled. His mother's voice had become strangely, piercingly clear. "I am rejected!" she cried again.

"No, Em'ly. Course not," Chayta said quickly. She took the Bible from Jonathan and fumbled through it for another passage.

"Psalms," Andrew whispered helpfully over her shoulder, his gray head nodding.

But Chayta suddenly spied the letter which lay on the page opposite the underlined scripture. Her eyes widened momentarily. She glanced quickly again at Jonathan and noted with relief that he seemed unaware of her discovery. The letter was addressed, in Emily's most ornate hand, to someone named Silas Will.

"Oooooh, Lord God!" Emily began to wail and sob.

"Momma!" Jonathan pleaded. "What did I do?" He looked at Chayta. "Did I frighten her?" he asked.

"Oh, no. You did fine. Just fine, hon."

"I did not!" he said with angry alarm. "I made her cry. I don't want to read more."

Chayta had closed the letter back within the Bible and had already found a new place for him to read. She placed the book gently in his hands again, pointing to a new passage. "It was just the wrong page, sweet-hon, you didn't know. It made her think of something bad . . . but here. Here is something real nice to read. Right there."

He hesitated, glancing again at his mother's agony-ridden face. He couldn't deny the horror in her voice when she had called, "I am rejected." She had cried out just when he had read that very word "rejected" on the page.

He looked down to where Chayta's finger now pointed to new words on another page. There were no underlined markings here. Perhaps it was a safe place to read.

He took a deep breath, then began, " 'The Lord is my Shepherd, I shall not want, He maketh me to lie down in gree'—"

"I AM LOST!"

Emily's shriek shattered the timeless peace of the Psalm and the Bible fell from Jonathan's hands to the floor.

"Momma, I'm sorry," he cried, ending with silent tears streaming from his eyes.

"I am lost," Emily moaned.

"You are no such a thing, Em'ly! You are not lost," Chayta rebuked, motioning Andrew to reapply the damp towel which had fallen from her thrashing forehead.

"Why is she lost?" Jonathan wailed.

"She is not lost, sweet—"

"She IS!" Inside he knew it was true. He could feel her panic when he looked at her, he could hear it when she cried out. She was being thrown away, rejected, like an uprooted weed. "Because of me," he cried, "because I read it."

"No, no, no," Chayta said sternly, turning and shaking him by the shoulders. But he tore himself from her grasp and bolted from the bedroom.

Chayta followed as far as the door. She watched him fling himself into the Captain's chair across the library, curling his body against its large leather arm. At length, she turned away, not knowing what more to do or say.

"Macaijah, get the Bible," she said tiredly. "No, wait. I will get it." She hurried to where it lay on the floor and bent down to pick up the letter which had fallen free. She examined it briefly again, shaking her head sadly, and tucked it again into the page of the book. She stood then and crossed the room, placing the Bible in Macaijah's arms, carefully reclasping it for him.

"Take this back to the shelf," she said, "then you stay with Jonathan for a while."

He nodded and turned to the library.

As he entered the library he was glad for the task of returning the Bible to the shelf. Something in Jonathan's anguish had inspired a new sympathy in Macaijah. But something about the way the boy refused to be comforted also threatened to sweep Macaijah away on a despairing tide. He did not want to feel out of control, so he ignored the younger boy crying in the chair and ascended the stepladder in an overly busy manner, taking his time to reinsert the Bible on its shelf. Soon he was finished, however, and had nothing left to do but descend. He descended slowly.

Jonathan continued to sob.

At the foot of the ladder Macaijah stared at the boy numbly, feeling helplessly sorry. For once the uninhibited emotions of his childhood friend seemed right. He also felt Emily's deathbed terrors were real. He quietly stepped toward Jonathan, standing just behind his shoulder. Maybe he had not been fair in his feelings of resentment for Jonathan, Macaijah thought. Maybe, especially on this night, he needed the kind of tender attention Chayta showed him, and maybe it was always right. Slowly then, he reached out toward Jonathan, but instantly had to blink back the stinging moisture that leapt to his own eyes. He paused, his hand poised awkwardly in the air, then quietly turned away and sat in a chair across the room.

Midnight passed. A grandfather clock ticked from a darkened corner of the library. Macaijah snored evenly from the chair near the fireplace.

Jonathan was fully awake. He had finished his crying and sat quietly erect in the armchair, resting his head against its tall leather back. His eyes were fixed upon the large oil portraits of Captain Barratt and Emily, hanging side by side on the wall. Outside, a cold April rain pattered against the side of the house. Jonathan chilled and shuddered as if the rain had swept unhindered through the walls.

For the first time in his life he longed for Captain Nelson Barratt, his tall, silent sea captain father whose strong name anchored the Barratt household, even though he was seldom seen. Until now, Jonathan could find all his needs met in Emily, and her gifts to him had been wrapped in warmth and tenderness. But he needed something less easily destroyed. He sensed his need for the Captain's strength now, that cool strength to stand tall above childish helplessness, to be silent in the midst of a howling storm, to be calm instead of terrified, to steer a steady course while others were blown about by confusing questions. As he continued to gaze up at his father's portrait, placed so commandingly above the room, he wondered where the Captain was on this night? Was he sailing to the West Indies, or to the Maine coast? Why wasn't he here? Especially now.

The Captain kept Emily in Bath for her health while his life was lived on the high seas, and when on land, mostly he was found at his portside quarters, far north in Boston. For these reasons Jonathan had come to accept that things were not as happy between his father and his mother as they might otherwise have been, and that he could expect to see his father in Bath two or three times in a year, and then for only brief visits.

A long ebony case rested upon the fireplace mantel. It reminded the boy of the Captain's last visit at Christmastime, some four months previous. He had drawn up to the house then, in a black landau pulled by a handsome team of six matched dappled grays. As the Captain stepped from his carriage, wearing a deep blue cape which swept from his shoulders to the ground, Jonathan was waiting expectantly by the edge of the drive. Macaijah had seen the coach approaching on the Martinsburg road and had run to warn of its imminent arrival.

"Avast, young man," Captain Barratt greeted gruffly, as if addressing a midshipman.

"Hello, sir," Jonathan replied in a small, worshipful voice.

Jonathan saw him as a towering man, though he was only of medium height. His facial features exuded such natural power that he seemed taller, even to grown men, when receiving a first impression of him. His eyes were large, gray, and wide-set and his nose came down in a straight line between them. His jaw was squared and jutted slightly forward. He despised the fashion of wigs, though his forehead was balding. His nearly black hair fell finely to his shoulders and he wore trim sideburns of gnarled black and gray whiskers. Wherever he turned his gaze, he commanded what he looked upon, just as his portrait in the Barratt library commanded the room, though he seldom occupied it.

The Captain stretched his cramped legs outside the carriage and surveyed with pride the Georgian mansion he had built for Emily. It was an imposing structure built of red Virginia brick, which set it handsomely apart from most of the other limestone-and-timber structures in Bath. The Barratt mansion rose three stories above the ground, counting the row of five gabled attic windows protruding at regular intervals from the long slate roof. It also contained a full basement, used for storage of firewood and surplus household furniture. On either end of the main body of the building, four massive chimneys towered above the roof, drawing the heat of the several fireplaces upward through the building. A fine ornamental cornice trimmed the edge of the roof all around. On either end of the main building, two symmetrical single-story wings extended outward, housing the slave quarters on one side, and on the other, the kitchen, or "galley," as the Captain liked to call it.

Captain Barratt seemed ever proud of this symbol of his wealth, which sat so conspicuously apart from the rest of Bath. But to Jonathan, everything about the house seemed too large. It made him feel small and insignificant. Everything, that is, except his mother, for as long as she occupied any of the fifteen main rooms of the mansion, she had the ability to fill that space with a feeling of home. Apart from her, it was not so.

"I have a gift for you, Jonathan," said his father, suddenly turning his attention back to the boy. "Uncle Ethan," he called over his shoulder, "see to that box."

"Yes, indeed," replied Ethan.

Uncle Ethan was a round-bellied little man with shoulder-length brown hair which he kept constantly hidden beneath a powdered periwig. He was an opposite of Captain Barratt in the wearing of his wig, and also in that his tastes in clothing were rather colorful and gaudy. He was slowly emerging from the door of the coach when the Captain asked this favor. That is as far as the little man carried his air of pomposity, for he never, ever failed to jump to do the Captain's bidding. And so he had immediately scrambled about and leaned inside the coach to find the gift.

He was called Uncle because he *was* an uncle. He was Emily's own brother. He had been a friend of Captain Barratt's since before he had married Emily. In fact, it had been Ethan who introduced the Captain to his sister, precipitating their courtship.

For the dozen years of Jonathan's life, and longer, Uncle Ethan had been the principal conductor of the portside business of Barratt Enterprises. This odd pair of entrepreneurs had turned out to be a near-perfect match. Ethan's sense of how and where to invest the wealth which Captain Barratt won from the sea had multiplied his fortune. Always, when the Captain made port, the two were inseparable, analyzing their finances, planning, deciding future directions for Barratt Enterprises.

Ethan emerged from the carriage with an oblong ebony box about one foot in length. He carefully stepped down the carriage ladder with the help of a uniformed Negro driver, and then marched past Captain Barratt to present the box to Jonathan with a pleased and polite bow. Jonathan was breathless with anticipation. His father had always brought gifts of fine furniture and furnishings for the house whenever he arrived in Bath, but as far as Jonathan could remember, this was the first gift Captain Barratt had given that was just for him.

"Shall I call Mother?" Jonathan asked, wanting to share the joyous moment.

The Captain looked puzzled. "No. No, you may open it now. Go ahead, young man. It's for you."

The boy's hands trembled and his fingers repeatedly slipped as he attempted to unlatch the small brass clip that held the lid. At last he opened it, and inside, lying in a bed of navy-blue velvet, found a brass spyglass. He gasped and a thrill swept through him. He immediately imagined himself standing on the deck of a tall ship beside his father, using his spyglass to sweep the horizon for signs of land or buccaneers. He looked up, full of gratitude, but his sparkling blue eyes darkened with disappointment. He found that the Captain had already become distracted by Uncle Ethan, who pointed in the direction of the Bath House Inn. Several new buildings were under construction along either side of the cobblestoned main street.

"Ah, yes," said the Captain. "We should do well to invest further here. How do you think it will grow, Ethan?"

"Fat," said Ethan with a pleased chuckle.

Jonathan encountered a vague empty feeling inside of himself. The Captain had turned away from his special moment of discovery to share something with Ethan.

For the next several days, as always during mealtimes when the Captain was at home, his mother doted on Jonathan's accomplishments. She commented proudly on every small piece of conversation that fell from his lips. She asked him to recite poetry, rules of etiquette, and stories and to demonstrate his grasp of mathematics and of the household ledger. She delighted in setting up demonstrations of his cleverness with characters and numbers on a hornbook, and beamed nothing but pure pleasure and enthusiastic applause for all of his performances.

But at Christmas, Jonathan had become bewildered by it all. As far as he could tell, his mother was alone in her delight over the progress of his educational and social skills. His father was merely tolerant. And he also noticed—because every time he noticed it he felt that empty feeling again—that by contrast, the Captain's eyes danced with pleasure when speaking with Uncle Ethan about any kind of business matter.

The boy had no understanding of the dimension of estrangement between his father and himself, because he had little true understanding of the estrangement between his father and his mother. What he did not know was that early in their marriage Emily had fallen in love with another man, one of Captain Barratt's own friends, that during one of the Captain's long voyages the friends had become lovers, and that Jonathan was the son of that relationship. No one had told him. Those who knew, Chayta and Ethan, had been sworn to secrecy on the matter.

Neither did Jonathan know of the subsequent duel fought between the Captain and the other man, upon the Captain's discovery of the awful matter, and that the Captain had spared the man's life only on his word of honor that he would banish himself forever to the wilderness. Had Jonathan known, he was still perhaps too young to understand what these seemingly innocent sessions of mealtime praise meant to the Captain. That each time his mother effusively praised his accomplishments she was really reminding her husband that though he had won a duel, he had lost her. Emily was not his, neither was Jonathan. In the way that was most important, both of them belonged to another man, a man who bore the name, Silas Will.

In the library Jonathan continued to gaze up at the portraits of the Captain and Emily. On this night all he knew was that his mother was sinking into an awful fever and that he had increased her torment by opening a book of terror, not meaning to, but nonetheless reading words which caused her to scream out, "I am rejected . . . I am lost." She was the one person in all the world who had been unswervingly faithful to him, but now, in her hour of desperate need, Jonathan had not been able to return an ounce of comfort.

His eyes roved up and down the portrait of the Captain. He wanted the portrait to speak to him, to tell him how he could make up for his terrible mistake, but he found no help from the picture on the wall. Neither from the Captain's nor from Emily's. From their tall gilded frames, they only dwarfed him and stared in cold silence to some place in the room far above his head.

A tear escaped his eye. Suddenly he became aware that his mother had grown quiet in her bedroom. In fact, he had heard no disturbance for quite some time. He got up stiffly from his chair in the library and tiptoed, so as not to disturb her slumber, to the open doorway.

Chayta drew in her breath sharply. It was still hours before dawn. Emily was suddenly dead. After weeks of faithful care, after many watchful nights and days, she had slipped away undetected, in a moment when Chayta had turned her back.

"She was jus' here," Chayta explained as Andrew sadly nodded, "then she was gone."

Gently Chayta closed Emily's staring eyes, kissed her lifeless brow, then slowly stood erect, unaware that Jonathan was watching from the doorway.

"Let's wait to tell sweet-hon," Chayta continued to Andrew, "let him sleep." But then she saw him. She moved carefully toward him in the doorway, reaching, not knowing how much he had seen or heard.

He stared blankly ahead, then suddenly wheeled and bolted away. Shortly thereafter the main entry door was heard to swing open and the sounds of rain and wind filled the library. Chayta ran from the bedroom, crossed the library and into the entryway. She called out of the open door, "Jonathan!" Then she hurried to the closet, flinging on her coat and scarf.

Macaijah arose sleepily from his chair near the hearth. "What is it?" he asked. "Jonathan's momma . . . ?"

"She died," Chayta replied, "and Jonathan ran out. We mus' find him now before he catches his death. Macaijah, you look in the barn, and after that, see to the springhouse. Andrew, stay here. He might return."

Andrew nodded.

She quickly took a small lantern from a nook by the door, scampered to the fireplace and lit it with a splinter of wood from the coals. Andrew let her out of the door, then reclosed it. Soon Macaijah entered the room with coat and cap.

"Check the stalls real good now," Andrew advised. When Macaijah was gone he returned across the library to take up a pose, hands clasped behind his back. Waiting.

Outside, Chayta crossed the semicircular drive to the cobblestoned main street of Bath. Stopping there, she cupped her hands and shouted up the hill between the dark silhouettes of the buildings that lay below the Bath House Inn.

"Jonathan!"

The rain muffled the call. Still she paused and held her breath, listening for a reply. The only sound she heard was the falling rain and distant thunder. Calling frequently, stepping on the slippery cobblestones, Chayta made her way to the top of the hill. By this hour all of the street lanterns were dark. Steadying herself by grasping barren rhododendron and lilac bushes, the old black woman managed to circle the Bath House Inn, holding her lantern high, calling frequently for Jonathan. She completed the full circle and paused to rest at the top of an embankment where the road ended at the entrance to the Bath House Inn. She called again, but as she did, her feet slipped from under her. She thumped down, sliding a dozen yards down the embankment, coming to a halt in the muddy road. Holding her lamp high, she called again, hoarsely.

"Jonathan!"

This time as she held her breath she heard the faint gurgling of the hot springs behind her in the darkness. Chayta turned and saw that the cavernous Bath House door stood open beneath the shelter of the Inn's main entry porch. From where she sat in the road she could smell an acrid trace of steam. She struggled to her feet and hurried to the door, leaning into the darkness.

"Jonathan," she called, softly this time. Her voice boomed back to her, rebounding from the low ceiling and wet walls within. She stooped and entered. At first her glowing lamp illuminated only clouds of ghostly steam, pungent with sulphur and salt, swirling past her and out into the rain. But then a faint chattering sound drew her deeper within. She glided through the mist toward the sunken baths where in the soft circle of light thrown by her lantern she found him.

He was naked. His fine clothes lay in a muddy pile by the pool. He had curled his knees to his chest beneath the steaming water. Only his rain-soaked head showed above the surface. The lenses of his spectacles were coated white with fog. Sweat stood in droplets on his forehead and upper lip, yet he shook uncontrollably, teeth rattling from an empty coldness in his bones.

Chayta hesitated, watching him for a moment, wondering what to do. Then, suddenly, she knew.

She hung her lantern against the wall, removed her scarf, her coat, unlaced her mud-caked shoes, and stepped into the pool. She waded slowly toward him, weaving back and forth like a tall ship, humming across the water the rich tones of an ancient African lullaby. The sound vibrated against the walls, filling the whole room with its wordless eloquence. Down into the warm depth she went, her arms reaching about him, gently pulling him close. There she began to rock him, slowly, almost imperceptibly, to the gentle rhythm of her tune. Occasionally she cupped her fingers into the healing water, lifting and pouring it slowly over his head. It washed down in warm streams beneath his clouded spectacles like the tears he could no longer cry . . . childhood had hardened into something less sensitive.

Part I

BATH
1784

"My spirit is grieved at so much vanity as is
seen here at Bath, by the many poor careless
sinners around me. The living is expensive."
Francis Asbury, *Journal*

1

The Exhorter

He rode the saddle with a zeal absent in the leg-weary animal beneath him. The horse, a solid brown mare, had been a gift, given to him days ago by a wilderness homesteader on the breaks of the Monongahela River. "Let her make her own pace o'er the mountains," the farmer had cautioned. If the rider had heard, he'd forgotten. His thoughts were not of the horse but of the road. He breathed the dust of it with relish, body bent forward, in contrast to the drooping mare, who ambled haltingly, pushed to the limits of her endurance. A second riderless horse carried packs and dragged a heavy travois behind.

As the man urged the tired mare forward with clucking noises and nudges of his heels against her flanks, his piercing blue eyes pondered what seemed to be his destination for the night. Pondered it with a good deal of wonder, for he had never seen its like. Ahead, magically serene in the gathering gold of sunset, lay the cobblestoned haven of Bath. Beneath the blankets of the travois shivered a fevered companion, in much need of the ministering waters of this place.

"We'll go to Bath, though it be a place of wickedness," the rider had said earlier that day.

He was no ordinary traveler, not a trader or a soldier, not a road-weary homesteader. This was a man with burning secrets, a man to whom time and death and danger mattered little next to the passion of his heart. For he believed the burning secrets he carried could change men into sons of God, and he knew, beyond doubt, that no greater sense of purpose was attainable for a man in this life. Inside, he swelled with a sense of importance, he was chosen, and the good news he was chosen to share was that any man, *any* man on earth, could become as he was . . .

He was an "exhorter," more commonly called a "riding preacher," ordained by the man who now lay fevered in his pack. By whatever commission, by whatever miracle of transformation in his own life, he believed God had personally summoned him to a life-and-death ride against evil. From the look of him, he had already tested that calling on the back trails of the wilderness and he looked ready to test it again in Bath.

Wild Kentucky was his home, where poverty and extreme difficulty were the norm. A steadfast and vigilant resistance to evil was the only virtue there. As he gazed with amazement upon the wealth of Bath, he saw at once that leisure and frivolity were the way of life here. To him, such purposeless living was an unforgivable sin in a world where too many people despaired, murdered, starved, and died from a broken will to live.

He seldom left his wilderness circuit where he saw a clear vision of his enemy at work in the principal form of whiskey. On the frontier, whiskey was a quick way for poor folk to make gains in trade. Kentucky farming took its toll in long, unpredictable seasons with only modest returns for backbreaking toil. There were constant dangers from hostile Indians, changing weather, outlaws, and few opportunities to relax. Whiskey was a popular item. But the gains of trading whiskey were temporary and in themselves intoxicating, eventually sapping the strength and vitality of any person who dealt with it. And without exception, somewhere along the chain of production and trade, whiskey became, irresistibly, the poor man's paradise. The Kentucky exhorter declared only one way to paradise: "Let God lead you to Heaven, and be drunk with the Spirit of God for joy in this life."

He rode slowly past the Barratt mansion until the hooves of his mare clacked against the first cobblestones of Bath. His mare stopped, stepped back gingerly, and dipped her head to sniff the strange surface. A fast-wheeling chaise suddenly clattered from behind them and surged up the incline, startling both trail horses, causing them to shy from the noise and the sudden motion. The rider was quick. He reined his mount sharply back so that his hand could shorten the lead rope on the second horse.

"Whoa," the man rumbled in his throat. It was part reassurance, part threat, for he would do what was required to control a horse.

He urged them both forward, up the slope toward the Bath House Inn. Their heads and ears were now erect with fear. They pranced, eyes rolling, but they obeyed. The sound of the travois scraping over the individual stones kept them on edge.

Two things appeared remarkable about the dust-covered man to passersby strolling the street. The first was his dress, the black long-tailed coat and black slouch hat, clothing that singled him out in any crowd as a man of God. The second was that underneath the hat the man's head was crowned by a remarkable mane of red hair. It was thick and combed back, falling in a loose cascade over the collar of his coat. A thick two-day growth of red beard sprouted from his jaw.

Midway up the hill the rider passed an elderly couple strolling arm in arm in the direction of the Inn. "Good evening, Preacher," the man said.

"Evening," returned the man in black, though he did not like to accept the title "preacher." Had his companion not been so ill he might have stopped in the road to inform the man of his true station as an exhorter. In his mind a preacher was a man who stood in a pulpit. This exhorter had never been in a church. He was a former Kentucky renegade who had met the preacher now ill in his pack on a Carolina road after some dark and bloody business had brought him low. The encounter with the "riding preacher" had dramatically changed him from renegade to follower of Christ. The same preacher who had led him to this transformation had one year later laid hands of prayer upon his head, ordaining him an exhorter, and commissioning him to spread the message of that transformation to the men and women scattered across the wilds of Kentucky.

The distinction between an exhorter and a preacher was not one that needed to be clarified to the non-clergy, but the red-haired preacher did not much recognize the difference between clergy and laity. And because he had ridden only his solitary circuit in Kentucky, he had developed more than one eccentric practice that would have disappeared in time, under the refining influence of a religious organization. For now, he was a one-of-a-kind lay preacher, schooled only by a voracious schedule of prayer, Bible reading, and the study of a book of rules by the Church of England's great horseback preacher, John Wesley. The book was appropriately called *The Discipline.*

The preacher who lay ill in the travois, had been sent to America by John Wesley. Upon arrival, Asbury found few Wesleyan preachers in America who were willing to leave the safety and comfort of their pulpits to go where the people were in dire need of the civilizing influence of the gospel. So he took to a horse, began making converts, and as soon as he observed one of his converts filled with the Spirit and purposes of God, he ordained him to ride as a layman and preach while the enthusiasm of the conversion was still fresh. These ordinations were subject to the weaknesses of the flesh, yet the preacher knew of no better way to have a spiritual awakening in America than to send forth those whom the Spirit seemed to select, taking the chance that at least some of them would become true men of God. Thus the designation of "exhorter" was employed, ordaining men to ride in order to demonstrate the legitimacy of their calling in actual ministry until such time as the fruit of it spoke for itself, good and bad.

The red-haired man and his companion neared the Bath House entrance. From the veranda above came the sound of chamber music and gentle conversation, as evening diners enjoyed a meal in the light of sunset.

The rider leaped powerfully to the ground, gathered the reins of both mounts, and tied them securely to a hand-carved hitching rail to one side of the bath door. His hand trailed for a moment along the handsomely carved rail. He had never seen its like. Then he walked back to the travois and gently lifted his fevered companion from the blankets. The man protested that he could walk, but the red-haired preacher refused to hear it. He carried him across the tiled patio and into the darkened basement of the Inn.

Mr. Lemuel Simkins stood behind a counter as the caretaker of the baths. He was a slightly built, soft-looking man who cared for the cleanliness of the place like a doting mother-in-law. He was just about to cross the floor and close the outer door for the evening when the preacher suddenly made his appearance.

The rugged man with the sick man in his arms walked past Simkins as if the bath belonged to him.

"This man is sick," boomed the red-haired preacher. "Might he be nursed in your waters?"

"Well, sir, I *was* closing the public door—"

"Closed!?" The preacher wheeled indignantly, causing the man in his arms to clutch his head with a cry of pain. "But this man is sick."

"Silas, please calm yourself," said the sick man weakly.

The preacher called Silas helped his sick companion to a bench beside the pool.

"I shall be calm," Silas growled, "when this man has taken a new measure of himself." He glared at Lemuel. "The Great God made these waters. Can you deny them to one so in need?"

"Perhaps, you may—"

"And do you have any idea *who* this man is?" Silas continued, moving toward Simkins.

Simkins shook his head.

"Then you must meet him. Come."

Silas walked over and steered the now submissive caretaker to the bench where his preacher companion weaved back and forth in a fevered state. "This is Francis Asbury, sent to America by the great John Wesley. This man has seen John Wesley with his own eyes. Heard him preach to forty thousand souls in the great rock quarry of London."

"Thirty thousand," Asbury corrected.

"Well. It was a goodly number," Silas affirmed. "And this man is here to reform this nation of dead religious bones."

"A preacher of the gospel," Simkins murmured knowingly.

"Not just a preacher. This preacher was sent from God and the anointed hands of John Wesley. Now who are you?"

"Well, I . . . I am Lemuel Simkins, sir, and you are welcome to make use of the bath, though it is now closed to the public."

"God be praised!" Silas shouted. "Changed in the twinkling of an eye. We are welcome."

"Thank you, Mr. Simkins," Asbury said, and smiled wearily. "I apologize for the inconvenience . . ."

"None required, Reverend Asbury. We . . . we do not see many preachers here."

"None like us, I am certain," chuckled Asbury. "Had my friend Silas here been in Bethlehem, our Savior would not have been born in a manger. Silas would have *made* room at the inn, I do believe."

"I am rebuked," Silas said.

"Mildly so. Mildly," Asbury replied with a dismissing wave. He leaned painfully against the back of the bench. "Silas, I fear I have a bad one this time. I shall need more time than I can afford."

"Then I shall stay to assist you."

"It would be good if you could fill my engagements for the next few days and report back to me."

"I am not one to speak for you, sir."

"Well . . . you can carry my greetings and news of my delay by this illness. If you could visit the O'Sheas and the meeting place near Martinsburg, it would serve me well."

"Then I will do it." Silas fell silent, thoughtful.

"I . . . know this will delay you on your return to your circuit. Perhaps you can find another good man to stay and assist me here."

"No. Think no more of it. I can ride harder to make up the time on my return to Kaintuck, but I am here to do your bidding in God's own name."

When Silas spoke of Kentucky, he always used the affectionate word many of the locals used, "Kaintuck." It distinguished those who chose to live there from those who merely visited or had never been there.

Lemuel Simkins closed the door to the outside and concluded his sweeping of the floor at the entrance. He politely approached the two conversing ministers.

"I shall leave the bath to your private use," he offered. "If I can serve you, I will be upstairs in the Inn."

"We will be in need of a room tonight," Silas said, "and a room for several days for Mr. Asbury."

"I shall see what is available, Mr . . ."

"Will," said the exhorter, "Silas Will."

2

The Burial

"Mark my words, Tibbet," Ethan Stillwell said, nearly shouting to be heard over the rumble of the carriage. "Bath is the very Eden of Virginia. An oasis, it is. A few months there and you will never wish to leave."

"Lord knows I shan't want to return to Boston over this same horrid road." Tibbet winced noticeably as the carriage bounced across a deep rut. His thin, stiff body seemed ill suited for carriage travel.

Ethan smiled at his secretary's discomfort. With a plump, bejeweled hand, he patted Tibbet's arm. "Travel does broaden us, now, Tibbet. Isn't that right, Jonathan?"

"Hmm?"

The young man seated across from them looked up startled at the question. His mind had been far away, the blue eyes behind his spectacles were glazed with daydreaming.

"Travel, Jon. I was saying travel broadens the soul. Do you agree?"

"Yes, certainly, Uncle." Jonathan searched the road outside the window for signs of Bath. He removed his spectacles and wiped them against the lace of his shirt. Fourteen days of late-spring travel, even in the well-built landau carriage, had left his eyes red from the constant road dust.

The years in Boston had matured him. His face was lean and handsome, the blond hair had grown thick and wavy about his temples. His eyes, though tired and reddened now by travel, peered about with alertness and curiosity. He was tall and slender, a sturdily built young man. But there was about him an air of hard-bitten skepticism, as though he questioned everyone and everything that came near him, putting everything in the world to some kind of test. He was determined not to be easily fooled, nor to follow any path without deliberation. To a fault, for in most cases he remained immobile. Full of motivation, but unable to act decisively.

"It won't be long now." Ethan spoke heartily, nibbling from a bowl of nuts beside him on the seat. "Barratt Enterprises will flourish here in Bath. The decision to move our enterprise from the sea was a stroke of genius. Genius, I say, Tibbet. You have to know that with the Captain's passing we were left with a great void of expertise on the high seas. But now, ho, the future looks stupendous with this young man at the helm." Ethan nodded toward Jonathan.

Jonathan tried to smile. The decision to move the business had been none of his doing. He merely signed the papers shoved before him by his uncle. He found his mind hostile to business, ever wandering. His inheritance hung like the weight of a chain around his neck. If only the Captain had lived, he would have taught him the purpose of it, he thought wistfully.

But Captain Barratt was gone. He died in the war, a casualty of the tragic battle of Penobscot Bay. The funeral of a hero, Jonathan discovered, becomes a grand occasion. Ethan made all the arrangements. Naval leaders and officers of the Continental Army crowded Boston's fine Old North Church. There were lengthy eulogies. In a quavering chant the elderly rector praised the Captain's heroism. Jonathan, then in his first year at Harvard, learned from the memorial service that his father had never done anything quite so fine as dying. Apparently the lifetime of loss by the members of his neglected family counted nothing next to the single moment of sacrifice when the Captain made his decision to fight and die for the nation's cause. So this was religion, intangible, personally useless, Jonathan thought bitterly. Every stranger in Boston seemed to accept religion's comfort in the loss of a hero, but Jonathan found it no comfort at all in the loss of his father.

But this was as he expected.

He craned his neck out the window of the carriage. Behind them, a team of strong English shires pulled a lumbering wagon. Two slaves trotted beside the vehicle, urging the horses forward. On the wagon bed lay a burnished wooden casket. Jonathan was taking the body of Captain Barratt to Bath. Though the Captain had never lived in his mansion in Bath, Jonathan believed in the rightness of his decision to exhume his body and remove it there. The Captain should lie beside Emily for as long as they were to be remembered on earth, he reasoned. And it comforted the young man, after all the years of absence, to at least have the memory of his father home from the sea.

"Tell me, sir," Tibbet asked anxiously, leaning toward Jonathan, "what sort of activity will I find in Bath? Other than business, I mean." He had grown obviously worried, having not seen much in terms of civilization since leaving Philadelphia four days earlier.

"Fine dining," Ethan interjected.

"Horse racing," spoke Jonathan.

"Ah yes, men of sporting blood," Ethan added. "I mean for the gaming side of it, you understand."

"I think my uncle is better able to answer you on this."

Ethan scowled. "Well, I think not, but let me say this about young Mr. Barratt here; he wouldn't say so, but he has been quite a horse racer. Legendary in Bath. After his mother, my dear sister, passed on, God rest her, well, we came back here every summer until the year Jonathan entered Harvard and had a wonderful time at the track. Jonathan riding. Me betting, of course. But what a rider he was. And what a horse. We still have old Merlin at the stable, I understand."

"I do hope so," Jonathan said, a thought that stirred some feeling in him.

"Ah, what a homecoming. What a fresh beginning, eh, Jonathan?" Ethan rubbed his fingers over the golden head of his cane with anticipation. "The direction we are moving is exactly the direction your father and I set down many years ago. 'Land, Ethan, land is the future,' the Captain used to say to me. 'When I am no longer able to sail the sea, I want to walk the land that I own. I want to walk for days and never see the end of it,' he said. Well, from Bath we will see it come true. But you will be the one to walk it, Jon. More land than you ever dreamed about."

"What do you mean? Just how much land do we own?" Jonathan asked.

"Jon, you signed the papers. We invested a good amount of our profits from the sale of your father's ships in land."

Jonathan nodded. It had been another legal document shoved in front of him by his Uncle Ethan.

"Providence has been kind to us, Jon. Had we not concluded the sale of the fleet at the time of the blockade, when Boston Harbor was still free—my Lord, Jonathan, we were able to name our price then. And only months later the British were on the run and American trading ships were bursting from every harbor. So many of them they could be had for a jig and a rum ditty. Sometimes I'm ashamed to admit how much we profited from that war. But who am I to question the hand of Providence? As the scripture says, "The Lord maketh poor, and maketh rich . . .""

Jonathan stared at him curiously. "Uncle Ethan, do you truly believe God made us rich?"

"I merely quoted a scripture, Jon. I was not planning to debate the matter. What can I reply?"

"I mean no disrespect, Uncle. Do you think God made us rich? Or did my father, Captain Barratt, and you make us rich?"

"What difference would it make?"

"A great deal of difference, I think."

"What difference?" Ethan plucked a nut from the basket.

Jonathan frowned, lost in serious thought. "Well, if God made us rich, then all that we have belongs to God, does it not?"

"I'm no student of the matter, Jonathan. And I have no Harvard training with which to debate the likes of you, but I believe who it belongs to makes absolutely no difference as to who spends it." He chuckled.

Tibbet tried to suppress a smile. "Well, now," he said eagerly, joining in the discussion. "It seems to me that if Providence gives wealth, then Providence may also take it away. The Lord giveth and the Lord taketh away, I believe it says somewhere in Holy Writ." He leaned back against the seat, satisfied with his own erudition.

"Tibbet, now, too much religion is a dangerous thing." Ethan yawned, waving a jeweled finger at his secretary.

"No, Mr. Tibbet has said something curious to me," Jonathan said solemnly. "Look there, at those people." He pointed out the carriage window. "Did God take the wealth from them and give it to us?"

They were at that moment passing an oxcart, one of many they had seen on the road. Such pitiful families, with their meager belongings piled high about them, were becoming common sights on the road. A growing mass of displaced people was fleeing the populous, inflation-ridden cities in the chaotic aftermath of war.

"Well now, Master Jonathan." Tibbet seemed flustered by this question. "Well now, sir, what is your own opinion about that?"

"I don't believe much of anything at all about it," Jonathan said flatly. He looked away from Tibbet, signaling that the disputation had ended, but he had lied. He was thinking very much about it.

He continued to imagine the multiplied hardship of these poor families in their carts. Each of them dreaming of land they could have and hold. Of something they could point to that fed and supported them, and displayed the results of their expended effort in tangible form. Land, self-reliance, independence, opportunity, these were the dreams they carried. As of today, they had their slow-moving oxen, their ill-fed children and unkempt clothing. They had cuts, rashes, insect bites, dysentery, and infections from exposure to the elements along the road. What's more, they still had a long way to go.

Ethan watched his nephew, trying to read his troubled thoughts. Trying to find a way to turn him to a brighter side of conversation.

"Do you know, Jonathan, these settlers are the key to our future wealth?"

Jonathan turned to him with a puzzled look.

" 'Tis true. Our Kentucky land scheme looked forward to this day when there would be such a great number of people moving to the frontier to settle it. With each settler passing through the Cumberland Gap, our investment in the land out there increases."

"These poor folk raise the worth of our land?" Jonathan asked rhetorically.

"Jonathan, it's the way of the world." He raised his hands helplessly. "The muscle of the poor, and the mind of the rich."

For as far back as Jonathan's memory reached, he could recall the occasional passage of oxcart families through Bath. When he was younger he had had no questions about it, but now he did. He remembered a particular time, though not the exact year or date, but an incident when he and his mother encountered such a family in the cobblestoned street above the mansion. The dirty-faced woman in the cart had stared at his mother as she stepped from her coach at a seamstress's shop, sporting a fringed silk parasol, a flowing, bustled hoop dress, and piles of ringlets upon her head—Jonathan could still see the poor woman as she pulled and brushed her fingers suddenly through her own impossibly matted hair, snarled with knots and pieces of sleeping straw. How painful poverty must be, Jonathan reflected. No doubt, on their journey to the promised land, when the poor passed through Bath they suddenly felt much poorer.

Meanwhile Ethan squirmed his rounded buttocks in the seat. The jovial atmosphere in which he flourished had fled the riding compartment and he wished to retrieve it.

"The Barratt mansion is a fine place, Tibbet. Of course, Jonathan"—he now turned back to his nephew—"you will find some changes."

"What changes?"

"Oh, many. For example, I have hired a new administrator for the Bath estate. An overseer, to be exact. He was to have arrived some months ago, and should already have things well in hand. A Mr. Bard Dugin. He comes with high recommendations."

"An overseer, Uncle? What could he possibly oversee in Bath?"

"That, of course, is well . . . part of the change. We have the farms under development now. Of course, this was as your father had always planned it." Ethan fidgeted, realizing he had failed once again to tilt the conversation in a jovial direction. In a tone of humble protest he addressed Jonathan. "You agreed, Jonathan, that I should have full charge of Barratt Enterprises. Now, of course, if at any time you should disagree with my decisions, you are certainly the one to—"

"Of course, Uncle," Jonathan replied.

"So I have, well . . . I have brought in more slaves."

"You have?"

"Oh, yes. Mr. Dugin has had no choice but to use them to develop our land, Jon, why else? Your father left you with some of the choicest lands in Bath. When we're finished, why, the Barratt holdings will be the envy of all the colonies."

"Certainly," Jonathan said, but he frowned as he said it. He saw no reason to change the land that surrounded the mansion. The meadows were green and pleasant in summer, the hillsides covered in every variety and shade of wildflower. But he decided not to resist his uncle at this moment. Barratt Enterprises seemed alien to him, but it was beginning to be impressed upon him that it was a growing thing. It did not diminish simply because he paid it no mind. It grew, and his name was on it.

"Bard Dugin has done a splendid job, wait and see."

"How is he with the slaves?" Jonathan asked.

"Why, as any overseer would be, he is firm. But that is quite normal. Indeed, necessary."

"You say 'firm.' I wonder about Macaijah," Jonathan mused, almost to himself. He had noted the hard calluses on the slave's hands as he drove the carriage that now drew them toward Bath. Most painfully, Jonathan had been aware of an impenetrable curtain that had grown between them. Macaijah addressed him as "master" and turned away when Jonathan tried to talk with him about the things they both had once enjoyed, horses, the races in Bath, and hunting with hounds in the surrounding countryside. Macaijah's dark, brooding attitude was disturbing to Jonathan.

"What do you wonder about Macaijah?" Ethan asked curiously.

"He seems, well, changed."

"Ah yes, well," Ethan began comfortingly, "life changes, Jon. Sooner or later we all face it. You have changed in the years since you left Bath. And Macaijah has changed. And, of course, all of it is not completely to our liking."

"But more slaves . . ." Jonathan turned the subject back to Ethan's earlier disclosure.

Just then the carriage lurched to a halt. Ethan and Tibbet bounced against each other on the seat. Jonathan leaned out the window to see why they had stopped.

A strange sight met his eyes. A man in black with red hair and a ragged growth of red beard stood in the road waving at them.

"What kind of man is that, Uncle?" Jonathan asked.

Ethan straightened himself from the unexpected jolt. Then he looked out the window.

"Ah, well, it's one of those meddling riding preachers," he said, mildly disgusted. "They seldom come so near Bath."

"A riding preacher?"

"I heard one preach once," Tibbet volunteered eagerly, "from a street corner in Boston, do you know. It was a rather loathsome sound he made, too. They call them enthusiasts. They follow the heretic Wesley in England."

"Wesley? A heretic? We did not consider him so at Harvard," Jonathan replied.

The red-haired man approached the carriage. "We have a delay," he said.

Jonathan opened the door and climbed out. He was happy for the chance to stretch his legs. Ethan and Tibbet clambered down the ladder behind him. Ahead of the carriage, a two-wheeled oxcart sat askew in the middle of the road, one wheel having broken from the axle.

"Sir," the preacher spoke to Jonathan. "Sir, we'll have the cart moved shortly. If you care to lend a hand . . ."

"Perhaps Macaijah would get the other slaves to help this man," Ethan suggested to Jonathan.

He nodded his agreement. "Macaijah," he said, "have the others help out here." The big slave sat in the driver's seat of the landau. He wore a driver's uniform and it would not seem proper for him to undignify it with a great deal of physical exertion.

It was then the preacher noticed the wagon following behind the carriage. He started toward it, as though to warn it also of the blocked road ahead.

"That is my wagon, sir," Jonathan said.

"Aye? Is it?"

"Yes. It carries a casket."

"God be praised, my lad. This seems a sign of God's care to have sent you to us in this way." He smiled slyly through the red whiskers. "It is a good day for any of us when the Lord uses us to do His will."

Jonathan frowned, suspicious of the gentle pressure he sensed in the man's voice.

"You see, young man, the wagon ahead bears the same sad burden as your wagon there. But without the same dignity. A grandmother, a godly woman to her family, has passed to glory. They have carried her body for two days now, not wisely perhaps, but out of love, you understand? Their desire is to bring her for a proper burial in Bath. As you see, the wagon is broke . . ."

"I do see that."

"If you would allow us to place her body on your wagon, that would lighten our load and allow the other members of the family, the children especially, a more comfortable ride. We would follow on, of course, as soon as we fix the wheel."

Jonathan saw no way to deny the request, though he cared little for the idea of a second body on the wagon with his father's casket. He wondered that this rough preacher spoke to him so easily about it.

"You may do what is helpful," Jonathan said, then turned back to the carriage and climbed in to wait. "My slaves will help," he said over his shoulder.

" 'Twon't be necessary," said the preacher. He hurried forward to where Jonathan's slaves worked to remove the broken cart from the roadway.

He reached within the cart and easily pulled out a stiff, blanket-wrapped corpse that had been propped in one corner. He carried her past the landau toward the trailing wagon. After tying her securely next to the Captain's casket, he walked forward again, stopping to speak to Jonathan at the window.

"Thank you, kind sir," the red-haired man called cordially. "May I repay your kindness by saying a prayer at the graveside for . . . for your departed one?" He gestured questioningly toward the wagon bearing the coffin.

"There'll be no praying," Jonathan snapped.

The preacher eyed him carefully but his face didn't betray his thoughts.

"God is merciful," he declared flatly, backing away as if lightning might fall from the sky on the carriage. He donned his hat and walked forward to assist the others with the broken oxcart.

Two hours later the caravan rolled into view of Bath. Jonathan watched the Barratt mansion come into sight and beyond it the familiar street leading up to the Inn. As the carriage wheels ground across the crushed limestone of the circular drive, Jonathan looked up at the magnificent Georgian house and felt a stir inside. He was glad to be home.

"Jonathan! Macaijah!"

Chayta ran down the steps of the porch as Jonathan stepped from the landau. She hurried toward him clutching her apron and dress. Andrew stood in the doorway. Jonathan welcomed Chayta's warm embrace with a smile. Macaijah climbed down from his perch on the driver's seat and stood to one side, waiting. It seemed he had to wait overly long for his mother to end her embrace with Jonathan.

"Oh, Jonathan. We waited and waited so long," Chayta went on. "This is your house now. Yours."

At last, Chayta looked toward Macaijah. He shrugged and turned away toward the luggage.

"Macaijah?" she said, moving to him and stopping him by the arm.

He whirled and looked at her with a small, masking smile. She did not smile back but scolded with her eyes. Then she silently returned to Jonathan and resumed her brightness.

"What is wrong here, Chayta?" he asked.

"Oh, I jus' don't know anymore, hon. I guess we all want things to be like they used to be when . . . Oh, but you are home now, Jonathan. It's a new day." She suddenly spied Ethan showing Mr. Tibbet to the house. "Welcome to Bath, Uncle Ethan," she said cheerily.

Tibbet's mouth gaped as he beheld the Barratt mansion. He now believed everything Ethan had promised him about Bath. He gazed up at the portico with wonder. In the meantime, Macaijah had begun to lift down trunks of luggage from the landau.

"Some things should not. change, Chayta," Jonathan said. "Macaijah, tell me about Merlin. Is he still the fastest horse in Bath?"

Macaijah grunted his answer as he lifted down a heavy crate, "No horse outrun Merlin, master."

"D____, Macaijah," Jonathan complained, emboldened in his speech to him in the warm presence of Chayta. "I haven't been gone so long as for you to forget my name, have I?"

"No, Master Jonathan," the slave replied, and continued on.

"You don't mind him," Chayta said, taking Jonathan's arm and leading him toward the house.

Jonathan was puzzled. "Tell me about the new overseer, this Bard Dugin."

Chayta would not look at him. She glanced away toward the house. "Come on in here, Jonathan. Andrew will be pleased terribly to see you."

Even Chayta seemed farther away from him now. With vague apprehension, he followed her into the house.

Jonathan was up at daybreak. After breakfast, he met Macaijah at the barn.

"Is everything ready?" he asked.

"Yes."

Without speaking further, they lifted the tools Macaijah had gathered and hiked up the hillside behind the house. The sun bore down on the morning fog, tearing it loose from the sheltering valleys and sending it slowly spinning skyward like floating shreds of cotton. The cool silence of the awakening countryside bathed Jonathan's face, refreshing him with the chill of morning. These hills were beautiful to him after so long in Boston. They awakened a sense of wonder at nature's unbidden loveliness, a wonder sharpened now by his sense of death's indifference.

The two men continued their climb in silence, their destination was a tiny white-fenced graveyard at the top of a ridge that overlooked the town.

Emily Barratt lay buried there. And soon the Captain would join her. Like the fog moving above the valley, they had been torn away from him.

"Do you see that?" Jonathan asked, panting from the exertion of the climb.

In the distance, a solitary figure knelt among the gravestones.

"One of those riding preachers," Macaijah said.

Jonathan strained to see through the fog.

"Is it the same one as yesterday? The red-haired man?"

"Too far to tell," Macaijah answered.

"He stands near my mother's grave."

As Jonathan and Macaijah watched, the figure rose, mounted a nearby horse, and rode to the top of the ridge. When they reached the small cemetery, he was nowhere to be found.

Jonathan and Macaijah measured a plot of ground next to Emily's grave, marking the boundaries of it with the point of a shovel. All morning they dug in the hardened earth. They worked mostly in silence except for grunts and the clang of metal against stone. As Jonathan dug he remembered his last conversation with his father in the cabin of his lumber sloop, the *Norwood.* It was the only time he had heard the Captain speak of his mother.

"Everything I took from the sea belonged to your mother. You know that?" he began. "I know you were there alone when she died . . . I understand she died hard. I do regret that I was not there that night."

"But you couldn't be there," Jonathan defended. "You were at sea. I know that now."

The Captain moved to the window of the cabin and stared out for a while at the harbor. "Late at night, when I am at sea, I come here to watch the water slip away behind my ship. And there is a path there, in the starlight. One can see where the ship has passed through, oh, for two hundred feet in the water, and then the trail is swallowed away. As if I had not been here at all.

"I used to think of Emily, while standing here. Oh, sometimes I still do, just like she is alive. It seems I think so very clearly when I am at sea. It is as if I can see directly into the heart of that woman. I see her face, too. Every detail of it, the sad turn-down at the corner of her mouth and the eyes, ready to laugh. And while I am here, I think of the perfect things to say to her. Words to bring those smiles to her face. You remember her smiles, don't you?"

Jonathan nodded.

"Like sunrise over the water. Her smile was that lovely," the Captain went on. "I have seen her smile that way, many times. When she was still alive, sometimes I would practice those words here, sometimes almost out loud, and in my mind I would see her smile back at me. I would repeat the things that came to me here until I was certain that I could say them to her face when next I saw her . . . but no. When I set foot on shore I began to lose them. By the time I reached Bath they were all gone. I couldn't seem to say what I wanted to say unless I was standing here at this cabin window." His voice faltered. "You know Emily never cared for the sea." The Captain took a deep breath before going on, then he looked directly at Jonathan.

"I have seen Emily give that special smile of hers many times, Jonathan," he said with difficulty. "Every time she smiled at you. How she loved you."

Jonathan felt himself impaled by this speech. He felt the guilt of a cornered thief. Not that Emily loved him, but that her love, her smiles for him had somehow defrauded his father.

Sweat soaked Jonathan's back as he continued to dig in the Captain's gravesite. His hands bled from painful blisters, but he did not slacken the pace. He welcomed the discomfort. It was the only thing he had ever done for the sea captain whose name he bore. It was an atonement.

That evening, as the sun touched the mountaintops, Macaijah, dressed in a suit and tie, drove the wagon with the Captain's body up the barren ridge. Jonathan, Chayta, and Ethan walked behind, their somber faces warmed in the yellow gold of sunset.

At the gravesite, they lowered the coffin into the ground by ropes. Then the three men picked up shovels and began to fill the hole with the fresh dirt. When they had finished they set a spired marble headstone into the earth. It read: Captain Nelson Barratt, 1729–1780. It stood next to the simple granite tablet that was inscribed: Emily Barratt, 1743–1771; under these dates were carved the Puritan skull and crossbones and the letters R.I.P.

As the others walked slowly back to the cart, Jonathan stood alone at the two graves. Another chapter of his life was now sadly closed. Here on the ridge overlooking Bath, his mother and father lay forever silent. The young man was still a boy. He had many questions to ask of them. He still wanted someone to be strong for him. He still felt the empty place inside.

He looked across the mountains into the gathering darkness. From somewhere farther down the ridge there came to him the sound of singing. Then he saw the red-haired preacher leading the family of the grandmother whose body had been transported into Bath the day before. The small group was headed for the far corner of the graveyard where a pile of fresh earth lay beside a hole. The words of the song floated to where he stood, and for a moment he listened.

"I am bound for the promised land. Oh, who will come and go with me, I am bound for the promised land."

Perhaps there was comfort in the religious song, Jonathan thought. One could hope to see loved ones in another land, a promised land, a life beyond this life. There was a part of Jonathan, he did not know how strong it was, but a part of him was ready to go there now.

The last rays of sun dropped below the distant mountains. Below him, the lamps of Bath began to glow in the gathering darkness. He bent down and crumbled a lump of dirt in his hand, so that the tiny grains streamed down on the fresh mound of earth. The approaching group continued to sing their mournful song. He brushed his hands clean, then turned away.

3

The Frolic

The frolic was Uncle Ethan's idea. He suggested that the move of Barratt Enterprises from Boston to Bath should be celebrated in high style. "We will invite everyone," he told Jonathan, "that is, everyone of merit. We'll introduce them to the rare opportunity to invest in Kentucky land."

A twelve-foot banner was hung above the Playhouse stage in the main room of the Inn which read: "Kentucky Land Company, a Barratt Enterprise." On the stage, jugglers and mimes whirled and grimaced as a woodwind quintet wafted dance suites and chamber music into the rustic ballroom. A table of smoked meats, cheeses, premium ales and liquors drew the men to a far corner of the room, where Ethan held forth on the vision of Barratt Enterprises and the wealth to be found in Kentucky lands. With a brandy snifter in one hand, his smoking pipe in the other, Ethan moved easily among the gentry of Bath.

"But you must understand," he was saying to Orville Hudson, the owner of the Bath House Inn, "we've taken our position at the precise moment in history when we cannot lose!"

"How can you say that?" Orville scoffed. "It seems a dangerous venture, if you ask me."

"No, my friend, it's not at all." Ethan smiled. "Forethought and planning will make this the best investment of our lives."

"But now that the war is settled, all we are hearing from Kentucky is talk about forming the state of Frankland out there in the wilds. Good Lord, what is this state of Frankland? It smacks of instability, if you ask me."

"It is an unstable area, yes. But an unstable investment? No." Ethan frowned thoughtfully. "Of course, it is still wilderness, it is still lawless, and we have made our claims there while it is still nearly worthless territory, but how long will it remain worthless? Boone, as far back as '76, tried to make a state of Kentucky. Clark annexed it as a county of Virginia and prevented him. Do you think we are the only company with an eye on the land interests of this area? No."

Edward Chase, a Baltimore banker, joined the two men. "How long will it take for the investments in the land to see a profit, Ethan? That's the difficult question here."

"How long? A few years, but let me say that since the end of the war, the process of settling that land has gained great impetus."

A crowd of distinguished gentlemen now gathered about, so Ethan moved to a place near the liquor table where he had set up a section of birch tree and a display of maps. On the table lay an Indian tomahawk. Ethan picked it up and chopped at the air.

"You have seen them passing through Bath nearly every day in their oxcarts and wagons," he said. "They are out there right now squatting on portions of our Kentucky land. Some of them are clearing it. They were not asked to do it. They volunteered, in a manner of speaking. Who else will clear it? You? Me? No, they clear that godforsaken land. They live on it. They settle their differences with the savages. But the error they make, and continue to make again and again, is that they are ignoring the established laws of ownership. They are out there marking trees with tomahawks." He made a slash mark across the birch bark. "They think they own things by their marks." Ethan paused and watched the reactions of his audience. "Why, just one small change in a mark on a tree"—he slashed the mark again, obscuring the original—"and we have 'your word' against 'my word.' What happens then to the principles of law and order concerning the ownership of land?"

He dropped the tomahawk to the table with a dramatic flourish. "What will happen to those primitive claims when Kentucky becomes civilized by law?" He picked up from the same table a wooden judge's gavel with one hand and a title document with the other. "Is a piece of malleable tree bark going to stand in a court of law against the well-ordered assertions of parchment and pen?" He rapped the table with the gavel. "Of course not! It is chaos out there, gentlemen. Chaos." He rapped the gavel repeatedly. "But we are bringing it to order!"

Jonathan walked over and stood behind Ethan. He studied a map on the table. Ethan had marked out the lands owned by Barratt Enterprises. Jonathan noted the names of certain places: Logan's Fort, the Green River, Cumberland Gap, and Crab Orchard.

"I say the scheme has merit," Edward Chase was saying as Ethan turned and noticed Jonathan.

"Ah, my nephew, gentlemen." He beamed, ushering Jonathan into the center of the group. "This young man, whom you all know, will lead Barratt Enterprises to new heights of prosperity."

Jonathan nodded uncomfortably.

Ethan raised his snifter and the others joined him in a toast.

"Come on, Jonathan," Ethan said, "it is time for introductions." He directed Jonathan toward the stage, while he signaled for the mimes and musicians to stop their performing. On a signal from Ethan, a French-horn player sounded a hunting flourish. The guests turned toward the stage and grew silent. Ethan stepped onto the stage.

"Ladies and gentlemen! I present to you Jonathan Barratt." There was polite applause and Ethan motioned for Jonathan to join him on the stage. "This visionary young man is the owner of Barratt Enterprises. Some of you remember his father, Captain Nelson Barratt, and . . . and his mother, my dear sister Emily. And now to announce the occasion of this celebration, I present, Jonathan Barratt." He stepped back and motioned Jonathan to speak.

Jonathan cleared his throat. "Bath is my home," he began nervously. "It has always been my home. There has been but one seagoing Barratt. My father. He was one of the very best, and when he made his great sacrifice for our country's cause, no replacement for his abilities at sea could be found."

There followed a strong round of applause. When it subsided, Jonathan continued. "I believe it is important to understand where one belongs. I belong nowhere, if not here in Bath. I hope that we can work together with you to build our new ventures in this land. My uncle, Ethan Stillwell, will administer all of that business. A fine man." Jonathan paused awkwardly. "I am glad he is with me." He stepped down from the stage without making a true finish to the speech.

"Fine speech, lad," Ethan said heartily, handing Jonathan a foaming tankard of ale. Ethan jumped onto the stage once again and signaled for the dancing to resume. Warmed by the ale and the music, Jonathan left the businessmen to wander through the crowd of frolickers.

"Young man," cried Orville Hudson, the innkeeper, "what a brilliant stroke you have managed in this land scheme."

"Thank you, sir, but I must say, my uncle's efforts are responsible for that," Jonathan replied.

"Don't be modest now. You have inherited your father's acumen, I can see that."

Jonathan smiled uncomfortably and moved away from him, skirting the main floor, which was filling with dancers.

"Jonathan!" A woman whom he recognized from years past as having been a friend of his mother's, approached him.

"Mrs. Chase." He smiled, with recognition. But she was more beautiful than he remembered her. By some art or magic, she seemed to have retained a youthful radiance. Her husband, Edward Chase, was a lucky man, Jonathan thought.

She took his hand warmly in both of hers, holding it near her breast. Her eyes moistened as she spoke. "Your mother would have been proud tonight. I was thinking, seeing you standing on that stage, so sure, so . . . so handsome . . . just how very proud she would have been. Oh, I am sorry." She dabbed her eye with a lace handkerchief. "You are to be congratulated, and as a friend of the family, I simply wanted to say welcome to Bath."

"Thank you, Mrs. Chase—"

"Estelle, dear. You are old enough to call me Estelle." She laughed.

"Yes . . . Estelle," he said, feeling a warmth on his face.

She released his hand slowly, her eyes continuing to inspect him as though everything about him pleased her.

Jonathan remembered Edward Chase, at that moment across the room with Ethan. He was suddenly acutely aware that they were in a room of many people. He turned away, but she turned as well and walked in step beside him around the perimeter of the dance floor. Jonathan searched for something to say.

"Will you stay in Bath all summer?" he inquired.

"Yes, I will be here," she replied cheerily. "Mr. Chase, however, will be returning to Baltimore."

Jonathan cleared his throat and moved on. So did Estelle, walking closer now, one hand resting lightly on his arm. He was charmed by this attractive woman.

"Do you still race?" she asked.

"Oh yes. I plan to again. My horse, Merlin, appears to be in fine form."

"Yes, Merlin," she recalled, "that lusty stallion of yours. I would like to breed that fine animal to my mare."

"You would?"

"Yes, I would." She laughed, stopping in front of Jonathan to ladle a glass of punch from a crystal bowl. "Name your price. It will be worth it, I'm sure."

He thought he caught an undertone to her words, saw an invitation in her eyes. They were not speaking strictly of horses. He stared at her lips, suddenly thrilled by how very full and sensitive they were as they touched the rim of her glass.

"My mare is in season," she said.

"Then we should arrange something soon."

"Yes, if we could—"

"Mother!"

A young lady in a blue silk gown, her thin brown hair tied in pink and yellow ribbons, walked up. She eyed Jonathan coldly over Estelle's shoulder. "Mother, where have you been?"

"Jonathan, do you remember Charlotte, my daughter?" Estelle asked smoothly.

"Could this be Charlotte?" he replied. "What a surprise." He took the hand the young lady offered, kissing it. Jonathan had seen her only a few times during the summers since Emily's death, and on no occasion had he a desire to speak with her. He remembered her only too well. They had taken outings together in the years before Emily died and she had been an unforgettable annoyance for him. He tried to find something more to say to her. "Surely this could not be the pigtailed . . . ?"

"Oh, do you remember the Sunday picnics?" Charlotte sniffed. "You were so amusing then. Such a priggish little gentleman."

Jonathan smiled blankly. "Priggish, was I?"

"Emily and I spoke many times about the two of you," Mrs. Chase interjected, "wondering what you would think of each other when you had grown. Now, here you are."

Jonathan turned to Estelle with an insincere smile, but she was not looking at him. She was looking instead toward the doorway.

"Oh, look. It is a riding preacher," she said with amusement.

Jonathan looked. The red-haired preacher whom he had met on the road near Bath stood in the doorway. He looked terribly out of place at this festive gathering. His long coat was dusty and his leggings spattered with dried mud. He removed his hat and moved well into the room, his boots clumping heavily against the polished floor. The celebrants backed away to give him room, as though he had some contagious disease. Whispered comments flew about, and soon the entire room fell silent as all heads turned to see this rare sight. As far as anyone could recall, this was the first riding preacher to cross the threshold of the ballroom.

"How amusing," sniffed Charlotte.

"I was told I could find Mr. Lemuel Simkins here," boomed the preacher, his deep voice ringing in the silence.

Orville crossed the now vacant dance floor, unsteadily because he had drunk himself tipsy. "I . . . I am the innkeeper here, sir. Lem . . . Lem . . . ah, Mr. Simkins is in my employ."

Simkins appeared quickly from the crowd and moved to Orville's side as he approached Silas. "This is Mr. Will, the preacher who brought a sick companion, some days ago. I allowed them the use of the bath," Simkins explained.

"Fine. Fine," Orville growled. "So what's the matter Mr. Will? What do you want? You'll find me as hospitable as a hellfire sermon on the sabbath day. That should suit the likes o' ye." A trace of drunken anger had risen in his voice.

Snickers laced the crowd. The amusement of the guests seemed to fuel Orville's temper. He took another step toward the preacher.

"I seek a room for the night, good sir," Silas said quietly.

"A room? You shall 'ave one!" Orville declared. "But I see you have a hat in your hand, sir. A preacher with a . . . 'at in 'is hand means a donation where I come from."

This scattered laughter throughout the room. The preacher's neck reddened.

"I am an exhorter. My companion, Francis Asbury, is a preacher of the

gospel of John Wesley's way. He is already a guest of this inn. I am willing
to pay—" he began.

"But I was off'ring to donate," Orville declared. "You will not accept?"

The red-haired preacher eyed him sternly. "I do humbly accept, and
thank you."

"Yer welcome. But, I also see . . . uh, seek a donation from you, sir,
Mr. Will. You shall join us in our frolic. How's that? Let that be the price
of your stay." Orville threw back his head and laughed.

The room buzzed. Some of the guests were amused. Others disap-
proved, knowing the pious reputation of this new breed of preacher.

Ethan moved up behind Orville's shoulder. "Orville, I think this is
unwise. There are more important things at stake here tonight. Send the
preacher on his way."

"Nonsense," blustered Orville, "the man hath availed himself of my
hospita . . . hospitality and I ask his in return. An eye for an eye. Eh,
Preacher?"

The red-haired preacher looked about the room. A light of inspiration
had suddenly grown in his eye.

"I shall join your frolic," he declared, removing his long coat and pushing it into Orville's arms. He removed his hat. The room grew hushed. His
eyes swept the guests and came to rest upon Charlotte. She stifled a tiny
cry in her throat.

With hypnotic energy, he strode across the floor until he stood in front
of her, his blue eyes piercing down into her terrified ones. The young
woman clamped a hand across her mouth. She looked helplessly toward
her mother. For the moment Jonathan could not help being slightly
amused by the preacher's choice.

Then, with surprising gentleness, the imposing face wrinkled into a
smile. The preacher took Charlotte's hand and asked, "May I have this
dance?" She stepped dumbly with him to the center of the floor, as
though she were powerless to do anything else. "Before the musicians
play"—the preacher's voice filled the room—"I would like to thank you
for inviting me to join your frolic. But as you know, I am a man who lives
in service to God. My life is not my own. I do nothing without asking the
blessing of my Lord God, in the name of His son, Jesus. He will speak His
peace to my heart if I am to do this thing. Shall we pray?"

He knelt abruptly to the floor, holding fast to Charlotte's hand. She was
biting the knuckles of her free hand to keep from crying out. She looked
pleadingly toward Estelle and Jonathan.

"Don't let him do this, Jonathan," Estelle murmured between clenched teeth.

Jonathan took a step forward, but the force of the red-haired preacher's prayer stopped him short.

"Almighty God. Maker of heaven and earth. Our Father which art in Heaven—" Charlotte slipped down suddenly to her knees in front of the preacher, breaking into silent tears as Silas roared on, "I pray in the name of Jesus, who lived and died sinless that we might live in the hereafter, and not suffer in chains and pains with Your enemy, Satan, the prince of the darkness of this world. I call Your divine attention, Lord, to this room, and to every person here in this room. And also to me, Lord God, Your servant in this room. You have called me to rescue souls as branches from the burning. To save them and exhort them to a life of holiness unto You, who art the True Holy One!"

A child near the stage began to cry.

Silas did not diminish the strength of his praying. "Now, Lord, I have been asked to join this frolicking business here. I . . . I am ready to dance, Lord. I am prepared to take this young maiden in my arms, though I do not know her name, and prance about this room to the pipers' music. Will You bless this trifling dance, my Lord? Will it please You?"

Silas bowed in silent meditation. The crying child had found its mother who now smothered its cries against her shoulder. Charlotte was sobbing pitifully against the back of her hand.

"Don't let him do this to her," Estelle whispered urgently to Jonathan.

He hesitated, but only for a moment. Inside he was seething with anger at the rough preacher who had gone too far in his humiliation of Charlotte. Even so, he felt himself quivering inside as he stepped to the center of the floor and stood over the two kneeling figures.

"I appeal to your sense of common decency, sir," he said, speaking as firmly as he possibly could. "Release this girl and remove yourself from this company at once."

Silas looked up in genuine surprise.

"You have embarrassed this lady deeply," Jonathan said, his temper rising.

Silas looked into the girl's face as he rose to his feet. Tears still streamed down her cheeks. "But look. See her sorrow. In such sorrow is true repentance." Charlotte wrenched her hand free with a loud sob and rushed to her mother's waiting arms. Edward Chase joined them and they escorted her from the room.

"I see it differently," Jonathan said to the preacher. "She is crying from embarrassment. Is that what God has called you to do?"

"I would embarrass anyone if it leads them to repent," Silas announced boldly.

Angry murmurs rose from all sides of the room.

"But you have angered every sensible man in this room," Jonathan cried.

"I am not afraid of men. I would anger you, sir, or any man if it might save one soul for God," Silas blared. He looked about the room as if challenging their anger. "I know where I shall spend eternity. Can any of you say the same?"

"You will speak to me, sir," Jonathan said, surprised at his growing boldness, "and to no one else in this room. I am the sponsor of this evening. I do apologize for the rudeness of Mr. Hudson. He has had too much to drink, but you, sir, have outdone his rudeness many times over. I ask you to leave at once, or I will have you forcibly removed."

Silas fixed him with a stare. Then, nodding calmly, he collected his long coat and hat and turned toward the door. Just before leaving, however, he turned and raised his boot a few inches from the floor and looked up to the ceiling. "I shake the dust from my shoes for a testimony against them, Lord!" he boomed. Then he looked once more around the room. "May God have mercy on your souls."

"Begone with ya!" someone shouted, and a chorus of men joined in agreement.

Jonathan followed him out into the dark street. The preacher stood at the steps.

"I asked you to say nothing more, sir. You did not show the decency to restrain yourself," Jonathan said.

"Young man," the preacher said, whirling about, close to Jonathan's face, "I can see the Devil's poison has darkened your mind." He looked down at Jonathan's hand, which still held a tankard of ale.

"Devil's poison? Oh no, sir, it is merely ale." Jonathan laughed.

Silas slapped the tankard spinning from his hand. "I know what it is, and I called it properly."

Jonathan struggled to control his anger. "If I were half as uncouth as you, sir, I would thrash you for this offense."

"Do what you are able," Silas challenged, looking at him carefully. "You speak properly, young man, but as for me, I would gladly appear uncouth and rude if I might save your soul from Hell."

Jonathan shook his head. He had discoursed too much with the scoundrel already. He turned aside, retrieved his empty tankard, and walked back up the steps into the ballroom.

Beneath the porch of the Inn, a figure stood in the doorway, watching the preacher untether his horse. She held her breath, her eyes large with fear. For a moment, she thought that she dreamed, but as the light from the upstairs ballroom window caught his face, she knew she made no mistake. As the rider mounted and cantered off down the street, Chayta stepped from the shadows.

"Oh, Lord," she moaned. "It's Silas Will."

4

The Letter

Macaijah plunged a glowing horseshoe into a pail of water next to the white-hot forge. A violent cloud of steam hissed into the air about him. His face glistened with sweat. His muslin shirt, soaked through with perspiration, clung to the thick, taut muscles of his chest. He pulled the iron shoe from the water and examined it. It was now cold and black.

Bard Dugin, the overseer, waited nearby, watching a stable hand who led a haltered mule to the forge. Dugin was a homely, sallow-faced fellow with straight brown hair, which nonetheless he kept studiously parted and combed close to his head with the aid of kitchen lard. He appeared rather gentlemanly until one came close enough to notice the dust that formed a paste in his hair. But the combed hair served to identify him, especially to the slaves, as one who worked with his mind, not his body. In fact, he was common-born and would have been a laborer if slavery had not given him a higher station in life. He wore a pistol, tucked always in full view at his waist.

Macaijah moved away from the forge, holding the shoe up to the light with a pair of tongs. He reached for a small shoeing hammer and approached the mule. With a strong, smooth motion he caught the animal's right foreleg and wedged it upside down between his knees. He carefully aligned the iron shoe.

Jonathan rounded the corner of the barn entrance. He was dressed in wine-and-black racing silks and held a riding quirt in one hand. He seemed surprised at what he saw and stopped short, waiting for Macaijah to finish nailing the shoe. But when Macaijah had finished nailing he continued to trim the mule's hoof with a pair of nippers.

Jonathan grew impatient. "Where is my horse, Macaijah?" he asked.

Macaijah glanced up at Mr. Dugin. "Caleb get him ready for you, Master Jonathan."

"Caleb? Who is Caleb?" Jonathan asked irritably. He now looked at Bard Dugin.

"Macaijah," Dugin said, "Mr. Barratt needs his horse."

Macaijah dropped the mule's foot and instantly moved away toward the opposite side of the barn, where Jonathan's horse, Merlin, was being combed in his stall by another slave. Jonathan followed him, puzzled. Macaijah had always cared for Merlin. He had spent long hours training the stallion. He had a natural way with horses and was himself an excellent rider. They had ridden together on a number of hunts during the summer before Jonathan had left for Harvard. It was then that Macaijah had taught Merlin to come at the sound of a special two-note whistle, rewarding him with a small crab-apple treat for repeating the trick. None but Jonathan and Macaijah had ever ridden the spirited animal. What had changed in the four years he had been away in Boston? More slaves and Bard Dugin, but what else?

"It will be good to race again," Jonathan said, hoping to stir some conversation.

The slave only nodded without looking at him and pulled a saddle and bridle from pegs on the barn wall, dumping them roughly to the floor. Then he stepped to the stall, taking the halter from Caleb, and led the snorting bay stallion out into the main area of the barn.

Jonathan had noticed, from his first day home, a disharmony with the slaves, including Chayta and Andrew, who had always seemed like a part of the Barratt family. He suspected several things accounted for this. From his days at Harvard, he knew that the war with England had spawned a new wave of sentiment for the abolition of slavery in the colonies. During his first year in Boston, the Pennsylvania government made provisions for the gradual abolition of slavery within its boundaries. Bath, of course, was remote from the centers of this conflict, but Jonathan had learned that slaves everywhere had their own channels of communication. Most of their information was carried by clandestine networks of runaway slaves who visited slave quarters by night. During the war more than 30,000 slaves had become runaways in Virginia alone. The abolitionist efforts of the Quakers, the Societies for the Manumission of Slaves, and the Revolutionary War cry for freedom from the King of England had prompted many runaways among the Negroes.

Jonathan's most immediate concern had been that Uncle Ethan's addition of field slaves to the household would threaten the easy familiarity which the Barratts had always enjoyed with their house slaves. Certainly this seemed true in Macaijah's case. A new field slave, Caleb, had been given his duties with Merlin. Jonathan knew he must set this right with Dugin, the overseer.

"We will hunt again, Macaijah," Jonathan offered. "Tomorrow or the day after, I will arrange it."

Macaijah nodded but continued fastening a bridle beneath Merlin's jaw.

Ethan's management of Barratt Enterprises was destroying something Jonathan did not wish to destroy, but as heir, he also felt the weight of responsibility more and more on his own shoulders. He promised himself to do something about it, soon. He took the reins from Macaijah and swung into the saddle, astride his favorite horse for the first time in four years. The well-muscled stallion danced sideways, carrying his weight with ease. Jonathan held him firmly as he tested the length of the stirrups with satisfaction.

"Is he a winner today?" Jonathan asked.

Macaijah was busily examining the horse's foreleg as he replied, "He gives enough to win. No more."

"Same ole Merlin." Jonathan chuckled. "Is something wrong with the foreleg?"

Macaijah stepped back. "He's fine."

Jonathan waited and stared down at Macaijah until the silence became uncomfortable and Macaijah at last lifted his eyes. "We will hunt together, Macaijah," Jonathan promised. "We will."

Macaijah looked away.

Jonathan wheeled Merlin about and let him clatter from the barn entrance.

"Win the race now, Master Jonathan," Dugin called. He was outside the barn examining a broken plow as Jonathan passed.

Jonathan nodded to him. He did not like this man Dugin. He seemed to be perfectly at home with slavery, and Jonathan felt one should at least be uneasy with it. It seemed one of life's necessary evils, with the emphasis upon "evil."

The racetrack could be seen from the Barratt barn. It was a straight quarter-mile track, situated beyond a thin grove of trees a half mile behind the Barratt mansion. The bright clothing of the women in the crowd could be seen contrasting intermittently between the distant tree trunks as Jonathan galloped toward them.

Mr. Dugin watched him go, then strolled with a steely ease back to where Macaijah stood near the forge.

"A gentleman's groom ye be now?" Dugin taunted quietly, his eyes fastened on the slave's face. His voice betrayed a sinister anger. "Ah, but what do I know, eh? I only been an overseer thirteen years. I only *thought* I knew a God-made smithy buck when I seen one. Right?" He chuckled good-naturedly.

Macaijah picked up the heavy forge hammer, turning it slowly in his hand, the muscles in his jaw quivering.

Dugin spat. He placed his hand idly on the hilt of his pistol and stepped forward to stand directly in front of the slave. "Now, how could I know the new master of the house here expected *you* to groom his horse all special? How, 'cept maybe you told me. An' you didn't. Maybe you wanted to teach the old overseer some new trick, like he was just an old dog, huh? Did you want to teach this old dog a new trick, buck?"

"No, sir," Macaijah said, laying down the hammer and listening with his eyes quietly averted.

"Do you know better than this overseer what's best here on the farm?"

"No, sir."

"Then maybe it would be good if you tell Master Jonathan, next time you see him, just how very happy you are to be at the forge."

Macaijah paused, then nodded his assent.

Dugin smiled. "That's good, buck. You can do good here if you learn lessons like this. You surely can. And we'll be movin' this here forge to the far end of the valley soon where the clearing is going on. Most everyone will agree to the wisdom in that because we break so many plows down there, don't you agree?"

"Yes, sir."

"Very good. Now get back on it, you've dallied long enough. I'll see that you get more work if you've got time enough for daydreaming."

Dugin turned and strode from the barn to where his horse was tethered at a rail outside. He swung into the saddle and walked the horse in the opposite direction of the track. He was headed to the far end of the valley to inspect the clearing operation. Most of the field slaves were employed there.

Macaijah remained frozen until Bard was out of earshot. Then he dropped his hammer to the dirt, untied his thick leather apron, and let it fall away. He then went quickly to a feed bag and lifted a bedroll from beneath it. At that moment Caleb emerged from one of the stalls leading a saddled gray gelding, one of the horses used to pull the landau. The slave's eyes darted nervously about. He dropped the reins of the animal before Macaijah and hurried to the corner of the barn entrance, peeking around to check Dugin's position.

"Has he crossed the road?" Macaijah rasped in a hoarse whisper as he swiftly lashed the bedroll behind the saddle.

"No."

Macaijah swung aboard the gray and rode him forward, halting just inside the barn door. The big slave's eyes searched the trees in the direction of the place where the Martinsburg road entered the forest. He spied a plume of smoke rising beyond there and noted it with satisfaction.

"He's crossed the road," called Caleb.

"You know what to do," Macaijah replied purposefully. He took a deep breath.

In the distance a starting pistol cracked, signaling the beginning of the race at the track. The crowd began to cheer. As if it were his own signal, Macaijah burst from the door of the barn in a headlong dash for freedom.

"Master Dugin! Master Dugin! Runaway!" screamed Caleb, running from the barn and pointing to the galloping horse.

Dugin looked over his shoulder from beyond the road, uncomprehending for a moment. Then he spun around and gave vigorous chase. Soon both he and Macaijah disappeared into the stand of timber at the lower end of the valley.

Caleb looked about carefully to see if anyone else had seen the runaway or the pursuit, but no one appeared from the house or the barn. All seemed quiet except for the cheering of the race crowd in the distance. He trotted to the back of the mansion and hid himself in a blooming lilac hedge. He had agreed previously with Macaijah that if Dugin took the bait and gave chase, he would not tell Chayta until as late as possible.

The race was over, Jonathan had won at the last minute by a nose. This was as Macaijah had predicted; Merlin gave the race just enough to win. Other races were now forming and the crowd was busy placing new bets. No one took special note when Jonathan and Mrs. Chase took prompt leave of the track and headed back across the meadow toward the Barratt barn.

Estelle drove her own chaise. Her mare was tethered behind. She stole sideways glances at Jonathan, who had all he could do to control Merlin, as the stallion had caught wind of the mare in season. A wreath of red roses tossed back and forth on the winning horse's withers. They drew up before the barn, Jonathan dismounted and led Merlin into the cool shade of the entrance.

"Macaijah!" he called. Hearing no stir, he called again, "Caleb! Mr. Dugin!"

Looking curiously around, he tied Merlin to a stall and then exited again.

"Seems we're all alone," Jonathan said, approaching the buggy.

Estelle Chase stood and held out her hands for Jonathan's assistance. "However did *that* happen?" she teased, in a way that made Jonathan wish he had planned the empty barn. He smiled up and extended his hands, allowing her to think what she wished. She took his hands in hers and guided them playfully to her sides.

Jonathan's fingers found the soft curve of her hips just below her corseted waist. He lifted her to the ground. She smelled of springtime lilac and he found himself leaning forward against the softness of her body.

"Come," she said, lightly pushing him away. "Bring my mare."

Jonathan moved to the back of the chaise and untied the animal. He led her into the barn, Estelle walking beside him, smiling. Merlin kicked and whinnied in his stall as they approached.

"Stay clear of him, Estelle. He can be trouble."

She hurried ahead to get out of the line of danger. "I will get the gate for you," she offered. "Which one?"

"There," Jonathan said, pointing to a stall deeper in the barn.

Estelle opened and held the door as Jonathan led the mare past Merlin.

The mare kicked at the stallion as she passed, frightened of the big horse with the rolling eyes and flaring nostrils.

"Sooner or later he will need some cooperation from her, don't you agree?" Jonathan asked as he set the mare free into the breeding stall.

Estelle suppressed a smile as he passed her. "It can be later or sooner, I suppose, if he knows what to do." She followed him into the stall.

The mare circled the strange stall, inspecting the four walls with her nose, then with a nicker she burst from the side door into the adjacent paddock. Jonathan turned and stepped toward Estelle. She was more alluring in the dim light. With a new sense of pleasure he recalled that this older woman had been a friend of his mother's. He felt strangely at ease with her. She cocked her head questioningly as he moved close. Neither breathed. He took another step and she held up a hand between them.

"Jonathan, I know you are a wealthy young man now, but you have never named a price for the use of your stallion. You don't mean to say that it has no value at all?" She was teasing.

"No." He stepped even closer. "I mean, if you wish to discuss price you should speak with my Uncle Ethan. My interest in horses is purely romantic."

She smiled expectantly. "Mine, too."

She did not resist as he slipped his arms around her small waist and covered her mouth with his. His face flushed hotly. She pulled free and backed away from him to the stall door. Her green eyes flashed.

"You certainly do not kiss like Emily's little boy!" she gasped, then came toward him, this time pulling him gently against her, taking his hand in hers and guiding it to the soft flesh of her neck, then lower toward the bodice of her gown.

"Mmm, Jonathan," she murmured.

He kissed her again, but at that instant heard someone in the doorway.

"Jonathan!"

His head jerked around to find Chayta standing there, tears streaming freely on her face.

"D____!" swore Estelle under her breath, stepping back, straightening her dress. "Do something about her!"

"He's gone!" Chayta cried, and the agony of her words tore at Jonathan's heart. "He's gone!"

"Who? Who is gone?"

"Macaijah! He run away on the trace. And Mr. Dugin right after. He'll kill him, Jonathan!"

"No!"

Jonathan leaped from the stall and ran to untie Merlin. "He won't kill him," he promised, though he had a terrible fear inside, recalling how he had overruled Mr. Dugin's role for Macaijah at the forge. Already in the saddle, he lashed Merlin, then had to roughly rein him around, remembering how quickly he had abandoned Estelle. She stood in the doorway of the stall now, glaring accusingly at the old black woman.

"Estelle," Jonathan called. "I am sorry. I will be back."

She softened. Until that moment she had feared he would rush off without a backward glance. She nodded and waved him on. "Go after him."

He raced from the doorway across the backyard of the mansion toward the trees where the Martinsburg road turned east. The Newtowne Trace, merely a trail, dipped southward through a series of small ridges and valleys as it turned toward the upper Shenandoah. He entered the trace at racing speed, letting Merlin pick his way. His eyes searched right and left ahead. By the stream of the second meadow beyond the trees, he rode right past the object of his search. He shuddered in disbelief, turning Merlin around.

Returning, he found the body of Mr. Dugin crumpled awkwardly by the trail. He dismounted and with horror unfolded the overseer's broken limbs. Blood oozed from at least a half dozen wounds. Jonathan glanced fearfully around the meadow. The man had been blown from the saddle in a volley of bullets. His horse grazed serenely, one hundred yards downstream.

Jonathan did not dine with Ethan and Mr. Tibbet that night, but remained brooding in the candlelit library. He sat in the Captain's old leather chair and stared up at the portraits of his mother and father on the wall.

Two voices spoke in his mind. One voice argued that he had done nothing, therefore he had caused none of this difficulty. Another, more powerful voice told him that he had caused all of it. It accused that whatever he did, whether something or nothing, he always seemed to cause pain. Jonathan waited to hear a third voice of reason. He looked to the portraits, but they spoke nothing. His head throbbed.

Chayta came quietly through the doorway carrying a tray of sweetmeats and tea. Her face was drawn and tired, but there was a calmness about her that had not been there when she had burst into the barn.

"Why did he run away, Chayta?"

She placed the tray on a small table and scooted it next to Jonathan's chair. Then she sat down in a chair opposite him.

"Macaijah become a man since you left. Even a man *born* slave wants to be something else, sometime. He might do something foolish."

"Macaijah was born a slave, I was born . . ." He was still gazing at the portraits. "But I don't know why."

"Don't talk nonsense, now. This place needs you, Jonathan."

"Sometimes I wish I had never been born."

"You stop that talk!"

"If it's true, why should I stop?" Jonathan shot back. He stood to his feet and began to pace the room. "This place needs something, but it doesn't need me. I tried to help Macaijah this morning. Mr. Dugin wanted Macaijah on the forge. I wanted him to tend to Merlin, like always before. Look what happened."

"Jonathan, that was Macaijah's doing, not yours."

"Oh? I meddled between him and Dugin. Dugin's dead now and Macaijah is accused of the killing. Chayta, believe me, I don't think he did it. At least I know he was not alone in it. But whatever, he's gone. It just seems I try to help, but only cause more trouble."

"Jonathan . . ."

"My own mother, Chayta, you were there. I made things worse when she was dying, for heaven's sake. Just trying to help."

Chayta looked up suddenly. "You can't never get that outa your mind, 'bout your momma, can you, hon?"

He swallowed with difficulty, hearing the deep empathy in her voice. "Oh"—he shrugged—"I . . . I can forget that." He felt like a little boy again. "But it doesn't matter. Something is still wrong with me. Even with the Captain there." He pointed to the portrait. "He told me when I was in Boston that all he wanted in life was to have Mother smile at him, and all he ever saw was that she smiled at me. It was like I stole something from him, but I . . . I don't know what I stole. I loved my mother. What the heck was wrong with that?"

Chayta looked up at the high ceiling and closed her eyes in a silent prayer. She was beginning to sense that the time had come to break a solemn promise to Jonathan's parents.

"Oh, forgetting all that," Jonathan went on. "Look at me now. I can't even take hold of my inheritance. Ethan does everything for me——like I am some kind of invalid. I just . . . I just sign my name here and there where he points his finger. I signed the sale of the Captain's fleet, for heaven's sake. Chayta, do you think I knew what I was doing? Heck, no. The Captain spent his life with those ships, and it was as easy as signing my name to undo all of it. And then the Kentucky Land Company. What do I know about that? Nothing. I've never been there, I have never even read the contract through. And here in Bath, Uncle Ethan still knows what is best, at least he says he does, but something is wrong here, too. I would do something about it, but I don't know what is right—or wrong, for that matter. I'll probably only make things worse."

"Jonathan," Chayta said, "would you please sit down. I am going to have a talking with you, I can see that."

"Talk. I will stand."

Chayta stood wearily and walked to the secretary. The large Bible already lay on top, unclasped but unopened. As Jonathan curiously watched, she opened the pages to a place where a bunch of wildflowers and a letter had been pressed for safekeeping. Long ago. Jonathan's mind went back to the night his mother died, when he had opened the Bible to this very same page. He did not like remembering it, and he did not like the Bible.

"Jonathan, you say you hurt your mother when she died—"

"I did. I read about being rejected and that is when she . . . she thought it was meant for her."

"That's right, hon. I remember it, too. But what you don't know is *why* she thought it was for her. Jonathan, she thought it was for her a long time before you read those words."

"What do you mean?"

"I know why she cried that way, Jonathan. 'Cept I told and swore a oath not to ever tell you. I kept Emily's secret from you. But now you keep sayin' you made everything worse for her. I know that's not true."

"It is true. Just like everything else."

"I don't know 'bout everything, hon. But I know 'bout Emily. I won't tell, 'cause of my oath, but I will tell you that if you want to know the truth about it, you can find it right here on this page where all this trouble started."

A feeling of alarm crept suddenly up Jonathan's spine. He felt strangely, as if the entire house was tilting. He could not stay away from the hated book, not if it held this secret. He woodenly moved toward the desk until he stood beside Chayta, looking down at the flowers and the letter on the Bible.

"Silas Will," he read aloud the name on the envelope.

"Do you remember?"

"No, I—"

"She called a name that night, Jonathan, remember?"

Slowly he did remember, and with a chill. "She thought I was Silas," he whispered with wonder. "She called me Silas."

Chayta moved to the other side of the secretary and looked up into his eyes.

"Your mother wrote that letter to Silas Will, sweet-hon. I was there when she did. But I know he never saw it. And now I must tell something more. That man, Jonathan, that preacher at the frolic who you throwed out, he is Silas Will. The Silas Will on that letter."

Jonathan stood to his full height. "My momma knew *him?*"

Chayta shook her head. "I did, too, Jonathan. That's all I can say and keep my oath. The rest is there for you to find. I will leave you now, but I will be in the next room about my business." She paused to swallow and her eyes moistened. "I love you, Jonathan, most times like you was my own. I will be here for you. Remember that."

She backed away from him to the doorway, and then disappeared, closing it quietly.

Jonathan looked down at the letter on the page, terrified. Did he want to know? No. And yes. What had his mother to say to this red-haired riding preacher, for heaven's sake? And what did it have to do with her torment on the night of her death? "Silas!" She had called for him. He could still hear the terror in her voice. Of course, he had to know her secret.

He reached down toward the letter, his hand pausing above it. Then his fingers moved toward the flowers. They fell apart at his touch, crumbling into flakes of multi-hued dust. Picking up the letter, his hands were trembling. He turned it before the glowing candle on the desk. Then he removed the yellowed letter from the envelope, unfolded it, and read:

April 16, 1762

My Beloved Silas,

You have gone to the wilderness or so I am told. If it is true and if by miracle this letter should find you, then know that I am begging you, return for me. I will follow you to the wilderness or to the end of the earth.

I would live here with my shame, bear my own punishment, I would even, God forbid, forget the sweetness of our hours together, and learn to call them abhorrent, but for something neither you nor I could have known when last together—I carried a child of our union.

How I feared the child would die within me when I knew what we had wrought. But what joy is now mine! God has seen fit that the child should be born—and a son. Yet now I am sick with desire that you should return to claim that which Providence and our love has wrought. I have named the child Jonathan—

Jonathan's hand closed upon the page, crushing it. He whirled to look again at the two portraits high on the library wall. As ever, they stared with placid indifference to a place in the room far above his head. He was quite alone in his discovery. The last to know.

5

The Seeker

A robin sang out in the darkness as if wakened by a dream. In the distance another answered. Soon every nesting bird in the neighborhood of trees had joined in a sleepy cacophony, heralding the approach of morning. Jonathan was listening in the Barratt library. Minutes passed while the songbirds continued. As if to honor their singing, a glow appeared at the top of the tall window curtains. It spread slowly downward across the Argentan lace as dawn grew in the sky, chased by colors of rose, orange, and finally the hard yellow light of day.

Jonathan sat in the Captain's chair, unshaven and disheveled, still in the clothes he had worn the night before. His mind swam with thoughts and images that whirled from the pages of the letter he had read the night before, and from the memory of his recent encounter with the red-haired preacher.

He was in the same chair in which he had sat the night of Emily's death. He heard again her fevered cries and the name that she screamed into the candlelit room: Silas. How could he now accept the truth that this uncouth riding preacher was the same man for whom his mother called? On his lap lay the Bible which Chayta had taken from the shelf, its page still open to the crumbled wildflowers and the letter. He pushed his finger through the withered flowers until they were only a fine chaff on the page.

" 'But that which beareth thorns and briers is rejected . . .' " he read aloud.

He wanted to tear the page from the book. His mother had died in torment, believing herself damned. And the man who was the cause of this terror now masqueraded as a man of God, damning others for their sins. Jonathan thought of his own harsh rebuke at the hands of this preacher, recalled the blow as he struck the ale tankard into the dust outside the Inn. And this man was his father?

Perhaps Chayta had meant to do him some service by this disclosure, but all Jonathan could feel was that something fine had been stripped from him, to be replaced by a thing so base and ignoble that he could hardly bear it. He was not the son of Captain Barratt. All that he saw around him, the mansion, the lands and fields of Bath, nothing was truly his by birth. But the Captain had left him his entire estate as if he were his own son. Why? It made no sense unless the Captain, like himself, had been unaware of Emily's folly. But no, Jonathan now understood the meaning of the Captain's long absences and his last conversation with him about the smiles Emily had not given to him. With a wave of anguish, he wondered how Captain Barratt had tolerated the very sight of him. But he had made him heir!

So this was his mother's torment when she died. She called for this man Silas, and she felt rejected by God for her wrongdoing. Jonathan had truly not been the instrument of her suffering, but he felt no better. There was now an ugly stain on the memory of his mother.

He stood and wearily walked to the window, looking out through the curtains at the brilliant morning.

Who was this Silas Will, this snake that had crept into the Barratt household so many years ago? His coming was a curse. His mother had borne that curse. And so had the Captain. Now it was Jonathan's turn. But what had Silas Will borne? Emily had called for him in her hour of desperation but he had ridden free, somewhere in the wilderness.

"He will be made to bear something now," Jonathan promised bitterly.

He turned and walked to the far wall beneath the portraits of the

Captain and Emily. From a mount on the wall he removed the Captain's dueling pistols.

Ethan shuffled into the library in his fur-collared bathrobe and slippers. He carried a ledger.

"Good morning, Jon," he said with surprise. "You appear ragged. Go easy on the ale, my boy, and a shave would do wonders, I might suggest."

He took a seat and was immediately beset by three slaves who had followed him into the room. The first was Andrew, who set up a clothes-horse, complete with his wardrobe and powdered wig for the day. Another took his hand and began a manicure. The third combed the ties and tangles from what was left of his true head of hair.

Ethan opened the ledger with his free hand.

"Did you hear, Jon," Ethan said with a chuckle, "that Orville got religion last night? It's true! Well, near true. He felt so condemned of conscience after the way things got out of hand at the frolic, he went after the riding preacher and persuaded him to return and accept the hospitality of his own home. And the preacher did it, too, by God. He came back. Imagine. The preacher in Orville's own house, with all that liquor, too. The other one, Asbury, the one who is quite sick with the fever, stayed at the Inn. It will be some time before he travels on. Should be entertaining to see if this religion takes hold."

Jonathan stuffed a pistol into his belt and turned, squint-aiming the other at the clotheshorse beside Ethan.

"Jon, my Lord, what are you doing?" Ethan asked with alarm.

Jonathan lowered the pistol. He drew it into the light that streamed through the near window, inspecting its flint and charge. "What do you know of these firearms?"

"They are old. Very old. Probably unreliable. Belonged to your father."

"Did he . . . ever use them?"

Ethan did not answer immediately. He seemed to be looking for just the right words. "Your father was not known to be a dueling man. He distinguished himself quite properly in other ways."

"They are well-made pistols," Jonathan observed. "This one has been fired."

"Well, he practiced with it, no doubt. Of course, he was quite capable of using it had he found the need."

Another slave entered the library. He carried a traveling trunk with a wooden crate of apothecary jars riding on top of it. These were some of Jonathan's belongings from Harvard, yet unpacked.

"Master Jonathan," he called.

"In there." Jonathan walked with him to the door of what had been Emily's bedroom, pointing the way with the pistol. "I will decide what to do with it later."

Ethan looked up from the ledger. "Things are proceeding well, Jon. Abercrombie has decided to invest. Chase is thinking it over, but I believe that is only a matter of time. When word gets around, they will fight each other for shares."

"They can have it," Jonathan mumbled.

"What did you say?"

"Nothing, Uncle." He stuffed the second pistol into his waistband.

"Now really, Jonathan, if you have some objections to these dealings . . . I only try to do what is best for you and for Barratt Enterprises, you know that."

"Yes, yes," Jonathan said coldly. "You do that quite well."

"Well, mercy me, the boy is in short humor this morning." Ethan threw up his hands, turning to Andrew. "Bring me the maps," he said, studying the ledger again.

Jonathan closed his fingers over the handle of the pistol in his belt and stalked from the library. He moved broodingly along the corridor. The lack of sleep had done nothing for his restraint. The man Silas had come unexpectedly, unbidden, out of the unforgiven past. And *how* he had come! As a loud, condemning riding preacher. To Jonathan, he was the embodiment and perpetrator of his worst torments.

His heavy steps led him down a flight of stairs and into the kitchen. He looked for Chayta. She stood deep in thought in the open doorway at the back of the kitchen. Jonathan came to the same doorway and leaned there, watching in silence the sunny road that stretched up the hill to the Inn.

"I hate him," Jonathan said.

"You mus'n't say such. He's your father."

"No, no," he said, "my father's dead."

Chayta turned and touched his cheek, her eyes filled with fear.

"I want to kill him."

"Jonathan, no!"

"And why not? After what he did. He made Emily suffer. He made the Captain suffer, and now he pretends he's a man of God."

"Poor boy," the old slave sighed, "and now you suffer, too. But you can't kill him for that."

Ethan opened the kitchen door timidly, a look of concern on his face. "Jonathan, my boy, is . . . is something wrong?"

Chayta replied, "We're havin' a talk, Master Ethan."

Ethan looked unconvinced. "Very well, very well." He backed out of the door.

Jonathan pushed past Chayta through the door to the yard, taking the steps two at a time. When he reached the cobblestoned street, he began to run. Merchants, sweeping their shops, stared at him as he passed. A young woman watering a planter box snickered to herself at the sight of the wealthy young Mr. Barratt hurrying up the hill, his fine clothes rumpled, his hair shaggy and unkempt. He knew he was seen in a distraught state, but he cared little. He no longer had anything to lose. He was Emily's illegitimate son.

A Baltimore coach waited near the top of the street. Edward Chase stood nearby, prepared to climb aboard. Estelle and Charlotte waited on the boardwalk. Jonathan passed on the opposite side of the street, hoping not to be noticed as he finished the last yards to the top of the hill. At the Bath House door beneath the main entry porch of the Inn, he paused briefly. Looking back over his shoulder, he saw that the coach had gone and so had Estelle.

Jonathan stepped into the steamy darkness of the Bath House. Inside, he moved to one side and waited for his eyes to adjust to the lantern light. Slowly the details of the room emerged. He could see that it was unattended and empty of bathers except for one man who sat up to his neck in the bubbling water near the far wall. His back was to Jonathan. On the bench, the black clothes of a riding preacher were folded in a neat pile. But the man was not Silas.

Jonathan's hand rested upon the handle of one of the pistols. He looked again at the back of the bather's head and imagined for a moment that it was indeed Silas' head. He took the pistol from his belt and aimed.

"Do what you will on that day," Jonathan whispered between clenched teeth. He returned the pistol to his waistband then walked across the floor toward the figure in the bath.

The man sat with his eyes tightly closed. He was much smaller than Silas. His forehead was high and broad, his face bold yet kindly. Thin brown hair streaked with premature gray cascaded from the top of his head. He was chilled with fever. His lips were cracked and bleeding from severe blisters. Jonathan paced to the wall, then back again to his original position.

"The footsteps of a troubled man," the preacher observed without opening his eyes. "What is your name?"

Jonathan paused, taken off guard. "Jonathan," he replied at length.

"Jonathan, I am Francis Asbury. It is good to make your acquaintance."

"Are you the same Mr. Asbury they say was sent from John Wesley in England?"

"I am. You have heard of my commission?"

"I . . . yes. At Harvard College we spoke much about John Wesley and heard of your coming. The feeling was, however, that Wesley's religion was more right for the British, who needed it more than we."

"Is that what they say?"

"Well, some do. In general it was doubted that you could repeat Wesley's work here in America."

"I was in hiding during the war because of that sort of talk. But thanks be to God it has been shown that the gospel I preach is from the heart of God to the heart of man and transcends kings and kingdoms. In a sense I do represent Mr. Wesley. He commissioned me. But I would not have ridden from Boston to Charleston to the edge of Kentucky and to the edge of my own ruin, in the space of one year, on that commission alone. I travel for my Lord, whose servant I am."

"Wesley himself failed to do in America what he has commissioned you to do."

"He had not experienced saving faith forty years ago, my young man. That makes the difference, or did you overlook that in your discussions at Harvard?"

"Perhaps we were unqualified to discuss it, sir. But it interests me. I . . . I seek God, a true knowledge of Him. But I see you are ill and perhaps I should speak with you at a better time."

Asbury raised a weakened hand from the water. "When the flesh is punished, the spirit grows strong. What knowledge do you seek?" He cracked open an eye.

Jonathan began to pace slowly. He saw an opportunity in this discussion. He was a kind of seeker, that was no lie, but what he sought had little to do with God. Did Silas masquerade as a man of God? That's what he wanted to know. Well, then, Jonathan would masquerade as a God seeker, to find out.

"My mother . . . who died many years hence," he began, "is she now with God in paradise? Or in some other place?"

After a thoughtful pause, Asbury asked, "Was she a godly woman?"

"She was religious. Not agitatedly so, but a good woman. She was always good to me . . . but when she died she screamed out that she was rejected by God. What kind of God would do that to her?"

"God did not do it—"

"Is God revealed in Holy Scripture?"

"He is."

"Does the scripture say that 'God maketh the poor and the rich,' some vessels 'created for honor and others for His wrath'?"

"The scriptures you have torn from their place in the Bible do not stand alone, Jonathan. They are part of a picture of God given in many thousands of words, over thousands of years by many men of God. Tell me, have you read the scriptures from beginning to end?"

"I have not."

"Then, how are you seeking God? Do you expect to find Him in the evils of life? In a tragic death? Do you think you shall find Him there? Hear this scripture: 'God is light and in Him is no darkness at all.' Seek Him in the light of scripture. Not the darkness of this fallen world."

Jonathan did not expect such a good answer from a riding preacher.

"Well, what of the darkness, Preacher Asbury? I did not have to seek for it. The death of my mother came when I was but a child. As it has for many. God has not come to me this way—"

"Oh, but He has."

"Begging your pardon, sir, He has *not* come to me with the same power as evil," Jonathan said bitterly. "God, we see 'through a darkened glass' . . . I believe your scripture tells us? But I have seen evil face to face. I saw my mother die, screaming that she was damned. I heard no words of assurance come from a God in Heaven. And how did that darkness come upon her, Preacher?" Jonathan was surprised at his own vehemence. "It came by the hands of religion, I say! It came by scripture. Tell me, where is the light that comes in the hour of need?"

Asbury's head was bowed and he remained quiet for a long moment in the water. "What pain you bear," he said at last. "As do so many in this land. I have seen many die as you describe. Tormented. Despairing. But there is truth to set them free. There is a saving faith which is the reason I ride this land. No other."

"You came too late for her. If this truth, this 'saving faith' exists, why was it denied to her? And tell me this, now, Preacher, was it the work of God that denied her that comfort, or perhaps someone on this earth?"

"It was not God—"

"I concur. It was then"—he bit each word—"someone—on—this—earth."

"But you can know the peace of God, Jonathan—"

"I am not here asking comfort for my own death!" Jonathan snapped. "What of my mother? Did God reject her, or is she with Him?"

Asbury was slow to speak. "I cannot say," he said gently, "but I pray she was not rejected."

"Then I am still seeking God. I should know what He did with my mother before I give Him my worship. That seems fair, does it not?"

Asbury spoke sadly. "You may never find what you seek, young man. You have a heart of stone. I would plant a seed there, but as yet I find no soil."

Jonathan's mind worked quickly now to get what he came for. "Perhaps this other riding preacher can find soil in my heart for planting."

"Silas?"

"Yes, Silas. The one who brought you to Bath. Perhaps I should spend more time with him. And I could leave you to a much-needed rest."

"I am afraid he is busy filling my place at meetings to the north of here."

"He will not be back?"

"In three days, if the weather is good. But he will not stay longer than to see that I have not expired here. He is under an urgent constraint to return to his circuit."

"And where is his circuit?"

"The most uncivilized part of this land . . . Kentucky."

"Kentucky. How intriguing. I have business there."

"Indeed?"

The words that he spoke next surprised even Jonathan. "Perhaps I might accompany the preacher to Kentucky." His hands trembled. The long night had exhausted him. "Do you suppose he would allow it, the preacher Silas?"

"You would have to ask him yourself."

"Yes, of course." Jonathan was deliberately quiet. When he did speak, his words were measured. "But you might help me by speaking to him first. You might explain that I am traveling on business to Kentucky. And that I seek God."

6

The Fowl Shoot

"Bring another," Ethan shouted.

A slave boy in a black and white house uniform ran to a nearby pile of wooden crates. Reaching inside, he trapped and extracted a European partridge. He held the fluttering bird aloft. Andrew tamped shot and powder into the barrel-works of a blunderbuss as Ethan leaned back in a stuffed leather chair beneath a tassled sunshade. He plucked a grape from a bowl beside the chair and peeled it expertly. From where he sat, Ethan looked down on fields of grain and newly planted orchards. Through a distant niche in the valley, the blue-hued Appalachian foothills could be seen, descending northward like a stairwell to the Potomac.

"Are you ready?" Ethan called. He signaled to the boy who clutched the struggling bird. The boy nodded.

Andrew ceremoniously handed the primed blunderbuss to Ethan, who raised it to his shoulder.

"Release it," he called.

The boy tossed the bird and threw himself prostrate in one terrified motion, covering his head and ears.

Ethan fired.

"D____-*nation!*" he swore. The partridge whirred harmlessly across the lush valley.

"Bring me another," Ethan ordered the frightened boy.

Sounds of hoofbeats were heard from below the hill. Jonathan rode into sight.

Ethan waved. "Jon," he called, "come try the shooting chair."

Jonathan reined Merlin to a halt near the canopy. "I must talk with you, Uncle Ethan."

"What brings you here, Jon?" he asked.

Jonathan walked to where his uncle sat. He stood looking down over him as he spoke. "I have come to a decision, Uncle."

"Yes?"

"I believe that I am old enough to take more direct interest in Barratt Enterprises."

"But certainly, Jonathan, and you are doing just that. Why, that is why we returned from Boston to Bath so you could be more involved in business."

"I mean learning about it, actually doing something."

A look of worry crossed Ethan's face. "But what do you want to do that you are not already doing? You own Barratt Enterprises, Jonathan."

"But I have never really done anything with it. When the Capt . . . when my father was alive, everything revolved around the sea. But now that the business is located in Bath, I want to learn about this land business. Take more part in the administration of my inheritance."

"I must say, the world is strangely fashioned. Those who must work for their bread complain against the injustice of life, while those whom Providence has blessed beg for work." Ethan laughed uneasily. "Well, certainly, there are things you can do. Why, I had hoped for this very time, when you would shoulder more of the heavy burden of Barratt Enterprises." He paused, trying to decide what to say next. "Have you anything in mind?"

"I had thought of something."

"Yes?"

"I should like to go to Kentucky, to see the land that we have purchased."

"Kentucky? But Kentucky is a wilderness."

Jonathan twisted Merlin's reins between his fingers. "I feel that firsthand knowledge of our investments will be valuable to us in the future, Uncle Ethan."

"You can't be serious about this, Jonathan. I don't think Barratt Enterprises stands to gain anything if you lose your scalp."

"I have made up my mind." He turned away and prepared to mount his horse.

Ethan got up from the chair. "One moment, Jonathan. You would never, now, do anything to jeopardize the investments your father and I have planned together all these years?" He folded his hands uncomfortably behind him and paced to the edge of the hill, looking thoughtfully across the farmland below. "You *are* my nephew and the owner of Barratt Enterprises, and I, merely in your employ, but there were certain items, uh . . . things in your father's papers that . . ." He stopped himself from saying more, feeling suddenly that he had said too much.

"What things, Uncle?"

Ethan smiled. "Well, nothing of great import, Jonathan, just instructions for the business, you know. I am only concerned for the well-being of your inheritance."

"I am sure of that, Uncle." Jonathan returned his smile. "And I don't plan to jeopardize it either. But I will be leaving shortly."

"Do you know anything at all about this land of Kentucky, Jon? It is a land full of savages, pagan, blood-rite savages who . . . why, they lie with carnivorous beasts and have monstrous offspring by them. You have heard these things, haven't you? They follow laws of a most inhumane nature, sacrificing infants and the elderly and such, worshipping demon spirits, roasting captive settlers—they have roasted them alive, Jon—and there are fever-laden swamps out there, and I have heard of depraved renegade bands that roam there of such a wanton nature as to make the rites of the savages pale by comparison." He paused. "Have you made a will?"

Jonathan turned to see if Ethan was joking. But Ethan's face was as serious as Jonathan had ever seen it, his fat cheeks red and puffing. Jonathan laughed. "And this is our promised land, is it? This savage country? The land you are selling with such vigor?"

Ethan instantly defended. "Well, it *is* being settled, Jon. You have lived all of your life among the comforts of civilization. A century ago this area around Bath was a hostile land, like Kentucky. There will be many fearful sacrifices necessary before Kentucky is a fit place to live. These are things that most of us who have lived long enough understand."

"Then I am more determined to see it."

"Dear God, you are serious. Then I will obtain for you an armed escort."

"I have already made arrangements for protection." Jonathan mounted Merlin. His heart raced. Perhaps this would be more of an adventure than he bargained for, but he had come too far now. There would be no turning back.

As the pleasant atmosphere from the dining porch filtered through the floor planks above him, Jonathan eased his naked body into the steaming waters of the bath. Across the same pool of water sat the Reverend Francis Asbury, looking much healthier than he had days ago. The tired and fevered look was gone from his eyes. The lip sores had nearly healed. On this evening, as he soaked in the healing waters, the preacher gave serious attention to a page of his leather-bound Bible.

Jonathan gave no greeting. He had come to the bath with the intention of finding Asbury in order to tell him of his firm decision to make the ride to Kentucky with Silas Will. At length, Asbury cleared his throat. He continued to squint intently at the scripture, then lamented aloud, "My Lord and my God." He looked up at Jonathan as if he now owed him an explanation for thinking aloud in his presence.

"Good evening, sir," Jonathan said.

"My young man, this passage in the Second Letter to Timothy seems written concerning Bath," Asbury said. "Listen to this." He began to read. " 'This know also, that in the last days perilous times shall come. For men shall be lovers of their own selves' . . . That seems to describe every trifling citizen of Bath, I fear, and here the writer describes those who are 'traitors, heady, high-minded,' and here 'lovers of pleasures more than lovers of God; having a form of godliness, but denying the power thereof: from such turn away.' "

Anger welled instantly in Jonathan. If anyone was high-minded, it was this preacher, he thought. He stifled a retort. Too much was at stake to risk offending Asbury now. He continued to peer calmly at the man from behind the steam-fogged lenses of his spectacles.

Asbury folded his Bible and placed it on the edge of the pool. He settled back into the water, addressing Jonathan directly.

"Orville, the proprietor of this inn, once a seeker of righteousness, has allowed the love of pleasure to pull him back into sin, I fear. He will not abide sound doctrine. Liquor spirits, frivolity, the trifling pleasures of wealth, all of these hold him in bondage. You, Jonathan, are the sole citizen I have encountered in this settlement who, though contentious, has a serious mind for God. Perhaps He ordained our meeting."

If Asbury had not been looking directly at him, Jonathan would have laughed at this assessment of his character.

"Perhaps," Jonathan said. "And perhaps the hand of Providence arranged my business in Kentucky. I'm, uh, fortunate that Silas Will is to travel the same road. And he possesses the same knowledge of God as you do, sir."

"Intriguing," Asbury observed. "You have praised what you call the hand of Providence. Would you not take a small step of faith and praise instead the hand of God?"

Jonathan thought for a long moment. Had he seen anything like the hand of God at work in his life? So many things had happened to him, so many twists, so many events, decisions, and actions had brought him to where he now stood. Had the hand of God orchestrated any of this?

"No," Jonathan answered. "I fear I must go in the opposite direction, sir, and call it rather the hand of fate . . . of mere chance."

"But why?"

"Because . . . well, suppose I were to call it the hand of God and declare that He had arranged my need to travel so that I could be with this exhorter of yours, Silas. In that case, I would be forced to ask what kind of God would move His hand in the trifling matter of my travel, but would not move His hand to save my mother's life. Or to give her the comfort she needed on her deathbed, at least. I do not wish to hate God." He paused. "So I will call it the hand of chance."

Asbury was hesitant to reply. Certainly this was not the answer he had expected. He chose his words with care.

"I will say this to you now, Jonathan, without fear of contradiction. God desires you for His Kingdom. He has created your quick mind for some great purpose. I will pray daily that you find that purpose."

"Perhaps Silas can reveal it."

"Only the Spirit of God can reveal the ways of God to a man, but Silas may well be His instrument. I will recommend your company to him when he arrives here tomorrow."

"Thank you, sir." Jonathan climbed from the bath and began to towel away the dripping water.

"Let me warn you concerning Silas," Asbury cautioned. "Don't expect his answers to be as temperate as mine. He is not highly schooled, though he is surprisingly well read. And he knows his scripture: it is his daily bread. Before the spirit of God overshadowed him, he rode with Jacques LeFevre and his cutthroat renegades. You probably know nothing of Le-Fevre, but in Kentucky he is known all too well." Asbury closed the Bible.

"But about Silas, now. While riding with me on a Carolina road some eight years ago, he experienced a saving faith as wonderful as any I have witnessed. Right there on the road. It was like the Apostle Paul, the way his life turned around. I needed others to help me carry this gospel, so I recognized the Spirit of God upon him and licensed him to exhort.

"Afterward, he rode back to the Kentucky wilderness to preach there. Time has shown his conversion to be sincere. I have rarely seen the like of it."

Jonathan noticed that Asbury spoke with great conviction about Silas. When it came to the judgment of a man's character, he thought, this preacher was subject to grave error. So Silas Will had ridden with rene-gades, had he? Jonathan could well believe it, and that perhaps he worked with LeFevre still. Not only would he have to guard himself against savages and robbers, he would need to be on his guard with Silas.

"I accept your word of caution," Jonathan said.

At that moment the door of the bath opened. A uniformed house slave entered.

"Sirs," he announced, "I have a message for Mr. Barratt."

Jonathan's eyes narrowed on the man. "Yes? I am Mr. Barratt."

The slave handed him a sealed brown envelope. "I am sent from the Chase household, sir."

"Oh, yes, well, one moment." He unfolded the note.

> Jonathan dearest,
>   Would you join me this evening at nine?
>   I will eagerly await your reply.
>   Estelle

He stared at the note. His mind and heart had traveled far since that day in the stable when Chayta had interrupted their meeting. He folded the note and laid it with his things on the bench.

"I shall reply later," he instructed the servant.

He pulled on his riding boots and gathered his coat to go.

"Shall I meet you and Silas here at the Inn? Midday tomorrow?" he asked of Asbury. "I will be ready to travel by then."

"Midday should be fine. Good night, Jonathan. You shall daily be in my prayers."

Outside, the moon had risen full above an approaching storm. It reflected on the cloud tops, outlining them on the distant horizon. The same light cast a soft blue moon path, which stretched before him all the way down the cobblestoned hill to his home.

He was suddenly moved by the beauty of the moment. It called to him and he felt a solace in it. He leaned quietly against a pillar of the dining porch, allowing the scene to touch him. Couples strolled in the moonlight. Across the street, a family walked homeward after dinner at the Inn. Their lanterns appeared and disappeared like bobbing fireflies. The breeze carried whispers, laughter, and the chatter of children. This was life the way Jonathan would choose it. This was home. Here was peace. And beauty. And the wealth to create more of the same. Beyond Bath, elsewhere in the colonies, life was hard.

Jonathan had not chosen Bath, nor had he yet created any part of it. It had all come as an accident of birth. As he basked in its beauty, his heart still troubled by the events of recent days, he felt that he owed something, or someone. But what? Or who? Who should be thanked? Emily? The Captain? Yes. Chayta? Andrew? Macaijah? Yes. He was beginning to realize that their lives had been more to him than the servitude required of slavery. Did he owe the early English colonists, perhaps? Lord Fairfax and Washington for discovering the springs of Bath? Or the hand of chance, or fate, or Providence, which had conspired to make Bath a haven of delight?

Jonathan decided that it must be some unknown combination of all of these things. The moonlit street confirmed this belief. Each cobblestone, uniquely defined by the moonlight, owed something to the unseen hands that had found, quarried, and fit them together. And to the minds that had conceived their order and usefulness.

It surprised him that he could feel this way. For a brief moment, the trouble within him had been replaced by quiet reverie. He was weary, bone-weary, but from the center of that weariness came a gentle exhilaration. He felt alive with these troubles. Alive. And now the beauty of Bath in the moonlight made him sense that there was also a debt for just being alive.

Who were these riding preachers to call Bath a sinful place? How dare they? What was sinful about it? Its beauty? Its peace? Wealth? Did God stand against these good things on a miserable earth? If so, then Jonathan stood against God.

Tomorrow, he would leave Bath of his own accord and ride an unpaved road to Kentucky. Why was he going? What was pushing him to do this? Perhaps it was only the hand of fate. And suddenly he was overwhelmed with the feeling that he was looking at Bath for the last time.

7

The Goodbyes

Silas emerged from a thicket on the ridge above Bath. He rode one horse and led another along a twisting game trail that traced the high ground through patches of mountain laurel, hemlock, and broom sedge. He had forsaken the road. His long-coat collar was up, his hat brim low. He held a Kentucky long rifle, and as he eased along beneath the towering stone escarpment, his eyes swept the countryside below for signs of movement.

Morning had broken hours ago, revealing somber skies. Even now dark mists were curling past the crags above him like wind-driven armies rushing to position themselves for an assault on the earth. At ground level, a moist breeze passed through the nodding grass and bushes, whipping up pollen which sharpened the air with pungent aromas. Silas breathed the pleasurable atmosphere with the frontiersman's awareness that it was the harbinger of a coming deluge.

Whispering like a guided arrow, a golden eagle swooped unexpectedly past him from behind, hugging the contour of the open ridge at dizzying speed. Twisting suddenly, the bird stabbed a fleeing rabbit, talons locked on the bleating animal. Then the eagle veered upward with a defiant scream and rode the wind into the cliffs above.

Silas watched in awe as the powerful bird soared to its aerie in the granite towers near the clouds.

"How beautiful Thy creation," he mused. "How awful the curse."

He turned his horse downward, onto a path which led to Bath's graveyard. As he descended the ridge, he leaned forward and returned his rifle to its saddle scabbard. At the white picket gate he dismounted and tied both horses. Then he moved away from the gate to the crest of the hill, where he could look down on the settlement of Bath.

He walked over the hill crest to where a jack-in-the-pulpit bobbed in the breeze. He plucked it and continued on, stopping to collect a violet, a trillium, a buttercup, a snakeroot blossom, until he had collected an entire bouquet of multicolored wildflowers. He paused, arranging them one by one in his palm until they presented the mix of color that pleased him. Then he returned to the graveyard.

He moved among the headstones with the familiarity of one who had been there before. He had visited the Barratt plot many times. But always before there had been only one marker, the one bearing Emily Barratt's name. Now there were two headstones. He stopped to read Captain Nelson Barratt's marker: "1729–1780."

Silas removed his hat and moved forward to Emily's grave. He knelt down and set the wildflowers in front of her marker, but before releasing them he stopped and withdrew his hand. Then he placed the flowers on the ground between the two markers. He stood up. The wind gusted and scattered his bouquet across the yard.

He was disturbed by this. He breathed in deeply, inhaling the fragrant morning air, holding it for a long moment as if undecided. Then he let it go in a long sigh. He nodded to himself as if trying to bring all of his will into agreement with the actions of the wind. He had been wrong to gather the flowers, he thought. He should be leaving this alone. Sin was sin and time had not made it right.

He firmly replaced his hat upon his head and left the graveyard.

Chayta was strangely quiet as she walked the corridor and entered the library of the Barratt mansion. She crossed the floor to the room that had once belonged to Emily. She stopped in the doorway without announcing herself.

Jonathan did not look up. He sat on the floor, surrounded by dozens of half-unpacked traveling trunks containing books, clothing, and other mementos of his Harvard life. He was deep in concentration as he put the finishing flame to the last of a half dozen pair of metal-rimmed spectacles he had soldered for the trip.

"They tell me Kentucky is rough country," he said, still concentrating. "I hope I don't need all of these spares, but I do intend to be prepared."

He finished a nosepiece and set the final pair of glasses on the floor to cool. He snuffed the focused candle he had been using to heat the metal. Then he turned to Chayta, for the first time noticing her tears.

"Now, Chayta, should this be a sad occasion? Truly?"

She shook her head. "I know you mus' go. But you're the last one. I can't help cryin."

Jonathan got up and went to her. In all of his turmoil he had forgotten that she too had suffered. Her only son was a fugitive with a price on his head. She too had loved his mother. And now Jonathan, who had been another son to her, was leaving on an uncertain journey. He took the old black woman in his arms and felt her tears soak through his shirt. Suddenly he knew that her life, far more than his, had been a life of losses. So much had been taken from her—home, family, youth, heritage, dignity, dreams, rights, choices. She was a slave. And as a slave, she had cared for him—and his mother. But the law that made her chattel had not required that she give them her love. And Chayta had loved them, with a love as deep as her sorrows.

Jonathan helped her from the room. He felt that he owed far more than he could ever repay.

Silas had arrived at the Inn. He leaned in the doorway of Asbury's room, scowling, arms folded across his chest.

Asbury, nearly recuperated, hobbled about collecting a few extra pieces of clothing into his worn leather saddlebags. Both men were dressed in knee breeches, waistcoat, topcoat, and riding boots. They were ready for the road.

"I say he should go his own way," Silas growled. "I have dangerous business."

"So it would seem. Are you certain that you were followed?"

"I only know that I saw one of LeFevre's men. No doubt about it. I recognized him from the raid on the Green River. He was in Martinsburg when I passed through, day before yesterday. LeFevre hasn't sent a man out of Kaintuck since Alamance. What you suppose he'd do it *now* for?"

"The raid and the hangings, is my guess."

Silas nodded, then betrayed a hint of pride and said, "First time anyone in Kaintuck ever had the gumption to put a check on that whiskey-foul reprobate. Ha. And it pleases me that they did it under the inspiration of scripture, too. God's men rose up!"

Asbury sounded a note of caution. "Not all of my fellow ministers agree that you acted properly, Silas. Some would turn the other cheek seventy times seven before bearing arms."

"Would they now?"

"They would leave such matters to the law of the land."

"There is no law in Kaintuck! You saw what Kaintuck law is like, up the head of the Monongahela."

"Yes, I did, and I do stand behind you in this, Silas. And, if necessary, I shall arm myself when I return to your circuit."

"You know that I would, as the scripture says, turn the other cheek, and have done so on occasion. But this man LeFevre is a demon. He murdered Simon Stern's womenfolk, members of my flock. I'll exhort with a Bible *and* a long rifle till LeFevre and all his bunch hang by the neck."

"So it is possible that LeFevre has sent men to ambush you. But this man in Martinsburg, could he have been sent for some other reason? Perhaps he was expelled by LeFevre, or was running away?"

" 'Tis possible, but not likely."

"This young man Jonathan seems quite fit. A companion may serve as protection, Silas."

"I will not bear the responsibility for him."

"He is a man in his own right. He says he has business in Kentucky. Inform him of your possible danger and let him decide if he should ride with you or not."

"You say his name is Jonathan?"

"Yes, perhaps you have seen him about. A handsome lad. Intelligent, with spectacles. All of our conversations have been of a spiritual nature."

"Then it most certainly is not the young man I have seen of that description," Silas muttered.

Asbury closed the straps on his saddlebags and attempted to lift them with some difficulty. Silas stepped in to take them on his own shoulder.

"Is it wise for you to return to the road today?" Silas asked.

"Bath has closed ears to the gospel."

"I also found it so."

"I grieve to see the manner in which these people partake of the sweet life, eating of the fat of the land with neither a sign of fear nor supplication to God. You and I need to go where souls are hungry, where sinners cry for salvation."

Silas acknowledged with a silent nod and turned from the room. Asbury followed. They descended the stairwell together.

"You say this young man seeks God?" Silas asked.

"Well, he is a seeker, yes. He may be a good distance yet from finding."

As the two preachers entered the main room of the Inn, Orville Hudson stood at the bar engaged in conversation with two young ladies. Seeing Asbury and Silas come into view, he frowned. The laughter of the young ladies suddenly ceased. They excused themselves from the room, while Orville busied himself with a cleaning rag.

"No need for pay," Orville spoke up curtly before they had reached the counter.

"Orville," Asbury said gently, "we are able."

"But I would not be able to accept. Godspeed to you both. Excuse me, I have things to attend." He walked briskly from behind the counter and disappeared through a door to the kitchen.

Jonathan raced for the barn. He was late for his noon rendezvous with Silas and Asbury. Merlin was saddled and waiting. Jonathan fastened his packed saddlebags behind the saddle.

He listed in his mind the things he had packed, afraid he had forgotten something: copies of Barratt Kentucky maps, a packet of six individually wrapped spectacles, the spyglass given to him by Captain Barratt, Chayta's raisin-crab-apple cakes, bread, cheese, and his oilskin rain slicker. Under his coat, he wore the Captain's dueling pistols in a shoulder harness he had made. He had a pouch of oak and pine tree shillings and had hidden a dozen eight-escudo Spanish gold pieces among his belongings. The last item packed was the letter: written by Emily to Silas.

He stepped back from Merlin to be certain he was ready.

"D____!" he swore. On the horse's right foreleg he saw a blood-crusted cut.

"Caleb," he called angrily.

The slave, who was cleaning another stall, poked his head over the gate. "Yes, Master Jonathan?"

"Caleb, what's happened to this horse?"

"The mare kicked him, I suppose."

Suddenly Jonathan remembered Estelle's horse. He felt a wave of regret for having put Merlin to stud. He bent to examine the leg closely. "Well, it is not deep," he said, frowning. "Let's see if he favors it."

Caleb led the horse in a wide circle within the barn. Merlin pranced with his usual vigor.

"He seems not to be bothered," Jonathan mused. "But he is fresh yet. From the look of it, I will have to go easy for a few days."

"Maybe he just needs a pine-tar remedy, master."

"Yes. Apply one," Jonathan said, and walked disgustedly out of the barn.

The tension of the coming encounter with Silas gripped him. He twisted his cold fingers nervously. What would Silas know about him? Did he know his true identity? Did he know he would be riding to Kentucky with Emily Barratt's son? Emily's letter seemed clear that Silas did not know of Jonathan's birth. But had there been other letters, letters not tucked away in the Bible? Or other meetings between Silas and Emily? And why was Silas a preacher? Was this another deception?

Jonathan heard the sound of a carriage approaching from the street. He looked up to see Estelle Chase heading toward the Barratt barn. Her daughter, Charlotte, sat next to her. Jonathan felt momentary panic. He had never answered Estelle's note. And now he had no time to explain, no time to make an adequate apology. He had hoped to slip away unnoticed.

Her chaise pulled up before the barn and stopped. She sat looking ahead, ignoring him. Jonathan glanced back over his shoulder into the barn. Caleb was busy preparing the poultice for Merlin's leg. Jonathan turned and stepped forward to Estelle's carriage.

"I am here to get my mare, Jonathan. Have her saddled, please. Charlotte will ride her home." She barely glanced at him and her head trembled as she spoke from what appeared to be the effort to maintain an icy attitude. "I believe our business together is quite finished."

"Yes," he replied. He called to Caleb to saddle the mare, then stepped forward to help Charlotte from the chaise. The girl smiled at him brattily and wandered away into the barn.

"Estelle, I'm sorry," Jonathan began. "My mind has been on many . . . on urgent business, even to this very moment."

"Yes, I know. Men always have urgent business."

Jonathan drew a deep breath and turned to see if Charlotte or Caleb was within earshot. Both were apparently in the stall with the mare.

"Estelle," he said, "would you mind walking with me to the oak there, so we can speak privately?"

She waited, considering it for a moment, and then offered him her hand so that he could help her from the chaise. She stepped carefully down each rung of the ladder to the ground. Jonathan walked with her around the corner of the barn. They reached the shade of the tree and Jonathan turned, searching his mind for something to say.

"Estelle, I have to go away. To Kentucky. I am leaving today. The other day, here, when you and I were together, I did not know I would be taking this journey. But when I received your letter, I did know. It did not seem fair to see you more." He noticed the anger soften in her eyes.

"But you were not even going to say goodbye."

He was silent for too long. "I . . . I was . . ."

She looked away. "It would have been a wonderful summer. At least you made me believe that it would have been. When will you return?"

"It may be months, Estelle. It may be . . ." He caught himself before he said the word "never." "I will hurry," he laughed, trying to disguise his fear. "I will be thinking of you."

She sighed. "Dear, dear, Jonathan. Kentucky is dangerous. Please take care."

She put her arms around him abruptly and pulled him close. He kissed her, but as he did so a scream sounded from the corner of the barn.

"Mother!"

Charlotte had rounded the barn, her face livid. She came running, clutching her long skirt in her hands. As she reached them, her foot caught a root and she tumbled forward to the ground. Jonathan hurried to help her up. Like a springing catamount, she uncoiled from the ground with an unintelligible screech, catching Jonathan off guard. With her fingernails she raked his face from forehead to chin, breaking his spectacles and leaving long red scratches to mark her disgust.

"Charlotte! Charlotte! Good Lord." Estelle rushed between them, slapping her daughter soundly several times.

"How could you?" Charlotte sobbed. "How? *Him?* Mother, what about Father? What have you—"

Estelle glowered at her. "Charlotte, you have made an utter fool of yourself, and of me. Get in the carriage. Now!"

"Mother—"

"Do as I say!"

Charlotte backed up, shaking her head in shame and disgust. Then she turned and stalked tearfully toward the chaise.

Estelle turned to Jonathan. "Oh dear, you are badly scratched." She shook her head and sighed helplessly.

Jonathan's head began to throb. He inspected his broken spectacles and felt his stinging face.

"I must go, I'm late." He tried to smile. "Tell Charlotte that I will seek a proper husband for her among the savages of Kentucky. Perhaps when I've healed, I'll forgive."

They both smiled wryly and turned toward the barn.

Merlin was ready. Jonathan went to his saddlebags and removed a leather pouch. He took out another pair of spectacles. Carefully, he put them on.

"Goodbye, Mr. Barratt," Estelle said.

"Goodbye, Mrs. Chase."

He swung into the saddle, nudged Merlin once, and the stallion bolted away from the barn.

It was now long past midday. He rode cursing himself as a fool for having, as the fool's proverb said, "shot himself in the foot" on the eve of battle.

Silas paced before Asbury in front of the Bath House Inn. Asbury, by contrast, seemed calm and unhurried.

Silas grumbled, "This young man who seeks God would do well to heed the scripture: 'Seek him early, while he may yet be found.' "

"He will be here." Asbury smiled. "He not only seeks God, he has business in Kentucky. Be patient."

"For your sake, my friend, I shall wait longer, but once on the road, I must keep to a schedule if I am to be in Logan's Fort for the hanging day. He will keep up then, or be left behind."

"That's between the two of you, but, Silas, in your discussions with the young man you may find him, oh, perhaps . . . intolerably educated. He will not be like most men that we counsel."

"He needs God like all men. And there is only one way to find God, educated or not."

Asbury nodded. "But he is full of questions, quite thoughtful ones, I might add."

"It will not take long to determine if his questions arise from a heart that seeks God, or from the sin of unbelief."

"But what appears to be unbelief can sometimes . . ." Asbury began, but at that moment a clattering in the cobblestoned street drew their attention down the hill. Jonathan rode the powerful black stallion with flowing ease up the cobblestoned grade. "Unbelief can perhaps be the cry of a wounded soul," Asbury finished.

Silas did not hear. The closer Jonathan came to them, the more his eyes narrowed with recognition.

"*This* is Jonathan?"

Asbury nodded. "It is." He moved forward to greet Jonathan and did not notice the snapping indignation in Silas' eyes. "Jonathan, I have been telling Silas of you. Welcome at last. Silas, this is Jonathan."

Silas' eyes mercilessly bore into Jonathan's as he dismounted from Merlin and stepped forward with extended hand. Silas cocked his head to one side, reading the telltale scratches on Jonathan's face with slight amusement. Jonathan felt his face grow hot, but he steeled himself to meet the preacher's gaze. "Good day, sir," he said.

"Are we pretending to be meeting for the first time?" Silas asked.

Asbury grew troubled. "What do you mean? You have met before?"

"What he means, Mr. Asbury," Jonathan cut in, "is that we have had several brief encounters here in the past few days. I certainly did not count any of them a proper introduction. I had hoped he would consider it the same."

"It was introduction enough for me," Silas retorted. "You and I both know that you are no seeker of God."

Jonathan felt his resolve wither beneath Silas' quick attack. But he shot back, "I am a seeker, as much as you are a man of God."

Silas turned away with a short, disgusted chuckle and gathered the reins of his two horses. "I know, Francis, that you did not intend for me to give time to this . . . impostor, who appears to have recently tangled with an angry bear, heh." He turned a sarcastic gaze back to Jonathan. "A she-bear, by the look of it. You know the urgent duties that call me. I must be on my way without delay."

"I understand," Asbury replied with quiet bewilderment, "but I do *not* know that he is an impostor. However"—he turned now to Jonathan for an answer—"I did gather from the nature of our conversations that you would be meeting Silas for the first time."

"I consider that is so," Jonathan asserted.

"Francis," Silas said, leading his horses near so that he could stand before his friend, "this young man has deceived you in order to obtain your favor. And I now deeply suspect his reasons for doing so. This"—he pointed—"is the very young man who ejected me from the licentious frolic the evening of our arrival. It is clear to me that he does not seek God."

"By what authority do you say that?" Jonathan asked. He stepped forward. "Are you God, who sees the heart?"

"No. I am merely a man who sees the fruit of a tree. By your fruit, you fight against God. You do not seek Him."

"I say that I do."

"Well, then, have you had a change of heart? That is a simple matter to know," Silas said, walking back to stand uncomfortably close to Jonathan. "If you seek God, you must begin at the door. I will show you the door. It is here." He pointed quietly to the ground between them. "You enter it on your knees."

Jonathan cast his eyes about for Asbury, who stood nearby, arms folded like a judge, brows knit in curiosity, waiting to know his response.

Jonathan felt very alone.

"I will explain for you," Jonathan said, "as I explained to Mr. Asbury, that I cannot bow before God when I do not know the truth about Him. I must first know what kind of God He is, or I bow my knee in ignorance."

"Better"—Silas exploded the word into his face so that Jonathan smelled his breath with it—"to bow your knee in ignorance and enter Heaven than waste your life ever learning, but never able to come to the knowledge of the truth. You might then be the most educated fool in Hell. You want to know the truth about God, Jonathan," he went on, "so that you do not have to bow in ignorance. What kind of God is He? I'll tell you. He is One God, above all, Creator, and He is Holy. He alone is Holy, absolutely without blemish."

Townspeople had gathered on the porch of the Inn and in the street.

So, Jonathan thought, Silas would use him to preach to the whole crowd. The thought of being used so, in the presence of his neighbors, insulted him.

"Nothing, *not one thing,*" Silas cried, warming to his subject, "nothing with a single imperfection can stand before God, and that must include you. For to see God today would mean damnation for you. There would be no choice in the matter, it would simply be done. But God loves you, Jonathan. He has given His Son, a Savior who died that you might live. Jesus Christ, the Holy Lamb of God who taketh away the sins of the world. If you humbly bow your knee to God now, begging His mercy, accepting His sacrifice for your sins, you shall someday *stand* before Him, face to face without fear, redeemed by that sacrifice."

Jonathan's knees trembled. He fought to control his own will over his body, for something made it want to kneel.

"You say you are a seeker of God? Well, here is the door. There is no other name under Heaven by which we must be saved. Now is the day of salvation."

Jonathan swallowed with a throat so dry it burned. "We are in a public place—" he protested.

"Christ *died* in a public place," Silas said. "Will you kneel? Or will you not?"

Jonathan felt confused and strangely, powerfully motivated to fall to his knees, throwing himself into the arms of Silas' God.

"You have sinned. You were born in sin. In sin did your mother conceive you—"

"No!" Jonathan cried. He took a step away from the preacher, and felt the spell of his words suddenly break at the mention of his mother.

"—there is only one choice to make," Silas went on. "As the scripture saith: 'Choose you this day whom you will serve.' "

"No," Jonathan coolly replied, "there is another choice. There are many other choices. I can choose to wait. To remain a seeker."

"Then you have made your choice," Silas said, moving away from him. "May God have mercy, you were shown the door. And plainly. There is nothing you can learn until you enter it."

He turned to Francis Asbury and his entire aspect changed as if he had dismissed Jonathan entirely from his mind. "Goodbye, my friend. God grant you many souls before we meet again." He embraced him.

"I know you must not be delayed," Asbury acknowledged. "I will explain the urgent nature of your trip to Jonathan. God speed you."

Silas swung his leg astride his mount. He gave Jonathan a final nod and with a wave to Asbury clattered away down the street.

Jonathan turned to his own mount, but Asbury leaped forward, placing a restraining hand on his arm. Jonathan turned again.

"It would not do well for you to follow him now," Asbury pleaded. "It would be dangerous."

"I expect danger," Jonathan said.

"I perhaps committed a grave error when I suggested that you ride with Silas. You see that both of his mounts are saddled. He rides one and rests the other. He must not rest long nor be delayed."

"My horse is more than a match for the two of his."

"But yours wears a poultice, and you yourself are wounded."

Jonathan swung himself into the saddle.

Asbury came nearer and grasped Merlin's bridle near the bit. "I beg you, reconsider. The consequences of this journey are the most serious that Silas is ever likely to face. He is not just preaching this time. He is organizing the men of his circuit against Jacques LeFevre, the man I told you about. They have captured and sentenced three of these murderers to death. LeFevre has vowed to kill Silas before he carries out the hangings."

"Did you receive the details of this story directly, or did you receive them from Silas?"

Asbury paused. "Well, of course, from Silas."

"And from no one else?"

"Why should that be necessary?"

"Because Silas Will is the greatest impostor here."

"I count myself a better judge of a man than that."

"Please let go of my horse."

"I am reluctant to, Jonathan. Something is wrong here. I fear some evil is at work to destroy a work of the Kingdom. Perhaps you are its unwitting accomplice."

Jonathan turned Merlin's head, and Asbury released his grip on the bit.

"Trust God, Preacher," Jonathan said with bitter irony. "I am sorry if I deceived you into believing that I seek God, but I do not deceive you in this: That man is an impostor and I will discover his true self."

With that, Jonathan turned Merlin in the direction Silas had taken. The red-haired preacher had already disappeared into the trees at the lower end of the valley.

Here and there on the dusty cobblestones, a sparse sampling of rain had begun to fall.

Part II

THE ROAD

"I hope I shall travel as long as I live;
travelling is my health, life, and all, for soul
and body. I am not well, but I am kept upright in heart . . . I am alternately in hope
and despair about it."

Francis Asbury, *Journal*

8

The Newtowne Trace

At the lower end of Bath's cobblestoned street, Jonathan was faced with a decision. Silas had disappeared. Which way had he gone?

Jonathan knew of only two roads to travel: the Martinsburg road and the Newtowne Trace. The trace was the more treacherous route, but it was the shortest to Virginia's Shenandoah Valley and the main colonial highway to the Kentucky wilderness. He guessed that Silas would take it and plunged ahead, guiding Merlin down a wooded hill between heavy ruts. He began to worry that the uneven roadbed would place extra strain on Merlin's bruised leg. He looked up at the dark sky. Things would become much worse in the rain. Suddenly, he knew that his clothes were too fine for such a journey in the raw elements. He wore a handsome suede riding suit with knee-high boots, a blue tricornered hat with a staghorn hunting medallion and small plume. These would not last long.

He planned to use his mount's superior strength at the very first to catch up to Silas. He could not be far ahead. Once having caught sight of him, he would then hang back, keeping him in sight and waiting for an opportunity to introduce himself again, this time in a manner Silas would not refuse.

As he rode, Jonathan wondered if he should tell Silas who he was. Certainly, that would alter the present stalemate. But how would it alter it? He knew so little about him. Was he really a changed man, a convert? Or did he ride in a preacher's clothes to disguise other motives? He reached the bottom of the first gully and broke into a canter up the far side then he entered a hollow and crested a side hill at the same pace. The warm summer air blew an occasional drop of rain against his face. But few raindrops were yet finding their way through the network of elm, oak, and pine branches above him.

This was adventure, he realized. The boldness of this step filled him with fear and exhilaration. He had loved his life in Bath, but there had been days of idleness and boredom. Not so now. He wondered if Macaijah had felt this way on his flight from Bath.

The road descended a long gentle slope into a grassy park. Jonathan's eyes searched ahead for a sign of Silas. He saw no one. He clucked to Merlin, spurring him into a faster run. They covered the distance quickly, the horse breathing hard, then again entered the forest and followed the trace up another ridge, slowing with the incline to an easy canter. The only sound was the sound of his own horse's hooves thudding on the trail, punctuated by the beating of his own heart in his ears. His eyes flitted back and forth, his ears strained to hear any foreign sound. From time to time he talked to himself in rhythm, "Where are you, Silas? Where did you go? I will find you. Where are you now?" He would make it a game, the hound and the hare. And no matter how quick the hare, the hound would stay close behind.

He entered and raced through a second park. Still no Silas. Now he grew worried. He splashed through a creek in the center of the meadow and noticed no fresh water marks on the opposite bank. If Silas were only minutes ahead of him, the water marks should still be showing.

"Blast." He had guessed wrong. Silas had taken the other route.

Jonathan knew he must decide soon whether to go back to Bath and try to catch him with an all out race on the Martinsburg road. But could Merlin's leg take the strain? He doubted it. One more park would tell. If he reached it and could not see Silas, he would return.

He urged Merlin even faster. They topped one wooded gully and entered a second. Pounding into the bottom of it, they suddenly came upon a lone oxcart, one of its wheels thoroughly mired in the black mud of a creek. The family had disembarked. Three children sat with their mother on the creek bank. The father and his young son were trying to position a stripped sapling pole under the cart's axle. The oxen waited placidly in the water.

Jonathan reined in hard, showering the mother and her smaller children with particles of black mud. "Apologies," he shouted. "Did a riding preacher pass this way?"

"No—" replied the boy, as the father tried to prevent him from speaking by clamping a hand on his mouth.

The man, sweaty and splattered with mud, released the boy and chuckled. "Well," he said, "figgered that answer oughta be worth somethin'. How 'bout a hand?"

Jonathan was already turning around. "I'm sorry," he cried. "But I will send help to you." He galloped back in the direction of Bath.

He topped the ridge and plunged into the next gully. He was becoming reckless now, trusting Merlin's savvy, giving the sporting animal his head to run as fast as he desired. He raced down a slope into the grassy park where earlier he had crossed the stream. As he leaned low, he saw in the woods to his left a dark motionless silhouette. He saw it only from the corner of his eye, but he knew immediately it was Silas. The moment of recognition passed like a chill through his body. Who was stalking whom? He felt an urge to ride on, pretending not to see him, but he took hold of his fear and reined in, plowing Merlin to a halt in the trail. He whirled to face the spot where he had seen the silhouette but now he saw nothing.

Merlin was blowing, sides heaving. Jonathan held his breath, eyes searching the woods, but there was no sign of Silas. Had it been imagined? Did the recklessness of his pursuit loosen his mind? No, he had seen him. He walked Merlin slowly back along the trace, and as he did so, Silas slowly came into view, sitting motionless on his horse. He had been concealed by the trunks of several red spruce. Jonathan stopped. He chuckled softly to himself. So Silas had tried to outsmart him. Well the hound had caught the hare.

Silas sat motionless on his horse, a statue of pure disgust. Then, swiftly, he spurred his horse forward. He swept past Jonathan and entered the trace on a dead run, the second horse panting behind.

"Mr. Will," Jonathan called as he passed.

There was no response. Jonathan turned after him, glad to have the chase in his hands at last. He followed through the hollows until they came to the mired oxcart. Jonathan was surprised to see Silas dismount immediately and tether his horses. Jonathan did the same.

"God be praised!" the woman sang out from the creek bank. "A preacher, and I prayed, too. I prayed God would send help and he sent a preacher. I attended society meeting regular back in Watkins Ferry, I did. God be praised."

Silas went straight to the sapling pole and positioned himself against it. "You drive," he said to the mud-spattered man. "I'll heave here."

Jonathan stepped up beside Silas and also took hold of the pole. The man whose cart it was looked at him with a quizzical expression.

"I found help," Jonathan explained with a shrug. "Go ahead, do as the preacher asked. Make speed."

The man shook his head and rounded the cart.

Jonathan turned to look Silas in the eye. "Mr. Will, I never properly introduced myself to you. My name is Jonathan Barratt. Of the Barratts of Bath, Captain Nelson Barratt . . . and Emily . . ."

He thought he detected a shrinking deep in the eyes, but that was all. Silas paused only slightly before answering.

"Mr. Barratt, go your way."

"I *am* going my way."

Jonathan stooped beneath the sapling, placing his shoulder against it.

"Hawh," called the man to his oxen.

They strained forward and Jonathan and Silas heaved against the axle with their lever. There was a loud sucking noise as the cartwheel pulled inch by inch upward. Then the whole cart surged forward, free of the mire. The woman and children cheered. The driver smiled happily.

"When the storm hits, give the ground a whole day to dry out before you continue," Silas shouted to the driver.

He nodded and waved gratefully.

Silas and Jonathan mounted again. Silas rode to where the woman sat.

"Did you read the Holy Bible this morning, ma'am?"

She blushed and turned her head ashamedly. "Well, I confess I did not."

"Read it and pray each morning according to the Discipline. Where are you going?"

"Abingdon, sir."

"There is a strong society of believers there. Prepare your heart, even as you travel. Be good soil for the seed of the Word that shall be planted.

God desires a good harvest from your family but you must prepare the soil. Good day."

"Good day, and thank you, Preacher," she said, blushing at his words.

Silas turned to go. Jonathan noticed the children were giggling and pointing to the fingernail scratches on his face. He had forgotten them.

"Mommy says you kissed the wrong woman," a young boy squealed with laughter.

"Joshua," the mother snapped, then smiled, embarrassed.

"Is that what Mommy said?" Jonathan repeated, loud enough so that Silas could hear as he rode away. "That should give her something to discuss with the believers in society meeting."

He spurred after Silas, and as he did the rain broke from the sky in torrents. It would be a long day.

As they rode, both Jonathan and Silas fumbled through their packs for their oilskin slickers. Jonathan unbound his from his bedroll and pulled it over his head. He donned his wool tricornered hat. Ahead of him the rain flowed evenly from the slouch brim of Silas' hat as he hunched against the downpour, concentrating his eyes on the ground before him.

So on they went. The rain continued through the afternoon and into the evening. Occasionally thunder rumbled through the clouds above, shaking down sudden heavy torrents through the tree branches above the riders. Their slickers soon became soaked through and both men were wet to the skin.

Jonathan squinted and tilted his head to see through the water drops that clouded the lenses of his spectacles. The rain picked up loose pine needles and particles of leaves from the trees above, and swept them across his field of vision. When he tried to wipe at his spectacles with his hand, he left smears on the glass. When his lenses cleared briefly he would check quickly ahead to see that no low-hanging branch threatened him for the next few feet of the trail then he would remove the frames and raise his face skyward to catch a cleansing shower. Shaking the excess rain from his face, he replaced his spectacles and resumed his squinting and tilting efforts to keep track of Silas' glistening slicker, which was ever disappearing before him into a haze of ground steam, rain, and whiplashing dogwood.

Without so much as a curious glance over his shoulder, Silas kept a relentless pace, uphill and down, along the twisting trace. As Jonathan fixed his eyes upon the preacher's hunched back, he saw in the ride a great challenge. He had chosen to follow. He would prove himself able to keep up.

Mile after mile wore on. When his horse slipped and stumbled with fatigue, Silas paused just long enough to leap to the saddle of his fresh mount and press on, with not even a glimmer of recognition that Jonathan was there behind him, keeping up. Several times, branches slapped the spectacles from Jonathan's face. Once he was forced to turn back and retrieve them from the trail, having not been quick enough to catch them with his hand as they flew away. He found them in the mud, severly bent, and stuffed them into a pocket. To follow the blurred image of the man in front of him seemed less trouble than to maintain his spectacles in the rain.

Unable to distinguish the trail with clarity, he found himself occasionally dodging branches that were not really there, wincing like a fool at a public whipping. But sometimes the branches *were* there. They sprang out of nowhere, to rake their needles across Charlotte Chase's fingerprints on his cheek. Tiny streams of fresh blood ran with the rainwater from the point of his chin.

His body began to ache. A shooting pain grew between his shoulder blades, increasing with each change in road elevation. His lower back throbbed, deep in the bone, as did the temples of his head. The insides of his thighs and buttocks grew raw from the ceaseless back-and-forth friction of the saddle. For relief, he stood as much as he dared on his toes in the stirrups, but sometimes when he did, the trail would unexpectedly dip and throw him onto the wet leather saddle, with an even more painful lurch. He would not stop unless Silas stopped. His bladder had long ago filled to capacity and he relieved it the only way he could. But certain discomforts he could not relieve. He held his bowels with increasing difficulty.

As a horseman he had been merely a racer and an occasional short day rider. Though he had hunted the woodlands and meadows around Bath, he had never ridden like this. Time and again he fought an urge to turn back, and this was only the first day on the road.

Darkness of night descended. Yet they were still many hours from Newtowne. Jonathan put on his spectacles again, so he could navigate the trail with some degree of safety in the reduced visibility. Surely Silas would stop to rest soon, he thought.

Night fell, but the man he followed showed no desire, indeed no need, for comfort. Jonathan saw that his head remained perfectly alert, as though he grew stronger with the miles. For Jonathan the adventure had already turned to punishing nightmare. Suddenly at the bottom of a draw, Merlin grunted and slid to a halt. Jonathan felt a soft impact on the horse's chest. In the dark he made out that Merlin had run into the rump of Silas' second horse. He listened through the wheezing and the dripping rain and heard, rising above them, the roaring of an ample stream flowing full in the draw. Silas' saddle was empty. Had he fallen? Jonathan forced action into his aching legs and slid to the ground, leaving Merlin standing free.

He felt his way past the horses in the muddy trail to the edge of the stream. He stopped, looking up and down, and with difficulty at last recognized the hunched form of Silas, squatted like a boulder in the rapid water near the bank. He was relieving himself.

"Son of a lowborn . . ." Jonathan muttered.

He plunged into the knee-deep stream and waded the rushing water to the opposite side, seeking a shallow flow for his own needs, but he had held his bowels so long that now they had ceased to demand relief. Jonathan discarded his slicker on the opposite bank and quickly undid his breeches. He squatted silently in the shallows, keeping his eyes on Silas. He could tell, even in the darkness, that he returned the gaze. He pushed his hand against his stomach. Sharp pains raced through his abdomen. At that moment Silas rose calmly from the stream and waded back to shore. Jonathan strained harder, cursing under his breath.

Silas untethered his mount and swung into the saddle. He gigged his horse and they lunged into the stream, splashing torrents of water into the air, which fell across Jonathan as they passed. Jonathan knew this was deliberate on Silas' part. He pictured himself drawing a pistol and killing Silas right there in the trail, but his anger turned to panic as he saw Merlin, dragging his reins, following the other horses up the trail. Raising up as far as he could, Jonathan cupped his hand and whistled the two-note signal Macaijah had taught him. To his relief Merlin stopped dead in the trail, whinnied, and trotted back into the stream, ears alert, nostrils flaring, looking for his crab-apple treat.

Jonathan called softly in the dark and the horse waded to where he squatted. Luckily Jonathan had thought to stock crabapples in his pockets. He slipped one beneath his nostrils and grabbed the dangling reins at the same time. Then he took an extra half minute to let himself down into the cooling water. It flowed around his aching buttocks like a gentle massage. Let Silas go his insane way for a while, he thought. He impulsively threw his entire body down, allowing it to be taken by the current. Still holding fast to Merlin's reins with one hand and to the nose bridge of his spectacles with the other, he allowed the stream to swing him around and baptize him from head to toe in its swirling waters. The force of it swept him downstream several yards, Merlin following obediently after, picking his way carefully through the rocks, tilting his head from side to side, trying to locate his master beneath the surface.

Suddenly a rejuvenated Jonathan leaped from the water with a shout. "Whooeee!"

Merlin grunted and shied backward, dragging him upstream. He stopped to gaze at his rider, now laughing and hooting like a madman, his waterlogged knee breeches clinging about his boot tops.

"We are in it, Merlin! We're in it to stay!" Jonathan shouted to his horse as he pulled up and fastened his pants. "We'll catch that old hypocrite. You and me, yes, we will!"

A kind of ecstasy had come over Jonathan. His aches and pains remained constant, but he had plunged himself into them somehow, he had dared and defied them, willed himself over them and now he actually felt greater. He felt childlike, giddy, and invincible—all at once. Searching the bank, he retrieved his useless slicker, but instead of donning it he bundled and strapped it behind the saddle.

"Buck up, old friend," he said to Merlin.

He swung into the saddle, feeling the fresh pressures against his open sores, but he held himself erect, placed his hat firmly upon his head, and spurred Merlin up the embankment.

They continued at the fastest pace Jonathan could safely manage in the dark. What was most important was that it was now his own pace, not Silas'. It felt good to be charting his own course. But would he catch him? He did not know. Maybe he didn't care. Besides, he had other business in Kentucky. One incline at a time, one ravine, one grassy park, one ridge at a time, that was all. He searched the ground with great energy, helping Merlin steer a course along the trace. Through ridge and hollow they continued, up and down. When he found a long park he did not race through it, he allowed the horse to proceed at a gentle canter. After several hours, at the end of a fine long park, they pitched up a steep hill, and when they had topped it, the land before them sloped gently eastward for miles.

"Shenandoah!" he breathed, slapping Merlin's rump with his wet hat.

As his eyes searched the rain, which had slackened now to a drizzle, he heard the faint click of iron on stone below in the dark brush thickets, which told him that Silas was moving ahead of him, not yet onto the valley floor.

He plunged through several small gullies, hoping to overtake him before he entered the wide expanse of the valley. But soon a rain-swollen stream blocked the trail. Once into it, Jonathan found that the water rose to Merlin's chest. In the middle of the crossing the horse lost his footing and swam downstream past the cut in the embankment where they should have emerged. Jonathan sensed a loss of strength in Merlin as he turned and struggled upstream. The great animal stopped several times, panting heavily, as he moved toward the cut. Reaching the cut, the horse sighed and grunted before surging with great effort up the bank. When they topped out, and at last entered the flat valley trace, Merlin was going lame.

A quarter mile beyond, Jonathan could see the dark silhouettes of Silas and his extra mount trotting along the trace. The dark outlines of several buildings loomed in the rain ahead. Jonathan assumed it was the Newtowne Inn, though he had never been there. He sighed, expecting that soon he would find rest and refreshment and that he might purchase a second horse to relieve Merlin of the whole burden of the trip. The sight of the inn buoyed his sagging spirits.

He leaped from his saddle and trotted on foot, leading Merlin. His own legs were fresh for the run and he made good time along the trace, though he became winded long before his legs lost their willingness to run. His side hurt but he clamped one hand to it and continued running until he covered a half mile to the point where earlier he had spied Silas. He stopped to catch his breath and peered ahead at the inn. A dog bayed from the road. What he saw next nearly forced him to despair. Silas was riding past the inn, turning south on the main colonial highway without even a pause.

"No," he moaned, "no, no." This was the moment to quit, to forget the relentless preacher, sleep the rest of the night, and turn back to Bath in the morning. "D____!" he bellowed straight up to the sky. The dog in the distance fell silent. Jonathan raced for the inn fueled by a surge of anger. He would not let Silas win, not now, not ever.

He would find a fresh mount in Newtowne, that was all, find it this night. Find it and pursue. His legs pumped, his lungs screamed, tears streamed from his eyes. Behind him Merlin cantered and grunted in pain. As he approached the inn the dog bayed and charged suddenly from beneath the porch. It was a large short-haired dog, solidly built with a crushing jaw. It came at him stiff-legged, white fangs bared. Jonathan hardly cared. He even felt a small pleasure at the dog's challenge. He felt gratitude to the hand of fate or chance or whatever had arranged this fitting outlet for his anger. The dog was armed with teeth and he snarled with a promise to use them. Without breaking stride Jonathan snatched a palm-sized stone from the trace. Then another. With perfect calculation he waited until the animal lowered its head and dashed for his leg. Then he let fly the first stone, sidearmed, with deadly accuracy.

Clack! It struck the dog square in the teeth. The animal's snarl turned to high-pitched screams. The sound was music to Jonathan. He was ready to chase this dog and Silas Will all the way to Hades. After all, it could not be much farther down *this* road! he thought. As he trotted to the inn doorway, the dog flashed again from under the porch, having sufficiently recovered to make an attack that was nearly silent, except for a rumbling growl. Jonathan dropped Merlin's reins and counterattacked.

"Cur!" Jonathan thundered, as if to wake the dead. He played the role with relish now. The animal broke and ran for the corner of the building, tail tucked between his legs. But Jonathan timed a second rock to intercept the animal in the center of its rib cage. Once again the animal's screaming filled the night.

But Jonathan did not enjoy beating the dog anymore. The howls, as it was, served a greater purpose. They woke nearly every inhabitant of Newtowne, and from the disturbance, if his luck ran good, he might purchase a fresh horse in a matter of minutes. Something he desperately needed to do. He listened with satisfaction to the clumping and thumping of boots on the stairs within the inn. Soon a lamp showed at a window. Then the door creaked open and the barrel of a long rifle emerged furtively, followed by the head and shoulders of a large man in a nightcap and gown.

"Put away your gun, good sir!" Jonathan called. "I am on a mission of law and order."

"Who be ye? State yer name! And what have ye done to my dog?"

"I . . . I am . . . Jonathan Gates of Martinsburg, sir. I am pursuing a dangerous criminal who passed your inn only minutes before me. He is even now making his escape on the road to the south and I am helpless to apprehend him without a fresh horse, sir. I am willing to pay."

"Never mind that! What have you done with my dog?"

The innkeeper produced a lighted lantern and hung it from an iron hook just outside the door, so that it gave him the advantage of seeing while not being seen.

"Oh, that, sir. Well, I was severely attacked. I . . . I was on foot and was forced to defend myself. Under normal circumstances I would not have stoned him as I did. I . . . uh, did it for the urgent nature of my mission." There was a pause. "He seems to be a fine, good dog, sir, truly. I think he will recover with only a few sore ribs."

Jonathan reached within his belt pouch and pulled out a large eight-escudo Spanish gold coin and turned it before the lantern. Such a coin was a valuable prize. Only the most wealthy could afford them. He had hidden a half dozen of them separately among his belongings for just such an emergency.

"This is yours, sir, if you have a good horse and saddle to spare."

"It's a highwayman for sure. Don't let him trick you." A woman's voice quavered from the dark behind the innkeeper.

"The highwayman is halfway to Strasburg by now, woman," Jonathan called out. "I am here with a lame horse."

"I have a horse for your doubloon." A second male voice sounded from behind the door.

"Quiet," commanded the innkeeper. "I shall do the trading here. What is the offense of the criminal you seek?"

"I hesitate to speak of it, good sir, in the presence of a lady. The crime is rape," Jonathan replied. "The man raped my own mother. I have chased him through the night, many times coming within sight of him, nearly close enough to apprehend him for the hanging tree."

Jonathan drew back his coat, revealing his pistols, in leather holsters, one beneath each arm.

The woman gasped. "I told you! The man is a highwayman liar!"

"Good," said the innkeeper. "Then I shall gut him and feed him to my dog for breakfast." He leaned out the door and winked at Jonathan. "Meet me at the stable entrance." He closed the heavy-beamed door.

Jonathan turned, giving a reassuring pat to Merlin, who stood by wearily shifting his weight from one foot to another. His proud head hung low with fatigue. Jonathan had never seen the horse so worn out. He walked to the stable entrance and waited for several long minutes. He was about to return to the main entrance when a sound told him the innkeeper had finally entered from the interior door. The stable door creaked open. The innkeeper, a burly man, stood half dressed in a nightshirt, with boots over his long johns. Several lamps illuminated the interior of the stable and

Jonathan noticed a black stable keep peering at him from the shadows of a stall. The barrel of a gun pointed in his direction.

"Come in," said the innkeeper. "This weather be fit only for crows and riding preachers."

"Amen to that, sir." Jonathan said.

The man looked Jonathan up and down. "You have ridden hard. Now, I care not, young man, if ye be lawful or no, so much as I care for the gold. Might I see it?"

Jonathan handed him the coin reluctantly, as though it meant everything in the world. A trick he had learned from Uncle Ethan when it came to negotiating price.

As the innkeeper examined the coin, Jonathan called to the stable keep. "Two shillings for you if you rub down my horse and double grain him before I leave."

The stable keep looked to the innkeeper for permission. He nodded, and the stable keep moved toward the feed bin.

The innkeeper eyed Jonathan carefully. "That horse of yours is a fine animal."

"Yes, he is."

"I see men on this road nearly every day who would kill for a horse like that, Mr. Gates."

"Mr. Barr— Ah." Jonathan caught himself quickly. "Thank you, I shall keep alert."

The innkeeper looked at him suspiciously. "I seldom see green young men of your standing on the road this far to the south. Least not alone. Not at this hour."

Jonathan was tired of his meddling. "Your name, sir?"

"I am Richard Holmes."

"Mr. Holmes, I have calculated the dangers of this journey well." Once again, he pulled back his coat to reveal the pistols. "What I need is a horse, and soon. And if I must purchase it from another occupant of your inn, I shall do so."

"Very well. There." He pointed Jonathan to a stall.

Jonathan looked. A thin, swaybacked sorrel mare stood pitifully looking at him.

"Mr. Holmes," Jonathan erupted. "Are you making a fool of me? I need a horse, not a bag of bones." He turned to leave.

"Not so fast, Mr. Gates," the innkeeper said, holding tight to the heavy

Spanish gold. "You would not ask for my own personal mount, would you? Other than this horse, it is all I can offer."

"For an eight-escudo, that *is* what I ask."

"But he be like a pet. My wife would not forgive me."

"Then he is well cared for, not like this crowbait!"

"True. He is well cared for."

"Show me."

"There." He pointed to another stall.

Jonathan again looked and this time saw a light bay English hackney. The horse, a gelding, appeared well bred and sturdy. He entered and led him from the stall, walking him around the straw-covered floor of the barn. Jonathan inspected each foot, one by one, opened his mouth and inspected the teeth. It was more than he had hoped to find under the circumstances of the hour.

"Fifteen years by the look," Jonathan lamented.

"Not a day above eleven."

"Then he has been given poor feed. Mr. Holmes, I have no time for dickering. The eight-escudo will buy four of these Tory horses and you know it. Let that satisfy your wife. I have to go. Do you have a saddle for him?"

Holmes strode to a tack shed and produced a saddle and bridle. Jonathan inspected the girth, cinch, and stirrups. All seemed reasonably well conditioned. He saddled the horse quickly. Satisfied, he led the horse to the door, where the stable keep held Merlin for him, in halter.

"Thank you, both of you," Jonathan said. He drew two Massachusetts oak tree shillings from his belt pouch and flipped them to the stable keep. With that, Jonathan mounted the English hackney, testing the security of the cinched saddle, and waited for Mr. Holmes to open the door to the road. "How far is it to the inn at Strasburg?" he asked the innkeeper.

"Two hours of strong pacing."

"Thank you, Mr. Holmes. The horse is gaited?"

"Fully. Good luck to you, sir, Mr. uh, Gates."

Holmes held the door and Jonathan clattered out into the night once more. As he passed the front of the inn, the dog growled from underneath the porch. Jonathan urged the hackney into a fast canter. Looking back, he saw that Merlin still limped, but at least it was no worse than before.

Two hours later the dogs of Strasburg welcomed Jonathan.

At the south end of town stood the Strasburg Inn and Alehaus. Jonathan had heard of its reputation while a student at Harvard. It was touted as a haven for highwaymen who paid a safekeeping bounty to the proprietor, a German ale maker, Hans Korbel. But Hans had served the Revolutionary War effort with such faithfulness that he had been vindicated of his past reputation.

At this hour, Jonathan did not care what reputation the innkeeper had established. All he desired was a simple bed, highwaymen or no. A lamplight still flickered in the main room of the inn. It was well into morning, but surprisingly, the inn still showed life. Jonathan stopped, dismounted, and tethered both horses. He entered by the main door. Inside, three men sat at a table throwing dice. One of them stood to greet him. This could not be the infamous Hans Korbel, Jonathan thought. He was a small, softlooking man who spoke in a soft voice as well.

"You seek a room?"

"I do if Silas Will is here."

"I do not know Silas Will." The man backed off a step, looking Jonathan over suspiciously.

"He is a riding preacher," Jonathan explained.

The man relaxed a bit, then added with a sly wink, "He may be here, I cannot say. Do you care to see our stable?"

"Yes, I would."

The man led him to the interior stable door. Jonathan took a lighted lamp and followed. Another lamp burned within the stable. Silas sat at a makeshift plank-and-barrel table where he worked over a pile of wadding, gunpowder, and shot, making ball-and-charge cartridges. The silence of the night was broken by loud snores. Two drunks sprawled in the straw. Silas looked up. For a moment Jonathan had the supreme satisfaction of seeing surprise and disbelief on the wilderness preacher's face, but only for a moment. Silas again bowed to his task.

"The stable will suit you, yes?"

"Just fine," Jonathan said.

He followed the man back into the inn, shutting the stable door.

"Wilhelm. Put up da man's horse."

"Yes, Hans."

Jonathan produced several pine tree shillings and laid them on the bar. Hans drew him a stein of ale. He gulped it down and felt his thirst slaked and his body soothed by its mellowing influence. He ordered another. With the second tankard in his hand, he went into the stable, where Wilhelm brushed down his horses.

"Double grain for both, and a fresh pine-tar poultice for my stallion."
Wilhelm nodded.

Jonathan took his bedroll from the saddle and sat on it, his back resting
against the wall. He sipped and watched Silas work. At length Silas looked
up. Immediately his face clouded with disgust. He stabbed his hunting
knife into the plank before him, rose glaring, and walked over to Jonathan.
Jonathan knew he had offended him with the drink and stood to meet
him, his tired muscles tensed.

"I do not intend an insult by this drink," Jonathan defended.

Silas only stared.

"It is no business of yours, but since you seem to want to make it so, I
will argue that I have ridden hard, I drink in moderation. Whatever is
wrong with a drink in its proper place anyhow?"

"Nothing," Silas said.

Jonathan was taken aback.

"It *has* a proper place."

Silas held out his hand to receive the tankard. Jonathan gave it to him,
curious now. Silas took the drink and backed away to a pile of fresh horse
manure. Slowly he poured the contents of the tankard over it.

"*That* . . . is a drink in its proper place."

Harsh, coughing laughter erupted from one of the darkened horse stalls
and a drunken voice called out.

"Don' never cross no ridin' preacher," the voice warned. "Don' never.
Heh, heh . . . cough, cough . . ."

9

The Dueling Pistols

Exhaustion crept through Jonathan's body as he lay on his bed in the straw. It set his muscles, stiffened his limbs. It began to throb in his head and in those delicate places where the saddle had rubbed through his skin. His face swelled beneath the rain-washed scratches. His eyes burned from the strain of seeing the trail in the night. His insides trembled from tightening a thousand times with fear at a thousand startling surprises in the dark of the Newtowne Trace, and now his brain began reeling with visions and voices: Chayta, Asbury, Andrew, Caleb, Silas, Estelle, the man at the oxcart, his religious wife, Holmes, Holmes's dog. They all barked in disjointed phrases that would have made sense had he the mental energy to capture and examine them one by one.

But the one tankard of ale he had consumed reduced his willpower and sent him deeper into slumber, where now in his dreams, interspersed with the people and events of the day, he saw his mother on her deathbed. He saw Asbury, then Emily, his mother; Chayta, then again, Emily; Holmes,

then Emily; Andrew, then Emily; the seductive Estelle, then Emily; Silas
—then suddenly Emily's death-ravaged face rose screaming into his: *"I am
lost!"*

"N-n-noo!"

A cry had wrenched itself from Jonathan's throat even as his body had
sprung erect on the bedroll. He stood trembling, staring into the blackness
of the stable. The lamps had been put out. Loud snores continued from
the sleeping drunks among the stalls, though a restless twitching and
snorting had taken hold of them. In their sleep they must have heard his
cry. It seemed to his waking ears that the cry that had ripped from his
breast was the cry of a child. As his eyes adjusted to the darkness, he
discerned the form of Silas. He was sitting on his bedroll, peering
strangely at him from across the floor. Embarrassment climbed Jonathan's
cheek in the dark. Eventually, Silas lay back down. Jonathan slowly
crouched and slid onto his bedroll. His eyes closed again and he soon
tumbled into helpless sleep.

Though he did not cry out again, twice more his body convulsed violently from dreams: once when the Newtowne innkeeper's dog bit into his
leg, and again when Estelle's daughter raked her nails across his face. Each
dream jerked him into a state of wakefulness where eventually his mind
would clear and his thoughts would focus. Then he would settle back
wearily, praying for a quiet reprieve in the world of sleep.

An iron hinge shuddered with a betraying groan and Jonathan's eyes
blinked open. He lay for an uncomprehending moment, staring toward
the wall, where in the darkness Silas had slept. The bedroll was gone. Gray
light from the open door behind him outlined the soft shadows of two
saddled horses being led from the stable. The door groaned carefully shut.

Jonathan leaped from his bedroll, rubbing his aching eyeballs with the
heels of his hands, wincing at the wretched pains that shot through all of
his limbs. He moaned quietly to the pain and to the unending challenge of
Silas Will and the road ahead. For a moment, he was seized by an urge to
lay down again, to cover his head with the blanket and sleep through the
day. He would forget Silas. But he shook the notion from his head and
dropped to his knees, fumbling beneath the straw for his discarded spectacles. He found them and put them on, only to discover he had rolled on
them in the night. They were bent so badly that he slung them across the
barn. They flew into an empty stall and shattered against the wall.

"Wha—"

A startled drunk popped his head from a pile of straw on the floor, peering out red-eyed, trying to locate the culprit that had disturbed his sleep.

Jonathan was bent over his bedroll trying to bundle it together. A good bit of straw still clung to it, but he wasted no effort to remove it. He leaped to his feet and ran across the barn.

"Keep!" he yelled.

"Quiet, for mercy's sake," the disturbed drunk bawled from his place in the straw.

"Keep!" Jonathan yelled again. "Four good pine tree shillings for your help."

The drunk lifted a weighty eyebrow at this, then fell to rubbing his temples from the pain of forcing expression into his booze swollen face. Jonathan fumbled with his overturned saddles and quickly strapped the bedroll behind the one that would ride the hackney. He frantically fished a spare set of spectacles from his saddlebags and slipped them over his ears. To check their effectiveness, he focused this way and that, then spying two bridles, he snatched them up and ran to the stall that held Merlin and swung it open.

Merlin's head recoiled at the touch of the bit to his sore mouth. Jonathan paused a precious moment, pondering Merlin's condition, then dropped the bridles and ran back to the tack pile. This time he returned with a hemp halter, which he fastened over his head. With that, he hastily led him to a hitching rail in the center of the barn. The still groggy drunk stumbled from the adjacent stable.

"I shore 'nuff could use the pineys, good feller."

"Saddle this horse, for one," Jonathan ordered, without even looking at the man.

The man moved on wobbly limbs to the saddles.

"The one on the right!" Jonathan barked.

"Le's see here . . . right, left . . . no . . . no, it's left—"

"Here." Jonathan leaned over and jerked up Merlin's saddle with one motion and threw it against the man's chest. He reeled backward from the impact but held on to it.

"For one shilling, or nothing," Jonathan said, looking him in the eye. "*If* you make haste."

"No call t' git nasty." The man calculated one shilling's worth of ale and forced his disobedient limbs into action.

Jonathan lifted the other saddle and hurried to the hackney's stall. He opened it and led out the fresh bay gelding. It nickered a friendly greeting as he patted its neck. At least this horse was ready for the day on the road. Merlin snorted and pawed the straw, bowing his neck at the sight of Jonathan stroking this new horse. Merlin would rise to the occasion, too, lame or not, but Jonathan would ride the hackney all day to speed his recovery.

When he had saddled the hackney he ran across the barn to check the cinch of the saddle the sleepy drunk had strapped upon Merlin. It was loose, so he paused to pull it tight. He slipped Merlin a crab-apple treat from his pocket, tossed a coin to the drunk, and led both horses to the barn door. It was unlatched. He slammed a heavy riding boot against the planks, causing the iron hinges to scream. The door flew open, rebounding against the outside of the barn, and he pulled the excited horses immediately into the fresh morning air. The drunk stumbled out to shut the door after him and called as Jonathan mounted up, "That ridin' preacher sho got the better a you las' night, I say. Hee, hee, heh . . . cough, cough, wheez . . ."

Jonathan spurred across the misty innyard toward the road. He clattered well into the road, then pulled to a sudden stop, realizing that in his haste he had passed two saddled mounts tethered to the inn's rail. He had assumed Silas would be at least two miles south by now. But he laid the reins over the hackney's neck and trotted curiously back to the innyard. Silas' horses stood waiting at the rail.

This was another trick, Jonathan thought. He quickly dismounted and tied his own horses beside them. Perhaps Silas switched horses with someone else at the inn in order to confuse and delay him further. He ran to the main door of the inn but found it bolted from within. Then, glancing repeatedly in every direction, he ran around the side of the building, where he spied a well-worn path leading to a wooden privy. He ran down the path to the structure and carefully opened its door. It was empty. He walked back to the innyard and stood there scratching his straw-matted hair, looking about. Then he saw him. Silas knelt beneath a spreading oak which towered above a grove of smaller trees in the corner of the innyard.

An early-morning mist rose hauntingly above the distant fields, surrounding the kneeling figure in a soft white haze. Above, pink-fringed clouds glowed in the paling blue of dawn. Nature had blessed the praying imposter with a morning of surpassing beauty.

Jonathan walked quietly, curiously forward, his boots crunching in the sandy loam of the innyard. The morning bird chorus disbanded, the birds finding light enough to fly one by one from their nests in the oaks to the sky above the fields. A cottontail bounded away in the wet grass.

Nearing Silas, he noticed that he seemed to be in deep concentration, an open Bible held in front of him. Jonathan crept closer and heard softly spoken words, too soft for him to understand them. If the man merely masqueraded as a riding preacher, he certainly did not avoid the finer details of the role. Jonathan felt the chill of the morning penetrate his still damp clothing and settle about his shoulders. He backed away quietly and returned to the entrance of the inn and there rapped lightly and steadily against the door. He was suddenly famished and bothered by the uncomfortable itch of his beard. At length he heard the rustle of skirts within and a hand removing the plug from a peephole on the door.

A female voice called, "Who is there?"

"I am Jonathan, I slept in the stable with the preacher. Can you fetch me something to eat? Anything?"

"Tee, hee, hee. Ya slept with the preacher? Haven't tried it myself. Ha-ha."

Jonathan leaned closer to the eyepiece and saw a woman with pock-marked skin and bulbous features. She wiped a toothless grin with the upturned corner of her apron. Traces of egg batter and ground wheat flour clung to her fingers.

"I must leave with the preacher . . . soon—" Jonathan entreated.

"Liked him that well, did ye? Tee, hee, hee."

Jonathan lifted a shilling to the small window. "Do you have something in the kitchen for me at this hour?"

She snatched the shilling through the peephole so quickly he was left staring at his empty fingers. The peep door had slammed shut. He pounded his fist once against the door planks and threw his hand up in despair. He was at her mercy.

Running his fingers wearily through his matted hair, he looked to see that Silas was still at prayer. He hurried to his saddlebags, disengaged the leather flap, and removed a travel box covered in soft kid leather. He opened it on the edge of the watering trough at the hitching rail. A polished brass mirror was set within the lid of the box. Jonathan looked at his beard in the mirror, the unkempt hair and the scratches on his face. He lifted an ivory-handled razor and a tortoiseshell comb from the box and set them to one side. He removed his coat and the shoulder holsters containing his dueling pistols and laid them across the hackney's saddle. Then he loosened his shirt until he could remove his arms from the sleeves, removed his suspenders, and let the shirt and suspenders hang downward from his waist.

With a glance toward Silas, to see that he was still there, he worked the handle of the pump until a stream of water flowed. Then he dunked his entire head under that stream. It was so cold to his skull that it ached, but he gasped and stayed under anyway, until with his free hand he had rinsed the straw and soil from his head. Then he straightened, took the comb, and ran it quickly through his hair. He took the razor next and began to carefully scrape the whiskers from the side of his face that was not scratched. The door of the inn swung open behind him. He turned with surprise. It was the toothless woman in the apron. She marched with a wooden bowl and spoon across the inn porch and deposited them firmly in his hands.

"I thank you," he said with gratitude.

She looked him up and down, and an amused, superior smile grew across her face.

"It'll stick to yer ribs," she said, and slapped her broad hand flat against his rib cage, playfully taking a pinch of flesh between her thumb and forefinger. "You need something to stick to these, I'll say. Hee, hee."

Jonathan was startled by her boldness, then he grinned, realizing she was a common woman, used to the rough atmosphere of the Strasburg Inn.

She backed up, wiping her hand in her apron, eyeing him with pleasure and amusement. Jonathan was famished. He bent to devour the gruel with great relish. It was hot and he was thankful for that. He divined certain ingredients from the taste of it as he ate; oatmeal mush, maple syrup, fresh warm milk, apple pieces, whiskey, and cinnamon. It was wonderful, especially after the fasting ride of the night before.

"It's delicious," he called to the woman as she disappeared within the inn.

He had swallowed nearly half the contents of the bowl when he looked up to see Silas mounting his horse.

D____ the man.

His first instinct was to drop everything and give chase, his second, to rip the hitching rail from the ground and knock the preacher from his saddle. That would give him time to finish his gruel. He enjoyed the thought of it. But Silas didn't leave the innyard. He walked his horse near to where Jonathan sat. Jonathan held his bowl invitingly up to him.

"Breakfast, Mr. Will?" he said cheerfully. "It's delicious. I will have a bowl brought for you at my expense."

Silas was staring at Jonathan's guns.

"Oh, I suppose you do not indulge in anything so unholy as . . . breakfast."

"Mr. Barratt. You should go back," Silas said. He spoke with a gentle tone of concern that disarmed Jonathan.

But as he spoke, Silas continued to fasten his gaze on the silver-and-ivory-trimmed handles of the dueling pistols, which gleamed from the saddled back of the hackney.

"I have business in Kentucky," Jonathan replied. "I am committed to go. Why should I turn back? I think we should ride together. What is so wrong with that?"

Silas' eyes remained fixed on the pistols. To Jonathan's surprise he had grown visibly agitated.

"Go back," Silas said sharply. He wheeled and cantered from the inn-yard.

Jonathan's eyes followed Silas' receding back. He shoveled the final spoonfuls of mush into his mouth. Then he threw the bowl and spoon to the inn porch and wiped his dripping chin with his hand. Slipping his arms into his shirt, he buttoned it quickly.

"My word, how does that buzzard live?" he mumbled to himself and his horses.

He hastily positioned his suspenders, restrapped the dueling pistols around his chest, and donned his waistcoat. He retrieved his shaving box, then leaped aboard the hackney and thundered down the road behind Silas. A half mile ahead, Silas cantered without a backward glance. Jonathan checked Merlin as he started and saw that his limp was barely noticeable, so he decided to experiment with the hackney's pacing ability. He found, to his relief, that the horse had a smooth, ground-eating four-beat rack on the relatively even surface of the road. It was fast enough to at least keep pace with Silas' canter, and perhaps exceed it. The hackney moved in the gait with disciplined ease, so Jonathan settled him into it as they ran southward through the broad Shenandoah.

Once again Jonathan felt the ripple of exhilaration. The aches and pains in his muscle and bones grew numb as they were pounded and massaged against the constant motion of the saddle. His blood flowed warm again. The storm-washed air was chill, but it smelled fresh and renewed, like Jonathan's spirits. The sun rose like a wine-red ball on the horizon and slowly warmed the mists, separating them from the corn and grain fields as he passed. By midmorning the warming smell of cultivated black river-bottom soil filled the air. Jonathan drank it in as a reward for his painful early rising. The road provided its own kind of reward as he let his mind drift easily with the passing beauty.

Occasionally he passed a farmer on horseback or a freight wagon.

And as he rode on, watching Silas' back growing nearer in the road before him, he wondered what it had been about the dueling pistols that had so disturbed the man.

The settlement of Woodstock was in sight when the hackney began to come abreast of Silas and his cantering horses. Jonathan felt pleased, knowing that Silas, who had never yet looked over his shoulder, would be irked to see himself overtaken in the road by this upstart traveler.

Jonathan drew up beside him, looked over at Silas, and waited to be acknowledged.

Silas only looked straight ahead.

"How far by tonight, or do you plan such things?" Jonathan asked.

Silence.

"Rocktowne? Surely not Staunton. Is there an inn between those two? I have never traveled this far south."

"Mr. Barratt, we are strangers," Silas said. "We each travel our own way. It is not road-wise to ask a stranger such questions."

Suddenly Jonathan found himself at the end of his patience. Something in the impassivity of Silas' response insulted him like the slap of a duelist's glove.

"Strangers?" he cried. "A d____ sight more than that, I would say."

Silas sharply turned his gaze upon him. "Don't curse in my presence, boy!"

"By what right do you instruct me, Mr. Will? Are you so much better than I? Well, I'm not deceived. I know the hypocrite that you are."

Jonathan's face flushed red, his stomach and fists tightened. All of his muscles were tensed as they had been when he had stoned the dog in Newtowne. Silas squinted at him, calculating, questioning the words and their meaning. Having unexpectedly opened this course of action, Jonathan decided to take it further. A smile spread slowly across his face.

"Mr. Will," he announced, "yesterday you asked me in the presence of Mr. Asbury if we were pretending to meet for the first time. And then you called me an impostor. Now today, in the presence of God, I ask you, are we *pretending* that you are a *stranger* to the Barratt household?"

Silas looked straight ahead, implacably.

"Or do we in fact hold something in common, Mr. Will," Jonathan went on, "something that makes us much more than strangers on the road to Kentucky?"

Silas continued in silence.

"And what might that connection be, Mr. Will?"

Silas turned his eyes back to Jonathan. There was an iron hardness there that told Jonathan he had gone as far as he had better go for the time. Jonathan was ready to quit. He felt he had finally stopped parrying and delivered a solid blow to the man. There would be time to follow it later.

They entered Woodstock side by side. Woodstock was the rallying point for the far-flung farms of the west-central Shenandoah Valley. The town was comprised of a store (which traded everything from farm implements to household items), two homes, an inn, and a small decaying stockade that had become overgrown with berry briers, indicating the absence of hostile Indian activity in the region. In front of the store, in the very center of the road, was a well with a watering trough. The road curled around it on either side. A small rough-hewn gazebo had been erected over the well. The gazebo was covered with climbing vines, with a hedge of lilac groomed in a circle all about it.

Jonathan and Silas hitched their horses to a railing near the gazebo where water stood in the moss-lined trough. Several speckled trout finned in the clear sunlit water but they darted for the shadows at the bottom of the log as soon as the horses touched their noses to the sparkling surface. Inside the gazebo a drunk loudly snored on a wooden bench, a crock of corn whiskey clutched to his breast.

Silas and Jonathan stepped around him to the well. Silas picked up a pewter mug which was placed on the edge of the well and began to work the pump until a stream of water flowed. He drank deeply of several cupfuls, always tossing the sediment that had gathered in the bottom of each cup into the street. Then he set the mug again where he had found it. Jonathan took his turn, looking about at the pleasant sight of Woodstock as he drank with full pleasure.

He observed a man, dressed in the loose linsey-woolsey of a working farmer, emerge onto the porch of the store. A sturdy English draft horse stood patiently hitched to a farm wagon in front of the store. Other than that, and except for the sleeping drunk, the street was deserted.

Silas had moved opposite Jonathan in the gazebo. He leaned on his arms, peering into the depths of the well.

"I knew some Barratts in Boston many years ago," he said, rumbling the words into the well in a begrudging confession.

Jonathan stopped drinking mid-gulp, delighted at this break in the stalemate. "My family came from Boston," he replied.

"The Barratt I speak of was a sea captain."

"Captain Nelson Barratt, one and the same. Did you know him then?"

"Those are his dueling pistols."

So that was it. "They are. You must have known him well to know that."

Silas paused. "I came from Ireland on his ship," he said, and turned from the gazebo to his horse.

Jonathan knew he had reached the end of Silas' willingness to talk, but he had one more question: "And did you know the Captain's wife? Emily?"

Silas stopped stock-still in the road. Then he turned about.

"Yes," he said, moving deliberately toward Jonathan. He stepped into the gazebo.

Jonathan feared he had jabbed too near the wound.

But Silas looked down at the snoring drunk.

"I knew Captain Nelson Barratt, and his wife. I was saddened to learn that they have both died. I . . . read their markers in the graveyard in Bath." He looked up at Jonathan. "But I did not know they had a son."

Now Jonathan was silent, pondering this. "The Captain was killed in the war," he announced. "The British sent him down on Penobscot Bay."

"I am sorry. He was a skillful captain, I reckon, though I was never a man of the sea. I judged him a strong leader of men. You should be proud."

"You knew him at least as well as I did," Jonathan blurted. Silas' eyes narrowed. He had not planned to say this, but he wanted Silas to know of the Captain and Emily's estrangement, and to begin to know that he was the cause of it.

"My mother raised me in Bath until her death. The Captain sent her to live there alone, to be near the healing waters for her many fevers, or so he said. We saw him seldom through the years. He was not there when she died." Jonathan remained calm in his delivery, watching Silas' face closely as he unleashed the story. "But I was there. She died in torment of her eternal soul, Preacher. It seems she bore the burden of some sin to the grave, and who knows, perhaps to Hades."

Silas was visibly shaken.

"What do you divine from all of that, Preacher?"

Silas turned as if searching for something to say.

The sleeping drunk on the bench rolled over with a restless snort, waved his arm blindly in the air as if fighting off invisible demons, and then slumped again into snoring oblivion. Silas reached down and took the crock of whiskey from his arm, unstopped it, and began to slowly pour the precious liquid over the rail. He seemed to collect himself as he did it.

"Mr. Barratt, have you ever heard tell of the sea of God's forgetfulness?" He did not wait for a reply. "This poor wretch hasn't heard, or he refused it when he did. His purpose in life is to get drunk, fast and painless. Whiskey is death, because this life is neither fast nor painless. It's cursed. This poor fellow, he wants to forget all the trouble of this life. He's not willing to stand like a man no more."

The drunk snored loudly, underscoring Silas' speech. "Whatever he endured in the past, he's allowed what the scripture calls 'a root of bitterness' to grow up within him and trouble him. Defile him. Oh, just a small back-up against God at first. Now the root has grown into a tree that is larger than life itself. Too large to remove.

"Now, the sea of God's forgetfulness? Why, that's a miracle. It comes from God, fast and painless—and once you know it, you are free from the past. You become a new creation in God."

Silas sounded suddenly humble and small in the shadow of the idea he expressed. Jonathan perceived that he wanted to hide behind it. "I do not know how I would live without it, Mr. Barratt," Silas said, glancing down at the drunk. "Like him perhaps. But I am not likely to be that stupid, to trade God's good gift for a sip of the Devil's drool. It's beyond me." He shook his head.

Silas corked the crock and bent toward the drunk, raising his voice. "Do you want a miracle from God, sir?"

The drunk moaned and stirred restlessly, cracking his eyes. He saw the crock in Silas' hand and reached for it. Silas let it go and the drunk settled back into the comfort of his slumber.

"He chooses," Silas intoned sadly. "Where is his family, his wife, children? Who can tell how many lives he has poisoned with his whiskey?" Silas eyed Jonathan again. "You have a root of bitterness in you, too, Mr.

Barratt. Cleanse yourself. Submit it to God's sea of forgetfulness, or it will drag you down to Hades."

Jonathan steadied his gaze into the preacher's eyes. "Perhaps I shall meet my mother there."

Silas turned livid and lurched from the gazebo. He mounted his horse, and spurred southward on the road without another word or a backward glance. Jonathan watched him go, walked over to the drunk, and dislodged the whiskey crock from his embrace. He tilted it up and drained the remnant into his open mouth. He swallowed the fire-hot liquid and let it burn his lips and throat. Then he replaced the carved wooden stopper.

"Pious old preacher, would you agree?" he said to the sleeping drunk, setting the empty crock on the wooden floor of the gazebo.

The drunk continued to snore blissfully. "I promise you this," Jonathan continued, "the past will rise from that sea of forgetfulness and come up on that old crust of a preacher."

10

The Mill Wheel

Following the exchange in Woodstock, Jonathan observed a gloom settle over Silas. The Kentucky exhorter pressed forward at the same obsessive pace, but from time to time, as Jonathan would overtake him on the road and observe his face, he detected a new darkness there. He had wanted to trouble this man, to make him suffer, but the gloom seemed to touch Jonathan as well. He did not understand why this was so, except that he was no longer sure that the man's religion was a masquerade. That made his attack seem less justified.

A few miles north of the settlement of Rocktowne, they passed another caravan of oxcarts. Several of the occupants called out a friendly greeting to the preacher, replete with scriptural ejaculations, hailing him to stop and hold ministry for them on the spot. But Silas dismissed their request with a short wave of his hand as he passed. He did not so much as pause, much to the vocal consternation of the raggedy occupants, who were used to being ignored by everyone on the road except riding preachers.

Jonathan, who rode behind, took note of this change in Silas with a degree of satisfaction, for it was the first evidence that the hard moral shell of the Kentucky preacher could be broken. He rode past the oxcarts himself, and observed firsthand the disappointment on the faces of the women, especially a young mother who held a sickly, coughing child. He noted the angry set of the jaw of the men against this man of God who had neglected to serve them in the manner of his high calling. Jonathan stood in his stirrups and yelled with his full lung power after the retreating preacher.

"Mr. Will! Preacher Will!"

He spurred the hackney into a gallop, surprised to note that Silas had also spurred his horse into a gallop ahead of him. He was running away!

"Preacher Will! These people need you!" He knew that Silas needed no reminder. This was a verbal stone thrown at his retreating back.

He galloped heedlessly on.

"They call for you!"

Jonathan followed until he realized that Silas was not about to turn back but was instead spending both of his horses at an imprudent pace on the road. Merlin labored to keep up, his leg still plaguing him with soreness, so Jonathan settled the hackney into his comfortable gait once more and watched Silas disappear around the bend in a storm of hoof-lofted dust. He was surprised and annoyed at this turn of events, but he believed that Silas' horses would tire and that within an hour or so he would come into view again. By holding to a sensible pace, Jonathan would catch him.

But hours passed and Silas was nowhere to be seen. Evening shadows gathered. He passed the granite quarries of Rocktowne at dusk and had still not sighted him. As darkness fell, Jonathan felt the valley floor rising beneath him as he entered the headwaters of the Shenandoah. Still no Silas.

He passed through a water gap on the upper tributaries of the river, its high walls of stone rising on either side of him. He pressed on through meadows and forests in the darkness toward Staunton. The town was situated in the uplands of the Shenandoah, near the watershed of the James River drainage. He thought perhaps he would find Silas at an inn near Staunton, calculating that it would be well after midnight when he arrived. Surely Silas would not go beyond there. But he was nowhere to be found in Staunton, even at midnight.

The Roan Springs Tavern was a fine inn, the best-furnished of all those Jonathan had passed on the colonial highway. It was the first he encountered after passing Staunton, and he took no time in deciding that he would spend the night there, Silas or no. It had been locked up for the night when he arrived, but an armed watchman stood guard outside. He seemed glad to see a guest arrive during his lonely vigil, though he watched Jonathan closely for signs of trouble. For a shilling he allowed Jonathan into the stable to care for his horses and then opened a small sleeping room to him in the main inn. Jonathan's bones ached to sleep in a bed; his feet, his muscles, his head ached. Let Silas go. Perhaps the world *was* a world of toil and trouble, as he said, but Jonathan would seek his share of comfort tonight.

The watchman poured them both a tankard of ale in the main room. Jonathan spread his maps on a large wooden table, which sat near the last embers of an evening's fire. He sipped his ale and studied his position on the road. Tomorrow he would pass through Lexington, Natural Bridge, Fincastle, and arrive late that night in Christiansburg at the junction of the Richmond road. At least he hoped to travel that far.

"Is it possible to make Christiansburg in a day?" he asked the watchman.

"Possible. But ain't likely," he replied. "One thing for shore, when ya pass Christiansburg, it ain't nice no more. I'd stay plum clear off the road after dark. Stay shore 'nuff clear. Highwaymen, renegade cutthroat runaways. Injuns, too. Time was when Injuns was all to worry a man. Now this godforsaken land has gone sour. It's all worse since the war."

"Sounds like toil and trouble."

The watchman slipped his eyes up on Jonathan curiously and spit a wad of brown tobacco stems into a small crock. He swilled a mouthful of ale and spit it into the crock after it.

"If yer findin' life too much toil an' trouble, young man, believe me when I say it, they's plenty on that road down there who'd take all yer toil an' trouble away fer whatever jingles yer pocket. Not even ask. Just do ye the favor." He drew his hand dramatically across his throat.

"In that case, they may find that it is I who do the favor," Jonathan said, with more conviction than he felt. He drew out one of his pistols and checked the charge.

"Don't see many like ye on the road. Smooth hands, well-bred horse, dirtied-up fine duds, fancy pistols, and such. Yer green and it hangs on ya like a chimney vine. I say fer yer own good, stay clear of the road after dark."

"Well, I thank you. But I am careful, and not quite as green as I seem," Jonathan lied. He hoped to give the impression that he possessed mysterious powers of self-defense.

Jonathan folded his map wearily, deposited it in his saddlebags, and forced himself to walk the one hundred steps to a springhouse that stood behind the inn. The water was cold as it cascaded over a wall onto a scrubbing floor, but he found soap and used it to lather the sweat and soil loose from his skin. Finally he shaved his face completely for the first time since leaving Bath. The scratches on his cheek had scabbed over and had begun to peel off at the edges. He noted with satisfaction that soon they would be gone and the tender skin beneath would grow tan in the outdoor weather.

He returned to his room and threw himself into a billowy feather-tick bed. Instantly he was lost in sleep so soft and wonderful he did not convulse or waken, even when his whirling dreams turned their visions against him. In dreams he saw Silas disappearing again and again around a bend in the trail. He saw Merlin grotesquely dragging a broken foreleg, bones protruding from the bloody flesh as he struggled to follow the constant tug of his master's halter. Then rose a strange dream of oxcarts full of screaming women and children calling for the preacher as they were being swept by the rushing Shenandoah through the center of Woodstock and over the roaring edge of a cataract, their cries only briefly disturbing Silas Will, drunk and sleeping in the gazebo, now beyond caring, his pious shell broken, drowning his anguish in whiskey. Jonathan saw himself in dreams, scrubbing his naked body before an open furnace, feeling the blast upon his skin, calling into the flames—"Mother! Mother!"—then turning his head and covering his ears so he would not hear a reply if there was one.

Somehow as he dreamed, as disturbing as his dreams were, he recognized the quality of dreaming and did not wake. The pressure of his exhausted body against the familiar feel of a bed confirmed to him through the night that he was only dreaming.

His body had not moved by morning and he did not waken until he heard the clump of boots down the inn stairwell. By then he was certain he had slept too long and leaped from bed, stumbling across his boots in the dark. There were no windows to his room. He opened his door and dressed by the faint light of the main room. After grooming and saddling his horses he was able to obtain a bowl of hot corn mush from the kitchen. He downed it with haste and mounted the hackney once again. He was much later than he planned to be in returning to the road but at least he felt well rested.

The road south of Staunton began to descend somewhat, for now it traveled through the James River valley in a downstream direction. The James River drainage resembled the Shenandoah's, but was not as expansive. There were more forests and fewer farms in evidence. At least for the first miles that he traveled. By late morning he began to notice one farm adjacent to another in rapid succession, with many more slaves at work than he had ever seen in his life.

He neared Lexington. Here he began to notice the faceless uniformity of slavery. Each slave labored barefoot, in identical tow-cloth garments, and each wore sun-sheltering hats of woven corn husk. The hats hid their individual features, so that an observer would not notice if the face was fresh or tired, healthy or in pain. Nothing showed but the rhythmic bending of their backs, all under the watchful eye of armed overseers. They cleared land, planted orchards, built fences of stone, herded sheep and cattle, cultivated crops of corn, barley, and tobacco along the colonial road.

Soon he arrived at a cluster of broad Georgian mansions and well-ordered streets and houses that formed the town of Lexington. He began to see, in a way he had not seen before, the kind of prosperity slavery could bring when it was employed in a vigorous manner. It presented a picture of marvelous industry for the passing observer, as long as one did not look at the human misery beneath a single hat of corn husk. This was the kind of slave-powered expansion Uncle Ethan envisioned for the Bath farmstead, and yes, Jonathan mused as he watched it in progress, it would be possible to achieve such dramatic results in Bath. But a nagging doubt filled his thinking about it. Was the further prosperity of his household, of the Barratt farm, worth the cost in human bondage?

Growing up, he had never seen slavery as anything but the natural ordering of life. Chayta and Andrew had tended to his needs as though Providence had ordained it. But he had seen Macaijah's growing restlessness. Now that he had run away, Jonathan sensed the injustice that had prompted such a desperate act. No court of law would acquit him of the murder of Bard Dugin. No court would accept the testimony of a slave against the coincidental evidence of his running away and Dugin's murder. Even if others had done the murdering, Macaijah was considered guilty.

I am part of an evil system, Jonathan thought sadly, but his mind saw no remedy. He began to sense, however, that a huge debt was building all across the land, growing from a root of bitterness into a giant tree. A debt of deliberately inflicted pain and misery that someday would have to be paid.

As he passed through Lexington and continued toward Fincastle, he inquired of everyone he passed if they had seen a riding preacher on the south road. By midafternoon he had received one affirmative reply, from an overseer guarding a group of slaves. As the slaves herded sheep through a water gap with a natural bridge of limestone spanning its top, the watchful overseer told Jonathan he had seen such a rider less than an hour before.

"Did he have red hair?"

He could not recall. The rider could not have been Silas. Jonathan could not imagine anyone not remembering his red hair, but he quickened his pace anyway.

By nightfall he had passed through Fincastle and knew that he would not make Christiansburg before stopping. He would continue until he found a suitable inn or some other stopping place by the way. He was tired and dismayed, but consoled by the fact that Merlin had nearly lost his lameness. He felt he would be ready to ride the next day if they continued their present pace.

Midnight came and passed and he had still encountered no public inn on the highway, though he continued to pass many farms. At last, he forded a tributary of the Roanoke River, stopping midway to allow both horses to take a long-overdue drink. A full white moon had reached its zenith, casting light and shadows over the water. Upstream, the wheel of a millhouse turned round and round in the channel with a grinding mindless regularity. As it churned, it sucked rivulets from the surface of the water that showered and splattered down from its glistening paddles like silver coins in the moonlight. He decided to stop for the night.

When the horses completed their drinking, he crossed the ford, dismounted, loosened the saddles, and unburdened both horses on the opposite bank. They sighed and grunted and rolled with ecstasy in the grass. After a while they stood again, splay-legged, and shook the dust from their backsides. He staked them out to graze along the riverbank, unrolled his bedroll beneath a tall elm, and soon fell asleep to the sound of the churning mill wheel.

The sound of splashing and snarling woke him from sleep. He sat up, snatched one of his pistols from beneath his bedroll, then felt quickly and carefully for his spectacles. He bent them into place over his ears. He let his breath go with a gasp of relief and quiet laughter as he recognized a pair of scrappy young raccoons disputing over the possession of a crayfish. Jonathan amused himself for a time watching their fierce bickering in the shallows, framed against the moonlit water. He lay down again, this time taking careful note of the precise position of his spectacles, in case he should need them again. He uncocked his pistol and placed it under his blanket. Shortly, he slept.

It was not yet dawn but he had come fully awake, eyes open, ears alert, blood pounding. The moon was down. He did not stir. Some instinct or dream or *something* had come over him. But he heard nothing. Saw nothing. Slowly he reached one hand from his bedroll and found his spectacles. He put them on. Then he reached under his blanket and found one pistol, then the second. He was inexplicably terrified. Gathering his courage, he scooted himself backward to disguise his body against the dark trunk of the elm tree. He turned to his right, to his left, straining his eyes to see in the darkness.

Then he noticed Merlin. The stallion stood stock-still on the bank of the river, ears alert, staring with flaring nostrils into the darkness at the opposite side of the ford. Jonathan looked, too, and slowly, as though ghosts materialized before his eyes, he saw riders, he could not tell how many, standing silently on the opposite bank. A chill ran between his shoulders to the base of his head.

Had they seen him? They made no move toward him, nor did they act as if they were aware of being watched. He wondered how long they had been there. Were they law-abiding or renegade? It was very late for civilized men to be about. They must be white, he reasoned. Surely not savage. Indians didn't ride.

Remembering the watchman's warning at the Roan Springs Tavern, he cursed himself for camping so near to the ford, and hastily strapped his shoulder harness into place, holstering his pistols. They hung heavily against his sides. Could he use them? He had never fired at a man. Growing up in Bath provided the experience of hunting game animals. It had been difficult enough to kill them. At Harvard he had participated in training drills with the student militia, but that was far from the real experience of war.

He felt himself trembling at the joints of his arms and legs. His hands tingled. A picture crossed his mind of Captain Barratt, the man of courage, standing at the helm of his ship in the thick of battle. Jonathan didn't have his blood or, he feared, his courage. As yet, the riders remained across the river, a temporary advantage. He knew he must use that advantage to secure his horses, at least Merlin, without attracting attention. He would run before he would fight.

Above the sound of the gurgling river and the mill wheel he heard the click of iron shoes against stone, and occasionally now a muffled word passing between the men. One of the riders unsheathed a long-handled torch from a scabbard by his saddle and set it afire; then a second torch was lit from the first. The flames leaped high, illuminating faces. Jonathan noted with a degree of relief that the men were dressed as farmers, gentlemen farmers in knee breeches and topcoats, but to his surprise and bewilderment, Silas Will was among them, his unmistakable red hair ablaze in the firelight. But strangely, he was their captive. His arms were bound behind him.

He counted five riders in all. Each one, except for Silas, carried a rifle. One of the riders who held no torch, a younger man, took a long drink from a whiskey flask. Then he tilted his head back and suddenly filled the night with a horrific scream. The scream was followed by gruff laughter from the other men who seemed to enjoy Silas' disapproving scowl. Another shot of whiskey, another scream, followed by more jesting and laughter.

Jonathan crawled from his bedroll and stole forward to the riverbank. He patted Merlin, who bowed his neck and pawed the ground, excited by the commotion and the presence of other horses across the river. Jonathan unstaked him and led him near the saddles. He lifted the first saddle carefully to his back, patting him and making murmuring sounds to calm him. His fingers fumbled for the cinch while he kept his eyes on the men across the river.

Strangely, all of the riders now entered the water, but instead of crossing the ford, they turned upstream and waded slowly toward the turning mill wheel. Seeing this, Jonathan became certain that they had no idea of his presence.

Taking advantage of their turned backs, he hurried through the essentials of haltering and saddling the hackney. He tumbled his bedroll together and lashed it over his saddlebags, then slipped a bridle over Merlin's head. Leading both mounts, he trotted along the bank upstream to gain a closer look at the riders as they waded nearer to the millhouse. He moved to the ford, which was as close as he dared come. He stroked

Merlin's nose to keep him calm. Then he peered into the darkness, catching partial glimpses between the moving horses and riders of something weird in the glow of their torches. On the spokes of the mill wheel turned the bodies of three slaves; they were men displayed like sides of beef bound to a spit. Their heads had been strapped to the paddles, feet to the hub, so that with each revolution of the giant wheel their torsos disappeared under the channel.

The men sat on their horses before the wheel speaking to Silas in words which Jonathan could not understand. They drifted to him over the troubled water as muted bass tones. He averted his gaze, but too late. One view of the disgraced bodies was enough. The image would remain with him as long as he lived.

He looked again. He could not tell if the slaves had been drowned there or killed elsewhere and brought to the wheel for display. But he knew this much: they had been dead for many hours. It occurred to him that they had been grotesquely turning there earlier in the night, even as the mill wheel's sloshing had lulled him to sleep. What had happened that night he could not guess, and Silas' involvement seemed an even greater mystery.

He drew the horses back from the water's edge to wait unseen near a thicket of lowland laurel. He wondered what he should do now. Perhaps blood was a strong bond after all. He felt Silas' helplessness, now bound to his saddle, and wanted to help him if he could. But he was quite outnumbered.

Suddenly, Merlin could hold his peace no longer. He hurled a trumpeting challenge across the water toward the other horses. The men fell silent and turned quickly to look in his direction, shifting their guns to the ready position. Dawn was beginning to lighten the sky, but Jonathan held Merlin quietly, sure that he was not yet seen against the backdrop of laurel. The two men with the torches turned and spurred their horses with splashing lunges toward the bank where Jonathan stood.

Suddenly the night shattered with explosions and flashes of yellow light that seemed to come from everywhere, from the opposite bank, from the millhouse, and from the thicket just behind Jonathan. All was screaming confusion as the angry needles of light stabbed toward the men in the center of the stream. They twisted and fell from their mounts. Merlin screamed and plunged from the bank, dragging Jonathan into the water. He grabbed the saddle and clung there, hiding his body behind Merlin's midsection. Then an eerie hush descended.

Jonathan crouched in the water and peered about. Above the water, tracers of blue smoke and wadding hung in the air where screaming balls of lead had passed moments before. Only Silas remained in the saddle, looking about, this way and that. Around him four riderless horses plunged helter-skelter, stirring a bloody froth to the top of the river. The torches floated downstream where they had fallen, still burning, but fading fast in the water. Now and then a hand or foot reached above the darkened surface, arched in death's spasm as the current slowly rolled four fallen riders downstream.

"Preacher!"

A voice rang out from the opposite bank. It was a voice familiar to Jonathan, but he could not be sure.

"Preacher, go your way!"

"Macaijah!" Jonathan screamed. There was no answer but the echo of his own voice against the wall of the millhouse.

Jonathan knew he was as good as dead, and Silas, too. If it was Macaijah, perhaps he would not kill his former master. Perhaps he had been more than a slave all these years. Jonathan had no other hope. He swung into his saddle and guided Merlin toward the thicket on the opposite bank. But instantly a needle of fire and thunder roared from the thicket, sending up a thin spire of water where the bullet struck, a scant yard in front of him. Jonathan held Merlin still. He turned to look at Silas, who stared back at him with amazement.

"Can you cut me loose?" he whispered hoarsely.

Jonathan pulled a knife from his belt, held it over his head so that Macaijah or whoever else lay in ambush could see what he was doing. He nudged Merlin near to Silas, reached behind him, and cut the ropes on his wrists. Silas stared steadily into his face.

"We are in the 'come-down' of a slave revolt here, Mr. Barratt. Do you know of it?" Silas whispered between his teeth.

"I know nothing."

Silas eyed him suspiciously, having heard him call Macaijah's name. "It would be well, and I mean well for the both of us, if we found ourselves on neither side of this thing. Understand?"

Jonathan nodded. In the cold breaking dawn he looked again at the bloated bodies of the slaves turning on the wheel. Then at the bloody water pouring through the ford below them. He wanted to race away toward Christiansburg, putting this place far behind him. But what of Macaijah? Was it him on the far bank?

"Let's go," Silas said, splashing his horse downstream.

Jonathan waited a moment more, searching the thicket on the opposite bank for some sign of his runaway slave. He held up his hand in a signal of friendship, but in the silence he felt the cold stare of an unknown number of rifles pointed in deadly aim at his heart. He turned Merlin downstream after Silas, who now galloped away on the road south.

By midmorning Jonathan and Silas entered Christiansburg. Unlike most of the sleepy farm settlements they had passed through, this community bustled with activity.

There were oxcart caravans and pack trains bound for Kentucky, farm wagons, coaches, frontiersmen, and local townsfolk. This was a crossroads community where the northern highway met the Richmond highway not to mention several southern farm roads and traces winding out of the tangled North Carolina mountains. At the very center of town, where all roads converged, they entered a large barren common. All of Christiansburg's traffic of necessity crossed here, for the settlement had few cross streets. Over the years, it had grown outward from this very intersection. Its buildings, which toward the center of town included a church, a constabulary office, several inns, stores, craftsmen's shops, and homes, had simply been erected along each of three main routes which radiated from the common—routes which, in turn, subdivided near the perimeter of town into a half dozen smaller routes.

"Why did those men have you bound at the ford?" Jonathan asked as they entered the common.

"There is a slave revolt here. The men were searching the road lookin' for sympathizers, and me being a stranger, they looked through my bags. That's where they found the petition. I've been signin' up folks against the slave trade in Kaintuck."

"What would they have done to you?"

"Just stick me in the pillory here in Christiansburg. Let the children throw dirt at me for a few hours. Nothing that hasn't been done before. But those bushwhackers back there, I figure they spared me because I had my hands tied by those slaveholders. Just the grace of God I'm still here to tell of it. Praise God for that. And what about you? That hollerin' buck, the one you called Macaijah, must have spared you, too. Who was he, if you don't mind my asking?"

"I don't know if it was him, but it sounded like a former slave of mine."

"A freed man?"

Jonathan paused. "A runaway."

Silas shook his head ponderously. "There's a mighty bad number of them these days. And I must say, not much good they can do in a slaving world. They go bad, most of them. I mean real bad."

Even as they spoke they passed a slave auction in progress. A half dozen slaves in chains waited their turn to step onto a block in the sun. The owners and bidders stood sheltered in the shade of an arbor. Some of the men resembled those at the Roanoke ford. Most were armed with rifles. Several groups of them stood in serious discussion. Perhaps news of the ambush had reached them.

"The road gets rough from here on, Mr. Barratt. Best you turn back." Silas looked at Jonathan steadily for his reply.

"I have business in Kentucky."

They had crossed the common and were turning due west on a poorly surfaced road. Silas suddenly spurred his mount into a gallop.

Jonathan spurred Merlin right after him.

11

The Duel

From Christiansburg the road became treacherous. Chaises and narrow-wheeled buggies never went beyond the western edge of town, only heavy-wheeled Conestogas and oxcarts. The rugged route was like an initiation fee that only the poor could pay. Extreme difficulty and pain were the accepted currency here. No doubt Silas would do well. The road was undisciplined. Its ruts wandered, sometimes fifty feet to one side or another of rocks, mudholes, protruding tree roots, and stumps. This was a luckless road, a desperation road, and they descended it at a full gallop. Following a long meadow, they both dashed under the clutching branches of a dead oak and plunged into a darkened canyon.

"Go back!" Silas warned as Jonathan pulled abreast.

The words bore a mixed load of irritation, exasperation, and real concern, Jonathan thought. Hearing them, he was surprised to find himself hanging back, an increased sense of dread settling over him. He still felt the effects of the death he had seen at the ford in the first light of day.

An hour passed, then two. Ingles Ferry came into view on the New River. Silas was far in the lead. Jonathan still followed. When he reached the ferry station, Silas had already tied his horses on the floating beams. He now stood blocking the entrance. The ferryman and his mule stood ready to draw the rope which would pull the raft across the flowing current by a wooden pulley attached to a tree on the far side. Jonathan drew Merlin to a halt.

Silas moved forward; he seemed distracted, troubled. Then suddenly he looked up, demanding, "What do you want with me?"

Jonathan replied carefully. "I have told you. I have business in Kentucky. I wish to accompany you there. You know Kentucky well . . . and besides, there is the pleasure of riding with someone who knew my father and mother. It seems quite natural to me."

"Unnatural," Silas mulled. "Unnatural. Why do you still follow me? It seems like a lot of trouble to me. This is not a frolic out here."

Jonathan dismounted. "I am following you for moral reasons, I suppose. Because I found myself in strange sympathy with your objection to slavery."

"Your morals and mine are not a whit of the same cotton, Mr. Barratt. Until you enter the Kingdom, your morals count for *nothing* in the eyes of God, and nothing to me."

Jonathan turned to face him, feeling his anger rising. He laughed it away. "You want to provoke me to turn back. I'm not fooled."

"Perhaps you are. We are of two different worlds. You are of this earth, I am a stranger to this earth. How can we ride together when you refuse to enter the door of God's Kingdom? I've seen many unregenerate men such as yourself run from the fear of God, which they feel when riding with me. *That* is natural. But you. You ride on."

Jonathan had no reply for a time. He knew that it was because this man was his own father, and that this man had caused his mother's suffering. Jonathan followed to even the score. The other reasons had taken him from Bath, but this one drove him to follow even when the road grew dangerous.

He turned on Silas with cold anger, "I have my reasons, Mr. Will. When I am ready, I will give them to you."

Silas' hand reached forward. It was not a fast move so much as an unexpected one. Jonathan stared dumbly as Silas reached inside his coat and cleanly pulled free one of the dueling pistols. Too late, Jonathan grabbed his wrist and held it firmly with one hand. They stood there, with the pistol held tensely between them. The ferryman shifted uneasily, watching them beyond earshot, near the riverbank.

Silas spoke. "These pistols you wear are made for shooting men, Mr. Barratt. Have you ever shot a man?"

Jonathan reached into his coat with his free hand and drew the other pistol, cocking it. "I am capable, if that worries you," Jonathan bluffed.

"Do you want to shoot me, Mr. Barratt?"

Jonathan shook his head in wonder. "What kind of question is that?"

"A good one. These pistols are not for hunting game, they are for killing men. You ask to ride with me. Why? I ask. And why should I allow it, when you wear your father's dueling pistols?" Silas' eyes suddenly grew narrow. "Do you want to kill me with them . . . as your father did?"

Jonathan was stunned. "What did you say?"

Silas did not reply. He stood, eyes fiercely blazing, and in a twinkling had wrenched the pistol free of Jonathan's grasp.

Jonathan was embarrassed that Silas had broken his grip. His voice rose with emotion. "If Captain Barratt had wanted to kill you, you would be dead."

"There is much you do not know, Mr. Barratt," Silas replied, turning the pistol around and handing it back to Jonathan. "Let it remain that way. Go back. Or take your own way to Kentucky."

Jonathan returned his pistols one by one to their holsters and replied coldly, "Why should Captain Barratt want to kill you, Mr. Will? I know what kind of a man he was. What have you done to cause the Captain's anger? Some deed that I may not be aware of, but which nevertheless plagues your own sinful conscience? Do you wish to confess the deed, Preacher Will?"

Silas' face flushed. "You may ride with me, young man," he snarled. "And your blood be on your own head!"

He whirled and stepped onto the planks of the ferry. Jonathan followed.

Silas whirled on him again. "And don't call me Preacher. I am an exhorter!"

Jonathan nodded once.

As Silas turned back to the ferry, he stiffened. "Look there, across the river," he muttered.

Jonathan looked where Silas now pointed. At first he saw nothing, just a clearing surrounded by trees where the ferry and the road joined. Then he discerned the outline of a man on horseback standing at the edge of the clearing watching the ferry. Even from that distance he could see that he was a black man with long, matted hair, his horse nearly concealed by brush.

"Runaway," Silas explained. "Most runaways in Kaintuck join LeFevre. I suspect this one's in cahoots with the ferryman. The ferry will stop close enough to the other side to make us sitting game for his long rifle. You best stay here and watch the ferryman while I cross. When I am over, I'll watch your crossing in turn."

Jonathan wondered about Macaijah. Would he turn renegade, too? He realized it was possible that he already had.

"I'll keep one of your horses with me," Jonathan said.

"I said you ride with *me* now, Mr. Barratt, not the other way round. You do as I say."

Silas pulled his rifle from its saddle scabbard and rested it over the back of his horse. He watched the opposite bank. Jonathan left the raft. It bobbed and gurgled under the shifting weight. He approached the ferryman. He was a graying man, fortyish, with hawkish eyes and a small chin covered by sparsely grown whiskers. His mouth carried a constant sour pucker.

"Take him over," Jonathan said.

"Preachers ride free," protested the ferryman, nodding toward Silas at the front of the raft. "They ride when others ride."

Jonathan tossed him a shilling from his pouch. "Take him now."

The ferryman glanced nervously across the water, stuffed the coin into his pocket, then cast loose the shore line and called out, "Haw!"

The mule leaned into its harness and the raft pulled free of the shore and into the current. Jonathan mounted Merlin and rode parallel to the mule path as the ferryman walked beside his mule. He could see that Silas had positioned himself for cover behind his horses. Jonathan continued to watch back and forth from the raft to the rider on the opposite bank.

As the raft neared the other shore, Jonathan noticed with satisfaction that the rider on the edge of the clearing suddenly vanished into the trees. Perhaps they had foiled an ambush after all. He tried not to feel too much satisfaction. There was still rough road ahead. The ferryman turned his mule about, hitched him to an opposite rope, and drew the raft back to the near side of the river. Jonathan paid for a second crossing, which proceeded without incident. On the opposite shore, Silas watched and waited, guarding the crossing just as he said he would.

Nightfall. They had come as far as Seven Mile Ford on the Holston River. Throughout the afternoon they had passed through the settlements of Newbern, Fort Chiswell, Evansham, and Mount Airy, with their collections of bleak log-and-mud cabins and fortifications. Milled lumber and paint were no longer in evidence. Most of the primitive structures had appeared newly constructed.

Jonathan felt strange as he passed through these settlements in his civilized clothes. Most of the people wore loose buckskin and linsey-woolsey cloth. They looked at him suspiciously as he rode by, but Silas, in the distinctive black of a preacher, seemed immediately accepted by the same folk. Jonathan decided he needed more suitable garments for riding this territory.

On the road itself things were different. About half of the fellow travelers they passed that day seemed to be of a distrustful nature. They regarded both Jonathan and Silas with dark silence. Jonathan wondered about these travelers. Were they criminals on the run from the civilized East? Or former prisoners sent from the Continent to homestead the land?

They crossed Seven Mile Ford on their horses; the river was high and treacherous. Once across, Silas abruptly left the road. They ascended a ridge. When they had topped it, finding a flat area nestled among a grove of pine trees, they dismounted and began to make camp for the night.

"Tether the horses apart," Silas ordered in a hushed voice. "Make it hard for thieves. Lazy as snakes, they are."

Jonathan unsaddled the horses and tethered them at the four corners of their campsite. After spreading out his bedroll, Silas built a small fire, pulled a flat rock next to it, and neatly laid out a swatch of cotton cloth, a knife, a powder horn, and a bullet mold. He pulled a piece of cold venison jerky from his saddlebag and waved Jonathan over to the rock.

"You should make cartridges," Silas grunted in a hushed tone as Jonathan came near. "It saves time reloading. 'Sides, you can reload on the run." He tore loose a bite of venison and began to chew. "Know how?"

Jonathan nodded. He had made cartridges in his militia training at Harvard. He laid his pistols on the rock, took the knife, and began to cut cloth patches, laying them in a row to receive premeasured powder and bullets.

"Who is this man LeFevre?" Jonathan asked as he worked.

"French Indian scout. Gone wild. He lives up in caves on the Green

River in Kaintuck. As long as he and his bunch stay in the caves, things go along good, but they come out now and again and play a bloody game all along the Wilderness Road from Crab Orchard on up to Danville on the barrens. Mostly they go after weak folks and women. Easy pickings."

"He wants to kill you?"

"He does."

"Asbury said you had been his friend."

"Never was a friend. I rode with him in Carolina, to fight the whiskey tax, long 'fore I knew the Lord."

"How did you cross him?"

Silas sighed heavily before speaking. "I discovered the truth about him. And that truth is a grim thing indeed. He has a melancholy and bloody passion toward women. Do you understand what I mean by that?"

"No, I . . . I do not."

"When he first came to Kaintuck, it was rumored he killed his own wife and daughters up on the Allegheny. Is that making things a bit clearer?"

"I suppose it does."

"I asked him outright about it as soon as I heard of it—that was about ten years ago—and he made a good story about Injuns. I found it too hard to believe that the man could butcher his own, so I took his side with the folk in Danville. Some won't ever forgive me for that. But I was without the Lord then. Then came the time in Carolina when we fought the whiskey tax. We had finished our fight poorly and were low-spirited. LeFevre and I rode together up the Holston River to the widow Harkness' cabin. She was a . . . well, a licentious woman, which seemed to please Jacques. She made a stout whiskey, which, I'm ashamed to say, pleased me at the time. I was untouched by the Spirit of God then and feeling the need of getting dead drunk. So I was drinking when he begins to abuse the woman. I remember yelling at him to stop it . . . but I had the Devil's drool in me . . . that's all I remember."

He paused. When he spoke again he was looking far off into the night.

"In the morning I woke covered with blood, the widow's. She must have fought him good, but . . . the man is possessed of demons. He . . . he cut her to pieces. That's how I learned the truth about Jacques LeFevre, and I have not hesitated to tell it to those who need to know."

"Why haven't they hung him?"

Silas looked up at Jonathan as if amazed at his question. "You must understand me now, there are sections of Kaintuck that belong to no one but outlaws. No decent folk at all. With no law, these people live lower than they should. Even the good folk. Only Christ on the inside makes them stand against the pull of savages."

"But surely a crime as outrageous as—"

"Ha! You're green. When these men drink, it's a contest to see who has the most Devil inside. LeFevre wins every time. He is boasted of by these. Ride into their country and put a stop to their bloody game and you have no friends at all. Soon you will be in the ground. It is no small thing to do."

"But you are hanging some of his men, aren't you?"

"Three of them, but by God's Providence we shall bring down the others as well. Some of my flock, Brother Stern and his family, were touched by this rotten bunch. I had prayed God's protection over my people, but when the Devil prevailed, I took it as a sign that God wanted Silas Will to put gunpowder into His Almighty service. Some of my flock went out and surprised part of the gang over at Crab Orchard. Got 'em trussed up at Logan's Fort for hanging right now, and when I do hang 'em, LeFevre's days are numbered in Kaintuck. People will know he can be brought down."

As he listened, Jonathan had quietly tied up his cartridges with lengths of fine thread. Now the small fire of pine cones and dead branches glowed red and popped. In the distance an owl hooted.

"It seems odd that you advise me to prepare cartridges," Jonathan mused.

Silas picked up one of the ornate dueling pistols and turned it quietly in the firelight. "A man must protect himself."

"Ah, that is it. To protect myself. And you are not enlisting me to help you against LeFevre?"

"If you or any other unregenerate man would help me subdue LeFevre, it would be good in the eyes of this world, but I am called to declare the Kingdom of God, and the Kingdom cares not for your good works. But all of Heaven rejoices over one sinner that repenteth. That is the only good work you can do. I have shown you the door and you turned from it, young man. You *must* protect your life now by all means, for if you were to die, you would enter Hades."

Jonathan chilled at the coldness of these words. They seemed especially frightening on this star-blanketed ridgetop. He could almost hear Heaven's door closing him out. "And you believe that?"

"It is the truth, young man. I would be a fool not to believe the truth."

Jonathan thought he had never met anyone with such strong and contrary beliefs. "How did you come by such thoughts?" he asked.

"I bowed at the door of Salvation. My eyes were opened." Silas stared steadily across the stone slab between them.

Jonathan looked away. He stretched his cramped knee and tilted his head back to look up at the stars above the pine tops. Each star a mystery, he thought. Countless cold mysteries there. Silas' constant turn of conversation to the "door of Salvation" agitated Jonathan. It induced feelings of being lost. Feelings of great distance from the stars and from the silent God of Silas' religion.

Jonathan stood and walked thoughtfully away to the crest of the hill. It seemed Silas sought to agitate those feelings of being lost, regardless of time or place. Normal life was twisted by this preacher-exhorter into a strange dream-landscape, wherein there would open an invisible door to the night sky: the door to the Kingdom, invisible to every human being except Silas Will. He had to admit, his words gave it a strange power. But he did not want to hear the words again. Stepping through the door, he feared, would not reveal a stairway to Heaven but rather a plunge into the void where his mother's dying words, "I am rejected," made the only kind of sense. Jonathan let his gaze creep down from the stars, down from the pine-tree tops. His ears filled with the cicadas' song, the sounds of crickets, and the distant call of a hunting owl. This was the world he understood. The coals from the fire glowed softly against the lacy delicate lichens clinging to the pine trees nearby. The world of wood, insects, and men was Jonathan's world. Silas had his strange "Kingdom."

Jonathan turned back to collect his cartridges and found that Silas continued to be preoccupied with one of the pistols. He turned it in his hand opposite the fire. Jonathan had the other in his holster.

"Your father and I fought a duel with these pistols," Silas said.

Jonathan was glad he had raised the issue again. "I did not know that," he replied.

"I thought that you did. I thought perhaps you wished to end what your father had begun with me."

"Perhaps I would if I knew his reason."

Silas looked up sharply. "And so you shall not know," he said with a weary smile. "I was not of the dueling class. According to dueling men, a duel decides guilt or innocence. But that was already known between your father and I."

"So you were guilty."

"I did not say I was guilty. Did you know that your father and I were friends?"

"I would have only *your* word on that."

Silas turned his back to Jonathan and held up the pistol in the ready position. It looked so strange for the preacher to be playing duelist, the more so because he handled the pistol with such ease.

"I asked him for ten paces," he said over his shoulder. "Sure killing range." He took a couple of steps beyond the fire. "That would have been . . . about here." He whirled and aimed the pistol directly between Jonathan's eyes. Jonathan fought off a flash of fear. He started to reach for the other pistol, but Silas continued talking.

"I aimed," he said, squinting at Jonathan with deadly aim, "but found the Captain standing there with his gun to his side. He was a dead man." Silas lowered the pistol.

Jonathan was puzzled by this. "Does that mean Captain Barratt was the guilty one?"

Silas walked past the fire and stood uncomfortably close to Jonathan's face. "I fired off to one side," he said. "Then your father raised his gun at me. He held *my* life in his hand, and asked if I would pledge myself to a solemn promise to go to the wilderness and never return to Boston again, that pledge in exchange for my life. I thought for a long time about it; I had not planned to live a wilderness life. But I *had* planned to live. I gave him my pledge. He never fired his pistol, he just lowered it. And I have never gone back on my word to him."

Silas placed the pistol in Jonathan's hand.

The coals of the fire had gone cold but Jonathan lay wide-eyed on his bedroll. The stars poured an icy influence upon his wakefulness. He wondered why the Captain had not fired on this red-haired scoundrel. Or worse, why had he placed his life in Silas' hands first, not even raising his own pistol? After thinking of it from every side, all the strange questions about the duel pointed to a disturbing pair of answers: either Silas was a liar or he and the Captain had truly been friends.

12

The Wild Folk

"Boone's axmen started there," Silas said. He pointed to a log-and-earthen fortification a short distance downstream. These were his first words of the day.

He had finished his prayer at first light that morning to find Jonathan mounted and waiting. They had promptly set out from their camp above the Seven Mile Ford, traveling silently at a hard pace through several ridge and valley systems until arriving at this very fortification on the east bank of the Holston River. It was now early afternoon.

"We can supply up here," Silas said. "Take the horses on, and I'll follow."

Then he dismounted and walked uncomfortably to a crude sapling privy constructed on the bank of the river. He disappeared behind a deerskin flap. Jonathan took the reins of Silas' horses and moved toward the fort.

It was a two-story log structure built in the open, with rifle notches cut through the walls on all sides. The second story overhung the first so that in battle the first story could be defended from above. This was a standard blockhouse structure. But this particular blockhouse had successfully thwarted many an Indian raid and in doing so had become a symbol of confidence for the settlers and newcomers to the land. They had named it the Blockhouse as well. Most of all, it was the celebrated place chosen by Daniel Boone and his axmen as the starting point for the Wilderness Road to Kentucky, cut some nine years earlier.

Uncle Ethan had talked about the history of this road. He had assured his investors that their Kentucky land investments would increase in value with the flow of settlers through the Cumberland Gap. Ethan had been right, Jonathan mused as he rode past dozens of loaded oxcarts and half camps on the meadow surrounding the Blockhouse. On a second road from the south, at that very moment, two more carts rumbled toward the meadow.

Jonathan took careful notice of the settlers. This ragged, hollow-eyed class of poor who had attracted his pity for years as they passed through Bath had now reached a land where they were no longer oddities. Here they found no buildings dressed with milled lumber, no neatly painted shops, no great houses, no well-tailored gardens or greens to remind them of their dispossession. Everyone here was alike in poverty and in having traveled so far. They seemed now to be enlivened by purposes within their reach. To build a sapling half camp, clear land for planting, to plant, harvest, trade, to sustain their families just one season, then perhaps to build a cabin next year, that was enough.

As Jonathan rode nearer he saw that, almost without exception, the typical despair in the eyes of those on the road had been replaced by a new light. Each cluster of men, women, and children were engaged in animated chatter, sharing ideas and techniques to advance their lives in this land of the clean slate. He dismounted, tying his and Silas' horses outside the Blockhouse, and waited, leaning against the rough beams of it, in the warm sun. A young man, perhaps thirteen or fourteen had followed him from a nearby encampment. Jonathan noted the boy's interest in his blue tricorn hunting hat with its tasseled staghorn medallion. The boy approached.

"Hello there," Jonathan said. "What's your name?"

"Thaddeus. Thad."

"You like this hat, do you?"

"Oh yes, I do, sir."

"Well, here, you can borrow it while I buy supplies." He placed it on

Thad's head. It was too large, slipping down over his eyes, but the boy adjusted it with a proud smile.

"Thank you!" he said, and trotted toward the encampment.

Jonathan went into the Blockhouse, passing beneath a wool blanket that hung in the doorway. Inside, in the semi-darkness, he felt the presence of other bodies, though he could not see them. He stood to one side, letting his eyes adjust. The air was heavy with odors of sweat, tobacco smoke, whiskey, and wood shavings. He could hardly breathe. The poor ventilation made him uneasy. He would have opened the door flap to allow in fresh air but the shafts of light streaming from the rifle ports revealed a room full of men clad in buckskin and linsey-woolsey who seemed to enjoy the atmosphere just as it was. They were gathered around heavy plank tables conversing in low voices.

"What can I do fer ye?"

A toothless little man in a bloody apron approached Jonathan from off to his right, surprising him. The man wiped blood from his arms as he spoke. On a table behind him lay a heavily antlered white-tailed buck, his entrails half scooped from his body cavity into an oaken whiskey barrel on the floor. The smell of the cooling guts suddenly hit Jonathan. He nearly gagged, but steeled himself against the smell. He spoke to the man.

"I would like to obtain small portions of bread, cheese, and meat for myself and grain for my horses."

"Haw," shrilled the little man. Many of the men in the room turned and looked his way. "Ye mus' be green as grass. 'Tain't no grain from here to 'Tucky what ain't fer seed. A green one fer darn sure."

Gruff laughter rippled from several tables.

"Grain-fed hoss makes good eats," a voice bellowed from a nearby table.

More laughter.

"'Member the time the Shawnee ate our hosses up the Blue Licks, Griz?"

"Yeah. Good thing he weren't grain-fed. Been a waste."

"Forget the grain," Jonathan said. "I am green . . . as you say. So green, in fact, that I pay my way in hard shillings. Perhaps I shall find what I need at Martin's Station."

He turned to go, but the man slipped nimbly in front of him, blocking the exit. "Shut yer big yaps," he hollered to the room, "or the whiskey barrel dries. This 'ere man ain't as green as he makes out. No, sir." He lowered his voice. "Jus' a little fun for a bunch o' ole geezers is all. I'll get yer supplies, and right quick, too."

Jonathan smiled and followed the man to a counter in front of a large pantry. He watched him pull down a rib cage of smoked venison. The man scowled at it in the dim light, then blew on it, flecks of spittle showering out of his toothless mouth as dust billowed from the dried meat. Jonathan shook his head in disgust.

"What? How now?" exclaimed the little man. His brows knit in a self-chastising expression. "Lets see some fresh backstrap fer the likes o' ye." He threw the rib cage back onto the shelf and pulled a piece of lean backstrap from underneath the counter. "Fer a hard shilling." He winked. Then he uncorked a crock of strong-smelling whiskey and poured some into a mug.

Jonathan was thirsty but held up his hand. "No, thank you. I am traveling with a riding preacher."

The little man leaned forward and whispered, looking about the room. "Preacher? Be he Silas Will?"

Jonathan nodded.

"Keep him out o' here. Some men's been lookin' fer him." The man looked frightened. "I'll bring the supplies to ye outside. Now best ye be gone."

Jonathan was suddenly fearful, choking on the smoky air of the room. He nodded and slowly made his way back to the door. He glanced one more time about the dim Blockhouse. Instinctively, he searched for the giant form of Macaijah, though he had no reason to believe the slave was heading for Kentucky. A black man sat in the corner. His long, greasy hair shone in the light from one of the gun notches. Jonathan could not see his face. He was clad in buckskin and sat drinking at a table with several whites. Jonathan thought it might be the same man who had waited to ambush them at Ingles Ferry the day before.

Outside, he spied Silas, surrounded by a group of settlers. He stood with them near their oxcarts, praying and talking. Jonathan walked across the grounds toward them, passing in among the carts and the scattered family groups. At the edge of the crowd several men drank defiantly from a whiskey crock. They did not seem pleased at Silas' presence.

"A man's gotta stand on his own two legs," one of the men muttered as Jonathan passed.

"That we know," a second man agreed.

The first tilted another drink from the crock. "Preacher and his holy talk is fer womenfolk. That's about it."

As Jonathan passed out of earshot he heard, "Gimme a good long rifle. Som'one else can do the prayin'."

"Yup. Pray that your aim improves."

A burst of laughter flew from the men.

"God wants good fruit from this land." Silas' voice drifted to Jonathan as he drew nearer. Silas stood on the back of a cart to preach to the small group of women and children. A few men loitered at the perimeter. "The Lord taught us to pray His Kingdom come on earth as it is in Heaven. And He has given all of you a new start in this land of Kaintuck, with a challenge to make it a more godly land than the land you left behind."

"Amen," shouted an enthusiastic woman. Many of the women nodded agreement.

"God knows your heart, good woman, and each of you. He knows you mean to make this land abound to His glory. At least you do in this moment. But what of the trials ahead? Will you still mean it if the crops fail? Will you rise up praising God each morning? Or will you lose your faith and turn to wickedness? Licentiousness? Evil?"

"No, Preacher!"

"No! I believe you do mean to follow Christ come what may!"

"Amen," shouted the woman.

"Amen," chorused the crowd.

"Amen," agreed Silas. "But I must warn you. Each of us must search our heart before God today. Some of you already have. Some of you are overcomers even now, by the Blood of the Lamb, Praise God!"

"In Him, I have overcome," declared a young woman. Her eyes filled with tears.

"I can see that you have," Silas said, his voice lowering. "I wish that I could stay to hear you testify of it, my sister, but I must be going."

"Mr. Will," Jonathan shouted.

Silas looked at him sharply, annoyed at the interruption.

"Mr. Will, you may minister longer," Jonathan said. "Your supplies are being assembled in the Blockhouse. I will see they get packed up for you."

Silas looked uncomfortable. "Yes, well . . ." He turned back to the crowd.

"Will any bow? Will any enter the Kingdom of Heaven today?"

"I will!" a young lad's voice sounded.

Jonathan recognized the voice and turned to see him. Thaddeus, still wearing Jonathan's tricorn, removed it reverently and bowed his head before Silas.

"Praise God," Silas shouted. "The Lord said, 'Suffer the little children to come unto Me.' Shall we pray?" They bowed their heads and Silas began to pray. Jonathan moved toward the edge of the camp. "Our Father, which art in Heaven," he heard Silas pray loudly, "we confess our sins before You this day, and ask that You write Your law upon this young man's heart, and upon our hearts anew today. Create a new heart within us. A heart that will believe when all else fails, a heart that will endure till the end. Forgive us our trespasses . . . lead us on a righteous road for Thy Name's sake . . . bring us to the Land of our Inheritance . . ."

"D____' religion's fer wimmen and children," Jonathan heard as he passed the men at the edge of the camp.

A short time later, at the Blockhouse, the storekeeper emerged with two tied bundles. Jonathan paid him with a pine tree and an oak tree shilling for each. The man's toothless face broke into a happy grin.

"Take car'y the Preacher Will, now," he croaked.

"Do you mean that I should look after him? Or that I should beware of him?"

"Tee, hee," chuckled the storekeeper. "A mite o' both, I reckon." Then his face turned as serious as Jonathan imagined it could ever become, and he blurted, "He's a man o' God fer d____' sure, he is. But Preacher Will, he ain't afraid o' no man. But some o' us is 'fraid fer him. There's them that wants him kilt." He sniffed and swallowed. "Iffen I ever git religion, I want it jus' like his'n. By God, I mean it, too!" The storekeeper waved his hand in the direction of Silas, who still prayed from the back of the cart. Then the storekeeper ducked out of sight into the Blockhouse.

As he took up the two bundles and adjusted them behind the saddles, Jonathan continued to observe Silas among the settlers. So it was mostly women who sought religion, he noted. A commotion interrupted Jonathan's thoughts. A large man was headed his way, holding young Thaddeus by one ear and marching him away from the group near Silas. The man's face was dark with anger. In his other hand, he clutched Jonathan's tricorn. The man stalked straight up to Jonathan, pushing the boy forward and shoving Jonathan's hat back into his hands.

"You and the preacher stay clear of my boy," he demanded.

Jonathan felt himself grow angry. "I only let him borrow this hat," he said. "Was that wrong?"

"A corst it be. I shan't have my Thad thinkin' he's high and mighty, puttin' on that hat. And the preacher, too. Gittin' Thad agitated. I ought to clout the both of you. If I catch you near Thad again, just like I tol' the preacher, you get no warning from me. I just start in. Thad!" The boy scurried after the man without a backward look. Jonathan was left shaking his head.

He brushed a hand through his hair, then donned his hat, unhitched the horses, and led them away toward Silas, who was bowed in prayer with the woman who had responded with enthusiasm to his preaching. As Jonathan neared, Silas finished his prayer, patted the woman's shoulder encouragingly, and then quickly strode to meet him. With a leap, he hoisted himself into his saddle.

"Where'd he go?" Silas asked angrily.

"Who?"

"The father of that boy."

Jonathan pointed. "Over there."

"There's one thing a man must not do," Silas seethed, holding his horse to finish his point. "You can reject God as a man, that is one thing, but you must not prevent one of the little ones from coming to Him."

Silas gigged his horse into a run in the direction of the oxcart where Thaddeus' father now stood with a group of men. They passed a whiskey crock among themselves. Jonathan mounted Merlin and followed him. Silas had reined in, dismounted, and walked up to Thad's father by the time he arrived. Jonathan could see that the man was nearly a head taller than Silas. The men around him looked rough and surly, in no mood for a lecture. Jonathan remained in his saddle watching.

"I want to speak with you, sir," Silas said politely to Thad's father. "There, by the river." He nodded to a spot several yards away.

The big man looked down with an uneasy grin. "Never knowed a preacher not to have something to say."

"I am not a preacher. I'm an exhorter, and the exhortation I have for you is hard. It might be better for you to hear it in private."

"If you got something to say, say it here."

"All right. I heard you from the back of the crowd boasting that if I tried to preach this gospel to a man like you, instead of to women and children, you would cut me down to size. Did I hear rightly?"

The man grinned to his companions. "Somethin' akin to it."

"Well, here I am," Silas said steadily, looking him in the eye.

The men standing there seemed uncertain. They glanced sideways and nudged one another, surprised.

"I got something to say to you from God's word," Silas went on, "and anytime you want to, you can start cuttin' me down to size."

The man stepped back. "I always heard preachers turned the other cheek."

"I told you I'm not a preacher. I exhort. Now hear me out. According to the word of God you have committed a sin. The Holy Scripture says it would be better to have a millstone on your neck and be cast into the sea than to prevent one of these little ones from coming to God. Your son opened his heart to God. His heart was tender and you prevented him." Silas' voice betrayed no uncertainty. "Hell is not hot enough for likes of you!"

The man turned his gaze away. His jaw worked silently. A red flush spread upward from his neck.

"He's my boy, now, mister," he growled.

Silas leaned in toward him and spoke with a hoarse intensity. "Your boy? Your boy is a gift from Almighty God. Your boy just felt his heart moved by the Spirit of God. He had the good sense to step forward and *you*, mister, put a stop to it."

The man looked helplessly at Silas. "I ain't havin' him like the women and children, always cryin' to God when he's supposed to be a man on his own feet."

"He can't be a man without God in his heart. What? Do you want him to be a man like you? You've yet to back up your boast to me."

The man looked sharply at him. "I'll fight you."

"Yeah, and you'd lose," Silas boldly taunted. "And you want to know why you'd lose? Because I'm right, and you're wrong. You need God, and good and right on your side to be a man. You got to get on your knees first to stand on your own two feet in this world. Get it right. Look at these men." Silas swept his arm in disgust toward the faces of the men gathered at the cart. "You want your boy to be like these? Suckin' whiskey to fill the hole in their guts. What they need is God, an' they aren't smart enough to know it. Your boy knows." Silas' voice grew soft. "Your boy reached out his hand to God, and you stood in his way. I can see that millstone around your neck right now." Silas put his hands at his own neck. "Can you feel it there?"

Silas let silence build. Then he turned to the other men and quietly commanded. "You men leave us alone here."

The men glanced back and forth at one another, each looking for one of them to stand up to Silas. None did, so they slowly, grudgingly gave ground. The man with the whiskey crock threw it disgustedly into the dirt and moved away toward another oxcart.

When they had gone, Silas turned kindly to Thad's father. "Except ye become as little children, you cannot see the Kingdom of God. That is God speaking to you just now."

Jonathan was amazed to see the man fighting back tears. His face had lost its hardness and he stood awkwardly, like a boy shamed before a parent. Thaddeus watched transfixed from behind the corner of the cart. Jonathan suddenly felt his own presence was an intrusion, but to move the horses away would distract even more so he stayed.

"Jus' leave me be," the man pleaded.

"I will not leave you be. Nor will God. Today is the day of salvation," Silas said. His voice continued to be quiet and reassuring.

"Another day. I . . . I'm not ready."

"You can only come to God when the Spirit draws you, mister. He is drawing you now. Don't grieve the Holy Spirit of God. Will you bow? We can settle this thing with God right now. But you have to pray, 'God be merciful to me a sinner.' "

There was a long silence. Then slowly the man let himself down to one knee. Then to both knees. Jonathan turned in his saddle, looking about. Several crowds had gathered at a good distance to watch. The man's friends stared curiously from across the way. Some of the women Silas had preached to stood watching, others bowed in silent prayer. Silas had turned the field into a church. He reached out, taking the man's head between his hands. To Jonathan it seemed a shocking display of tenderness, especially from Silas.

"God be merciful to me a sinner," Silas prompted.

"God . . . be merciful to me . . ."—the man's shoulders began shaking—"a sinner."

"You are forgiven," Silas quietly declared. "The Holy Word of God says you are now in His Kingdom. Now, stand on your feet," he ordered.

The man stood.

"Don't be ashamed. Look at me." The man did as he was told. "I am Silas Will, servant of the Most High God. Who are you?"

The man wiped his eyes on his sleeve, then took Silas' extended hand. "Thom Keating."

"You are a man, Thom Keating, more of a man than I took you for, frankly. You showed courage to repent here publicly as you did. I would be proud to call you friend, and to visit you and your family wherever you settle."

"Up the Kentucky near Boone's Station is where we're headed," Keating said. "Jus' the boy Thad an' I. His mother died back in the Watauga."

"I will come to find you when you settle there, Thom. There will be the work of finishing your faith. But for now, read the scripture. Do you have a Bible?"

"My wife had one."

"Find it. Read it and pray an hour before daylight each morning. When I find you again, your spirit will be strong as an eagle and we will win many souls together."

To Jonathan's utter amazement, Silas unashamedly embraced the man. Then he turned to his horse, mounted up, and rode toward the ford of the river. Jonathan followed. He waved his tricorn hat at young Thad, but the boy did not see him. His head was buried in the arms of his father.

Across the Holston River, Moccasin Gap cut through a low ridge into the Clinch River valley. Silas and Jonathan entered the gap and two hours later forded the Clinch River on the other side. They crossed the river valley and ascended a steep grade into the Powell Mountains. Several times Jonathan stopped, looking back, and found that three riders followed at a distance. He pointed them out to Silas. Each time, Silas merely nodded and rode on. Toward evening, they passed Powell summit and descended toward Wallen Ridge, the last ridge between them and the Cumberland Mountains. They stopped to water their weary horses at a hillside spring. Jonathan produced his map of the region and began studying it.

"We try for Martin's Station tonight," Silas said.

"But that is near the Cumberlands. Still twenty or twenty-five miles."

"We will go it in the dark."

From the map, the terrain looked rough. "That seems treacherous," Jonathan said.

"Um-hm. But if that's LeFevre's men following us back there, we will need to put some miles between us. They're too lazy to ride in the dark."

"How do you know that?"

"Evil men are lazy. That's why they are evil. Being good and upright got to be too much for them, so they quit. Murder? Why, it's easier than peacemaking. Robbing's easier than the sweat of the brow. Lying's easier than truth telling. The only thing hard about evil is the final reckoning. An' a lazy man never thinks that far ahead."

Jonathan shook his head in wonder and weariness. "This much I am willing to wager. Those men are lazier than you, Silas Will. That's a sure wager." With that, he resigned himself to the bone-bruising prospect of riding the Wilderness Road in the dark of night. He folded his map and stowed it in his saddlebag. As Jonathan prepared to mount up, he noticed a rustling in a patch of whortleberry bushes near the spring. He pointed it out to Silas.

"A bear?" Jonathan whispered.

"Naw. Horses would spook if 'twere."

Jonathan led Merlin until he came close to the bush. It continued to shake and rustle. Whatever was under the leaves was not yet aware of him. Then, to his surprise, a child's small hand reached up to pluck one of the blue-black berries from a branch.

"Hello," Jonathan said.

The hand continued to pluck berries, ignoring his greeting. He leaned carefully over the bush and drew back the branches. A scrawny boy and girl of perhaps six or seven years of age were up under the foliage. They were totally naked, brown-skinned and covered with filth. Berry juice was smeared all around their lips. Their dark hair was matted in long, kinky clumps as though it had never been trimmed. When they saw Jonathan, they leaped up with fright, squealing like wild animals, and scampered away through the bushes.

"Hey," Jonathan called and ran after them. Their weird shrieks caused the hair to rise on his neck.

"Come back," Silas barked.

Jonathan stopped and looked around at Silas. He had mounted his horse, uneasily searching the road with his eyes. "Come back to the road," he said to Jonathan.

Jonathan hurried back through the whortleberry bushes and mounted Merlin. "Those children are like animals," he said.

The squeals continued from bushes farther off. Suddenly the children broke into the roadway. They paused, sighted the two men, then darted up the steep embankment above the road.

"Half-breeds," Silas muttered. "Half black. They're wild all right, but they belong to Molly. That's what I make of it."

"Molly?"

"A whore. Lives somewhere near this pass, but I never knew she had children."

"They appear to be deaf," Jonathan observed. "Neither of them heard me call."

Jonathan nudged Merlin forward. As he approached the place where the children had crossed the road, he pulled in, letting his eyes search up the hill. To his surprise the two children stared back at him over a fallen log at the crest of the embankment, not twenty feet above the roadway.

"Hello," he said, wiggling his fingers in a friendly gesture.

Suddenly a large, wild-eyed woman stepped into view, towering just above the children's heads. She leveled a long rifle at Jonathan's chest. Her arms were as large as a man's; her face was ruddy, small-eyed, thin-lipped, and maned with stringy brown hair. Her big-boned body was draped in filthy, tattered buckskins which looked as if she had eaten, slept, and bathed in them for years. If she had bathed at all.

"What the h____ you lookin' at?" she demanded. She spat a long stream of tobacco juice to one side, keeping her eyes fastened on Jonathan.

"I . . . ah, thought the children were . . . might need help."

"H____ you did!" She cocked the rifle.

"Well, now that I know they are well protected, that's all I need to know, I will—"

"GIT OUT!" she finished.

"I certainly will," Jonathan said politely. He was already moving forward.

He glanced back at Silas, who appeared to be chuckling quietly to himself in the saddle. Now the woman spotted the preacher.

"Silas Will!" she bellowed.

His gaze jerked up at her. "What do you want with me, Molly?"

"Nuttin'." She spit another stream of tobacco. "I'm a d____ ole whorin' sinner and I know it, so git on past 'ere."

Silas began moving. "I'm going, Molly. I will pray for you."

"Don't go a prayin' neither. Ya holy ole buzzard. Jus' stay clear o' Cumberland Gap fer yer own good, that's all."

Silas stopped instantly in the trail without turning around.

Jonathan, who was ahead, stopped and turned.

"Stay clear of the gap?" Silas repeated.

"An' Martin's Station, too."

Silas turned to look at her. Was this a warning?

"I ain't sayin' it fer you, ya d____ holy fool." Molly spat. "The Sterns was kin o' mine. It's time LeFevre got what's due 'im, that's all. Now git yer a____ on down the road."

Silas stared at her, wondering if he could trust her word. To Jonathan it rang true, but he was amazed that lifesaving Providence might come from such an unlikely source. Molly was the first to give up her locked-in stare with Silas. She disappeared behind the crest of the embankment. The two wild children remained staring at Jonathan and Silas until both riders had disappeared.

13

The Killing Ground

"Kaintuck," breathed Silas.

It lay below them like a huge unmade bed, a patternless quilt of hills and valleys marked by meadows sporting massive red oaks and set about by multi-hued forests of ash, beech, hickory, maple, white oak, and towering tulip trees. The whole of wild Kentucky seemed jumbled together at their feet, crosscut by rivers that ran like silver threads, all of it rolling away to the wrinkled horizon.

"Injuns call it 'happy hunting ground,' " Silas continued. "See the bluff there?" He pointed to a wide meadow beside the Cumberland River below. A band of dark blotches grazed across the grassland.

Silas and Jonathan rested their horses atop the five-hundred-foot bluffs of Cumberland Gap. They had taken Molly's advice and avoided Martin's Station and the Wilderness Road as it passed through the Gap. At midnight the night before, having descended Wallen Ridge, forded the river, and crossed the Powell Valley in the dark, they camped near the base of the Cumberland Mountains. Then this morning they had ascended the steep north shoulder of the Gap, climbing on foot, sweating, slipping, leading their struggling mounts straight uphill through forested tangles of mountain laurel and dogwood. Their reward was a spectacular view of the Kentucky wilderness known only to a few frontiersmen. After an appreciative silence, Silas spoke again.

"Some say Kaintuck is Cherokee for 'dark and bloody ground.' Some say it means 'happy hunting ground.' I suppose for the hunter, one just about means the other, a 'bloody ground' is a 'happy hunting ground.' "

A warm gust of wind blew suddenly from below, causing both men to grab their hats.

"Injuns hunt down there," he continued. "Warm weather brings them up the rivers from the Ohio in canoes. They leave their farms and their farming ways behind. They always turn bloody in Kaintuck, and they are always on the move. Settler's a new kind of breed here in this land. Injuns don't live here; they just come to hunt, to kill, to lay store for winter. Hunting's quick and easy. Game's plentiful. They kill and butcher for days on end and then celebrate a day or so, that's when they get truly dangerous. Then they pack their canoes with meat and head down the rivers again. Leave a pile of carcasses to rot. You can smell killin' ground along the rivers for miles."

He pointed down to a river nearly between their feet. "Mostly Cherokee there on the Cumberland. The Shawnee hunt out there along the Green. They're dangerous. Fought for the British in the war."

He pointed west and swept his hand to the north. "Salt River, the Kaintuck, and the Licking River. Shawnee mix it up there with an occasional Erie and Iroquois. This is savage land. When they meet, they fight. The rest of the time they hunt. A few years back they got together to raid settlers. That's bound to happen again one day."

Jonathan let his eyes search the grand vista in silence. The land looked serene, beautiful; he wondered that so much violence was bred upon it.

"So this is your home," he asked at length, "this 'dark and bloody ground'?"

"I s'ppose I belong here now."

"How long did it take, then? I mean, after the Captain forced you to leave Boston and come here?"

"You mean, how long did it take before this land grew on me?"

Jonathan nodded.

"Ten years. That happened after my conversion."

"What good can a preacher—or an exhorter—do out here?"

"Same as anywhere. Fight the Devil and build the Kingdom."

"What about hunting LeFevre? That seems a strange calling for a man of God."

"I'm against those who threaten the work of God in Kaintuck. White or Injun. Injuns, they need a chance to repent. They are savages, pagans, they worship devils. Sooner or later it comes to bloodshed, but I don't care if they be Injun or white. Every man must bow before God. God did not call me to fight, but if my flock is attacked, I fight. LeFevre or Injuns or the Devil himself."

"Where is LeFevre out there?"

Silas pointed northwest from the Gap. "Up on the Green. Settlers are afraid of him or else they tolerate him 'cause whiskey trades better than farmin'. That's the Devil's quick an' easy way, the broad road to destruction." He looked at Jonathan. "What's your business here?"

Jonathan got to his feet. The question made him uncomfortable. "Land," he mumbled. "My uncle has bought tracts of land here."

Silas eyed him suspiciously. "There's other trades that's got the Devil in them. Like speculating."

"I am a businessman," Jonathan returned.

"Nothing belongs to us in this world, Mr. Barratt. 'Tis either God's or the Devil's. You choose." He stared at Jonathan. "You, too, are on a road to destruction."

Jonathan turned away to his horses without a word. The reproach seemed misplaced, yet it stung. Was he wrong to hold land in Kentucky? He recalled Ethan's words to the investors in Bath: "Just one small change in a mark on a tree and it's your word against my word." Was that shrewd investment or some kind of evil? Jonathan felt he should be angry with Silas for meddling where he didn't belong. Yet strangely, for the first time, Jonathan wanted this man's approval.

After descending the mountain and crossing the Cumberland River, the Wilderness Road became much easier. Jonathan pressed the pace, taking the lead. Silas and his mounts labored to keep up with Merlin, who had now regained his full strength and seemed to grow stronger with each mile.

As evening descended and shadows grew across the meadows, they passed herds of buffalo, deer, and elk emerging from their daylight beds to find watering holes, pastures, and salt licks. Wolves flashed among the trees and black bears ambled out of their way. Grouse and quail clucked and whirred from cover to cover as the horses approached. At dusk they turned from the road into a thick patch of white pine to make camp. They used the fallen needles to cushion their beds. The bare tree trunks let them see out to an open meadow on three sides while hiding them from view.

They tethered the horses separately. From their bedrolls, they could watch them silhouetted against the starlit meadow. Jonathan chewed on a piece of backstrap. He tried a piece of bread, but it was dry and crumbled into choking dust in his mouth. He threw it away. He walked across the open meadow to a small stream, where he drank, washed his face, felt his stubbly beard, and with watercress leaves freshened his teeth. Then he returned to his bed and lay down wearily.

Silas spoke. "Tomorrow night we reach Logan's Fort. That will be as far as we travel together."

Jonathan did not reply. He stared into the darkness, thinking about the letter he carried in his saddlebags, the one written to Silas by his mother. Should he give it to him now?

Suddenly Merlin tossed his head and snorted. Jonathan looked up.

"Could be bear," Silas said. "Or lion."

Jonathan lay down again. Bear and lion were no trouble. A mournful wail floated across the meadow, bringing Jonathan again to a sitting position.

"Then again, could be wolf," Silas said, chuckling softly.

Jonathan lay down again.

"Shawnee believe they can actually become animals through their religion. Howl like wolves sometimes, snort like buff'. But I believe I'll just get up here an' watch a while."

Jonathan's eyes closed. He felt he would not care if the whole Shawnee nation attacked them. He was so bone tired he would just as soon die in his sleep. As he drifted into slumber his last weary thought was that perhaps his sleepiness was laziness, and that he was, at heart, an evil man. Perhaps he was indeed on the broad road to destruction, as Silas said. It felt like *some* kind of road to destruction.

The next day Jonathan woke refreshed. This was their last day of travel together. There were still unfinished matters between him and Silas. But when, he wondered, was the right time to raise the past from the sea of forgetfulness?

At midday they were within a few hours of Logan's Fort.

They dismounted in a lush natural pasture beside a stream. Over the years, the flowing water had cut a broad depression in the meadow, so that now the stream bed flowed twenty feet below the bank. They turned the horses loose and watched them pick their way down the flood banks to the water.

Jonathan spoke. "Would you care to know when I first heard your name, Silas Will?"

Silas took in the question, his face implacable. Then he turned his back and moved slowly away from Jonathan.

"I was twelve years old," Jonathan continued, following after him. "My mother called it out from her fever bed. She called 'Silas, Silas, where are you?' I had never heard of Silas before."

Silas waited quietly for a while. The songs of birds filled the air around the meadow. "What do you . . . why do you tell me this?"

"Well. Of course, because you knew my mother. These were some of her last words. I thought you would care to hear them."

Silas bowed his head and shook it slowly, side to side.

"You don't wish to hear them? Well, *you* are the one who tells people things they don't wish to hear. You know so much more about sin and evil than I. Tell me, whatever did you take from my mother that she never could recover? Even to her dying day? I was there, and I heard her calling for you. Not for her husband. Not for me. For you. *Silas!*"

Silas shuddered as the shout echoed.

"Then I found that you were a man of God, the one who tells everyone they are on the broad road to destruction. You say the wages of sin is death." Jonathan's face grew red. He clenched a fist against his leg. "Well, she died, Silas. And whose sin did she pay for? Some holy man made her think she was damned to Hades, and she died screaming, 'I am rejected!' "

The echo of the shout rebounded around the meadow. He drew his breath and shouted again, "I am rejec—"

Jonathan sprawled backward, spectacles flying from his face, and he landed on his back over a rounded stone. The impact forced a cry from his lungs. He rolled slowly in pain to one side. He lay for a moment, his ears buzzing, his eyes refusing to focus. As he turned to look up at the blurring image of Silas, all he could remember was that Silas had turned suddenly; he could not remember seeing the fist at all. His jaw ached. His neck, which vibrated with shooting pains from the base of his head to his shoulder blades, told him where he had been hit. He put his hand to his mouth and it came away dripping blood.

"You will not ride with me further," Silas said, breathing heavily, his face flushed. He swiftly turned and descended the cut in the stream bank to get his horses.

Jonathan struggled to his feet. He wobbled awkwardly after him, gathering strength as he went. When he caught up to him, Silas was preparing to mount. He stopped and turned, surprised to see Jonathan at his elbow. Blindly, desperately, Jonathan swung his fist. It caught Silas on the jaw, spinning him against the horse. Then Jonathan leaped, grabbing the preacher's neck and tumbling them both to the ground beneath the horse.

The animal squealed and shied away. The two men wrestled over and over on the stream bank, punching, blocking, wrenching this way and that. With a lunge, Silas broke free. He stood with clenched fists. Jonathan stood, too, more wearily now, and advanced toward him, fists raised in a boxer's stance. They circled one another. Jonathan struck at Silas' head but he ducked the blow. He swung again, and again. Then he calculated Silas' ducking motion and caught him with a glancing blow to the forehead. It broke the skin there, and also on Jonathan's knuckles. Silas, frustrated by this well-calculated boxing, hooked viciously, catching Jonathan's left shoulder. The force of the blow threw him backward. He felt it bruise deeply. He backed away, his arm paralyzed and limp.

Suddenly Silas charged, head down. Jonathan tried to sidestep but too late. Both men landed on their backs in the muddy shallows. Exhausted, they struggled to their feet. Silas leaned forward and reached down into the bottom of the stream. Suddenly he sprang, slinging mud into Jonathan's face and eyes. Some of the ooze squeezed between his eyelids into his eyes before he could close them. Blind, Jonathan stumbled to the bank. He tripped and fell to his knees in the cold water. As he raised up, he heard Silas retreating up the bank. Jonathan dipped his head into water, opening his eyes to wash the mud from them. He raised up. Though his vision was still blurred, he saw well enough to move toward the bank again. Silas had mounted his horse.

"I will come after you," Jonathan rasped.

Silas gazed at him, truly puzzled. "No you won't. I was an unregenerate young man, like you on the road to destruction. I sinned with your mother. That was long ago. I take no pleasure in recounting it."

"Sin!" Jonathan yelled it so loudly his lungs hurt.

Silas shook his head. "I owe you nothing now," he said. He turned and cantered his horse across the meadow.

Jonathan picked up a rock from the stream bed and threw it after him. "You owe her! It was a h____ of a lot more than sin to her, you holy b_____." He hurled another rock. It landed far behind the retreating rider. Then he sat numbly on a large rock in the stream bed. The pounding hoofbeats receded in the distance. He put his aching head into his hands. Tears ran from his eyes. "It was not sin to her," he said to his broken reflection in the water.

He sat in the stream. The water washed sand and mud from his eyes, washed down his bleeding, dirty face. It hid the tears he cried for Emily, for her pain, and for the boy who lost her. Finally, he got up and started toward the bank to hunt for his lost spectacles. His jaw ached and his shoulder throbbed.

He moved stiffly from the water, across the flat flood bottom to the embankment. Downstream, Merlin and the hackney grazed contentedly in deep grass. The climb up the twenty-foot cut was difficult; he bent his painful joints forward against the steepness. Halfway up, a foul odor caused him to stop. What was it? The smell stirred a recent memory. In his mind, he saw the inside of the Blockhouse, smelled again the cooling guts.

He jerked his head up. An Indian knelt at the top of the bank, his hunting bow drawn and pointed at Jonathan's chest. Dried blood caked the Indian's forearms. His hair was long and hung to his shoulders. Jonathan started to reach for one of the pistols on his chest, then realized the utter stupidity of it. A release of the wrist on the part of the skilled hunter would bring instant death.

It was then that he noticed another Indian behind the first. He wore a breechcloth and had a strip of feathered scalp lock down the center of his shaven head. He seemed to be a completely different kind of Indian from the first. He was muscular and he carried a fine British-made rifle. The Indian was placing Jonathan's fallen spectacles curiously upon his nose.

14

The Reunion

The first Indian lowered the bow as yet a third savage emerged from the woods to Jonathan's left. This Indian wore a scalp lock similar to the second, and was armed with a rifle. He trained it on Jonathan. The second Indian, who had discovered the spectacles, slowly stood erect, looking with wonder through the damaged panes.

The Indian with the bow abruptly turned and trotted down the steep flood embankment. He collected the reins and lead rope of Merlin and the hackney. The other two approached Jonathan and without ceremony bound his hands behind him with a strip of rawhide. All of Ethan's dire warnings about savage Kentucky came suddenly to mind.

Jonathan watched despairingly as the first Indian eased himself into Merlin's saddle. The other two hunters prodded Jonathan toward a pine grove at the edge of the clearing. There they quickly bound him to a tree trunk.

All three of them, the two scalp-locked Indians and Jonathan, settled down to watch the other Indian experimenting with Merlin. The Indian leaned over the horse's neck, speaking words into his ear. Merlin cocked his ears forward and backward and pranced nervously in a circle at this unfamiliar voice. The Indian threw his weight forward and backward several times, trying to simulate the motion the horse was supposed to take. Merlin snorted and pawed at the ground. Then the brave tucked his legs backward, accidentally striking Merlin's tender flank. Instantly the animal shot forward, nearly leaving the rider in midair. The reins were lost, the lead rope on the hackney dropped, and the man's feet flew freely to the rear as he clung to the saddle, bouncing on Merlin's broad rump as the great horse reached full gallop past the trees where Jonathan was tied. Suddenly, Jonathan pursed his lips and whistled a two-note signal as Merlin came by. The horse took two bone-pounding lunges to come to a stop. This catapulted the bow-and-arrow Indian through the air for fifteen feet. He landed, rolling end over end.

Jonathan held his breath, afraid to look at his captors, and as Merlin trotted over to nuzzle him for a crab-apple treat, he had to stifle an urge to laugh. His own imminent death removed humor from the situation. The brave with the spectacles swung his long rifle into Jonathan's face, pressing the cold muzzle against his cheek. However, this dislodged the metal spectacles, so that they slid to the end of his nose. Ridiculously yet innocently, he held his rifle in one hand and adjusted the frames with the other, all the while glaring at Jonathan, the cursed whistler.

Angrily, the second scalp-locked brave drew a knife and approached Jonathan, sending a flash of new fear racing through Jonathan's blood. This was death for sure, he thought. But no, the brave's blood-crusted hands placed the knife near his throat, slashing the lapel from his coat, which he used to place across his mouth. Another rawhide thong was then tied to secure it there. By then the fallen Indian joined them, dusting himself off. He grunted something which broke the three of them into modest laughter. Then they spoke together through a combination of words and hand signals. They seemed to be of different tribes.

The Indian with the long hair, who had tried to ride Merlin, took the horse by the reins and trotted away on foot. No whistle from Jonathan was possible now. He despaired to see his great horse vanish. The remaining braves caught the hackney and tied him in the trees out of view. Then they returned to Jonathan's side and settled down to wait. They spoke together in low voices, their eyes constantly roving the open meadow from one end to the other.

Jonathan wondered what they planned for him. He struggled mostly to keep his fear in check, but death or enslavement seemed a real possibility. He had some reason for hope in the fact that these Indians were hunters; they did not wear war paint. But Indians were known to turn treacherous without warning on the "dark and bloody ground." So Silas had told him.

For the next two hours, Jonathan carefully studied his two captors. In contrast to the other one, who had a full head of hair and wore a finely finished doeskin robe, these two had shaven heads with a scalp lock which ran from the forehead to the base of the neck behind, where eagle feathers were tied into a decorative badge. The remaining strip of hair was fortified with bear grease so that it stood straight up on their heads, giving them a countenance that radiated ferocity.

The braves were naked except for a deerskin breechcloth held at the waist by a rawhide thong. Both were armed with metal skinning knives and British rifles obtained through some past contact with white traders or redcoats. The soft leather straps that held their buffalo powder horns were decorated with blue, jasper, and vermilion beads and crude tattoos set with patterned hedgehog quills. They wore tall leather moccasins that reached almost to their knees. The leather was rough and undecorated except for a single squirrel tail that hung at the calf of each leg. The leather covering their shins was heavy and scarred from scraping rocks and brush, and was splattered with clots of blood.

They continued to wait and as they did they squatted together whispering and gesturing over Jonathan's spectacles. The Indian who had tried them on seemed impressed with their powers, though one glass pane was cracked diagonally from the fight with Silas. The brave voiced whispered exclamations, repeatedly and insistently to his companion, who then tried the spectacles on his own nose and responded with a wrinkled scowl of disfavor.

Soon, however, the first Indian quit explaining his discovery to his skeptical companion; he simply peered this way and that through the metal frames. Periodically he sighted his rifle at selected targets across the meadow, nodding and murmuring with satisfaction to himself. Hours passed. Horseflies darted in and out, hovering before Jonathan's eyes. He shook his head to shoo them away. Ants began to bite his haunches and his ankles, having crawled upon him from the trunk of the pine tree. Then came the sound of pounding hoofbeats. As the sound grew nearer, the two Indians stood up and looked to the edge of the meadow.

Suddenly, rising in a cloud of dust over the flood bank of the stream in the center of the meadow, came what seemed to be a magnificent and terrifying warrior horseman. At first, through blurred vision, Jonathan could make out only that it was a gray horse with an expert rider. But as horse and rider pounded nearer he distinguished other details. The rider rode bareback at a full gallop. He was much larger than any of the Indians who had taken him captive, and he was black.

The horse hunched and grunted to a near-stop at the edge of the trees and the rider leaped free to hit the ground running in Jonathan's direction.

The other Indians fell in behind him as he ran. The Negro drew a long silver-bladed knife from a sheath at his waist as he came near, and Jonathan strained his blurring vision to see who it was. Then he recognized Macaijah, kneeling before him, inserting the knife between his jaw and the thong that bound his mouth.

"Jonathan," greeted that familiar voice.

The gag dropped from his mouth and for a long moment he stared in disbelief. Then joy.

"Macaijah!"

Macaijah reached around and cut the thongs that held his hands and those that bound him to the tree. Jonathan stood slowly to his feet. The Indian with his spectacles handed them back, uttering some words Jonathan assumed were apologetic.

"How is it you are here? With these . . . savages?" Jonathan put on the frames and looked again at Macaijah.

The runaway slave looked offended by the question. "Come to the river. We can talk on the way," Macaijah said sternly.

Jonathan worked to hide his uneasiness as he retrieved the hackney and led him to the edge of the trees, where Macaijah waited in the saddle of the gray. He did not feel safe with his former slave, especially when he recalled the death of Mr. Dugin, the overseer, and the hail of bullets at the Roanoke ford. Now Macaijah was giving orders.

The two hunters had already departed. They trotted in the distance along the edge of the meadow.

"Who are the Indians?" Jonathan inquired.

"The two are Powhatans," he said, nodding after the scalp-locked braves. "Watch what you say in their presence. They understand English."

Knowing of the Powhatan tribe, living in Virginia for generations with the colonists, he was not surprised to learn they understood English. But he was surprised to find them here in Kentucky.

Macaijah continued. "The one who brought Merlin to me at the camp is Tenskwatawa. He is Shawnee, the brother of Tecumseh."

Jonathan comprehended no significance in this. "Who is Tecumseh?"

"A Shawnee warrior and chief who is hunting in Kentucky now. Tecumseh and his brother Tenskwatawa will unite all Indian tribes who hunt here. I have crossed from Virginia with the Powhatans to live here among the Shawnee."

Jonathan remembered that Silas had predicted a unity among the Indian tribes the day before as he had surveyed the land of Kentucky from the bluffs of Cumberland Gap. Silas seemed to fear this development. Yet as Jonathan contemplated it, it seemed inevitable that the Indians would unite. He recalled that the once great Powhatan tribe had been decimated through a series of wars with the settlers of Virginia. The treacherous conflict which had begun one hundred and fifty years ago, with the very first English colony at Jamestown, had continued until the present, until now the Powhatan threat was no more than that of a few scattered bands of outlaws. Apparently some of them now saw the possibility of stopping the advance of white civilization through tribal unity. He also had heard that runaway slaves in Virginia had formed friendships with the Powhatans and other Indians. Apparently Macaijah now circulated in this fellowship of outcasts. More than the Indian influence, it was the influence of the other runaways that Jonathan feared in Macaijah.

"Do you wish to be a free man here in Kentucky?" Jonathan asked, glancing sideways for the impact of this statement upon his former slave.

"I will die free, Jonathan."

They rode in silence for some time. Jonathan felt that this man beside him was a stranger, not the friend of his boyhood. But that had been coming for a long time. They had grown apart in Bath. Something about Macaijah now, a new air of importance, was attractive to Jonathan. Even a brief freedom had changed him, that was obvious.

"Macaijah?"

"Yes, sir?"

Jonathan assumed the 'yes, sir' had slipped from him out of habit. "Did you kill Bard Dugin?"

Macaijah was quiet for a long time. "No."

Jonathan sighed. "Chayta will be relieved to know that."

After another long silence Macaijah said, "I didn't mean to help them. I didn't know they would kill him."

"How did it happen?"

"I knew the others were waiting on the trace, but I told them I didn't want him dead. Some of them had old things to settle with Mr. Dugin. Other slaves who worked for him on other farms. I thought they would beat him, as he had done to them."

"I see."

"I can never go back."

Jonathan nodded slowly.

"I killed some of them on the river that night."

"So it *was* you at the Roanoke ford!" Jonathan swallowed dryly, recalling the scene of ambush.

Macaijah turned to look Jonathan directly in the eye, sending a chill through his former master. "I kept the others from killing you. They wanted to kill you when you first came to the ford and you lay down to sleep. They thought you was a planter, but I knew Merlin, even in the dark, and I told them no. I knew it was you."

Jonathan believed him. Never mind that he wanted to believe him out of mortal fear of what Macaijah had become; since the time of his runaway Jonathan had hoped that some thread of loyalty still existed between them, a thread of understanding on Macaijah's part, that to the Barratts he had always been more than just a slave. Yet he wondered, how strong was that thread?

"Did you know the men on the wheel?" Jonathan asked.

"They were runaways, like me. One of those who helped me leave Bath is here with us in camp. A runaway. You will see. But he has oathed never to speak to a white man for the rest of his life. He says I should do the same."

"But you are a free man, you will decide for yourself about that."

"Yes."

Perhaps it was the new land they were traveling in, or the fearsome size and strength of Macaijah in this savage place where it counted for so much, but Jonathan realized that he was seeing Macaijah as an equal and that he, the slave's former master, wished him well in his newfound freedom. No matter that he had won it with outlaws, and with a horse stolen from Jonathan's own stable.

"I'm proud of you, Macaijah," Jonathan said.

The sound of these words broke the hardness from Macaijah's face. In its place a smile grew. He reined his horse next to Jonathan's and extended his hand as they continued to ride. Jonathan clasped it warmly, returning the smile. For a while they rode together in silence. Jonathan basked in the warmth of this unusual reunion. Encountering Macaijah now seemed so much more than coincidence, more than the hand of chance.

Macaijah broke the thoughtful silence. "Tenskwatawa said you ride with the one called 'the Whiskey Warrior,' and you fought with him. Your face is bloodied."

"Whiskey Warrior." Jonathan reached up to feel the raised bumps on his cheekbone and forehead, and to massage his aching jaw. "Yes, I believe that is him. His name is Silas Will and he is my father."

Macaijah looked at him quizzically. "Your father?"

"Do you remember the night Emily died?"

Macaijah nodded carefully, collecting the memory, his mind not having recalled it for many years.

"Do you remember the letter I found in her Bible that night? The letter addressed to Silas Will? She called his name. Do you recall that?"

Macaijah shook his head. He did not remember.

"Chayta knew. She gave me the letter and told me of Silas Will. He had come to Bath as a riding preacher. 'Whiskey Warrior' is a good name for him."

"If he is your father, why did he fight with you?"

"He doesn't know he's my father. In fact he doesn't *want* to know. He knows that I am Emily's son, and he thinks Captain Barratt was my father. I am waiting for the right time to deliver the letter from Emily. But I may have waited too long."

"You are sure he is the same Silas Will of the letter?"

"He is. Chayta knew him when he was with my mother, and she discovered him in Bath when he came there not long ago. He is the same red-haired preacher who stopped us on the road when we returned to Bath with Captain Barratt's body. Do you remember the man?"

Macaijah's eyebrows raised in recognition. "That man is your father?" They rode in silence for a while. "You will go after him?"

"Yes. I need to be at Logan's Fort tomorrow. Silas has gone there."

"I will go with you until you reach the fort," Macaijah offered.

"You won't ride with me more?"

"I am to join the Indian nation. I belong there more than with settlers."

"Or renegades," Jonathan added.

"I want to tell Tecumseh and his brother Tenskwatawa that they can meet your father, the Whiskey Warrior. I will be going to their hunting camp down the Green River. Tenskwatawa and his brother Tecumseh are against whiskey too, and they turn Indians back to their religion to resist whiskey and the white man's way. They know that the preacher Silas has turned many white men from whiskey. They say he is strong medicine. They would be pleased to meet him."

"I am not sure Silas will listen to me now," Jonathan said, rubbing his aching jaw. "But I will look for a way to tell him of this and see if he will answer me one way or the other about such a meeting."

They arrived at an Indian killing ground beside a tributary of the Green River. Jonathan was relieved to see Merlin securely tied to a tree there. Buffalo, deer, and elk bones were piled on the bank of the stream. In the water were two hide-covered canoes, piled high with meat and ready for travel downstream. A black man hovered near the campfire. He had long matted hair and a full beard. He made no acknowledging gesture as Jonathan and Macaijah approached.

Jonathan leaned toward Macaijah and said in confidential tones, "Do not mention Silas to the runaway there. He may be one of LeFevre's men. Silas is hanging some of LeFevre's men and LeFevre wants to kill him for it."

As Jonathan and Macaijah unsaddled their horses and prepared to stay the night, Tenskwatawa and the two Powhatans threw their few remaining belongings into the canoes and prepared to leave.

Jonathan approached Merlin, unsaddled him, checked him for damage he might have suffered at the hands of the unfamiliar Tenskwatawa. He was satisfied to find nothing amiss and staked him to graze by the water. Opening his saddlebags, he unwrapped a new pair of spectacles and put them on. Then he straightened the old pair and took them to where Macaijah stood with the Indians on the near bank of the stream. He held out the spectacles to the Powhatan warrior who had discovered their corrective powers.

"It is a gift," Jonathan said.

The Powhatan took it and carefully placed the frames upon his nose, tucking the temples behind his ears. He mumbled several words seemingly to himself as he looked about. Then he said to Jonathan, "I see as the hawk."

The other Powhatan and Tenskwatawa shared a laugh between them, exchanging words in Indian language. They ridiculed the man for his weakness or perhaps for his use of a white man's device. The Indian with the spectacles addressed himself to Jonathan once again. "My eyes will watch always for your enemies," he said.

Jonathan smiled. He extended his hand.

The Indian raised his hand in a signal of friendship, then accepted Jonathan's handshake. He turned and entered a canoe with the other Powhatan, launching it from the bank. Tenskwatawa manned one craft with the bearded runaway, and the Powhatans shared the other. They stroked to the middle of the current and soon were flowing silently downstream.

"Indians are not horsemen," Macaijah said. "The river is their highway."

Soon it was dusk. The shadows of evening grew long, muting the green of the land beneath the darkening sky. Jonathan and Macaijah settled into an early camp. Jonathan eased his aching and bruised body onto his bedroll and was asleep before the first star appeared. They would ride for Logan's Fort before first light.

15

The Whiskey Warrior

The ruts of the Wilderness Road rambled in a northwesterly direction, parallel to a long line of trees. A lone rider picked his way back and forth following the line of least resistance through the meadow. It was Silas. For the first time, he seemed weary of the road. His stooped shoulders matched the shuffling gait of his horse. No homecoming smile brightened his face when Logan's Fort came into view. Now that he was finally within sight of his urgent destination he seemed to have lost his passion for it.

Behind him was a long road, ridden in haste with the added discomfort of a thorn in the flesh, a messenger of Satan, to use the words of the scripture. His bruised forehead and bleeding lip reminded him of the toll the ride with Jonathan had taken on him. Ahead of him lay other roads, roads that would take him into the backwoods to the far-flung settlers that made up his flock. And immediately ahead of him at Logan's Fort was the added burden of an awesome civil responsibility. He called upon his spirit to rise stronger within him, for he was reminded with every step that his flesh was weak.

He passed by an oxcart at a half camp in the clearing. Many temporary camps surrounded the fort. Here newcomers to Kentucky waited for guidance and protection at the fort, while they sought out their claims to a piece of land to call their own. In the gathering shadows as he passed, he heard the soft giggles of children beneath a canvas canopy preparing for bed. The glow of a campfire illuminated a broad-boned mother scrubbing filth from a naked boy who stood in a small tub of brown and soapy water. The boy screeched and pulled at his mother's hand as she turned his head this way and that, applying the soap with a bristle brush. She rapped him sharply across the skull until he became quiet and cooperative.

Silas smiled, unseen as he moved past in the dark. Dozens of half camps were scattered in haphazard fashion across the clearing, wherever a convenient patch of ground presented itself. Friendly campfires dotted the darkness all around the stockade in the center of the clearing. Silas guided his horses on a serpentine path among the camps until he neared the stockade.

In front of the gates he stopped and dismounted before a crude gallows. Three nooses swung from a crossbeam, stirred by the evening breeze, the same faint breeze that carried the sweet sound of laughter and singing to his ears from the campfires across the clearing. Above him the brilliant stars cast down their blue light. In the distance a settler's dog bayed mournfully. He turned away and walked slowly through the gates of Logan's Fort, leading both of his horses.

In the center of the grounds four torches blazed upon stands at the corners of a large iron cage. In the cage sat three men. At each corner of the cage stood an armed guard. The central area of the fort was surrounded by five log structures and a storehouse. One building housed an inn. There was also a stable and a fenced stockyard. Each of the four corners of the stockade was a blockhouse structure. The two guards on the near side of the iron cage stood as Silas approached. They were both young men.

"State yer name, sir," said one of the men, leveling his long rifle.

"It's O.K., Nate. It's Preacher Will, come back," said the second. "Welcome back, Preacher."

Silas nodded tiredly, not bothering to correct him on the "preacher-exhorter" issue.

"Excuse me, sir," said the one called Nate. "I'll fetch Logan." He hurried toward the inn.

"Bose! Stable the horses," ordered William.

One of the guards, an old wrinkled black man, came around from the far side of the cage. "Good to have you back here, Silas," he said. "Things ain't right when you go."

"Things ain't right all over the world lately," Silas said, eyeing the criminals.

Bose seemed surprised to hear the tone of resignation in his voice. He took his horses and led them toward the stable.

"Silas, you look as though you've been in a tussle, sir." William tried to divert Silas' attention from the cage. He knew something there was going to disturb him.

Silas ignored him. He squinted in the torchlight at the three renegades in the cage. One was a renegade slave; the other two were white. He was well aware of who was in the cage: the same men he had put there following his raid upon LeFevre some months ago. But one of the men, a large white man with pitted skin and thick leering lips, now sat like a huge child on the floor of the cage cradling a crock of whiskey in his arms. As Silas touched the bars of the cage, the drunken renegade growled and chuckled in a slavering stupor.

"What is this?" Silas asked.

"Logan gave it to 'im," William replied carefully, apologetically. "Said it was his last wish. Said it would keep him quiet tonight, at the least. He's been a hard one to control, sir."

Silas' hand fell against the iron bar with a dull ring. He leaned his forehead against his hand. "How am I to carry out the law on these men when our own souls are fouled by the Devil?"

He pulled himself erect and turned toward the inn. A stalwart man with bushy gray eyebrows hurried toward him with Nate at his side. It was the Mr. Logan who had organized the settlers to build this very fort which bore his name.

"Silas! Silas, welcome back," the man called, extending his hand.

Silas walked past without acknowledging him. Logan looked flabbergasted, looked about for an explanation, and received a hand signal from William indicating the offending drink he had given to the condemned man. Logan slapped his own hand to his forehead and grimaced.

"Silas . . ." he began, but then he just threw up his hand and said nothing.

Suddenly William seemed to remember something and hurried after Silas. He caught him near the entrance to the inn. "Silas," he said quietly, "Silas, sir?"

Silas grunted as he continued tiredly toward the inn.

"The other two, Silas. The other renegades there, they ain't asked for no whiskey. They . . . they said they would like to have . . . well, prayer."

Silas stopped cold. He turned to William, then turned farther to look at the other two men in the cage. One black runaway, one white. They leaned soberly against the bars watching him. Silas blinked, swallowed with some difficulty, and then managed to reply in a voice that was husky and gentle.

"By all means. See them to my room."

Part III

KENTUCKY

"I saw the graves of the slain—twenty-four
in one camp. These poor sinners appeared to
be ripe for destruction. I received an account of the death of another wicked wretch
who was shot through the heart . . . These
are some of the melancholy accidents to
which the country is subject for the present;
as to the land, it is the richest body of fertile
soil I have ever beheld."

Francis Asbury, *Journal*

16

The Gallows Sermon

As the sun cleared the treetops a crowd stood expectantly before the gallows outside Logan's Fort. More than two hundred men, women, and children, residents of the fort and of the temporary half camps, gathered to witness the full penalty of the law upon LeFevre's renegades. Every able-bodied settler was present, with the exception of a half dozen delicate-minded mothers and their children who would not be coaxed out that morning by arguments touting the civil importance of the event.

Kentucky was a hard land. Life and death hung by tenuous threads here. To the early settler, to the man and woman who left the civilization of the East and entered this untamed wilderness, justice became as essential as bread and meat. The darker lusts and passions of the human heart, passions which a savage country so often unleashed, must not be allowed to afflict the innocent without penalty. It was everyone's burden. Thus, the settlers counted it a privilege to witness the ultimate execution of the law. Later, they could tell of it while gathered around campfires and at hearthsides with strangers and neighbors; they could say in hushed and sober tones that they had seen justice done and, by saying it, reassure themselves that ultimate decency ruled the dark and bloody ground.

To their children, from time to time they would invoke the garish memory of the dying criminals in order to induce some change of behavior of far less than life-or-death significance. A good lesson for the young, they would tell themselves, a lesson to prevent evils in the coming generation, though the passion of the telling produced its own evil. For these, and for less noble reasons, many settlers had waited extra days at the fort, in order to be present at this ominous daybreak. At the edge of the clearing two horsemen emerged unnoticed by the crowd. A white man and a former slave. Macaijah and Jonathan stopped to observe the crowd.

"The Whiskey Warrior has a strong enemy now," said Macaijah, surveying the gallows.

"You know of LeFevre?"

"Heard of him in Virginia. Just that he trades with the Shawnee."

"Whiskey?"

After a silence: "The Powhatans say its long rifles."

"So that is why the Indians tolerate his whiskey trade?"

"I don't know."

Jonathan took a deep breath, surveying Logan's Fort and the gallows across the stump-filled clearing. A haze of campfire smoke hung in the morning air. Through it, he saw a line of men troop from the gates of the stockade.

Silas led the way. He was hatless, clad in his black long coat and carrying a Bible prominently under one arm. His long red hair was combed and shining in the morning sun. He stepped firmly up the stairs to the gallows. Six guards followed him, each holding an arm of the three convicted murderers. The three were bound and black cloths were tied over their heads. Two of the men walked cooperatively, but the third, a large man, fought his captors all the way. His voice carried across the hushed clearing like the bellowing of a captive bull. Two of the guards had to return from the platform to help drag him up the steps. The crowd waited, hushed as the guards wrestled the man into position. Once they had his head in the noose it still took three men to hold him.

"They will never put that rope on me," Macaijah said, watching this terrible action with agitation. "I will ride to Tecumseh and talk of a meeting with Silas, then I will come back to find you," he said, and rode into the forest.

Jonathan gigged Merlin and cantered in the direction of the fort, weaving among the half camps until he arrived at the back of the crowd. There he dismounted. Silas stood at one end of the gallows gazing somberly at the men now in their nooses. Every now and again the large man roared again.

"Get on with it! They got it coming," Mr. Logan yelled from the front of the crowd.

An angry chorus rippled across the gathering. "Yeah, hang 'em!" "Kill 'im like they killed the Sterns!" "No mercy!"

Silas raised his right hand, holding the Bible high above his head, and the noise of the crowd fell to an expectant hush.

"Don't be guilty of the sin of vengeance, Mr. Logan," Silas said, his voice full and clear on the morning air. " 'Vengeance is mine' saith the Lord, the only Righteous Judge."

Jonathan noticed that Silas' cheek and lip bore swollen knots and his left eye was black and blue and opened only by a slit as a result of their fight. But his voice sounded strong and full of energy.

Suddenly Silas' words cracked like a whip through the air above the crowd. "When we carry out the righteous judgment that God demands here today, the murdering demons of Hell which drove these three men will be loosed—"

The bullish renegade roared again. Silas waited patiently until the man fell silent. "I said, demons will be loosed here today to seek a hateful soul among you to possess."

"Send me to Hell, Preacher!" screamed the man. "Go on, send me to Hell!"

A terrified hush fell over the crowd at these words.

"Examine your hearts before God," Silas reproved quietly. "Remove the vengeance." He pointed at Logan, who blanched and swallowed with difficulty. His wife moved next to him, supportively, holding his arm. She glared disapprovingly at Silas.

"They got it coming!" she shouted angrily.

"Only because the word of God demands it," Silas warned. "We obey the Word today. No man is worthy to condemn, only God."

"I killed the girl! Send me to Hell, Preacher!"

"Be silent, demon!" Silas commanded, walking next to the struggling man. "If you speak again I will have your mouth bound shut!"

Then he turned on the gallows to look down at a gaunt, hollow-eyed man in the front of the crowd, supported on either side by a frontiersman.

To this man he repeated, "John Stern, God is judge. Don't you sin. If any man has a right to vengeance it would be you, John. It was your family"— he paced across the gallows again speaking—"but no man has the right to vengeance, for all have sinned."

Jonathan craned to see the man called John Stern. He trembled pitifully, eyes swimming.

"Go to H____, Preacher!" screamed the condemned man, now laughing crazily.

Silas walked the length of the gallows in silence and stood before the renegade. He nodded to William, who stood behind the man. He reached forward and bound a strip of cloth over the black hood so that it gagged the mouth of the roaring man. He struggled against it and continued to emit sounds but was unable to shout aloud anymore. Among the crowd Jonathan saw silent terror on the faces of children and of adults as well. Merlin snorted, rolled his eyes and tugged back on the reins in Jonathan's hand. The very air seemed thick with death. The remaining two renegades stood quietly the entire time, heads bowed, their hoods stained with tears.

Silas held the Bible aloft once again. "Men and women of Kentucky! The Holy Scripture of God is our strength to do this thing! We send no man to Hell. Hell is the judgment of God alone. But it is the Book that tells us a life shall be the payment for a life. These men have taken lives, and they shall pay with their lives.

"God is the giver of life, God the creator of life, God made the world in the beginning! The Bible says it was a good world!" He thumped the book twice, dramatically, and held it in both hands before him.

"So what of death? Whence cometh death? How did murder enter the heart? It came from the enemy of God, Satan, that old serpent the Devil! *How* you ask? How did the Devil get into God's good world and spoil it? Somebody let him in, that's how. The Book tells us that a man . . . and a woman stooped to open the door. The first man and the first woman committed this sin. They broke God's law and from the beginning they were told that the wages of sin was death! And so it was, for God does not lie."

"Get it over with," shouted a buckskin-clad frontiersman with disapproval, standing with Mr. Stern. "We ain't here fer no sermon."

"Then leave!" Silas said firmly, pointing to the fort.

Several others spoke up noisily against Silas' words.

Silas' eyes sought them out. "Are your hands so sinless that you could stand here and send these men to their deaths bound and helpless?"

"They deserve to die!"

"Yes! But so do we all." He held the Bible before him and launched into a strong exhortation. " 'In sin did your mother conceive you,' so says the Book. 'All have sinned,' so says the Book. 'The wages of sin is death,' so says the Book. Men and women of Kentucky, we are *all* under the sentence of death! 'It is appointed unto man once to die and after that the judgment,' so says the holy word of God. No man stands clean before God on Judgment Day! But I show you a mystery. It is also in the Book of Books. 'If we confess our sins He is faithful to forgive our sins and to cleanse us from *all* unrighteousness!' "

Silas walked close to the first of the two weeping renegades. "All unrighteousness," he repeated. "Yours and mine. I tell you the mystery of the shed blood of Jesus Christ, 'though your sins be as scarlet . . . they shall be as pure snow.' Take comfort in the word of God."

He placed his hand on the man's shoulder in silence. From the crowd now there was no sound.

Then he turned and walked near to the other penitent renegade, placing his hand similarly on his shoulder. " 'Though your sins be red . . . like crimson, they shall be as wool!' "

Now Silas turned to face the crowd once more. He shouted, "The dying Christ on the cross between Heaven and Hell . . . heard a cry for mercy. He turned to the criminal who died at his side and said, 'Today shalt thou be with Me in paradise.' Men and women, I say to you he lived no worthy life in this world to gain this entrance to Heaven. He simply asked mercy, and found mercy. He entered the door of eternal life. The same as the purest saint who ever lived. This is a mystery, but I say upon the authority of the word of God, and the innocent Blood of the Lamb, these two sinners who have called upon the mercy of God shall receive mercy in His Kingdom!"

"No," shouted a woman's voice.

"Yes, woman! Yes! Say yes!"

"No mercy!" cried the woman. "They should have no mercy!"

"Woman, understand what I say. We will not spare the lives of these men today. Today they die. But I assure you, these who have repented before God have found peace with God! They will die and go to paradise no matter what they have done. If *that* is not so, then God is not God."

He turned, placing his hand upon the head of the condemned man on his left and prayed. "God, receive this sinner. Look upon his heart. Give him comfort by Your Holy Spirit now, in the hour of his death."

He walked solemnly to the other and laid his hand upon his head. "Father God, grant him Your peace and the knowledge that he shall soon be with Thee."

Silas paused, then he quietly looked over the crowd again, looking the men and women individually in the eye. He walked forward and stood at the edge of the platform. Many now hung their heads, unable to bear his gaze. Some wept openly. Jonathan was awestruck and horrified, unable to fully comprehend the significance of what he saw and heard. He only knew that he had never seen Silas quite like this. The event was macabre, frightening. Somehow only the commanding figure of Silas, now pacing on the gallows, made sense of it.

Silas spoke again, more subdued now. "Men and women of Kentucky, on the last night of October, these three men with Jacques LeFevre and ten others, men who must still be brought to the hanging tree—"

"Yes." "Yeah." "Amen!" chorused the people.

"—most of you know that they drank, yes, they drank themselves licentious on whiskey until they let loose the demons within. Whiskey which they purchased . . . and I learned this only last night . . . whiskey they purchased from *you*, Mr. Logan!" Silas pointed an accusing finger.

Gasps ran through the crowd.

Silas held up his hand for silence. "The rest of you! God sees your lying hearts! How many of you secretly make whiskey to trade with LeFevre and the Indians? How many? Examine your hearts. Repent of it! Repent, I say, or run from here! Don't risk your soul by watching these men die when you have made a secret pact with the Devil! It weakens me to know you are out there. Don't hold yourselves high and mighty. Humble yourselves as these condemned men have done.

"On that night of October, these whiskeyed men came upon the cabin of John Stern, a man who steadfastly resisted their evil influence. John is one of my own flock. I can testify, he made no compromise."

Silas turned to look at John Stern. "May God help you, John, to forget after today the things you saw done to your loved ones. To find some rest for your soul."

He turned back to the crowd. "It was whiskey that turned these men into beasts. On that night they found pleasure in the screams and cries of Mrs. Stern and her daughters. What they did was unspeakable, and I say this to you with sadness, their sin was so great it cannot be put right in this world."

With that statement he walked back to the first penitent renegade. The white man. He removed the tie that held the cloth over his head and then removed the cloth. The man squinted in the bright sun and looked into Silas' face with red-rimmed eyes.

"Look upon those consenting to your death, sir."

The man glanced tearfully over the hushed crowd. Many in the crowd turned their faces away.

To the crowd Silas shouted. "Look upon this man!" Then to the man he asked, "Do you have any last thing to say?"

The man's eyes began to flow with even more tears and he shook his head no.

"You did not live right as a man," Silas said. "Now may God help you to die as you should."

He moved to the black renegade and removed his head cloth. "Do you have a last word to say?"

The man looked terrified but shook his head that he did. With great difficulty he worked to force words from his mouth. At last he said in a nearly whispered voice, "I say this . . . Mrs. Stern, almost dead, she say out loud so I hear, some others hear . . ." Across the crowd such a hush had fallen that these soft words were heard by everyone with penetrating clarity. "She say, 'Tell my John . . . I love him,' she say . . . den she say, 'I see Jesus . . . an' Momma, too.' "

Now sounds of subdued crying rose throughout the crowd. The man himself began to shake. Jonathan brushed his hand quickly beneath each eye and turned to stroke the nose of his nervous horse. He felt as if he had been drawn into Silas' invisible Kingdom, that now he stood in it, like it or not. It was all around him, and as real as Merlin's snorting fear. On the gallows Silas quietly stood with his arms embracing the man who had spoken. When he released him the black man looked up and said, "Now I can die."

Slowly Silas approached the raging man. He signaled William, who cut the gag and the tie on the head cloth. Silas removed it and found himself face to face with the broad-faced renegade.

"Any last words?"

The man indicated nothing, not even that he heard; he just stared back crazily into his eyes.

"Do you wish to repent?"

The man suddenly spat into Silas' face.

Silas turned away, wiping his cheek with the black head cloth. He threw it down from the gallows near Mr. Logan. Then Silas raised his Bible high above his head.

"A life for a life," he cried!

Beneath the gallows the old black stable hand, Bose, swung an ax once, cutting the ropes which held the plank upon which the three condemned men stood. Shrieks went up from a few of the watching crowd accompanied by moaning and the sound of children suddenly crying. The three bodies dropped, jerking the nooses tight about their necks, their weight rebounding them upward several times as they spun and wriggled in death throes before the crowd. Silas stood with head bowed.

Suddenly, not from the gallows but from the front of the crowd, came the sound of choking. Silas lifted his head to see what was the matter. Logan fell to the ground, his hands clutching his throat. His wife began to scream uncontrollably, and clamped her hands over her ears as if the sound of her own screaming was frightening even her.

"It's the jerks!" shouted Silas with triumphant recognition. He leaped from the scaffold. "God's struck him with the jerks! Pray, Logan, bow your knee and pray!"

"God—I am a sinner, save me, God," Logan gasped.

"He's not a sinner," screamed Mrs. Logan, pounding Silas with her fists.

"He is, too! Hallelujah!" Silas bent over the prostrate Logan. "But now he is a child of God!"

"What have you done to my Henry?" Mrs. Logan sobbed.

"God's done it," Silas cried with elation. "Gave him the jerks. Whooeeew! He'll be just fine, ma'am. Better than you ever knew him!"

"But he *was* fine!" she bawled, she pounded him again futilely.

"No, woman, he was bound for Hell!" Silas leapt up, throwing back his head. "All Heaven rejoices over one sinner that repenteth! Here's another one for you, Lord, here's another!"

"Make that two sinners, Preacher," a penitent voice said, and a man stepped forward, hat in hand, to kneel beside the fallen and twitching Logan.

"Praise God!" Silas was running back and forth like a child. Behind him the three bodies swung limply at the end of their nooses.

"Me, too, Silas." A third man stepped forward, weeping. "I'm a goin' a quit my ole still . . ."—his voice broke—"an' . . . an' I truly mean it, by God!"

"Kneel at the cross, sinner man. Repent and let God have you, and clean up your tongue while you're at it! Wheee-oow! God's cleaning up Kaintuck! Wheee-oow!" Silas cried.

As the shouting continued, people began to hurry away from the intense atmosphere. Some hung back curiously while still others pressed forward, drawn to the scene. Those who were already of Silas' flock vocally encouraged the prayers of the repenting sinners and raised their shouts of praise to God for giving them this harvest of souls.

Something caught Jonathan's eye at the edge of the clearing. At first glance he thought it was Macaijah. It was a black man on horseback watching from the edge of the trees. It was not Macaijah, Jonathan concluded, because the man had longer hair and rode a sorrel horse, not a gray. He resembled the runaway at the Indian camp. Leaving the shouting revivalists at the gallows, Jonathan mounted his horse and made his way across the clearing. When he was halfway across, he saw the man bolt suddenly into the stand of trees. Jonathan drew one of his pistols and gigged Merlin, racing after him.

At the edge of the timber he found a small game trail and plunged ahead on it. Once inside he was thrashed repeatedly by brush and low-hanging tree branches as he dodged this way and that, clinging with all of his skill to the saddle. After a while, he stopped to listen for the sound of hoofbeats. He heard nothing, but as he strained to hear, he felt a sense of danger creep along his spine. He tried to shake it. He turned Merlin back toward the safety of the fort.

But as he did so, he saw in a distant meadow a half dozen riders. Two were black men, the others white, all armed with long rifles. In the center of the group was a small, unimposing figure. He bore no visible weapon. His flowing hair must have once been raven black. Now it was mostly gray. His skin was smooth and white, like the skin of a child. He had a broad forehead and large, darkly circled eyes. He was clean-shaven. He wore buckskin leggings, moccasins, and a finely embroidered blouse. He sat among the men in a calm and thoughtful pose. One arm crossed his chest; the other elbow rested on it, so that his thin fingers drummed against his cheek.

Jonathan felt a shiver run through his body. This sinister figure, he knew, without being told, was Jacques LeFevre.

17

The Tomahawk Claim

The day had long passed. Since sundown, Silas had been brooding by the fire in the main room of Logan's Inn. In spite of the warm June weather, he shivered. A blanket was wrapped around his shoulders and his feet were thrust in a basin of warm water. He had made it clear that he wished to speak to no one. William stood guard at the door, keeping settlers from crossing the room to where he sat.

Every half hour Mrs. Logan arrived with a fresh pitcher of hot water for the foot basin. Each time she threw out the cold and poured in the hot, she managed to spill a scalding drop of it on Silas' bare foot. "Oops-a-daisy," she exclaimed each time, with total sincerity. Then she went on about how unnecessary it seemed to convert an already good Baptist like her husband. *And* by the *jerks,* of all things!

"God's ways are above ours," Silas said, wincing from the tender scald on the top side of his foot.

When she returned one final time and opened her mouth to speak, Silas interrupted. "Mrs. Logan, you speak as a worldly woman. Go submit yourself to your own husband. See how he answers you, now that God's got a hold of him." She flounced around angrily and hurried from the room.

Jonathan watched from a seat at the end of the meal table opposite the fireplace. He, too, wondered about the strange antics that had taken hold of Logan at the hanging. He wished Silas had shown more patience in answering Mrs. Logan's questions. For more than an hour he had been turning Emily's letter over and over in his hand, trying to work up his courage to deliver it to Silas, a quarter century after it had been written. During this hour of internal debate, Silas had not given so much as a hint that he knew he was there. He thought about the letter once more. Did he still want Silas to know that he was his son? Surprisingly, the answer was yes. Then why did he hesitate?

Jonathan felt himself standing at a critical threshold. He had only to speak or simply hand the letter to Silas and leave the room. But he hesitated. Once the letter was out of his hands he could no longer protect it. If Silas did not want to accept the truth, if it threatened his position of ministry among the settlers of Kentucky, he could "lose" the letter accidentally or destroy it and claim that he had not read it and there would remain no proof. Jonathan decided to test the waters first. He would speak to him now. It would be the first exchange between them since the fight in the meadow. But deciding was one thing, doing another. His mouth had turned to cotton. He still had to force himself across the threshold of silence.

"Silas? Er . . . Mr. Will, I meant to say."

Silas had been holding his head in his hands. He lifted it slowly to look, not at Jonathan, but to his side of the fireplace, indicating that regrettably he knew where he was, but would not favor him with his whole attention.

"Mr. Will, I have something important . . . to give to you."

"You have given me quite enough. You have given me hindrance to the work of the Kingdom. I would like to be rid of you."

William took several menacing steps toward Jonathan and stood ready to act on a further word from Silas. For a while, Jonathan was silent. He could wait for a better time to deliver the letter. He tucked it into his inner pocket. "I was captured by Indians after you left me yesterday."

"Shall I remove him, sir?" William asked.

Silas looked up at William, then at Jonathan. He sighed heavily. "No. I will hear this."

William nodded and walked back to his station near the door.

"The Indians call you Whiskey Warrior. Did you know that?"

An amused smile pried at his lips. "Who calls me that?"

"Tecumseh."

"Tecumseh? What do you know of Tecumseh?"

"He is a great Shawnee warrior, a chief. He and his brother, called Tenskwatawa, who was with two Powhatan warriors—"

"Powhatan? There are no Powhatan in Kaintuck."

"There are at least two, at present. I've met them. They have come to visit Tecumseh, who wants to unite all the tribes." He noticed Silas' face grow concerned at this. "They were with Tenskwatawa hunting on the upper Green River, and they captured me."

"Captured?"

"I was escorted, you might say. I was asked to arrange a meeting between you, the Whiskey Warrior, and Tecumseh."

"Ho! What kind of story is this?" Silas replied. His voice was sarcastic but he looked eager to believe. Jonathan assumed that the name Whiskey Warrior flattered him.

"Tecumseh and Tenskwatawa are not only trying to unite the Indian tribes, they are trying to turn them against whiskey." Silas had become rapt over this revelation. "They say you have the power to turn men from whiskey—"

"Not I. It is God. I help . . . some."

"Very well. That is why they wish to meet with you. They want to know the secret."

"They do?" This seemed to excite Silas.

"They do."

Silas hunkered back into his blanket. "Like Simon the sorcerer, they do. To learn my power they will have to bow before God." At that prospect, he brightened. "Now, it could just turn out to be a good witness to those pagan heathens and their puny devil-gods. Ha, ha!" His eyes glowed into the fire at this prospect. Then he turned serious. "I shall make it a matter of prayer."

"When will you know?"

"I can't tell you now. I will be leaving in the morning to make a circuit of about fourteen days. When I return I will give you an answer."

He pulled the blanket around him, making it clear that as far as he was concerned the matter was concluded.

"But what if the Shawnee have gone by then?" Jonathan asked.

"That's in God's hands, not mine."

This answer frustrated Jonathan. "Very well, but God has seen fit to put an opportunity for the peace of this land in your hands. This is an unusual possibility for friendship between the settlers and the Shawnee. I believe this is an urgent matter."

Silas turned his head toward him. "You do? And just how many hours have you spent in prayer for that wisdom? I have to spend time in prayer. You say you were captured by Injuns. How can I know you are telling the truth? Whiskey Warrior. I have never heard the like."

"If you act soon you may win the help of the Shawnee against Le-Fevre," he replied. "And I saw LeFevre today at the hanging. He and some of his men were watching from the woods."

"Not surprised. Ha. He knows God is driving him out of the land. His days are numbered. But these Shawnee, if they fight whiskey like you say, they must fight LeFevre. I would not have to win their help unless they are dealing treacherously with us. They are known for that! LeFevre trades more whiskey to the Indians than anyone in Kaintuck."

"Yes, but he also trades guns."

Silas was silent a moment. "How did you learn this?"

"From a runaway slave of mine, actually a slave of my father's household which I inherited. He is accompanying the Powhatans here in Kentucky. He wants to join the Indian nation. He is the one who told me all that I am now telling you about Tecumseh and LeFevre."

"A runaway slave, wants to turn Injun? Runaways usually go to Le-Fevre. Are you sure this runaway of yours is not one of his?"

Jonathan realized this was possible, but somehow he believed Macaijah told the truth. "I have no reason to doubt him. He told me that LeFevre sells guns to the Shawnee yet they have reason to oppose him for selling whiskey as well. You are both alike in this aim, and a visit from the Whiskey Warrior might change the balance against LeFevre among the Shawnee. You might begin a friendship between the Shawnee and the lawful settlers of Kentucky."

"You are a clever young man. In this world, cleverness means much, but in the Kingdom, prayer means more. I will seek God's wisdom in the matter and give an answer when I've returned from visiting my flock. When I know the will of God concerning a thing, you will see me do it without a backward look. There is nothing else for a man of God to do."

Jonathan was relieved that Silas was going away for a time. He had grown weary following him and welcomed time to himself.

Silas departed at dawn, and for the next three days, Jonathan explored the small fort, talking with the permanent inhabitants and the settlers who temporarily camped outside. Each day brought new settlers to the fort on the Wilderness Road. And each day, a few of those who had been waiting left for the trackless wilderness to find land on which to begin their new lives. There were a half dozen weathered frontiersmen camped in tents near the gate who took turns describing choice meadows and valleys they had found while hunting and trapping. For an agreed-upon barter arrangement, these men would guide families to the very same areas to stake out a claim.

As day followed day, Jonathan began to widen his knowledge of Kentucky and of the momentous process of settling it. He spread his Kentucky Land Company maps on the table in the inn. As he studied them, he realized that Ethan had cleverly laid claim, in the distant courts of Boston, to the choicest land around the fort, land that was now being cleared and farmed by squatters. Jonathan decided to investigate further, but without tipping the settlers off to the nature of his curiosity. He knew he must investigate more.

He befriended one of the grizzled trappers, a wrinkled, twinkly-eyed man by the name of Joburn. Each day he paid Joburn to guide him to a particular area which he had noted on his map the night before. It was Kentucky Land Company land, claimed by Uncle Ethan. Joburn was happy to do whatever was asked for the shillings Jonathan carried, and so they rode a circuit of their own making, in ever-widening circles about Logan's Fort.

A great human price was being paid to extract a living from this land. If it was indeed a promised land, all it promised was to bear a crop if, and only if, every man, woman, and child swung an ax from dawn till dusk. The promise required that a family waste no time building a cabin the first year, but rather live in their sapling half camps until a crop was planted. They endured the winter by hunting, dressing game, mining salt from the licks to preserve meat, digging a food-storage cellar, felling timber to increase tillable land, froeing the timber for cabin beams, tilling the soil, planting, weeding, harvesting, spinning yarn, weaving cloth, sewing, dressing hides, quilting, rendering animal fat, dipping candles, making soap, carving utensils, forging tools, remaining constantly vigilant against Indians and renegades—all so that in the end they could look about on all they had done with satisfaction, because *this* was their land. Who would tell them it was not?

By the trunk of a solitary spreading oak Joburn reined in the hackney Jonathan had loaned him. Like most woodsmen in Kentucky, he had no horse of his own.

"Yonder be the land o' Hiraim Jessup," Joburn said, adjusting a quid of tobacco in his jaw. "From 'ere thataway."

Jonathan saw two carved wooden crosses under a nearby tree. "How do you know that?"

"Everybody knows Hiraim. Been 'ere ten . . . nope, eleven year. Makes the best whiskey ya ever did see! Boone comes by 'ere now 'n' agin, totin' ole Tick-liker seventy mile, jus' ta get a taste. Dja like o' see some?" Joburn's eyes twinkled at the prospect.

"I am a mite thirsty. But what are these crosses?"

"Them're fer John and Cobb, Hiraim's boys. Tortured and kilt by the Shawnee same year's they got Boone's son, James. That was back about, oh . . . seventy-three. Yep. Seventy-three. First year Hiraim was out here. Ole Blackfish was chief. New chief, now, stopped the Shawnee from torturin'. Ain't stopped 'em from killin' none, though."

"So, if you know whose crosses these are, then you can know whose land it is?"

"Shoot, no."

"So, well . . . how would one know, say if a stranger came by?"

"Wal 'ats easy. Looka here." He pointed to a blaze cut into the bark of the oak, head high on the trunk. "Ya see how he cuts a 'J' here? 'J' fer Jessup an' so forth. Then he marks an arrow through it thataway. Ya go down thataway till you come to the corner o' his claim. There'll be another mark 'n' arrow tellin' you whar ta find th' next 'n. An' so forth."

"I see." Jonathan peered hard at the mark to make out the exact significance Joburn had described. It was not easy to see the arrow in the "J," but slowly he made it out. "What if someone came along with a knife and carved away all the marks that said this was Hiraim's land? Seems easy enough to do."

Joburn suddenly squinted at Jonathan with a penetrating curiosity. 'Who th' h____d go do a thing such's 'at?"

"Well, no one. I am just . . . asking. Just learning your ways out here."

"I'll tell ya our way, son. I'd blow the man's innards all over this 'ere meadow in hog snort fer that! So'd any two-legged man in Kaintuck."

Jonathan swallowed nervously, nodding that he understood. "How about some of Hiraim's whiskey?" he suggested.

"Sure."

Joburn wheeled about and led them down a path through the trees at the edge of the meadow.

As they rode toward the best whiskey in Kentucky, Jonathan was remembering the frolic in Bath. He recalled the tomahawk and the tree trunk Uncle Ethan had set up that night for his demonstration. Suddenly he needed no answers as to what it had all meant. He knew only too well, and the thought turned into sickness in his stomach.

A week later, as Jonathan and Joburn rode back toward the fort one evening, a two-note whistle sounded from the woods. Immediately Merlin pranced from the trail toward the trees, ears erect.

Jonathan fought to bring him under control. Joburn, the seasoned woodsman, already had his long rifle cocked and held at the ready.

"Whoa, Merlin. Whoa." Jonathan finally turned Merlin back to where Joburn was standing at the edge of the trail.

"Somethin' took hold a yer hoss, boy. Dja 'ear that soun'?"

"I did. Now listen to me, Joburn."

"I smell Injun," Joburn said, gripping his rifle.

Jonathan sniffed but smelled nothing. "It's not an Indian . . . but a friend of mine, Joburn. You must promise not to shoot. Understand?"

Joburn spit viciously. "Shawnee?"

"No. He . . . he is a former slave. He is traveling with some Powhatan Indians."

"Who heared o' Powhatan in Kaintuck?"

"Joburn, I need your word that you will not shoot when I bring him to you."

Joburn eyed him through this explanation with growing interest. "Iffen you say. An' iffen he stays friendly."

"Fair enough."

Jonathan turned and rode toward the trees.

Macaijah emerged and met him in the open.

Jonathan smiled, extended his hand, and Macaijah took it.

"It's good to see you again," Jonathan said. "Are the others, the Powhatans, with you?"

"In the trees," Macaijah said. He nervously regarded Joburn in the background as they talked.

"Tecumseh says he would like to meet the Whiskey Warrior. He is camped at the Bends of the Green for hunting," Macaijah began.

"Silas is giving the matter to prayer. He left the fort, but will give me an answer when he returns."

"Tenskwatawa says Silas is a Holy Man."

"He will like that."

"I will find you again when you have an answer."

"Good." Jonathan looked around at Joburn. "I think you should meet my companion. It would be good for you to know one of the settlers here. And the other way around, too, if you catch my meaning."

"I must return. But there is one thing more."

"What is that?"

"When Silas comes to the Bends of the Green he should be well armed and have men with him. He will understand when you tell him we are at the Bends. LeFevre's caves are near the Bends."

"I see. Do you think it is wise to go through with this?"

"I can't answer that for you."

"What do you know of this man LeFevre?"

"It is bad between Silas and that man."

"I see." Jonathan did not like the sound of this. "Come meet my friend Joburn."

Macaijah eyed him skeptically.

They turned and rode slowly to where Joburn sat. As they drew near, Joburn eyed Macaijah's size with amazement.

"This is Macaijah. Macaijah, Joburn, of Logan's Fort."

"Hello," said Macaijah.

"H'llo, y'rself. Never seed a black Injun afore."

There followed an awkward silence. Macaijah suddenly wheeled around, nodding to Jonathan as he galloped back into the trees.

"Wal, 'e ain't all *that* friendly," Joburn observed.

Jonathan grinned. "You ain't either."

Silas did not return in fourteen days as he had predicted. He did not return in twenty. In conversations with Logan about his delay, Jonathan learned that his circuit had taken him to the northwest, to settlements between the Salt and Kentucky rivers, all the way to the Falls of the Ohio and back. It was no wonder he was overdue.

Jonathan continued to scout the squatters on Kentucky Land Company lands. He learned the landmarks and marked his maps with their family names and tree markings. He determined not to leave Kentucky until he had covered the entire mapped area around Logan's Fort. He might have accomplished that goal before Silas returned—except for the arrival of an unexpected visitor to Logan's Fort . . .

18

The Jesting Spirit

"Klaus! Don't tell me this is the fort," Ethan moaned.

A smartly uniformed Hessian soldier pondered a map, looked up at the clutter of half camps, stumps, and wayward ruts surrounding the stockade in the clearing, and cried curtly, "Logan's Fort. Yes. There!" He pointed to it as he spoke, folding the map.

"No, Klaus," Ethan protested dryly. "We must have taken a wrong turn."

"No. This the fort, sir."

Ethan turned dourly to Andrew, who sat opposite him in the wagon. "This is not a fort, for G___ sake! It's the outdoor privy of civilization!"

"Ha, ha!" roared Klaus.

Andrew smiled modestly and quipped, "Then you will know what to do here."

"Yes," Ethan replied, and turned impishly toward Klaus and raised himself from his seat for a moment.

The men laughed like schoolboys on holiday. The weeks they had spent on the road, facing the natural elements together, had created a camaraderie among them, but had also reduced their sense of humor to the scatological. Ethan waved Klaus forward. Still hooting, Klaus spurred his horse away from the wagon to lead his column of six mounted Hessians toward the fort. The wagon driver cracked his whip over the heads of four magnificent English shires. Ethan's opulent wagon lurched after the Hessians.

It was a strange sight indeed. Nothing like Ethan's wagon had ever been seen on the Wilderness Road. There had been oxcarts and heavy-wheeled Pennsylvania Conestogas rumbling through Cumberland Gap, but the Stillwell wagon was one of a kind. It had been conceived by its namesake, Uncle Ethan Stillwell, for his hastily, and somewhat urgently, planned trip to Kentucky. He was not the kind of man to abuse himself on horseback, so he designed a wagon to gentle the Wilderness Road upon his backside. Constructed on the undercarriage of a heavy-wheeled freight wagon, it was sturdy enough to survive the rigors of the primitive road. But the wagon was designed for more than endurance. Mounted on the front half of the wagon, just behind the driver's seat, was an exquisitely decorated riding car. The genius of its design was that while the wagon bounced through streams and ruts, the riding car and its occupants were kept from the harsher jolts of the road by iron-leaf springs mounted to beams set in the bed of the wagon.

Ethan proudly dubbed his creation the Stillwell wagon, and considered it a prototype, a vehicle for wealthy travelers who desired to see the wilds of Kentucky on a lark. He, of course, proposed to manufacture it.

As the Stillwell wagon rumbled across the clearing, settlers scrambled from their half camps to gawk at it and its strange rowdy entourage. Six mounted Hessians preceded it, while four loaded pack mules were tied behind. They were followed closely by four mounted civilians: a Mr. Cartwright, who was a cartwright by trade; a Mr. Ledbetter, the surveyor who had mapped the claims for the Kentucky Land Company's original expedition here during the Revolutionary War; a Mr. Abercrombie, the Barratt Enterprises lawyer from Bath; and Mr. Tibbet, Ethan's personal secretary. Finally, six more mercenary Hessians comprised a rear guard.

For most travelers of the Wilderness Road, the journey was one of desperation, necessity, fear, and hardship. But Ethan Stillwell had taken extraordinary measures to ensure that his journey would proceed as an overlong picnic. He had brought along, in the rear portion of the wagon and on the backs of the mules, enough fine wines and meats, as well as tents, cooking wares, and changes of clothing, to make him feel at home in the wilderness. Even so, he was happy to be done with travel for a while, even if Logan's Fort was something of a disappointing destination.

The entire train moved across the clearing and disappeared within the walls of the stockade.

Jonathan had spent the day scouting alone near the headwaters of the Green River. By midmorning he found his way back to the very campsite where Tenskwatawa and the Powhatans had put their canoes into the water. He hoped to encounter Macaijah and explain to him that Silas was long overdue. Perhaps together they could ride to find him.

But he had ridden the day long and had not seen Macaijah, or anyone at all. As he approached the fort that evening, he dismounted outside the gate near Joburn's tent. The frontiersman sat stirring the contents of a small black kettle on the fire.

" 'Ave some stew," Joburn insisted, ladling up a wooden bowlful for Jonathan.

"No, thank you, Joburn, I shall—"

"Whaaa?! Why, this 'ere's my famousest dish. Sit yourself on down."

Jonathan let Merlin go unattended and squatted by the fire to humor Joburn. He accepted the bowl, absently blew on a spoonful, and drew the hot stew into his mouth.

"Joburn, do you know your way down the Green?" he asked, chewing curiously.

"Shore nuff. How's the stew?"

Jonathan was puzzled by the texture of the meat on his tongue.

"Heh, heh," Joburn chuckled with satisfaction. "Not just what you 'spected, eh? But good."

Jonathan did his best to chew the small chunks of tough meat. They had a muddy taste, but he hesitated to insult the cook. "It's . . . it is good."

"Heh, heh, it's copperhead."

Jonathan chewed more slowly now, thinking it over. He shoved the meat to one side of his mouth so he could speak. "Why not grouse, Joburn, or deer or . . . buffalo?"

" 'Cause the d____ cuss nearly bit me, that's why, an' any critter that bites Joburn is goin' a get bit back! Hee, hee! Naw, I kinda like it for a change. How 'bout you?"

Jonathan spit the chunks of meat into his hand and tossed them into the fire.

"That whatcha think, huh?" Joburn looked pained, but conceded, "I reckon it could use some he'p from ole Hiraim Jessup." He pulled a whiskey flask from his bedroll and applied the contents liberally to Jonathan's bowl, and to his main pot of stew.

Jonathan grinned at this ploy and gamely spooned a taste of the broth into his mouth. But as he did so, he noticed Joburn was suddenly fumbling to hide the flask. Silas stood a few yards away, watching them. He was covered with road dust. A hot red flush crept across Jonathan's face. He hated feeling wrong when he knew he was right, but his red face went along with how he felt, not how he thought. He spit his mouthful of stew back into the bowl.

"Silas! Fourteen days and you'd be back, huh?" he said. "It has been nearly twice that, by my count."

Silas nodded.

"Well, you are back," Jonathan said, rising to his feet, "and safe. That's good."

"I had been away from my flock too long," Silas said. "There were many needs, more than expected. But I came to tell you I will visit a family near the Bends of the Green tomorrow. I hear the Shawnee are there. I thought you might go along. That is, if you still want to."

"Of course. But that will take us near LeFevre and his caves. Is that wise?"

"That viper won't keep me from the Lord's work."

"But . . . he intends to kill you."

"Only God knows my appointed day. I fear God, not man."

"But LeFevre may have a spy here, watching for you."

"How 'bout Joburn here?" Silas said, half in jest.

"H____, I ain't one of his'n!" Joburn said, quickly offended.

"No, of course not," said Silas, "but any man who uses whiskey strengthens LeFevre's hand in Kaintuck."

"Now, that goes just a mite too far, Preacher," Joburn seethed. The humor had left his eyes.

"I said it, and I stand behind it," Silas shot back.

"When do we leave?" Jonathan interjected, to ease the tension.

"First light," Silas said.

"I'll be ready."

" 'Ave some stew, Silas?" Joburn needled mischievously.

Jonathan wondered how Silas would respond to this obvious provocation. The exhorter had seen the whiskey go into the stew.

"No, thank you," Silas rejoined.

Jonathan waited for the thundering rebuke he was sure would follow. None came. Instead Silas explained, stealing a sideways look at Joburn, "I have partaken of Joburn's stew in the past, but I believe *without* the fortification?"

"Oh, ho, ho, no!" Joburn heartily agreed. "No fortification for you, Preacher, no sirree!"

"Exhorter, I am an exhorter." Silas' face repressed a smile as he spoke and the tension melted away.

For Silas to make light conversation with Joburn concerning even the remote possibility of his having ingested whiskey in copperhead stew, surprised Jonathan. This was as close to compromise as he had ever observed Silas to come. Perhaps the preacher felt sorry for the tension he had created between himself and Joburn and now put down his vigilant spiritual guard as a gesture of conciliation. If this was so, perhaps a human being lurked behind the holy exterior of the preacher—or exhorter, or hangman, or whatever he was—after all. Jonathan hoped to see more of that.

But at that moment a distraught young woman spotted Silas and now approached from a nearby half camp. She carried a crying infant in her arms.

"Preacher?" she entreated. "My baby's taken fever, bad. Can God make it well?"

"Yes, He can," Silas said without hesitation.

"Oh, thank God," the mother said, tears of relief spilling from her eyes.

"Who is the child?"

"Collin. He's my only boy."

Silas gathered the child in his arms. "I will pray for him," he said, and walked with the woman toward her camp.

Jonathan and Joburn watched him go. Joburn emptied his bowl of copperhead stew into the fire, sending a hissing cloud of steam into the air.

"H____fire," he said, "if I ever go gittin' religion, I'll prob'ly git it as bad as his'n."

Jonathan turned and gathered Merlin's reins. "Guess I'll be on the Bends of the Green tomorrow."

"Say your prayers," Joburn called after him.

As he continued across the clearing to the stockade, Jonathan's mind began to worry whether Macaijah would find them and arrange the meeting with Tecumseh while on this trip to the Bends of the Green River. He hoped Macaijah still wanted to find them. He knew LeFevre did. Suddenly these thoughts were banished at the sight of the Stillwell wagon surrounded by settlers and the uniformed Hessians. A certain familiar pattern in his mind told him instantly: this was the work of Uncle Ethan. He drew close enough to read the carved wooden plaque fastened to the rear of the wagon: "KENTUCKY LAND COMPANY, Barratt Enterprises."

"Stand back," barked a Hessian guard as Jonathan reached to touch the sign.

He drew back cooperatively and began to work his way around the huge wagon, mingling with the curious settlers. When he saw the riding car he laughed. The entire wagon was audaciously painted black and trimmed in gold, though mud caked the wood. Nothing else in Kentucky bore paint, but this ridiculous vehicle somehow warmed a spot in his heart toward Uncle Ethan's extravagant application of Barratt wealth. He needed to feel this small affection, especially now that he had learned the nature of Ethan's land scheme. Ethan would discover soon enough that the heir of Barratt Enterprises had grave reservations about the Kentucky Land Company. The main door of the inn was ajar. Several Hessians stood in the doorway and several more had gathered outside. They seemed to be positioned to keep the curious settlers away.

"Mr. Barratt!"

Abercrombie, who had been idling with Mr. Tibbet outside the inn, recognized Jonathan even in his newly acquired wilderness buckskins and hailed him as he approached the inn.

Jonathan steered him quietly aside. "Where is Uncle Ethan?"

"Inside."

"Whose are these Hessians?"

"They are Ethan's." Abercrombie motioned to a tall blond officer, who stepped politely over to where they stood. "Klaus, this is Jonathan Barratt, of Bath."

"We haf found you!" Klaus exploded, beaming.

Jonathan smiled back. He liked the man immediately. His face was large and ruddy, his eyebrows bushy above pale blue eyes. There was a boyish, yet strong quality to his face.

"Where is Ethan?" Jonathan said.

Klaus led him to the door and motioned his soldiers aside. Jonathan stepped across the threshold and waited before crossing the room. Uncle Ethan sat at a table with Logan. Ethan's map was spread before him and as he spoke he was pointing diligently.

"This fort could become a center of commerce," Ethan was saying. "Everything passing on to the Falls of the Ohio must pass through here. Here can be established a supply center, a trade center, so the farmers may come here for their farm implements and staples. You should build a mill to make lumber in this place. Soon every housewife in every squatter's cabin will want a house made with proper lumber."

"But that time seems far off," Logan said.

"Far off? My good man, look around you."

Jonathan realized that Ethan was wise in keeping the settlers away from this conversation. None of them could afford to think of exploiting the growth of Kentucky while still facing the struggles of survival. They could only do what desperation demanded, and might rise up angrily against Ethan for his very attitude. Ethan, however, was not without his security. He had his private army of Hessians. Jonathan crossed the room unnoticed.

". . . and don't let these squatters squat on any old place their wagon happens to stop around the fort. Line them up out there. Line them in rows. Show some order. Impose some rules. You want the very sight of Logan's Fort to reflect stability and security! After all . . . it's your good name, sir."

"If it glorifies God, then I am for it," spoke Logan softly, his conversion at the gallows still fresh in his mind.

"Oh, it does," Ethan said immediately, cocking his head slightly, wondering what had prompted this religious sentiment from the man. Then he spied Jonathan. "Jonathan!" He leaped to his feet.

"Sit down, Uncle Ethan. And please don't let anyone know of our association."

"What?"

"Mr. Logan," Jonathan said, "please do not reveal to anyone that I am acquainted with this man. That is most important."

Logan knit his brows. "Why, Jonathan?"

"Would you allow us a private talk, Mr. Logan?"

"Of course. Need to be gettin' on supper anyhows. God bless you, Mr. Stillwell, and you, too, Jonathan."

"Thank you." Jonathan turned to Ethan and pulled a tomahawk from his belt. He laid it on the table. "Uncle Ethan, call Klaus, your Hessian man, over here."

"What is it?"

"Just call him over."

"Klaus!" He looked entreatingly at Jonathan. "What is wrong? I traveled far and this is how you greet me?"

Klaus had come to stand next to the table. Jonathan handed Klaus the tomahawk. "Use this to remove the lettering from the back of Ethan's coach. The sign that says KENTUCKY LAND COMPANY."

"Do as he says," Ethan added. "But why, Jonathan?"

"Because your life is in danger, Uncle Ethan, and mine, because my name is on that wagon. Look at this map." He pointed to a place on the Kentucky Lands. "Here are the Clarkes, Richard and Barbara, and they have three children. Last year they were living in a half camp, now they have built a brand-new cabin here in this meadow and have planted a corn field . . . over here. They are clearing an acre here. They have made use of a spring and channeled water to their fields and to the cabin. Took them two months of digging in cold ground last spring—"

"What you are saying is there is a dispute over who owns this land."

"Not a dispute, Ethan. A probable war."

"I'd call it a dispute. It is the kind of thing the courts will settle once they are established here. This place certainly can't endure much longer without government."

"It is a dispute if you take one case at a time."

"Of course, Jonathan. That is how we must keep it. One dispute at a time."

"There are too many. Look, here's Hiraim Jessup's place. They say he makes the best whiskey in Kentucky. Been here since Boone came ten years ago. Buried two sons right there. You tell him that he has an unlawful claim to this land and he will become judge and jury. Believe me, your Hessian guard will not be enough to stop him if he tells a few of his neighbors about the nature of our enterprise. Now, over here you have Nathan and Mattie Bangs. There's John and Wreatha Heck, these are the Walshes! There are scores of families on this land you have claimed, Uncle Ethan. I have been visiting them for weeks. All of them on Kentucky Land Company land, but, Ethan, they have claimed it!"

"If they have, then I can assure you their claims are not legal," Ethan replied evenly. "Ours are. And, Jonathan, great family names and wealth have been put at stake in this. Those well established forces are solidly behind us, but if we threaten their interests in this matter, well, they can, and I mean in a trice, make Barratt Enterprises less than penniless, do you understand? Neither you nor I would own anything."

"I didn't know you had risked so much in this scheme, Uncle."

Ethan grew red. "I've done nothing illegal in this land venture, Jonathan. But if it is overturned for some reason, there are obligations. The amounts involved would finish us."

Jonathan breathed deeply. "Whatever I decide in this will be my responsibility, not yours."

"No, you're wrong in that. I have already made many decisions and given assurances. The foundation for this land venture was laid when your father was still alive, Jonathan. All of my personal integrity is at stake."

Jonathan was quiet. The problem was more complex than he had imagined. He had never been involved in the land company. Ethan had handled everything. Now he would have to become completely involved, no matter how much of a burden it was.

"Uncle Ethan," he said. "I am leaving tomorrow to ride with a preacher to the Green River. I want you to do something for me while I am gone."

"Oh?"

"Do precisely as I say to do."

"And what is that?"

"Tell no one what your true business is here."

"I understand."

"But I want you to visit the lands around Logan's Fort which are part of our survey, and I want you to personally introduce yourself to the squatters who are living there and give me an account of them when I return."

"With respect, that seems quite a waste—"

"To avoid bloodshed and a great tragedy is not a waste."

"I do not understand. There are many ways this thing can be presented in order to avoid such nastiness."

"Do as I ask." Jonathan had never been so insistent with Ethan.

"All right."

"And, Ethan, I want half of your Hessian guard to be prepared to ride with me at first light."

"But they have traveled far—"

"I will need protection."

"Yes, sir."

It was late, and Jonathan had completed his preparations for leaving in the morning, but he had been unable to locate Silas. He felt he should inform him of the Hessians who would be making the ride with them to the Bends of the Green. After seeing Ethan and his entourage to their quarters, Jonathan made his way to Silas' room in Logan's Inn.

As he stood in the dark passageway outside the door, he heard a strange sound. He leaned an ear to Silas' door and heard it again. It was a kind of muffled cry, a moaning sound, uttered in a free-flowing melodic pattern. He recognized Silas' voice, but the tone of it was disturbing, as of a deep, grieving lamentation.

After listening for several minutes he decided to try the door. It unlatched silently and swung open. He held it open just enough to peer into the room. Silas was kneeling in the middle of the floor. A lone candle burned on his nightstand. An open Bible lay on the floor before him. He held his sides and rocked back and forth. Jonathan was stunned by the sight and transfixed by the sound. He could not imagine the spiritual realities that might motivate this kind of prayer. But strangely, he felt for the first time that perhaps his own deep terror of God was well justified. Encountering God was always one or another kind of torment. He had hoped to discover otherwise.

". . . Cleanse me, O God . . . purge me of sin," Silas moaned, "cleanse me of foolish jesting that fouls the purity of Your Son, Jesus Christ. When I see him, I know how I have failed You, my God, so utterly failed. How my prayers are hindered, how my spirit weakened, my mind darkened, my words dulled by the filth of this world which hateth You, and which I have whored with in my mind! Search me . . . know my thoughts . . . try me, though as by fire . . ."

Jonathan pulled the door shut and let the latch fall quietly back into place. Why? What was this about? He slipped away to his room. For another hour he lay awake on his bed. When he did finally sleep, it was a restless sleep. Several times in the night he jerked upward in bed, hearing the sound of that mournful singsong prayer. What loss, what failing, could evoke such a cry?

19

The Bends
of the Green

Smoke and mist shrouded the clearing around Logan's Fort. It hung curled in mixed patterns, gray, cold, and motionless above the ground. Only a few sleepy-eyed men stirred so early in the half camps, scattering sounds across the meadow of coughing, hawking, and spitting away the night's phlegm as they prepared to build their breakfast fires.

From a camp near the trees the sound of an ax splitting a piece of pine crackled with perfect clarity upon the dead air, once, twice, and the hollow echo answered, once, twice, from the wall of the stockade. A hound bayed, then yelped, then fell silent as someone threw a curse, and a stone. The stockade gates stood open, having swung wide before a trace of dawn yet lighted the sky. Silas had already gone out with his saddled horse for his morning prayer.

Now across the clearing came the sound of grunts, snorts, and hooves on gravel as Jonathan emerged from the gates, followed by Klaus and six uniformed Hessians. They were all on foot, leading their saddled mounts.

No one spoke. In the paling light Jonathan could see Silas kneeling near the trees at the far edge of the meadow. With the Hessians in tow, he wound a path through the half camps toward the kneeling figure. When the troop had advanced to almost within earshot, he held up his hand to Klaus, then he and the other soldiers held back.

Jonathan dropped Merlin's reins and proceeded alone on foot. Something about Silas' prayer was different this morning. He was not kneeling beneath a lone tree as usual but rather before a small sapling cross. Jonathan crept near and saw that it was a fresh grave, an infant's grave. He remembered the grieving prayer he had heard the night before. He remembered also the face of the young mother with her infant son as she had approached the preacher at Joburn's campfire.

"Can God make him well?" she had asked.

"Yes, He can," Silas had affirmed.

His prayer failed, Jonathan thought. And now he blamed himself. Jonathan knelt on one knee by the grave, removing his hat. To his way of thinking, God was more to blame. At length Silas looked up, indicating that he had finished his prayer. He notice Jonathan kneeling by the grave.

"Do you pray?" Silas asked.

"Not much. I do, I suppose, but . . . not like you do."

"Of course not," Silas said, dusting his hat and standing. "You have never prayed that first great prayer, which would make you a son of God." He placed the hat upon his head. "A son would speak daily with his father, would he not?"

He fixed his moral gaze upon Jonathan, but Jonathan thought only of how ironic these words were, "A son would speak daily with his father." This father did not even know his son. Jonathan thought of the letter he still carried and knew that the time to deliver it would come soon. Son to father.

But Silas had spied the Hessians. He was taken aback. "What is this militia?" he asked, startled.

"These men are in my employ," Jonathan said. "They are Hessian mercenaries and will ride armed escort for us."

"Hessians? Are these the Hessians who fought us?"

"Yes, if you mean in the war with the British. Washington defeated them at Trenton, but Klaus here, and his men, joined Washington after that. Fought the British beside us. They fought better for us than for the British. They are good men."

"Well, but I do not need good soldiers." Silas turned to his horse. "I need Gideon's Army."

"Do you mean that you do not want them with us on the Bends of the Green?"

"That *is* what I mean. Send them back." Silas mounted up.

"But it seems foolish not to take them, when they are here and armed to protect us."

"The ways of God often look foolish to men with worldly eyes. You should know that by now!" With that, Silas turned and rode into the trees along a game trail.

"Wait," Jonathan yelled angrily, but he could see that Silas was set upon his decision. He scrambled astride Merlin and galloped quickly to where Klaus and his men stood ready.

"Klaus, report to Ethan," he panted, "tell him that we decided to ride alone to the Bends of the Green. If we are not back in five days, mount an expedition to find us. Is that clear?"

Klaus nodded professionally. "Yes, sir."

Jonathan wheeled around and raced after Silas. When he caught him in the trail he pulled Merlin in short beside him.

"You—" Jonathan seethed at this stupidity. He dared not complete the names he felt urged to call him. "You—" he yelled again but still could not think of a proper finish. "You can be so . . . *stupid,*" he said at last.

Silas watched him through these antics, unamused. "God has been talking to me and I have only partway listened," he replied evenly.

"Oh! Well, that explains it quite well! You hear voices telling you to reject common sense! Of course."

Silas rode for a time in silence, then he answered in total earnestness. "It came to me while riding alone, as it often does. I . . . began to see that I did not need many men to bring LeFevre to justice; I only needed the right men. Men who believe as I do, so that we are as one. Men who do not defile themselves with the world, who do not touch unclean drink, who do not despise me in their minds because I follow the counsel of the Lord."

Jonathan shifted uneasily in his saddle and ducked his head to avoid a low branch.

"One night on the trail," Silas continued, "as I was pondering these things, my Bible fell open to the book of Judges and I read from that very page about Gideon, who selected a great army of thirty-two thousand men to fight the Midianites, who were oppressing God's people. But when God had finished selecting *his* men, there were only three hundred left. Three hundred out of thirty-two thousand. But the three hundred won the battle and it proved to everyone that God's way was above man's way. I can't express the joy I feel when something like this happens and I sense that the Holy Ghost is using me. I am to gather Gideon's Army!"

At that point, the trail narrowed and Jonathan was forced to fall into single file behind Silas.

"But you and I are not writing the Bible," Jonathan entreated, trying to bring the present reality to bear, as he understood it. "This is Kentucky, not Israel. We have LeFevre, not . . . the whatever you called them, and you are not Gideon."

Silas did not respond. He was digging in the saddlebag for his Bible, which he shortly produced and opened as he rode along. After several minutes the trail crossed a meadow and Jonathan moved up beside Silas once more.

Silas began to read aloud. "And Gideon said, '. . . if the Lord be with us, why then is all this befallen us? And where be all His miracles which our fathers told us of, saying, "Did not the Lord bring us up from Egypt?" But now the Lord hath forsaken us, and delivered us into the hands of the Midianites.' And the Lord looked upon him, and said, 'Go in this thy might, and thou shalt save Israel from the hand of the Midianites: have not I sent thee?' "

Silas shut the Bible. "Evil has befallen my ministry in Kentucky because I have compromised. I have compromised in my heart. I have begun to love the world in small ways that have hindered my prayers with God. My people are oppressed by LeFevre and they say, 'Where is the Lord to deliver us?' I have already started to collect Gideon's Army, Jonathan. These are men of God. Not many, but they won't be afraid of the Devil when he roars. They have pledged to go into LeFevre's caves with me come October, after harvest, and in the final come-down they will smite him like Gideon smote the Midianites! And so, I do not compromise anymore. Another man, not of my calling, might do differently, but I will turn away the help of anyone who does not belong, with all his heart, in God's Army."

Jonathan rode in silence, afraid to ask the obvious question. He didn't have to.

"You are not in God's Army, Jonathan," Silas said.

There was no vindictiveness in his voice when he said it. Rather there seemed a twinge of regret. But he had spoken as if he had given it much thought and there was to be no appeal. This was Silas Will speaking life the way he would live it. Or perhaps end it, Jonathan feared.

They rode the rest of the day without speaking.

The trail proceeded directly to the headwaters of the Green River and followed the river for most of the day until the Green bent away to the south. In midafternoon they trekked the rim of a high plateau to the southwest. Throughout the day they saw numerous herds of buffalo and elk grazing in the open parklands. The lone red oaks which stood in the open were scarred from the horns of rutting buffalo and elk bulls. Every meadowland spring was a muddy wallow for these plentiful animals.

Jonathan noticed how sparsely populated this area was. It was as beautiful a land as that which he had explored around Logan's Fort, yet they had sighted only two settler cabins and one seemed abandoned. Jonathan attributed its lack of population primarily to the fact that it lay far from the Wilderness Road. Then there were the problems of the Shawnee and LeFevre. It might be a long time before settlers were willing to homestead here. In the back of his mind Jonathan began to arrange the various elements of a plan—the Green River Road plan, he called it. Perhaps there just might be an equitable solution for the investors of the Kentucky Land Company as well as for the many squatters who now lived on Barratt-owned land.

Jonathan marveled over the size and richness of Kentucky. He was thankful that it was so large and unspoiled. He felt a growing sense of proprietorship now that he understood how much of Barratt Enterprises was at stake here. He enjoyed the thought of taking over the reins of the Kentucky Land project from Ethan. He continued to dream of the Green River Road and its route to the Bends of the Green. First, the grip of fear over this territory had to be broken by driving LeFevre from his cave hideout and by befriending the Shawnee nation. Such achievements would multiply the value of this overlooked region of the promised land. As evening fell, they came upon the river again as it bent back toward the west. Ahead, where it intersected their southwesterly route, the river flowed through a dark valley in the plateau.

"The Bends of the Green," Silas said, pointing through the long shadows of evening.

They made camp in a grove of hardwoods on an open plain so they could see any approach made upon them.

"No fire," Silas grunted as he spread his bedroll on a pile of leaves.

Jonathan spread his bedroll likewise.

"We will sleep early and rotate watch," Silas said. He pulled his long rifle from its scabbard and checked its priming and shot.

"The Hessians would be keeping watch for us tonight while we sleep if you had allowed them along," Jonathan prodded.

Silas stayed quiet for a moment; then he retorted, "In those flatland uniforms they'd also draw the attention of every renegade and savage to our whereabouts."

A wolf howled mournfully from the distant rim of the Bends.

"Silas?" Jonathan could see that Silas sat staring at him in the dark. "Why didn't God heal that woman's child?"

Silence. Then: "Who can say?"

"But you believe God can do that sort of thing?"

"Yes, I do."

"But if He can do it and you prayed for the child and it died, what kind of God would do that?"

Silas gathered his reply in the dark, while the crickets sang and the stars began to rain their subtle influence. "There is no such question 'What kind of God would do that?' " he grumbled. "There is only to know God, and you have refused that knowledge."

Jonathan looked inside himself as best he could. Did he refuse? Not by his way of thinking. "I have not refused. I seek God. When I find Him I will not refuse to bow unless He is some kind of devil, and *that* is my question. To refuse to heal that infant seems, if you will pardon me, devilish!"

"He did not refuse to heal it, boy."

"Then God was unable?"

"I don't know. No."

"What kind of God do you know, Silas? This Gideon's Army God who speaks to you on your horse? You say you know Him."

Silas was cornered. He took a deep breath. "I have never put it to words, but God could have healed it, that I believe, but He did not, because He sees much more than we see."

"What did God see?"

"Let me finish, boy! I don't know. He sees the beginning and the end of things and He is doing what is best from all that He sees. But we also work with Him to make His Kingdom come on earth. Somehow our work is important. Our prayers. I jested that day, my mind wandered from the Lord. My prayers were hindered."

"You jested? What do you mean?"

"I jested with Joburn about the stew."

Jonathan felt sick. What an awful, ugly, impossible standard of conduct.

"My Lord! What was wrong with that?"

"It was worldly jesting. It showed a love of the world in me."

"So because of that, God killed a child?"

"No! You don't understand. He would never kill a child. I know in my heart. He would not! But there is an invisible war that goes on around us while we live here on earth. God and the Devil battle for the souls of men. There will never be peace. God promised to destroy the Devil and the works of the Devil."

"Why won't God finish it now?"

Silas was thoughtful for a moment and then suddenly leaped upon his bedroll and bent over with an excitement Jonathan had never seen in him before.

"They asked Christ the same question," he said. "Look here, watch right down here." He bent over the dark ground in front of him. "What I show you now, you should never forget."

Jonathan uncoiled from his bedroll and crawled forward, looking down to where Silas' hands bent and stroked the soft grasses beneath the tree.

"A parable explains it," Silas said. "Christ said the Kingdom is like a sower who sowed good seed in a field . . . but in the night his enemy came and sowed weeds among the wheat. See, here . . . here are the good grasses"—his hands stroked the fine grasses—"and this pennyroyal here . . . is like the weed." One hand closed upon a large mint-leaved pennyroyal stem. "The pennyroyal is the weed, the evil. It is the sickness in that child. Look at it, you know I can pull it out, but look what happens when I do."

Silas yanked the pennyroyal up by the roots. It exploded from the ground, showering both of them with dirt from its spreading roots.

"This is what Christ said," he went on. "In the parable, the people urged Him to pluck all of the weeds from the wheat field, but He said, no, let them grow together till Judgment Day because to pull them out now will destroy much innocent wheat. Look. See the grasses that have died here because I pulled up the pennyroyal?"

Jonathan could see hundreds of them lying like scattered straw in the starlight.

"Now, you and I are like God," Silas went on. "We know that the pennyroyal roots grow under the ground, tangled beneath the other grasses. We cannot see them, but we know they are there. Right?"

Jonathan nodded.

"Then, in that same way, God knows the roots of evil that have grown around every sickness since Adam and Eve. Yes, He can heal the child. Yes, He can make the cripple walk, the blind to see, or heal anyone who is sick. It is not a question of can He do it? Yes, He can. He can remove LeFevre by a stroke of lightning from Heaven. He can. He can purge the world of sin and death right now, but He doesn't do it because all have sinned and we are all so tangled with the corruption of sin that He would destroy us and the whole world in that selfsame moment. We would be like the small grasses you see here. The evil is gone. But so are they."

Silas was breathless with his explanation. "Now you tell me, what kind of God would do that?"

The question seemed to hang in air before the face of its original asker like a revelation: "What kind of God would do *that?*"

Silas continued, "If God healed that child and knew that the roots of its sickness were tangled like hangman ropes around many other lives—I don't know how, underground, like roots we can't see, but God knows all of the debts of sin to be paid in this world, and He said the wages of sin is death—what kind of God would heal that child knowing that He would lose many lives in the doing of it? Or worse, lose eternal souls forever to his enemy, the Devil? Knowing God as I do, I must believe—though I cannot see it—I must believe that the child in the ground back at Logan's Fort is in the arms of God tonight"—his voice faltered—"and that we have somehow paid the lesser of two terrible prices."

He settled back upon his bedroll. So did Jonathan. It was a lot to think about. They both listened to the insects and to the yapping of a pack of hunting coyotes. The midsummer breeze swirled about them like warm fluid.

After a while Jonathan sat up. "I'll keep first watch," he said, rising and walking away from the fire to the edge of the trees. As he lowered himself into a squatting position near the base of a pine he noticed that he was trembling. He trembled from the inside out, strangely weakened by Silas' logic. He inhaled deeply of the fragrant summer night and settled back against the tree, letting his thoughts run freely like the whispering breezes. Suddenly Silas and his God felt warm to Jonathan. Something in the wilderness preacher's description of the roots of evil fit the dilemma of life like a perfectly matched key. Since his mother's death Jonathan had found that everything good, everything alive, was indeed tangled in a noose of death. This was not a new thought but for the first time, as Silas had spoken, Jonathan had opened himself to the further idea that death was *not* God's doing. Opening this door had flooded his fearful mind with the light of new possibilities. Always before, by his way of thinking, death had been God's domain. Naturally. Emily had been taken by God. God was the God of death, the God of unjust suffering, and the God of Emily's dying torment. But suppose, just suppose, God was not the evildoer. Then what kind of God was he? Maybe God had an enemy after all, a very clever spirit-enemy that had coiled itself like a serpent around the very things God loved most. In which case God was a victim, not helpless, but holding himself in check, not engaging in revenge upon his enemy in order to save at least part of his creation. In that case, God was a sufferer, weeping as the scripture said Christ had wept, himself feeling the sting of death. Could it be that he was good? Could it be that he cared? That he watched his creation everywhere and searched for an ally among men to help him pull one small root of evil from the ruined garden without destoying the innocent wheat? Might it be that God found such small victories worth his divine attention?

For once Jonathan was not asking his questions in bitterness, not throwing them angrily into the face of God as if he expected no answers. Rather, as Jonathan asked, he was filled with a strange new hope. Not yet faith, but hope. He was surprised to find that something deep within him hoped desperately, even conspired, to find the answers to be "Yes! That *is* the kind of God he is." He choked at this realization and sensed a flood of emotion ready to fill his eyes.

Suddenly Jonathan became aware that in his deep concentration he had unknowingly slipped forward to his knees. His arms were wrapped tightly across his chest. He was both warmed and afraid to find himself unexpectedly kneeling at the door of the Spiritual Kingdom Silas had first pointed out to him in Bath. He remembered the preacher's humiliating public demands that he pray and prove himself a sincere God-seeker. Jonathan pushed the remembered voice away from his precious state of mind. He was not answering Silas' demand that he enter the Door; he was answering an inner voice far more compelling. Looking backward through time, as from the stern of a sailing vessel, it seemed that every path he had ever taken, every trace, every road, had been bent and twisted beneath the invisible, warring influences of faith and doubt, and the stronger of the two, the one allied more with life than death, had brought him to this moment of wonder. This was a turning point. It seemed he must now choose to ally himself with that gentle, healing influence. Still trembling inside he closed his eyes and whispered, "God, be merciful to me, a sinner."

He felt a weight leave him when he said it. It was as if he had finally given up a load he had not known he carried. Looking upward to the stars, he felt tears on his face. The stars seemed different now. They watched him, like the eyes of a cloud of witnesses who had been waiting to hear these words from the beginning of time.

"God, be merciful to me, a sinner," he whispered again, but the effect was not the same as the first time he said it. The buzzing of the cicadas rose in his ears. They had grown suddenly loud and insistent in the summer night, as if demanding an explanation for what this strange moment meant. He looked about, once again aware of his immediate duty and of the dangers for which he must watch on the Bends of the Green. He was not sure what the moment had meant, but in time he would know.

A hasty breakfast of hoecake and blackstrap was consumed as the two men saddled their horses. By full light they made their way across the plateau to the rim of the Bends of the Green.

The Green River wound in a series of horseshoe bends below them through a valley of lush grass and magnificent hardwood stands. Herds of game were browsing their way back to the valley walls from morning watering along the river. This was a hunter's paradise. Soon they slipped over the edge of the valley on a well-worn game trail which passed through a strip of white pine. A telltale odor wafted to them on the breeze from below.

"Killing ground," Silas rumbled.

They descended the rest of the way on the open hillside, stopping to view the long valley on either side of the river for a sign of the Indian camp. Jonathan used his brass eyepiece and at last found something that looked suspiciously like a pile of bleaching bones on the bank downstream.

"Have a look," he said, handing the eyepiece to Silas and pointing to the area.

Silas took a short look and nodded, handing the eyepiece back. "Fire circles," he said. "They have long gone."

He led the way to the bottom of the valley on a line to the campsite. Soon they were at the river, among the rotting entrails and bone piles of the butchering campsite. Circles of fire showed where each skin lodge had been erected. The site bore no day-fresh footprints.

"I would say they left two or three days ago," Silas mused.

He walked across to a pole with a buffalo skull set upon it. A small fetish of bird bones and herbs dangled from one horn.

"They serve false gods," Silas mused. "Any but the true God is a devil and a liar. I will meet them here when it is God's time. This is enemy ground, but I claim it in the name of Jesus Christ!"

He removed the fetish from the buffalo skull and threw it toward the river.

"Let's be on with the business of the Kingdom," he said, making for his horse.

In an hour they had left the Bends of the Green and entered a chain of low-lying hills and valleys due north of the Indian camp. As they traveled they encountered a set of oxcart tracks which showed faintly through the grass. They followed them to a long clearing, at the upper end of which lay a cabin and a barn, the homeplace of Marvin Stalker and his family. A good Christian home, Silas avowed with pride as they rode toward it. But the nearer they came, the more concern that showed on Silas' face. "This is not like Marvin," he mumbled.

Jonathan saw that the homestead had once been neatly cleared but now it was overgrown. A pair of goats, some piglets and chickens wandered about the cabin. A field of corn grew down one side of the meadow, interspersed with squash and pumpkin vines, all of it choked with a thick growth of weeds and pennyroyal.

On the far side of the meadow was a field of stumps. Each had been dug about and burned but none of the stumps had been removed. Now they were overgrown with berry vines and tall grass.

A hundred feet from the cabin, Silas stopped his horse. He looked about, puzzled, almost as if lost.

"Hello, the house!" he called, using the accepted backwoods greeting.

There was a flurry of activity inside the cabin. A hound bayed and scrambled out the front door in their direction. A pretty young woman appeared next, adjusting her threadbare gingham dress and pulling back her hair. The young woman was shoved roughly backward by the barrel of a long rifle as a haggard older woman elbowed her way suspiciously in front of the young one. She pointed the rifle at Jonathan and Silas, and then hollered toward the woods to her right.

"Marvin! Come 'ere, hurry!"

"Maggie, it's me, Silas! What's wrong here?"

"Silas?" The woman's eyes took a moment to focus with recognition. "Oh, dear God Jesus!" wailed the woman. Then she bellowed, "Why the h___ ya come *now* for? It's too late!" She threw her gun into the dirt and disappeared within the cabin.

The young woman reappeared in the doorway. She continued to pull at her hair and then stooped to retrieve the long rifle, her face flushed with embarrassment.

"Hello," Jonathan greeted with a friendly voice.

The girl looked to be about nineteen. Compared to her mother, she seemed the one ray of light in this bleak setting. Her hair was golden red, her eyes sparkled despite her fear. She stood poised in the doorway as though on some other threshold, the threshold of a radiant womanliness. If the harshness of Kentucky didn't crush the tender bud before blooming. The girl ducked suddenly back into the cabin. A large bearlike man lumbered from the woods toward the house.

"Dear God, drunk as a skunk," Silas growled. "Marvin, you backslider!"

20

The Stalker Still

Marvin stumbled blindly toward the cabin, whiskey crock in hand, miscalculating every rise and fall of his neglected field until it soaked through his whiskey-sodden brain that there were two riders standing at his door. One of them, in a voice like thunder, had called him a backslider. He attempted an immediate and full stop of which he was totally incapable, and covered another twenty yards by a series of overcorrected steps which jerked him forward, backward, left and right.

At last he stood still, weaving, puffy-faced, eyes gone bleary, nose sniffing trouble like a bruin in a pigsty. His eyes would not focus properly, but he made out the dark suit, slouch hat, and flaming-red beard of the exhorter Will, come a-calling. This was trouble.

"Drop it, Marvin!" Silas bellowed.

Marvin clutched his crock protectively to his breast. "No!" he wailed, and lit out for the trees again.

Silas spurred after him as he zigzagged among the half-pulled stumps. A sober man would have known it was no good. Silas overtook him, reached down, grabbed the nape of his guilty neck, and hoisted him to his toes. Holding him against the saddle, he plunged on, using the power of his horse to guide the hapless backslider, still clutching his crock, into the trees. Jonathan watched with dismay. He nervously nudged Merlin toward the open door of the cabin. The young lady peeked her head about. Her hand was clamped tightly over her mouth, suppressing—he could not tell which—mirth or tears.

"I am sorry," he blurted. "I . . . I will see what I can do." He felt ridiculous for having said that. He gigged Merlin and bolted after the men, who had now disappeared from sight, though Marvin's loud protestations could still be heard echoing from the trees.

He entered the woods along a faintly worn pathway and did not have to travel far to find them. Marvin knelt before a crude whiskey still, pleading like a child for Silas to spare it. Jonathan reined in and dismounted.

"Silas, please! You don't unnerstan'," Marvin begged in a drunken whine. "I . . . I . . . I . . . Oh, God A'mighty, don't go an' do it, don't, Silas, don't!"

A small fire burned under a potboiler. Beside it sat an open barrel of fermented corn mash. A crude tent of brass covered the boiler and a looped condenser tubing took the steam away from the fire, passing it through a cold-water bath in a hollow log. At the far end of the log, a newly crafted oaken cask collected the distilled drippings as they emerged from the end of the tube. There was a small stack of empty casks waiting there for use, their inner linings having been torched, then smothered to form charcoal. A number of newly carved oaken staves lay nearby with a small froe and mallet.

Obviously the still had consumed much, if not all, of Marvin's time. Worse than that, Marvin was one of Silas' Kingdom-convert farmers. He had once put his hand to the plow, but now had turned back and, as scripture said, was no longer fit for the Kingdom.

Silas jerked an ax from a nearby chopping block. His face flushed angrily. He swung the ax and the cask of mash exploded, showering the trees and splattering Marvin with globs of its sweetly fermented corn and malt mixture. He swung again.

Jonathan ran forward, placing a supportive and restraining hand on Marvin's shoulder. He felt as Marvin did, he wanted to drop to his knees and plead with Silas. He had never seen a still. He had never been enchanted before by these promising and mysterious aromas. He wanted to understand the distilling process, to examine and discuss it philosophically, to defend it to Silas as a medicinal art that wasn't necessarily a devil's art. Next, the barrel of straight whiskey exploded with a sigh and a liquid gush.

"No!" Marvin cried, wincing as if his own body were being broken by the ax.

The brass tent on the potboiler split and sailed spinning into the underbrush with a metallic ping. Another blow split the hollow cooling log. The bubbling pot of mash was kicked over, spilling its contents into the fire. Jonathan put his hand to his eyes. If only this had been Hiraim Jessup's still, he thought. Hiraim Jessup, upstanding citizen and the man with the best whiskey in Kentucky. By *his* example Jonathan might be able to make his arguments stand before this tide of holy wrath.

But Marvin, the pitiful figure on his knees, was Silas' irrefutable argument. Marvin the backslider, drunk at midday on his own product. He had slurped up the straight whiskey like a dog at his vomit. And there was other evidence against him: the neglected field of corn, the half-cleared lot of stumps, the filthy cabin, the haggard and slovenly wife, all testified to the truth that whiskey was exactly what Silas called it, "the Devil's drool." Now Silas walked toward the stack of fresh-made casks.

"Naw, Silas! Not *them!*" Marvin bawled helplessly.

"And why not?"

" 'Cause look at 'em. They're a fine lot of work. I was a cooper, you know? Back in Old Town, I was."

"You were more than that right here, Marvin! When I left Kentucky, you were a praying man. A king, a priest to your household. You hunted, you worked this farm. Now look at you. Look at this place."

"Aw, Silas," Marvin said, "LeFevre's been here. He barters them casks, full or no."

"Oh, he does, does he?"

Smash! The ax whistled butt first, shattering the crock in Marvin's hands. His jaw sagged in drunken amazement. He gazed down at his empty fingers, wiggling them to see that they were still attached. Whiskey cascaded in a dark stain down the front of his pants.

"All right, Silas," he said in a thin, resigned voice. "An' just who's gonna deal with LeFevre now? Tell me that."

"We are."

"D____ right!" Marvin cried with sudden bitterness. "Ever'body deals with LeFevre now, 'cause nothin' else pays. Hard work don't pay."

"Backslider!" Silas accused, pointing a finger at his nose. He advanced threateningly. "Repent of that now, Marvin."

"All right! I repent, I repent."

This turnaround by Marvin was just what Silas had asked for, but obviously not as sincere as the preacher would have it. "Repent to God," he prompted, "not to me."

Marvin simply wanted relief. Silas and his godly demands placed too much guilt on his drunken mind. But he had learned that repentance was the formula to a clean slate with Silas and his God. "I repent to God! Forgive me, God," he said, and sounded as if he meant it.

Silas stood panting, still flushed from destroying the still. He looked down sorrowfully on Marvin's kneeling form. "Marvin, how could you do this to yourself, to Maggie and the kids?" he asked, his voice husky from exertion. "And when you had God in you, too? How could this happen?"

Silas seemed to be asking this last question of himself. He had been totally transformed from renegade to exhorter by this message of repentance and forgiveness. Its power had never failed to correct him when he was tempted to go astray. He counted himself to have never truly lived before he met Asbury on that Carolina road and had experienced the exhilaration of entering the Kingdom of God. He assumed that the experience would have the same effect upon the life of any man who knelt at the door of Salvation and prayed: "God, be merciful to me, a sinner." How, then, could Marvin Stalker backslide? Silas needed an answer.

The exhorter stepped forward and with one arm embraced this backslidden member of his flock, pulling his disheveled head against his chest. The exhorter tilted his own head upward and called in prayer to God. "Hear the prayer of this drunk backslider, Lord! See his heart. In his heart he means to repent. See his heart, Father God, see his heart."

Then he stepped back and looked down at Marvin again. He shook his head. "We have to help you, Marvin, I can see that now. We have to turn you clean around." Silas gripped the handle of the ax once more. "Put you on the right road." With that, he turned purposefully toward the stack of new oaken casks.

"No, Silas!" Jonathan heard the words leap from his own mouth. He was thinking of the possible consequences with LeFevre, who was losing not only his whiskey maker today but his expertly coopered casks as well. This seemed a needless provocation. "That would not be wise," he cautioned.

As he spoke, he saw that Maggie Stalker had come through the trees and now stood to one side. He wondered how long she had been there. Two young children clung to her skirt. The older girl watched from behind her shoulder, holding a bundled infant in her arms. Silas paused at Jonathan's words but only for a moment. He drew back the ax. Jonathan leaped forward and threw his arms about Silas' shoulders, pinning his arms to his side. He locked his hands together around his chest and held on with all his might.

"Get off of me!" Silas roared. "No more compromise with the Devil."

He ran with Jonathan clinging to his back until he rammed him against the trunk of a tree. The blow loosened Jonathan's grip. Then Silas jerked sharply to the left and right and slung Jonathan backward to the ground. Before Jonathan could regain his feet, Silas leaped free and swung the ax swiftly.

Jonathan scrambled to his feet, too late. He slowly walked back to the still, stepping among the scattered staves, which lay broken and splintered across the ground. With dark foreboding, a conviction arose within him. He saw the splintered staves lying scattered on the ground just as he had seen the shoots of uprooted grass the night before. Silas had taken this evil by its root and had pulled it out, when he knew there was a price to pay for such action.

Marvin drunkenly lamented, holding his head in his hands, "Oh, I done so wrong."

Jonathan walked numbly forward until his face was only inches from the preacher's. He said quietly so only Silas could hear, "You've gone too far."

"Not far enough," Silas shot back.

"Do you see what you have done?"

"I make no compromise with the Devil!"

"Silas, last night you told me the Kingdom is like a field of wheat. Remember? Or did you forget what you told me never to forget? You ran roughshod, plucking up evil by its root here. The whiskey still is gone, but the Stalkers are all tangled up in the roots of that evil. What will become of them when LeFevre finds out?"

Silas' face blanched. This blow seemed far more telling than any Jonathan had landed. The man of right and wrong was caught off guard. Momentarily he averted his eyes, but not before Jonathan saw in them a shadow of doubt.

But it was only for a moment. Silas quickly regained his composure. "Marvin!" he barked authoritatively.

Jonathan did not press his attack. He had seen the exhorter's weakness. Silas had trapped himself. For the sake of Marvin, who had repented and lost his still, and for the well-being of his wife and children, Silas had no choice but to finish what he started. Because he had removed evil by its root, no matter what doubt he might feel now he had to act as if he was right. Jonathan would keep quiet and help salvage the situation, but he would never see Silas quite the same again.

"Marvin, on your feet. We have work to do," Silas said.

"On my feet?"

"Yes," Silas said, helping him up by the arms. "We, meanin' you and me, are going to clear some stumps out of this field here. Maggie, do you have another ax?"

"Get it yersef, Preacher." She turned and walked stonily back toward the cabin.

"Now, Maggie! Do you want to see this man back on his feet again? Do you want a good Christian husband again?"

She did not answer but continued to walk away.

"I'll get the ax," Jonathan offered. He looked at the daughter. "Can you show me where it is?"

"I'll bring it to you," she said. She hurried away after Maggie.

Silas helped Marvin to his feet and, dragging the ax in one hand, he led him toward the half-cleared field. Jonathan collected the reins of Silas' horse and Merlin and led them toward the hitching log at the cabin. The young woman hurried from the house and disappeared around the back of the cabin. She reappeared carrying a single-bladed ax. Jonathan left the hitching log and walked to meet her. She seemed too embarrassed to meet his gaze. She held out the ax handle to him. He reached slowly to take it.

"What is your name?"

"Melody. Melody Stalker."

He noticed again how pretty she was. Her eyes were bright and emerald green.

"I am Jonathan Barratt," he said. He put out his hand to her. "Melody is a beautiful name for a beautiful girl."

She seemed pleased with the compliment, then grew embarrassed about it and withdrew her hand. "I ain't beautiful," she said, "so don't say that. I am *not* beautiful," she corrected herself self-consciously. "I know how to talk right, I just forget."

"Perhaps you and I can find some time to talk. I'd like that."

"Well, if you stay, of course."

"I'm sorry for the way things happened here today."

"Are you with Silas Will?" she asked.

He hesitated, afraid of her displeasure. "Well, yes, sort of . . ."

"He's always tried to help Poppa." She spoke with obvious affection. She evidently did not share her mother's anger toward Silas.

"He is a good man," he agreed. Feeling both good and bad about Silas, he tried now to think of the good in order to have something in common with the girl.

"LeFevre's worse than a pig," she spat out suddenly. "I can't see how Poppa even talks with him."

A cold fear touched Jonathan when she mentioned LeFevre. "Has Le-Fevre seen you?"

"He *looks* at me," she said, and shuddered. "An' Poppa acts like nothing's wrong with him." She stepped back from Jonathan, alarmed, as if she had confided too much. He was a stranger.

"It's all right," he said, and smiled reassuringly. "LeFevre's days are numbered."

He turned away and walked toward the field, where Silas and Marvin were already at work digging and severing the roots of a stump. He looked back to see Melody staring after him from the doorway of the cabin. Just looking at her stirred something in Jonathan. But the thought of the Stern women and of the widow Harkness, who had been murdered by LeFevre, drove the joy from his heart. Melody was in danger. More danger than she knew. He would have to run from the thrill she made him feel, and run right now, or else he would have no choice but to stay and make a stand, placing himself between her and LeFevre. A knot of fear grew in his stomach.

Marvin's mules strained and brayed against their harness, digging their tidy hooves into the loose soil repeatedly until the towline they drew against the stump was taut enough to sing when plucked.

"I see it! I got it!" Jonathan hollered. He swung his ax once and severed a taproot beneath the stump and it suddenly popped free, sliding easily from the hole onto level ground. The mules dragged it away toward a burn pile.

The afternoon shadows had lengthened across the Stalkers' meadow. The three shirtless men in the stump hole had removed four stumps from the field by that time, and Marvin had sweat himself sober. Jonathan discovered that when the effects of the liquor wore off, Marvin was a man of decent thoughts and instincts.

"Let's take a break," Marvin suggested. "Water's in the cabin."

Silas frowned, not wanting to stop work so soon.

"It's all fer nothin' here, Silas," Marvin said, removing his hat, wiping his brow.

"What do you mean by that?"

"I mean, I lost the cabin, the barn, everything we are working for here. All of it belongs to someone who ain't never shed a drop of sweat on the place."

"Who?"

"I don' know. Land companies. I hear they got all our land sewed up. When I heard that, why, that's when I went an' quit on my Jesus. Why should I care so much when in the end some rich man takes it all anyway?"

"Wait now, who told you about this land-stealin' business?"

"LeFevre."

Silas spat hard.

"Naw, Silas, it ain't only him. I heard it from MacKinzou and Boyce, too. Both of 'em's been up at Boonesborough and face-to-faced it with ole Dan'l Boone. They say he's quittin', leavin' Kaintuck! He oughta own it all for what he done 'ere. He built the Wilderness Road, but no, he had his land stole from him. Ever' one of his tomahawk claims is gone to some land company. I tell you, it breaks the fightin' heart outa me. LeFevre's right about this one thing, Silas: if it happened to old Boone, nobody's gonna holler when it happens to me. Like LeFevre says, 'Law ain't no kinda justice!' "

The three men pulled on their linsey-woolsey shirts. Jonathan was glad he had abandoned his fancy riding suits at the fort. He did not want to be identified as a rich land stealer.

Silas remained thoughtful until they began to walk.

"I heard this about Boone myself," he said soberly. "It just might be true. I will know soon because I will be traveling Boone's Fork, but true or not for Boone, says nothing about your farm.

"But let's say the worst happens, say it is true you lost your land here. What should we do? Well, just as always, the people of God should band together and fight fire with fire. Every man on my circuit is ready to defend your claim on this land, Marvin, as long as you keep yourself unspotted from the world. But you gotta quit listenin' to LeFevre."

"Stay with me here, Silas. Don' let me backslide again."

"I'll stay as long as I can, but God will keep you when I am gone."

"But He didn't do so good last time."

"Marvin . . ."

"I know. It was my doin'."

Jonathan could see to it that Stalker got back his land. But how to do it without revealing that Barratt Enterprises was behind the Kentucky Land Company was another matter. He didn't care to imagine what would happen if Marvin learned who held title to his land.

They arrived at the threshold of the cabin door. Marvin leaned in and called, "Melody, fetch some water."

"Yes, Poppa."

"An', Maggie, rustle up some vittles fer us menfolk."

There was no answer.

"Maggie!" He grew red and leaned in the door. "Maggie, we got visitors. Now hop to it!"

Silas took Marvin by the shoulder and pulled him back out the door. "Marvin—"

"Unruly woman—"

"Marvin, be gentle with her. Go easy," Silas said.

Maggie had appeared in the doorway. She was disheveled, sour-mouthed, sipping from a small cup of whiskey.

"Why don' you tell 'im how we lost the land?"

"I did, Maggie. But they say maybe it ain't so."

"Oh, it's so all right. It's so. Ever' hellfire preacher knows that. Bad news is always a good bet. Right, Preacher? Good news is when yer dead, except unless you get that ol' bad news again. Some people's lucky. We ain't."

"There's no luck about it, Maggie," Silas soothed.

"We get the bad news on our way to hellfire, that's us—"

"Maggie, now shut up!" Marvin barked.

"Marvin," Silas warned.

Maggie smirked at the two of them and took another sip from her mug.

Melody appeared in the doorway with a wooden bowl of water and a ladle. She was dressed in a dirty apron, her hair tied back, suds showing wet at her knees and on her elbows. She glanced at Jonathan. She seemed pitifully embarrassed, and rightly so, at her parents and the condition of the cabin. She seemed so out of place here, Jonathan thought. She reminded him of the beauty of Bath. She belonged there.

Marvin filled the ladle with water, gulped it, refilled it, and passed it to Silas. Silas drank and handed the ladle to Jonathan.

"Maggie," Silas said, continuing to study her face with concern.

"Oh, it's too late for me, Preacher." She seemed to be on the verge of tears. "Why don' you get yersef on down the road where some good Sunday people are?"

"I'm right where I belong, Maggie. You just need a hand for a while. You and Marvin here."

"I need more than that," she snorted, laughing at her own private meaning.

Silas stepped forward into the house. "Come in here, Marvin, Jonathan. Let's give Maggie a hand."

"Now you get out," Maggie snapped. She tossed the remnant of her whiskey into the dirt. "This is my cabin."

"Come on, Marvin," Silas urged.

"You heard her, Silas, she wants to do it hersef!"

"You get in here, Marvin!"

"Get out," Maggie warned. "Now I mean it."

Marvin stepped in the door reluctantly, fearing Silas' displeasure more than Maggie's at the moment. Jonathan peeked over his shoulder. The cabin was dark and dirty; it stank and flies buzzed about. It was sparsely furnished with one rocking chair, a rough plank bench, and a table. In the middle of the floor sat a pail of soapy water. Silas picked up a bristle brush and got down on his hands and knees.

"Come on, Marvin," he said, "let's you and me scrub up this floor for Maggie. Make her feel better."

"That's women's work—"

"Get a hog bristle, Marvin, and bring that soap over here." ·

"All right, Preacher, I'm a-gettin' my ole hog bristle," Marvin said. He stood for a moment; a sudden mischievous light came in his eye. Then he reached for the pail of suds.

Impulsively he dumped the entire contents of the bucket on Silas' unsuspecting head. The two smaller children squealed with surprise and delight. Silas spit suds from his mouth and rose to his feet, spluttering and shaking soap from his eyes. He whirled around to find his attacker, suds dribbling from his red hair and beard. Marvin hung back, fearful now, the grin fading from his face.

There was a moment of tense silence. Then Silas said calmly, "But you missed the dirt, Marvin." He pointed to the floor plank in front of him.

Everyone in the room erupted with howls of laughter. Suddenly Melody stood before Jonathan, playfully holding out a brush to him.

"For me?"

"Yes, you. She wants you to scrub," Silas said. "Get down here where you can do some good."

Jonathan shook his head, grinning, but dropped to his knees and began scrubbing a plank next to Silas. Marvin grabbed another brush and joined them.

"Scrub, scrub, scrub!" Silas chanted.

"I will put supper on," Melody said to her mother.

"No, I will," said Maggie. "You take the children."

"Scrub-a-dub-dub, three men in a tub," sang Marvin, "who do you think they be? A farmer, a preacher, a—" He stopped, pointing to Jonathan.

Jonathan thought for a moment, caught off guard. "A . . . a . . . farmer and an *exhorter*," he corrected, "and a son of a preacher," he said.

He looked suddenly at Silas, who wore a puzzled frown.

Jonathan shrugged. "It rhymes. I guess."

"It rhymes, sort of," said Marvin, and he sang, "Rub-a-dub-dub, three men in a tub, who do you think they be? A farmer, a preacher, a son of a preacher, that's who they all three be!"

"An exhorter," Silas corrected.

Before the women finished preparing supper, the Stalker cabin was once again a fit place to live.

Sunset burned from orange to violet to cool purple in the sky, the colors radiating upward from the horizon as the sun disappeared. This magical glow filtered through the trees and passed across the faces of Jonathan and Melody as they strolled the ridge behind the Stalker cabin.

She looked at the sky. He looked at her. The golden light intensified the blue-green of her eyes. They shimmered in the evening glow, bright with laughter and energy. Jonathan carried a pole across his shoulder from which hung water buckets at either end. He had found his way to be alone with her, suggesting that she show him to the spring so he could replenish the water supply for the cabin.

"Is it a long way?" he asked, feeling awkward and unsure of how to begin their conversation now that he had succeeded this far.

"No. Just over the ridge."

The riotous song of tree frogs rose from the base of a brushy slope beyond the ridge.

"The spring is there," she said, pointing down the hill.

Jonathan turned to mark the position of the trail in relation to the barn and cabin behind them. He was developing the instincts of the wilderness. The vast unmarked stretches of virgin territory had taught him to learn the lay of the land wherever he went, as naturally as he would have looked for a street address in Boston or Baltimore.

"I don't see this place the way most folks do," Melody said as they began their descent. "Most folks came here for the land. They all want land, land. Well, look across there. There's a half a day's land between us and the next cabin. That's more than I would ever want."

They stepped carefully over a log that lay rotting across the path. Jonathan reached out to take her hand. She seemed surprised. It was obvious she was not used to being looked after. His hand closed around her slender fingers. She took hold of her skirt and stepped across the log. They resumed their walk. He wanted to hold her hand longer as they walked but feared she would not feel the same. He let it go.

"It's people I care about," she went on. "Like the way you and Silas came here today. It made a difference in everything. It's the same old land, same cabin, same spring"—they stopped on a small rise next to a pond as she continued—"but it's not the same. Do you understand what I mean?"

"I hope I do. It is better?"

"Oh yes. I think tomorrow will be twice as hard for me when you have gone, having all this land to myself again."

She turned away and descended the last part of the trail on the run. He hurried after her as quickly as he could with the empty buckets.

"The spring is over there."

"You mean you don't draw water at this pond?"

"No. The drinking water comes from over there behind those trees. From a cave."

Jonathan walked in the direction she pointed until he came to a cave with a mouth about ten feet tall. A breath of cool air came out of its depths upon his skin, chilling him. He bent down and began to fill the buckets in the crystal water that emerged from an underground source. A heavy oaken cask cooled in a pool.

"What is this?"

"Bourbon."

"Is there more in here?"

"No. Poppa's saving this one. Maybe we should smash it. Poppa's not strong against temptation, you know."

Jonathan considered it as he filled the second bucket. "No. Let's leave the cask smashing to Silas."

He lifted and balanced the buckets on the ends of his pole and carried them to the edge of the pond, then turned and walked toward Melody. She stood holding her hands crossed before her. He came close, stopped, looked into her face, and reached out, taking both of her hands in his. He said nothing. How soft her cool palms were against the palms of his hands. Her eyes, and the sensuous promise of her full lips, held him rooted to the spot.

"Why did you come here?" she asked.

He wanted to tell her everything, wanted her to know about him, care about him and why he had come, but if he told her everything about Ethan and the land company, would she understand? He was silent, then spoke more frankly than he ever thought he could.

"Silas Will. He does not know it, but he is my father. I followed him here, but I haven't told him."

"He's your father?" She was astonished, ready to be delighted.

"Yes. Do you think I should tell him?"

"Of course. Well—why shouldn't he know?"

"It seems to be the kind of thing he wants to forget, especially being a man of God. Do you understand?"

Melody did begin to understand. Her eyes darkened with an inner conflict. She did not want to know anything bad about Silas, but she would not know Jonathan if she refused to hear this.

"I don't understand," she said.

"My mother was Mrs. Nelson Barratt, not Silas' wife. I have a letter from my mother which she wrote to him years ago, telling him that I was his son. But she never found a way to get it to him here in Kentucky. So I came here to find my father, in a sense. I decided that before I gave him the letter I wanted to know more about him, what kind of man he was, how he had—well, how he felt about my mother."

"And what did you find?"

Jonathan sighed. "I found out many things. But I know that I will never learn what Silas felt about my mother. Perhaps if he knew I was his son, and if he could somehow be proud of me . . . but how can a preacher who hates sin be proud of a sin? I guess all that is left for me to do is give him the letter."

"I hope he . . ." She paused, not knowing how to finish. "Will you do it soon?"

"I will."

"I hope everything turns out well for you," she said soberly.

"Thank you."

His hands slipped up her forearms and beneath them to rest upon her slender waist.

"You know, I also came here to see this land, Kentucky," he continued. "It is an awesome land. A wonderful and terrible land. And you, Melody, you are as beautiful as the land, yet somehow so out of place in it."

"Don't say that."

He smiled. "I'm glad you're here. I'm glad I found you here."

He bent his head slowly forward, staring into the eyes that seemed deeper than mystery. She closed them as his lips touched hers. He kissed her tenderly at first, then passionately as he became filled with desire for her. The stars were spreading their blanket above them with a million crystal lights. He held her against his chest, stroking his hand through her fine red hair. Suddenly she stiffened and whispered quietly, "Someone is there, Jonathan."

"Where?" he whispered, reaching for one of his pistols.

"Near the cave."

"Don't move."

He was amazed at the poise she showed. She was terrified but continued to embrace him so that whoever approached would not suspect that they had discerned his presence. He was sure that the pounding of his heart was being heard by her, so close to his chest, and that she knew he was also terrified. Jonathan turned his head above hers, his eyes searching the brush near the mouth of the cave. Then he saw it. A form crept toward them. His blood screamed with panic, but he held the urge to run in check. He was sure that whoever was creeping toward them had seen them for some time and had the advantage of cover. Jonathan hoped for the advantage of surprise.

"Get ready to drop to the ground," he whispered.

She nodded her head almost imperceptibly against his chest.

"Now."

She dropped flat against the ground. Jonathan drew his pistol, cocking and aiming it at the oncoming figure.

"Jonathan!"

He lowered the pistol.

"Macaijah! Use the whistle, for heaven's sake!"

21

The Burden

"It's all right, Melody," Jonathan said, helping her to her feet. "He's a friend."

"I'm fine," she said, panting as she brushed dust particles from her dress. "You're sure he's a friend?" She was looking at Macaijah suspiciously, knowing that runaways in Kentucky usually kept company with LeFevre.

Jonathan released her and stepped forward to meet the looming figure. "You gave us a start."

"I'm sorry," Macaijah said in a low voice. "There might be some of LeFevre's men about. I didn't want them to see us meet."

"Do you know they are here?"

"I saw a man at the broken still who I know to be one of his."

"That means we are in grave danger here, Macaijah. Today, Silas smashed Mr. Stalker's still and now LeFevre will be stirred up for revenge. Who will he strike?"

Macaijah nodded seriously. "You and Silas were seen leaving the Green River by Tecumseh's scouts. I bring a message from Chief Tecumseh for the Whiskey Warrior. Tecumseh will come from the Ohio to the Bends of the Green at the second full moon. This will be his last hunt before the long shadows."

"You're beginning to sound like an Indian yourself, Macaijah. That will be September . . . near the end of September," Jonathan mused.

"Tecumseh will meet the Whiskey Warrior then."

Jonathan drew a long breath. "There is nothing to do but get his answer now. Come along." Jonathan hoisted the water buckets on their pole and led Melody and Macaijah along the dark path to the cabin. Macaijah loped past him and stealthily assumed the lead, holding his rifle at the ready. Jonathan noticed that the former slave had exchanged his linsey-woolsey pants for a pair of fringed buckskin leggings and tall moccasins.

At the cabin, Macaijah waited in the darkness beyond the candlelight that glowed from the doors and the unshuttered windows. Jonathan removed the buckets from his carrying stick and placed them outside the door. He signaled Macaijah to wait and entered the doorway with Melody.

"It ain't wise to be out like this, Melody," Marvin said, scowling his disapproval as soon as they appeared. He was obviously worried.

"I'll take the blame for that," Jonathan said quickly. "I met a friend while at the spring. He brings a message of importance for you, Mr. Stalker, and you, Silas." He turned to the door. "Macaijah, come in!"

Macaijah ducked his head in the door. His shoulders barely fit between the posts. The two children ran with fear to Maggie's lap. Marvin and Silas rose tensely to their feet, uncomfortable at the presence of this runaway black.

"This is Macaijah. He is a friend, a former slave to my household in Bath," Jonathan said. This explanation offered little, if any, relief to the Stalker family. Marvin continued to stare nervously at Macaijah. "We need to talk," Jonathan said. "Outside." Silas and Marvin picked up their long rifles and followed Macaijah quietly out.

"Come along," Jonathan said. He led them across the field to the still. When they were all gathered there, Jonathan turned, and the others followed his example, to look back toward the cabin with its glowing candlelight. "LeFevre will soon know you aren't making whiskey or casks here anymore, Mr. Stalker."

"God help us."

"I think we can be sure of it. Macaijah saw one of his men here at the still at sundown. He has, no doubt, gone to tell LeFevre by now."

"I didn't expect to hear from him until winter," Stalker said.

"The farm is in great danger. LeFevre can choose his time if he wants to strike back for this change you have made! Now, I need to know, Mr. Stalker, are you going to stand behind this change in your life?"

"Of course he will—" Silas interrupted.

"Silas! I have to hear it from him," Jonathan replied. "And I have to hear it now. Mr. Stalker, are you ready to make a stand against whiskey, or will you backslide when LeFevre shows up?"

Marvin shifted his feet in the dark. His knuckles whitened around the stock of his long rifle. "I ain'ta gonna backslide no more. No more, Silas."

"Praise God!" Silas breathed.

"Then we need Gideon's Army here now, Silas. Not in October," Jonathan said.

"They'll come the end of October. After harvest. They all have farms of their own to tend."

"Then how will you defend this farm?" Jonathan said, his anger rising. "We are not enough to make a stand! And if LeFevre finds out you are here, after hanging three of his men, he will want to settle a score with you. And I hear he likes to settle it on the heads of women and children! Do you want *them* in the middle?" Jonathan pointed toward the cabin.

"Let me pray about it."

"Pray about it? All right, pray about riding to Logan's Fort tonight. I want to get a message there. Tell them I want my Hessian guard to ride here immediately. They may not be Gideon's Army, but they can probably hold LeFevre off until you get them here."

"What is it you are offering to do?" Silas asked.

"To stay here. To bring my Hessian guard from the fort. They can work the farm. We can finish this field by September. And they can guard the place day and night."

Marvin was listening carefully. He liked the sound of this proposal. Silas saw the wisdom in it as well. Reluctantly, however, for he had rejected the Hessian guard once before. They were quite the opposite of Gideon's Army.

Jonathan concluded, "It's either that or we pack everybody up and retreat tonight for Logan's Fort. This place will not be safe until LeFevre hangs."

They fell thoughtfully quiet for a while.

"What do you want to do?" Silas asked, looking at Marvin.

"Well, I put myself into this ground. I sure would like to see it come up good like that." He looked at Jonathan. "How could you do all that for me?" he asked.

Jonathan thought about Melody. He wanted her safe. He would do it for her sake. He would also do it to study the future of the Kentucky Land Company and a possible solution to the dilemma over expelling squatters. And though Silas had forced the issue, Marvin had made his own stand against whiskey.

"It's not something I would do for a backslider," Jonathan said, at last, sending Marvin a grim smile.

From the darkness across the still Silas said, "I'll be riding for the fort tonight," and turned to go.

"Silas. Another thing," Jonathan said. "Macaijah has brought a message for you from Tecumseh. The Shawnee will be camped at the Bends of the Green at the September full moon for a week. They would like to meet the Whiskey Warrior."

Silas closed his eyes and scratched his neck as he thought it over. "I have to ride the Boone's Station circuit. I . . ."

Macaijah spoke up. "If you agree to meet Tecumseh, I will bring warriors here tonight. We will stand guard until Jonathan's soldiers arrive."

Silas turned tiredly, but with a look of amused surprise in his eyes. He glanced from Jonathan to Macaijah. "All right. Tell Tecumseh I will meet him at the September moon."

Jonathan accompanied Silas to the lower end of the Stalkers' meadow. The exhorter led his horse, saddled and ready for the midnight trek to the fort. Ahead of them Macaijah was a dark silhouette receding to the south, toward the river, where he was to obtain the help of his Powhatan Indian companions that night. The air was warm and moist. A breeze whispered through the nodding grass at their ankles. Jonathan pulled a newly sealed envelope from his pocket and handed it to Silas. "Give this to Ethan. Or Klaus, the Hessian leader, if Ethan is not to be found."

Silas tucked it into his saddlebag.

"Will you go on to Boone's Station from the fort?"

"Yeah," Silas grunted.

"Will you have time to complete the circuit before the moon of September?"

"Unless I have delays."

Silas readied to mount.

"Silas. Before you go, I have something else to give you."

The exhorter turned away from the saddle, waiting, regarding Jonathan curiously.

Jonathan reached into his shirt and pulled out Emily's letter. His hand trembled. He hoped Silas didn't notice.

"This means . . . well, this letter is to you, Silas. It was written to you by my mother, Emily, not quite a year after you last saw her."

Silas' face had turned to stone. He seemed not to breathe. Then suddenly he exhaled with a sigh and took the letter, stuffing it quickly into his inner coat pocket. He turned and mounted.

"Read it in the light of morning," Jonathan said.

Silas waited, as if uncertain, looking away, across the dark plateau.

"The letter was written for you to read, Silas. I've wished many times I had never read it. I should warn you, the letter carries a kind of weight, a burden . . ."

Silas turned sharply.

". . . but I believe it is your turn to carry it."

They stood looking full at one another as the wind gusted around them. Then Silas broke away. He nudged his horse into motion. Horse and rider were swallowed in the black of night. The soft sound of hooves pounded into the distance, and finally were heard no more above the whispering of the night wind in the grass.

22

The Compromise

Macaijah returned with the two Powhatans. They patrolled the Stalkers'
meadow throughout the night.

When the sky brightened at dawn lonesome clouds floated in the blue,
shifting from one shape to another as they moved northward, high above
their own shadows on the ground. It was a day for seeing omens in the sky,
a day for worry and hope, as everyone waited for the Hessians to arrive.
Melody walked beside Jonathan, pointing to a cloud-lamb which changed
into the shape of a fish as they watched it. This delighted her. Then she
pointed out a fence post and rail, a canoe and a pair of soaring birds. He
thought the birds resembled vultures, and he saw a large pair of evil eyes
looking from the same cloud in which she saw a laughing man. He kept
his impressions to himself.

Throughout the day Macaijah and the Indians took turns sleeping in
the barn and watching the perimeter of the meadow. Just before sundown, the sound of hooves and wheels drew everyone from the cabin and

barn. The men clutched their rifles nervously. In an orderly line, two abreast, the Hessians rode into view. The Stillwell wagon followed behind. The children danced and hugged one another. Marvin and Maggie embraced. Jonathan pulled Melody close, and kissed her forehead.

Joburn rode with Klaus at the head of the column of six Hessians. Ethan and Andrew were in the wagon. Abercrombie, Tibbet, Ledbetter, and Cartwright flanked the wagon, and the other six Hessians brought up the rear. In the written instructions Jonathan had requested that Ethan and Abercrombie come with the Hessians, but Ethan's entire entourage had made the trek. They were all armed.

As the caravan rumbled up the long meadow, Jonathan grinned and glanced sideways at Melody. No Kentucky homestead, he was certain, had ever witnessed a parade like this. Melody squeezed him again. With a shout, Andrew leaped from the wagon. But it wasn't Jonathan he sought. It was Macaijah. The old man threw his arms around Chayta's boy and cried unashamedly.

Ethan, however, kept a discreet distance from Macaijah. He recalled the fate of Bard Dugin in Bath. Jonathan had told him of Macaijah's presence in Kentucky, but seeing the giant Negro now, in this savage land, was no comfort.

After a night of talk and a breakfast of corn bread and applesauce, Macaijah and the Powhatans departed, promising to return by the full moon of September. Jonathan began to look ahead with anticipation. While waiting for Silas to return, he wanted to make plans for the Stalkers and also for Barratt Enterprises. He felt reasonably sure that LeFevre would not risk an attack with the Hessians present. One whiskey maker was hardly worth that much effort. Jonathan hoped Silas had been right in his assessment of evil men, that they were too lazy to attack unless weakness was shown. He noted the sun passing high overhead and wondered if by now Silas had read Emily's letter. Did he know now that Jonathan was his son? How would it change him?

August arrived. Thunderstorms swept the land in the early evenings. Foliage renewed, and late-summer wildflowers appeared across the pennyroyal meadows of the Green River.

Jonathan established a work schedule for the homestead. The Hessians were divided into two groups and rotated daily: a day of work, a day to rest and be at the ready for any attack from LeFevre. When working in the field, Marvin led them by example, handling his ax and shovel with great gusto. He was, overnight, a man with a new purpose.

Caleb, the wagon master, handled the large and muscular shires, setting them to pull the loosened stumps to the burn piles and to drag fallen timbers to a station near the cabin where Mr. Cartwright froed them with an expert hand. Ledbetter assisted him. As the stack of milled timbers grew, Marvin Stalker made plans for adding to the cabin. Joburn killed and butchered a buffalo at a salt lick in the lower meadow. He built a smokehouse and made jerky of part of the meat. He salted and stored the rest of it in the Stalkers' underground larder. After completing this task, and refusing pay in shillings from Ethan, he returned to Logan's Fort.

Maggie was overwhelmed by the assistance provided around the cabin by Andrew and Tibbet, Ethan's secretary. They kept the interior immaculate and assisted in the meal preparations each day. In their spare time they made small but important improvements, planting flowers, inlaying a flagstone walkway to the door, fencing the yard area, and building pens for the pigs, goats, and chickens to keep them from their habitual running through the house. From time to time Maggie would simply stop, take up the corner of her apron, and touch a tear of gratitude from her eye as she surveyed the transformation of her once dreary world.

Following breakfast each day, Jonathan huddled with Abercrombie and Ethan over the Kentucky Land Company maps. They set up a table of planks near the barn, where the Stillwell wagon was parked.

"Find a way to give free and clear title for this land claim to Marvin Stalker," Jonathan said on the morning of their first meeting.

"You don't mean that!" Abercrombie protested.

"He does," Ethan told him, in a firm answer that surprised both Abercrombie and Jonathan. "We will do as Jonathan wishes. Perhaps we can purchase the parcel out of Barratt profits from the venture, if there is no other way."

Jonathan smiled. He was beginning to appreciate his uncle's shrewdness. Business was a game of give-and-take, and Jonathan understood what Uncle Ethan had done to him: *giving* him what he wanted but *taking* it from his own profits by the same stroke. Finely done. But Jonathan had expected as much from Ethan. He had nurtured this land endeavor since the days when Captain Barratt was alive. He would not give anything without exacting a price.

But Jonathan wanted to win much more than the Stalker property in this game of give-and-take. He intended to accommodate every squatter on Kentucky Land Company lands—the Stalkers, Hiraim Jessup, the Hecks, the Bryants, the Hogans, every family. And he believed all of his investors could still realize substantial profits. He had a plan.

"Ethan, you and I will take Ledbetter today and establish the exact boundaries of Mr. Stalker's claims on our map," Jonathan continued. "We will define his boundaries separately within the bounds of the claim you have already made here, and in legal terminology, Mr. Abercrombie, you will find some kind of action we can take to give him this claim."

"There is only one action available to us under the law," Abercrombie advised.

"And that is . . . ?"

"Prior claim."

"But *we* have prior claim," Ethan prompted.

"True. It is well established. We claimed this land years before Stalker arrived here. There is no legal basis for his owning the land at all."

"Then we must find another way to accommodate him," Jonathan said.

"Why? And how?" Ethan protested.

"Uncle Ethan, look here." Jonathan ran his finger in a line on the map from Logan's Fort to the Bends of the Green. "Do you see how little land is claimed along here? This is wild land, and inaccessible. Most of the lands you have claimed lie along the Wilderness Road. It's the road that gives the land its value. It is safer and more useful to live near a road. But as to the land along the Wilderness Road, none of it is better land than you passed through on your way here from Logan's Fort. Don't you agree?"

"It looked good, but we haven't scouted it for water yet," Ethan cautioned.

"We can do that," Jonathan replied. "Assuming that it has good water and soil, then a new road through here would make this area multiply in value. Let's call it the Green River Road."

Jonathan was full of excitement, but Abercrombie and Ethan remained skeptical.

"Don't you see it?" Jonathan pleaded. "We file special claim to this land now. Secretly. Then we return to Baltimore to mount a road-building expedition such as the Wilderness Road. We can convince our investors of success by the example of success along the Wilderness Road! But this time we will not be in the way of a massive settler uprising."

"That would be listened to," Abercrombie admitted, "if you have information that can be proven. Not just talk."

"It is there. We can get it," Jonathan insisted. "Only now, when we open up this area of ours with the new road, we inform every traveler of the special rights they can have by settling on our land. The agreement they sign with their claim would not give them the land outright, but the opportunity to share in the increased value of the land as long as they developed it. In a number of years they would be given first opportunity to purchase it with their share."

Ethan and Abercrombie were silent, frowning for a long time. Ethan drummed his fingers on the map. "It will take a large commitment from all of us to build a road. And why do it when we don't have to? We can make a fortune on our present plan."

"To avoid stealing land from settlers simply because they don't know the finer points of the law."

"Jonathan, knowledge *is* wealth. It *is* fair. Sometimes it seems unfair, but it is fair."

"It is unjust that a man like Boone could be tossed from the land he claimed with a tomahawk. He won it, defended it with his life. He buried his children there, Ethan, and opened up this entire country. We couldn't come here if it wasn't for Boone. I say it *is* unjust! And I am willing to wager our entire fortune on the idea that the law will, if not now, then someday, see to it that this great wrong is made right. If that isn't what the law is about, then it is not the law of civilized men."

They remained silent on that point for a while.

"Jonathan, the law is well proven on this point," Abercrombie warned.

Ethan frowned. "It makes no sense to me to walk away from a fortune that lies before us ready to yield its fruit, simply to earn another possible fortune by risk and sweat and toil. Who has ever heard of such a thing? Why should we do it?"

"Because it is right—"

"Oh, my Lord, Jonathan!"

"All right, then," Jonathan challenged. "Do it because it is smart. You may well lose this fortune you believe you have already won. I say, you *will* lose it."

"How so?" Ethan and Abercrombie were both alert now.

"The squatters on our land are living there in ignorance. Tragic ignorance, if you will. But you, gentlemen, are also ignorant of something very important," Jonathan declared, "and that is that the settlers won't come to court one case at a time, as Boone did. No. Because these Kentuckians have a very formidable representative."

"There is none," blustered Ethan.

"Yes, there is."

"But they have no formal government."

"True, but there is a man who unites them. He travels among them, he knows them, and he will make their case with such eloquence that you will not be able to take their property by prior claim or by any other claim. You will lose it."

"Nonsense." Ethan bounded to his feet.

"It *is* nonsense," added Abercrombie, "because the law *must* back our positions."

"It probably will back it," Jonathan agreed, "but with a representative defending not one but many claims all at once, your investors will win back their investment only. They will lose the profits you promised, because there will have to be some kind of legal compromise to benefit these settlers. Barratt Enterprises will be the loser. That you can rest assured of. That is why it is smart to head off the action by making our own compromise, the Green River Road."

"My Lord, Jonathan. Who are you talking about?" Ethan asked. "Who is this representative?"

"His name is Silas Will."

Ethan's face showed surprise at the mention of this name, though Jonathan thought he tried to disguise it.

Ethan shrugged. "You are speaking of the preacher, of course."

Jonathan nodded. What did Ethan know of Silas? he wondered. "Do you know him?"

Ethan smiled to himself, looking away. "I know who he is. The same man we met on the road to Bath, and at the frolic."

"That's the one."

"I knew that you left Bath with him. Tell me, now that you have ridden all this way with him, how do you know he will unite these squatters? Has he made a threat?"

"Believe me when I say he will do it. He is already looking into the matter with much concern."

Ethan's eyes narrowed shrewdly at Jonathan. "Abercrombie, I would have a word in private with my nephew."

Abercrombie looked back and forth between them. "Of course," he replied. "I shall wait at the cabin."

He walked away, leaving Jonathan staring uncomfortably at Ethan across the plank table.

Ethan waited quietly, purposefully, until Abercrombie was out of ear-shot, then he spoke in a tone of soft finality. "So, Silas Will is your father."

Jonathan actually rocked backward with surprise. This was the last thing he expected to hear.

"Oh, come now"—Ethan smiled—"you figured an old weasel like me would make it his business to know, didn't you? Besides, the Captain told me . . . years ago. He was drunk. He told me of the duel, and how he ran this Silas Will off to the wilderness. I knew why you left Bath for this God-forgotten land. But I let you do it, regrettably, of course." He tried to smile. "I followed you because I feared for your safety and your inheri-tance." He sobered. "No young man such as yourself wouldn't try to find his own father. So you've found him finally."

Jonathan looked away. His uncle's tone of voice was sympathetic, but something made Jonathan not want to trust it. Ethan cared for him, he knew, but he cared for the life of luxury and wealth even more.

Ethan began to pace. "Jonathan, I want to confess something to you. You see, because I knew about the conditions of your birth, I never thought I would have to deal with you at all about Barratt business. The time the Captain was drunk, why, he said he would disinherit you and I always took that to be more than ale talk. So when the Captain died in battle, I was most unprepared to learn that he had made you his sole heir, and left nothing that was directly mine. I confess that I made preparations to have you removed from the will, disinherited. I went so far as to have legal papers prepared in Boston."

Jonathan gazed at Ethan. In the game of give-and-take, Ethan had placed his hand upon everything Jonathan had, to give or to take. The game was up. Would he really do such a thing? Why hadn't he done it earlier? Jonathan wondered.

"I hid the documents away," Ethan said. "I did not file the claim against you. I did it for Emily, I suppose. You are my sister's son. And because Captain Barratt had clearly left you his fortune, I did it for his memory, I suppose, and to honor my years of service to that noble man."

Ethan paused, gathering his next words even more carefully. "The way it has been, you have left all the business to me, Jonathan, you've never really shown any interest at all. That made everything just fine. But when suddenly you did show interest, and when you left to come here, I be-lieved you might very well put this entire enterprise in jeopardy, so it no longer mattered to me that you were Emily's son. You were becoming, if you will pardon . . . a b_____d in my eyes. I took those disinheritance documents again and read them over. I saw that the case was solid."

Jonathan wanted to say something, but he wanted to hear the rest, just as honestly as Ethan was capable of telling it.

"But then something happened to me," Ethan went on. "I don't know. I visited several squatter families around Logan's Fort, as you asked. And something has happened to you. I see you differently here in Kentucky. You are not the same aimless young man of just such a short time ago. Of course, I'm not certain that your business sense is sound. You give away entirely too much. This Green River Road is quite sketchy yet. But I like what I see in you. You remind me more than ever of your fath— of Captain Barratt."

He paused, as if just discovering a new idea. "You know, Captain Barratt knew me well. Perhaps that is why . . . why he made you his heir. I cannot say, hmm."

He averted his attention upon the thought for a moment, then continued, looking at Jonathan with sober eyes. "I'm a faulty old weasel, Jon. No doubt about it. And I'm not getting younger, I'm getting set in my ways. But I like your ideas about helping the settlers. There's a new kind of challenge in it for me. Maybe, just maybe, it can be made to work . . ."

He took a deep breath and smiled a relieved sort of smile. "When we get back to Bath I would like to invite you to a fine drink of schnapps and a bonfire. We'll burn those disinheritance papers and put the whole matter to rest between us."

Jonathan saw something new radiate from his uncle's face. Until now it seemed Ethan's purpose in life was the expansion of Barratt wealth. But something new had gotten ahold of him. He had caught a vision of something more. Kentucky was a land offering hope and a new chance for justice and liberty to its ragtag lot of settlers. Ethan, he guessed, wanted to share in that, perhaps start in at the beginning and help shape it.

Jonathan felt humbled. "Uncle Ethan—" was all he could say, then he reached out and embraced him.

"Now, now let us understand—" sputtered Ethan. "Let us understand something here—" He finally disengaged Jonathan's arms and stepped back.

Jonathan was beaming, undaunted.

"This idea of yours," Ethan went on, assuming his most serious business posture, "this Green River Road, I must say it sounds good. On the face of it, it just might provide a solution to the difficulties of the original plan.

But there are some grave legal entanglements. Very delicate, now. Mind you, you can still learn a thing or two from old Uncle Ethan!"

"I certainly can. I will not take another step without you."

Jonathan extended his hand. Ethan smiled and shook it warmly.

The Hessian soldiers were not only sharp fighting mercenaries but hearty drinkers by reputation. Sooner or later their indulgence in strong drink was bound to place a strong temptation before Marvin Stalker. Jonathan anticipated this and did not want it to happen. He was investing too much of his own time and resources on the promise that Stalker would not backslide to the bottle and let the farm return to ruin. Especially for the sake of Melody. Jonathan had to admit reluctantly that when it came to Marvin Stalker, Silas was right about whiskey. Jonathan had graphic memories of their arrival at the run-down farm in the meadow and the slothful drunkenness of the delinquent farmer.

Several evenings after their arrival, Jonathan came upon Uncle Ethan doling out cupfuls of grog for the Hessians from a barrel stowed in the rear of the Stillwell wagon. Ethan himself had opened a bottle of apricot liqueur after supper, with Klaus as his privileged guest. They sipped delicately. Jonathan normally would have joined them, but under the circumstances, he became upset. He took Ethan and Klaus to one side to speak with them about the special situation.

Klaus understood the dilemma immediately and offered to forgo drinking to honor Marvin's religious stand against backsliding. He assured Jonathan that his men would miss the grog but would comply without complaint. It was a kind of combat sacrifice. Ethan, on the other hand, objected. He said the soldiers had run their supply of grog low and the abstinence would serve them well anyway. He saw no sense in making this concession to Stalker since he neither shared nor understood the religious sentiment.

Jonathan had no doubt that Ethan and the soldiers would find their way to their cups on the sly. He did not want it that way, so he made the "great compromise."

The problem, he said, was one of the mere appearance of temptation before the eyes of the Stalkers. Recalling the cask of bourbon still cooling in the cave spring, he saw a way to serve both sides at once; each evening four soldiers would fill all of the water barrels needed for the household the following day and, having done so, would go into the cave and relieve

Marvin Stalker of a portion of his eighty-proof temptation. One measured slug per man, Jonathan said. The men would rotate this duty each day.

And so it was done. Quietly and without mishap. Until one evening, in mid-August. One of the Hessians returned alone, running from the spring. He was out of breath and appeared quite shaken. Jonathan was summoned to the barn to hear his story. A man had been waiting in the cave for them when they entered. The stranger was polite enough, and unarmed, but insisted that he speak with the young man who had hired their services on the Stalker farm. Klaus had refused to even acknowledge the man's request and ordered him from the cave, but as they all emerged, they could see nearly thirty armed men on horseback gathered on the far side of the pond. They seemed to be quietly awaiting a signal from the stranger in the cave, who apparently was their leader.

"What does the man look like?" Jonathan asked.

"Gray hair with some black in it, and he has eyes—"

"LeFevre!"

"He said I was to bring you to him."

Jonathan wondered what would be done. He had not anticipated this, and he felt his solution to the liquor question had made hostages of four of his prize Hessians. "I will go, but you, absolutely not," Jonathan said. "He wants to weaken the defense here at the cabin, but that is the last thing I will allow. You stay here. Arm everyone who can be armed and defend from the barn. Hitch the shires to the wagon and hold them in the barn. I am going alone. If things go bad here, wait until daylight and retreat to the fort. Now, bring everyone from the cabin!"

"Yes, sir!"

Jonathan spoke with much more command than he felt. He took one of his pistols, loaded it, and stuffed it into his belt. Ethan walked with him toward the trail leading over the rise to the spring.

"D____n!" Jonathan swore.

"Are you sure you should go, Jon?"

Jonathan drew a deep breath. "Those men's lives are in danger because I compromised with the Devil."

"What kind of talk is that?"

"Silas talk. He says this is no ordinary war here with LeFevre. He says it's spiritual war and that's why he is going after this Gideon's Army of his. He says men who have compromised with liquor will not be able to defeat LeFevre."

"Surely you don't believe—"

"Right now, I wonder, Uncle Ethan. I wonder. I should have honored his way in this thing whether I believed it or not. At least now I could face this snake without that awful doubt in my mind."

"You can't go in there like this, Jonathan. You're beaten before you start. And let me remind you, it's not only your life at risk here!"

"I know that," Jonathan snapped, his fright growing. He straightened his shoulders and glared at Ethan. "I will play this thing as LeFevre plays it. If he plays Silas' Devil, so the heck will I. If he is in that cave to make a fight of it, I will at least see that this ball of lead goes between his eyes."

Ethan shuddered. He was not a man of violence.

Jonathan looked searchingly at him. "Uncle Ethan. Would you . . . ?"

Ethan waited for him to finish.

"Don't mock me now."

"Of course not."

"Ethan . . . ask Marvin and Maggie to pray for me, for all of us. I mean . . . I . . . no need to tell him about the bourbon, for heaven's sake. No. Just . . . see if he would pray. It might . . . do something, I don't know." He hesitated a moment, then walked away.

"Of course I will." Ethan called after him and hurried himself toward the barn.

As Jonathan moved toward the ridge, terror hounded his every step, whispering, taunting him on the evening breeze, chilling him with waves of panic and an urge to break and run for his life, away from this madness, away from the Stalkers and their farm as if none of it had ever mattered to him. Better to be lost in the wildness of this land than to carry this burden. He topped the rise and saw the riders gathered on the far side of the pond just as the Hessian had said. Something about the way they lounged so easily in their saddles, without fear, knowing they held the power of greater numbers, triggered a change in Jonathan.

He neither slowed nor hurried his pace but began to descend the path on the balls of his feet. He let his boots crunch loudly on the gravel to announce his coming. The muscles in his neck, shoulders, and chest tightened, his fingers tensed, flexed, and tingled. His skin was covered with a warming perspiration. Now he was ready to fight to the death. Not in any physical sense, not even strictly of his mind, but in perhaps a spiritual sense he felt tired, deeply, unutterably tired of living in a world where the sweetest and best things of life were held at the mercy of such evil men. He could think of no better time or place to fight and die. He almost wished for it.

Suddenly he was powerful. Inside of him, a source of tears and laughter welled up together and flowed in a river of icy rage. It was a rage under control, he could direct it at will. He felt every fiber of his mind and body fully alive and at his command. He had never, ever dreamed this state of being existed. He always thought that terror could overwhelm him in the end. Now he knew better, and he would never again be perfectly afraid of anything.

His eyes swept across the men on their horses, then he turned toward the cave. He saw that a torch lit up the inside of the cave. He moved steadily toward it and paused at the entrance. Klaus silently leaned on his rifle looking grimly at him. The two other soldiers waited, gripping their weapons at the mouth of the cave. The man Jonathan had seen on the day of the executions at Logan's Fort, the man he took to be Jacques LeFevre, sat unarmed upon the cask of whiskey further back in the cave. He was casually opening wild hickory nuts with a small shiny blade.

Jonathan stepped into the cave, keeping his eyes locked upon LeFevre. He stepped near to Klaus and spoke quietly, "If it comes to a fight, he dies. That is all I ask."

Klaus nodded, but then whispered back in his thick accent, "He wants talk."

Jonathan did not want talk. He wanted LeFevre dead. He took hold of his rage, checked it, and stepped forward.

LeFevre looked him over with wide unblinking eyes as he approached, all the while nibbling at particles of hickory nut in his hand. The renegade's face confused Jonathan. He looked too human to be a demon, Jonathan thought. But a strange human. He had the appearance of having been put together from parts of several people, some pleasant, some weirdly unpleasant. In contrast to the unkempt bushy-bearded renegades who rode with him, he was clean-shaven. His gray and black streaked shoulder-length hair was neatly combed. He was not a large man, but there was strength in him. His hands were slender-fingered and pale like a woman's, his skin was oily and smooth. The skin of his face seemed young for his years except for dark semicircles that wrinkled the skin beneath his protruding eyes. His mouth appeared ordinary enough, except when he opened it to speak; then it seemed to curl between two contrasting expressions, pain and vengeance.

"Tell Silas Will I let him take Stalker from me, and I show mercy. I am Jacques LeFevre. I wish I were not, but I am. Why does Silas come for me? He makes my life misery. I show mercy. I let Marvin go. If I was the bad man, I would not do this. Would I? No. You tell Silas, will you?"

"Tell him?" Jonathan said, with complete uncomprehension.

LeFevre leapt up. "Tell him I am good! I have never done these things they say," he screamed, beside himself with Jonathan's apparent stupidity.

"All right," Jonathan said evenly, "I will tell him that you left the Stalkers in peace. That you did not—"

"I have many friends," LeFevre went on as if Jonathan had said nothing at all. "If Silas chase me, he will find it is so. Tell him, do not believe John Stern. He is a blind man. He did not see me. He did not see my men. I *know* who killed the Stern women." LeFevre spoke without emotion. Only a jerking of his eyes, inconsistent with his words, betrayed his agitation. "The Shawnee have always been the butchers. They tortured my family."

"I will tell Silas your words." Jonathan spoke calmly now.

"Whiskey kills Injuns, heh, heh." LeFevre said, stooping to pat the oaken cask. He seemed to be seeing a memory. "It shames them. When they are shamed they lay down and die. Why does Silas say I am bad man? I shame the savages. I make the land safe."

"I can't speak for Silas."

Jacques did not hear. As Jonathan watched, LeFevre's eyes seemed to struggle back to the present from some faraway place. He assumed a strange, thin voice. "I kill him. He begs my mercy down on his knees, or I kill him like—" He choked off the word. "He hangs innocent men. That is great crime. I kill him."

"Shall I tell him that?"

Jacques moved suddenly toward Jonathan. "Who are you?"

Jonathan knew fear again. He drew on images of Silas, recalled moments of the exhorter at the frolic, on the Newtowne Trace, on the gallows, at the still—somehow these memories brought a special strength for this very moment. "I am Silas' son," Jonathan said boldly into LeFevre's face.

Jacques' eyebrows shot up in surprise. Then his hand flew in a blur to Jonathan's throat, the point of his small blade pressed against the soft underside of his neck. A trickle of hot blood ran down his wrist. Jonathan's hand reached for his pistol.

"Fool!" screamed LeFevre.

Jonathan's hand stopped moving.

LeFevre stepped back, lowered his knife with a shrug and a chuckle. "I am no fool," he smiled smoothly. "I could have killed these men. I let them live. I come here where you could kill me. I only want to tell you some things, that is all. Tell Silas I could kill you, but I show mercy. But I will not show mercy to Silas. Tell him it is too late. I want him because he hangs my men. A life for a life. You tell him that."

With that he turned and strode from the cave. A horse had already been brought near for him. He mounted and rode away with his men.

August turned to early September. The air had begun to dry and the corn leaves rustled with creeping brittleness in the cooling breezes. The work at the Stalker farm continued. The stump field was cleared and plowed. The Hessians now worked with Marvin to channel seeping springs from the surrounding woods into irrigation ditches to his fields. Jonathan and Ethan organized daily surveying trips with Ledbetter and two accompanying soldiers, in order to scout the Green River Road project. Each day took them farther from the cabin and required harder riding for them to return by the time darkness fell. One day when they had reached a point nearly midway to Logan's Fort, they smelled the odor of rotting flesh.

"A killing ground," Jonathan said. "But it would be unusual to find one this far from a river."

One of the soldiers pointed to a number of circling vultures and Jonathan signaled the entire party to follow him in their direction. As they neared a grove of trees suddenly a wave of revulsion swept Jonathan. He pulled Merlin to a halt, not wanting to go any further. On an earlier occasion, he had seen a sapling half camp near the spot where the vultures settled and massed on the ground. As they approached again, a half dozen coyotes scattered away from the site and melted into the trees.

"My Lord." Ethan wretched, with awful anticipation.

Jonathan took his knife and cut a strip of linsey-woolsey from his undershirt. He tied it over his nose. The others did likewise. Then slowly the troop of them rode forward, starting and stopping as their eyes progressively revealed exactly what they hoped not to find. An entire family lay massacred. Their decaying bodies lay face down, in black swarms of flies. Painted lances were stabbed through their backs and their scalps were torn away.

"Savages!" Ethan sobbed.

They did not wait. They dismounted and immediately began to dig and scrape with their tomahawks a shallow grave for the first body they found.

It was a young man. Probably a son. They covered him, piling rocks on top of the loose dirt to keep the scavengers from digging it up again. Looking about, they counted five bodies in all, three boys, two men. They went to the next body. All at once one of the soldiers began to wretch uncontrollably. He ran from the half-camp shelter into the meadow, where he fell to his hands and knees, remaining useless for the rest of the time, crying uncontrollably. Jonathan and the others finished burying the bodies.

As they steeled themselves to the shocking sights and continued the grisly task, Jonathan noticed upon the ground something that began to confirm his growing suspicion. He pointed out to Ethan the deep round impressions.

"See here? Horses. The Shawnee do not ride."

Jonathan walked to the tent flap of the half-camp shelter, lifted it, and looked inside. In the shadowy dimness, his eyes took a while to adjust. Then he saw it, the thing that had made the soldier turn and run. In the shaded area within, obscured by a swarm of buzzing flies, were the dismembered bodies of a mother and daughter. Their severed parts rearranged beneath their heads in a pattern that could only have originated in the mind of a madman.

"LeFevre!" Jonathan choked.

"No. The Devil," said Ethan.

23

The Caverns

The settlers of Logan's Fort recoiled with news of the massacre. Jonathan arrived there to organize a fact-finding expedition, but the story had no sooner left his mouth than it was repeated outside the inn and subsequently spread through the half camps at the speed of a flash fire. The settlers and residents would have nothing of a fact-finding mission; they would have a bloody reprisal.

Jonathan stood fast against the idea. He explained to an assembled mob that the facts of the crime were not absolutely clear and that what was needed was a small company of two or three men to accompany an expert tracker on the cold trail. A reprisal would stand a much better chance of success if it took advantage of the information provided by the smaller company. They could mount a well-planned attack later. He was shouted down. He mentioned that an October raid was even now being organized against LeFevre—if he turned out to be the guilty party in this case—by none other than Silas Will. He was shouted down again.

Before first light the next morning, a company of fifty-four men, which accounted for two of every three able-bodied men at Logan's Fort, set out for the scene of the crime. They had reached a compromise with Jonathan. They convinced him that if they could not establish the killers' identity at the scene, they would quit the armed chase and do as he suggested. So he led them to the site. He sent Ethan and the soldiers back to the Stalker farm.

At the scene, several of the men set about exhuming a corpse. Seeing it was scalped, they immediately blamed Indians. Jonathan was afraid of this. The men wanted to believe the Indians had done it. Jonathan could see how a murderer such as LeFevre might use their natural fear and hatred of Indians as the perfect disguise for his own grisly passions. It was Joburn who set them right. He found that an oxcart had been driven from the half camp. Evidently it had been loaded with the family's stolen possessions. The killers had shown little fear of detection. The trail was plain enough to follow at a full gallop.

With whoops and cries for vengeance the men from the fort set out. Jonathan rode with them. For him it was important to erase any lingering doubts in his own mind about whether or not LeFevre had done it. If they were bent on quick vengeance, he, at least, would go along to satisfy his own questions. The trail led parallel to the Green River. They followed the river for two days before turning abruptly northwest, climbing a wooded ridge. The horses had grown tired from the hard pace, as had the men. They traveled without great caution and thus happened suddenly upon the mouth of a large cave. Shots rang out, scattering the pursuing men.

Two black renegades were all that could be seen guarding the mouth of the cavern, but the entrance was high enough above the trail so that they found it easy to hold off the settlers. So after about a half hour of futile firing, the settler group sent up two teams to flank the position at the cave's mouth. As soon as they did so, the firing ceased. The defenders fled within the cave.

For two days the men blockaded the entrance, and sent in teams of pursuers with torches. They found the cave deserted but uncovered well-stocked storerooms and living quarters, which they summarily destroyed. Their searches led them deeper and deeper into the wonders of the cavern, with less and less hope of finding the breathing renegades.

They found Indian totems, human scalps, and piles of humanlike bones in a number of rather ceremonial-looking places. There were bark-wrapped Indian mummies, pottery, and wampum about. Evidently Le-Fevre made use of ancient Indian ceremonial sites for his own purposes now.

On the second day of the search one of the teams emerged from another entrance to the cave several miles west on the ridge and they knew then that the cave was a honeycomb of escape routes. All of the killers had slipped between their fingers like a fistful of copperheads. Discouraged, they drew rough maps of their explorations of the caves and returned to the fort.

As they rode homeward they discussed the wonders of LeFevre's cave. The huge echoing chambers presided over by cathedral-like pillars of stone. The underground rivers populated by strange sightless fish. Some of the men produced albino beetles from their pockets, which, they avowed, would fuel enchanted storytelling about the firesides back at the fort. And all agreed that someday they would return to mine the rich deposits of saltpeter that abounded within the caves. The consensus was that they had indeed found the lair of LeFevre the renegade and that someday they would hunt him down with a more carefully organized force.

Jonathan left the group at the Bends of the Green and turned across the plateau alone toward the Stalker farm. Before departing, however, he expressed his fear that Silas Will's October raid on LeFevre would have little chance of surprising the renegades now that their caverns had been thoroughly sacked. And worse, in the meantime a nest of criminal hornets had been dangerously stirred up on the Stalkers' doorstep.

The men found it hard to look him in the eye as he spoke these things. They were the very ones who shouted him down at the fort. He suggested that he might call upon them, at some future time, to redress what their tomfoolery had wrought. They nodded their unanimous assent.

The September moon appeared. Each night as it rose, Jonathan sat watching the sky with Melody. They had found a pleasant routine together each evening. Following supper they would go to the barn to listen to the stories of the Hessians and their travels, then they would walk hand in hand down the center of the meadow until they arrived again at the cabin. There, they sat on a log bench, recently fashioned by Ledbetter and placed on the new porch. Each night Jonathan and Melody were the last to retire.

Since the discovery of the massacred family, Jonathan felt an increased need to hear Melody's voice, her ideas, her wishes and dreams. They

seemed warm and simple and good. She gave his troubled mind a welcomed focus and a reminder that there was a reason to endure against the
growing threat around them. He thought more and more of taking her
away from this place. He began to know that he could not bear to leave
her side until he had seen LeFevre dead and buried. Then he would not
want to leave her for long.

Each night the moonrise showed more full, reminding him that Silas
would be coming back from his northward circuit soon to meet Tecumseh
on the Green.

The moon was three quarters full when Macaijah returned. He arrived
at night as Jonathan and Melody sat on the porch. Jonathan heard the
sound of his approaching horse and recognized his form in the moonlight
even when he was at the lower end of the Stalkers' meadow.

"Eeeyo! Macaijah," he called across the meadow.

Macaijah returned his two-note whistle and Merlin whinnied in the
barn, kicking against his stall.

Jonathan bid Melody good night and went out to meet Macaijah at the
center of the meadow. He was joined there by Uncle Ethan, Klaus, and
Andrew. But a change had occurred in Macaijah. He had shaved his head,
leaving only a scalp lock down the middle. A bundle of eagle feathers
dangled behind. His torso was bare and he wore tall leather moccasins and
a leather loincloth.

"I and the Powhatans are to become brothers to the Shawnee," Macaijah explained to the astonished group. None knew how to answer him.
He was a fearsome sight. He appeared grim and haggard but smiled
warmly when Andrew extended his hand.

"I cannot stay. Tecumseh is moving on the Green River now," he went
on. "I was with them on the Ohio five days ago. LeFevre came there. He
made a promise to bring Tecumseh a supply of British long rifles in October."

There was a long moment of silence.

"What is wrong with Tecumseh?" Jonathan suddenly demanded.
"Does he want to rid his people of whiskey, or give them long rifles?"

Macaijah stood quietly, surprised at Jonathan's display of temper.

"Tell me why Silas should meet with him now." Jonathan said.

"You ask this of me?" Macaijah grew irritated at the tone of the question.

"I do ask you." Jonathan's eyes blazed in the moonlight. "You are the one who follows this great Shawnee leader. You say he and his brother are spiritual men. Yet they council with LeFevre, who is a true savage. A murderer! If Tecumseh wants war, then let LeFevre bring him all the rifles he wants. He also brings whiskey to shame the Indian. LeFevre raids settlers and blames it on the Shawnee. He says the Shawnee killed his wife and children. Tortured them—" Jonathan was shouting.

"Tecumseh forbids torture."

"Then why does he council with LeFevre . . . who tortures in the name of the Shawnee? He massacred a family of settlers near here, Macaijah. He butchered a mother and daughter. That is his way. I know it is not the way of the Shawnee. Yet LeFevre scalped the people and left Shawnee lances in their backs! Then you tell me Tecumseh holds council with him. He plays Tecumseh for a fool!"

Macaijah turned angrily, and in a single leap landed astride his dappled gray. "We will soon know the fool," he said, biting the words. Then he galloped away.

As the sound of hoofbeats faded, Ethan approached, placing a cautioning hand on his shoulder. "Jon," he said, "he was your friend."

Jonathan removed his spectacles and massaged his fingers wearily across his eyes. Then he looked up at Ethan. "LeFevre's our enemy. That we can count on. But we don't know yet who our friends are."

The next four days passed as days of high tension on the Stalker farm.

Jonathan ordered extra precautions taken in all activities. He reduced the number of Hessians on work detail to four instead of six, so that the others could keep a more thorough watch. He had the soldiers destroy the remaining bourbon in the cask at the spring, taking no more chances with Silas' God. He ordered Melody and the children to stay in the immediate vicinity of the cabin. He told the men not to move beyond the perimeter of the meadow alone. He ordered half of the horses to be saddled and ready for action at all times in the barn.

Still he did not rest easy. During the day he was in constant motion about the property, inspecting the progress on the irrigation ditches, checking the corn and squash in the field, inspecting the work on the new addition to the cabin, and huddling with Abercrombie and Uncle Ethan over their Green River paperwork.

His evening walks with Melody stopped. They continued to talk together on the bench at the cabin, but Jonathan was agitated, unable to respond as warmly as he wanted to with her. So he brooded, listening to her talk, but listening more to every unusual sound in the night.

"You have done right, Jonathan," she said.

"Do you think so?"

"Yes."

"I've done too much."

"How can you do too much good? So much is needed here. Look at what a difference you've made."

That is what worried him. "This place has become more than a farm. It's too well ordered for this wild area. Now it has become like . . . like a warning signal to LeFevre, and perhaps to the Shawnee as well, that they will not be here on the Green River for much longer. But the fact remains, they still are. And if they want to strike out against something in anger, this is where they will strike."

Melody was quiet, sensing the truth of this.

"And, Melody, I will have to leave for the winter. If I left the Hessians here, they would not be able to hold this ground until we can build a fort here. I have business to attend in Bath before I return. If LeFevre is still alive, how can I leave you here?"

"Don't," she said, softly stroking his arm.

He turned and pulled her close to him, wrapping his arms around her. So much had intruded between them since their magic night at the spring. So many things that he wished he could forget but could not, even in this moment when he held her. Her soft breath on his cheek reminded him of how much he wanted to hold her in a world at peace. It reminded him of everything he was fighting for, and then it reminded him that the fight still lay ahead.

The sound of an approaching horse aroused him.

"It's Macaijah," Melody whispered.

He released her and turned to look down the meadow. He saw Macaijah in the light of the full September moon. In the distance, far below the Green River, a line of thunderstorms stretched from horizon to horizon. Lightning played across the breadth of it, momentarily silhouetting the horseback warrior. He rode directly to the cabin until his horse stood before Jonathan and Melody.

"Silas has come to the Bends of the Green," he said curtly. "I thought you would want to know."

Jonathan kissed Melody's forehead, then rose to his feet. "Will you ride with me?" he asked.

Macaijah nodded.

Jonathan smiled in the darkness as he turned toward the barn.

An hour of darkness remained when they arrived on the plateau above the Bends of the Green. The lightning still flashed to the south. Rumblings could be heard across the distance. The storm grew nearer. Silas knelt in his morning ritual of prayer on the top of a barren rise. Jonathan and Macaijah pulled their horses to a halt and dismounted at a respectful distance, then squatted on the ground to wait for daylight.

"Tecumseh knows nothing but lies from white men," Macaijah said, leaning toward Jonathan as they watched the kneeling figure. "I have told him that there are honorable white men. He would like to meet one, but he will have to test him first. Until then, LeFevre still has a hold on him."

When gray finally lightened the sky to the east, Silas stood stiffly to his feet. He stretched his shoulders one at a time. Without looking at either of the men, he spoke to them.

"I came alone," he growled irritably, then turned away a few steps to look down on the Shawnee hunting camp. "But since you're here," he said. "Go tell that heathen chief that I refuse to meet him on his mumbo-jumbo ground. Tell him I'll meet him upriver, there, in the open spot." He pointed.

Jonathan wore an amused smile as he and Macaijah stepped forward. They looked to the place where he was pointing.

Macaijah swung into the saddle. "I will tell him."

"And you." Silas swung around to face Macaijah. "You need to get right with God. These Shawnee worship false pagan gods. Look, they got you half naked now."

Macaijah glared at Silas. "Pagan gods did not make a slave of me," he said, then jerked his horse around and descended the game trail toward the river.

"Neither did God," Silas hollered after him, finding his answer somewhat late.

He shrugged, looking at Jonathan, "He talks back to me . . . like you."

They were suddenly looking at each other, Silas squinting at the young man he had seen so many times, but this time was different. He searched the face anew, with wonderment, perhaps looking for a trace of himself there. Whatever he saw, Silas grew uncomfortable and finally had to turn away, clearing his throat.

"We . . . we need to prepare about this meeting here today. Tecumseh needs to hear the gospel straight and without compromise."

Jonathan took a few steps forward until he stood a few feet away, looking down at the same camp. "Silas, I . . . uh . . . LeFevre has—"

"I know. I heard all about the massacre."

"And about the raid?"

He nodded with disgust. "I figure LeFevre's left the caves now."

"I tried to stop them. You can hardly blame them, though. After what LeFevre did. But they wanted to believe the Indians had done it."

"So did I. LeFevre had me believin' the Injuns killed his family till that time down in Caroline, when we both got whiskey-wet an' I saw the Devil in the man. I told the truth about him then, but Lord knows, the Injuns make it easy for him sometimes. They can butcher, too. Believe it."

Silas moved away to his saddled horse and climbed astride. Jonathan whistled for Merlin and followed suit.

"Well," Silas said, "you came all this way. Come along."

He turned and led down the game trail.

24

The Savage Test

Choosing the ground was the first test. Would Tecumseh come to Silas? Or would he be offended by the demand to come to the meadow chosen by the Whiskey Warrior?

Silas had crossed Kentucky for this meeting. He assured Jonathan that if the chief did not come to the site he chose, he would leave without a meeting. It was a matter of principle, he said. He wanted the pagan to respect the gospel from the beginning. He did not want to "cast pearls before swine," as the scripture says. Jonathan and Silas reached the chosen meadow and dismounted. The preacher pulled his Bible from his saddle-bag and began to pace about, quite affected, mumbling prayers beneath his breath. Jonathan waited quietly. After an hour Silas quit praying and eyed Jonathan with a look of defeat.

"I thought it was important to choose the ground," he said. "Perhaps not."

But Jonathan had spied his answer. He pointed. A procession approached from the hunting camp. In the lead was a handsome young Indian who bore himself with great dignity. Jonathan immediately knew this was Tecumseh but he was surprised at his youth. From the look of his face he guessed him to be not more than twenty. He wore very fine deerskin leggins and moccasins. The leather had been chewed to a downy-soft texture. It was otherwise unadorned except for buckskin fringes along the side of the leg. Around his neck was a heavy leather yoke, inset with long ivory bear claws. Fastened to the yoke was a deerskin cape of matching texture and fineness. He wore on each wrist a broad bracelet of hand-beaten brass and triangular earrings hung from each ear. The earrings were made of delicate bird bones and feathers. His hair was neatly trimmed to fall in front of, and just behind, his ears. A scalp lock of hair, braided to accommodate a single file of perfectly matched eagle feathers, swept from the center of his forehead to the back of his neck. He was a handsome, intelligent figure.

Following him at one shoulder was his brother, Tenskwatawa, and over the other an old man, totally naked except for a mask made of painted birch bark. Dark holes were cut through the bark for his eyes and mouth. His body was painted in red and black designs, and he carried a woven reed basket. Behind him were about a dozen hunters in hunting dress, none as fine as Tecumseh's. Macaijah and his two Powhatan companions followed at the end of the procession.

Tecumseh walked to the center of the ground and sat down cross-legged. Tenskwatawa squatted behind his shoulder and the masked man opened his basket. The hunters arranged themselves to watch from behind. Suddenly a flame was produced by the old man to light a small pile of shavings on the ground in front of Tecumseh. He accepted a pipe from the man and lit it from a shaving. Looking up, he motioned Silas to join him. Silas walked forward and sat down directly in front of him. Jonathan moved forward, too, but as he did so, Macaijah came to his side and guided him to sit behind Silas' shoulder as Tenskwatawa had done opposite him. Then Macaijah sat likewise over Silas' other shoulder. From this arrangement it appeared that Macaijah was considered to be part of Silas' entourage. He was not yet a full member of the Shawnee, Jonathan noted.

Tecumseh took a puff from the pipe and passed it to Silas. Silas took it, drew a polite puff, and handed it back. In the meantime the painted old man in the mask began to chant. Then he shook gourd rattles from his basket and began to dance in a circle around the seated hunters. Silas eyed him and made no attempt to hide his displeasure. Tecumseh took this in and spoke in suprisingly good English. "Old Man speak with spirits."

"There are many spirits, sir," Silas said, "but only one God."

"One God, many faces, many spirits."

"No. One God. There are two kinds of spirits, those that belong to God and those that belong to the Devil. The Devil is God's enemy." He held up his Bible before Tecumseh. "The Book of God, the Bible, says to try the spirits to see if they be of God."

"Try spirits? What is 'try spirits'?"

"A test," said Silas. "To try is to test."

Tecumseh nodded once. "I will try spirit," he said.

The shaman now produced a small basket from the larger one, which he opened and placed on the ground. A number of snakes began to crawl out of it and immediately the air was filled with nervous buzzing. They were rattlesnakes.

"Old Man know God spirits," said Tecumseh proudly. "He come from across the Great River." He nodded to the west. "When . . ." He held up ten fingers, then four.

"Fourteen," Silas supplied.

Tecumseh nodded. "Fourteen . . . Tecumseh . . . Old Man pray, that same day I kill five white men in battle." He held up his long rifle and showed five scalps hanging from the polished stock.

Now the Old Man began to reach out and grab the crawling rattlesnakes, placing them in parallel rows. They writhed and struck at him but he arranged them deftly, without harm.

Tecumseh reached across the ground between them and touched Silas' Bible. "The Long Robes teach me. I read your Book of God. It is good. There is much bloodshed."

Silas was growing agitated, beset by the buzzing of the rattlesnakes, the pagan dancer, and now from Tecumseh's knowledge of the Bible through the Catholic "Long Robes." The French Catholics had been among the Indians for many years, Silas knew, but to him their religion was an apostasy, having gone backward into paganism.

"There is bloodshed, yes," Silas admitted. "It is a book about the Great War. The battle between God and His enemy, the Devil."

The buzzing of the snakes grew suddenly vicious as the Old Man began to dance among them. Quickly, lightly, he leaped forward and back through the gauntlet of snakes. Their tails quivered nervously. Then suddenly the dancer stopped at the far end of the row. He threw off his mask defiantly. He looked at Silas and began to walk toward him. Slowly, each foot was placed down and—once! twice! again!—every snake took aim and buried its fangs in his passing ankles.

"Aiiiieee!" screamed the Old Man as he completed his walk. His eyes rolled back in his sweating brow and he pranced in mystic ecstasy.

Jonathan looked at Macaijah. He was sweating and trembling. The veins in his head bulged with fear. He turned and sent a look in Jonathan's direction that indicated he did not know this ceremony was in store. The Old Man snatched his snakes from the ground and placed them back into the basket. The final two he hoisted over his head and began to dance toward the group of hunters. When he reached where they sat he passed the snakes in and out, around their faces and heads, chanting and dancing all the while. They sat unmoving. Macaijah's two Powhatan companions were among the group thus tested. Beads of sweat formed on their foreheads as the Old Man worked his ritual.

Tecumseh nodded appreciatively. "He gives power to hate whiskey. It is good medicine for young men, but the old no longer believe. Whiskey Warrior can change them." He nodded to Silas, who made no visible response.

The Old Man had finished his dance with the hunters and now moved back to his large basket. He reached within and pulled out a small black gourd. This he placed in front of Silas with a flourish.

"Drink, 'death angel,' " Tecumseh said, pointing to the gourd.

Macaijah leaned forward. "Mushroom," he said so Silas could hear. "Death before you swallow."

Tecumseh now regarded Silas seriously and steadily.

The Old Man danced toward him, bringing the two snakes near his head. Tecumseh explained. "I tell Old Man about your Book that say take up serpents and drink deadly drink without harm. Whiskey Warrior has strong medicine?"

Smoothly and quickly, like the striking of a snake, Silas unsheathed his knife and struck the heads from the two rattlesnakes as the Old Man held them. Then with the toe of his boot he tipped the contents of the gourd onto the ground. The Old Man leaped back and threw his headless snakes to the ground. He stood waiting for Tecumseh's verdict.

After a silence Tecumseh spoke, "You do not try spirit?"

"The Long Robes taught you wrong, Great Tecumseh," Silas said calmly, wiping the snake blood from his blade on the heel of his boot. "That scripture is about accidental snakebites and poisonings. No man can put God to such a foolish test. That is the Devil's way. If you read all of this Book"—he held up the Bible for emphasis—"then you know the Devil, God's enemy, tempts God with such foolishness. Jesus Christ was tempted by the Devil to throw Himself from the high cliffs to prove He was of God. But the Lord replied, 'Thou shalt not tempt the Lord thy God.'" Silas' voice had risen to the level of a sermon delivery. "It is not God who must prove Himself, Tecumseh. It is his enemy, the Devil."

The sound of the river's constant flowing now became the only sound heard as everyone awaited Tecumseh's reply.

"You speak hard," Tecumseh replied. "You do not try spirit. You say 'try spirit,' but you do not."

"I turn men to God. That is all."

"You are Whiskey Warrior. You fight whiskey."

"I fight whiskey, or snakes or anything that keeps men from God."

A naked and sweating Indian runner approached the group from downriver. He arrived at the meadow and knelt to await a signal from the chiefs. Tenskwatawa motioned him forward and he knelt before Tecumseh in quiet conversation.

Jonathan leaned toward Silas' shoulder and said, "A fine sermon, Preacher."

Silas gave him a look of mild pleasure. "Exhorter," he corrected. "That was an exhortation."

A sudden flash of lightning struck the southern plateau just across the river to Silas' back. Thunder shook the earth beneath them. Tecumseh rose to his feet, signaling that the council was unexpectedly over. All of the others in the field followed his lead and rose to their feet as well.

Tecumseh looked across at Silas, who was now standing. "You must go," he said. "LeFevre attacks the cabin of the man called Stalker."

"Melody!" Jonathan's thoughts ran hot as he whirled away toward Merlin.

Silas stood still, eyes narrowed at Tecumseh, questioning where he would stand in this conflict. The chief crossed his arms coldly on his chest.

"Now we will test your God, Whiskey Warrior," he said.

25

The Come-down

It was midmorning. A column of smoke rose above the ridge in the distance as Jonathan left the Green River valley and urged Merlin across the barren plateau. He watched the plume spread into the sky and scanned the surrounding landmarks. He was dreadfully certain that it came from the Stalkers' meadow.

He bent low in the saddle, ascending the plain at racing speed, his mind washed in tides of regret and vengeance. The regrets made him want to run the other way, the vengeance drove him unmercifully forward. He whipped Merlin with a lash. The angry air howled around his ears and stripped tears from the corners of his eyes. After several miles Merlin settled into a strong, even canter no matter how hard he lashed him. Jonathan realized that he had pushed Merlin to his limits of endurance. He would do no good to push the killing pace any longer.

As he watched the roiling smoke ahead, his mind began to search for strategies. He would preserve Merlin's strength for the necessary action ahead. He would circle the meadow and approach from the trees. From cover he could assess LeFevre's position and strength before deciding how to engage the renegade band. He rehearsed these things in his mind and prepared himself for the awful possibilities ahead. He pulled his pistols and checked their charges several times as he rode. He felt to see that his pouch of prepared cartridges was ready for use.

By midday he reached the upper plateau. Just before entering the line of trees that enveloped the base of the ridge below the Stalkers' meadow he turned in the saddle as he rode and saw two riders pursuing him from the Bends of the Green. Farther behind them he thought he saw a lone runner but he was not certain. The line of approaching thunderheads now darkened half of the sky behind him, and lightning flashed on the Green River where that morning the meeting with Tecumseh had taken place.

He pulled Merlin to a halt. The great horse was heavily lathered and wheezing. Jonathan felt a wave of tiredness sweep him. He had not slept at all the night before and now with this hard ride he felt drained of fight. He waited for many long minutes until Macaijah and Silas caught up. When they drew abreast they halted their panting horses. There was no greeting; the three were grimly silent. Suddenly the sharp crackle of rifle fire sounded from the upper meadow.

Jonathan raised his fist and shook it. Silas and Macaijah nodded their understanding. The rifle fire meant that the defenders had not been subdued and this flushed the riders with new determination to get to the battlefield and add their guns to the fray. Jonathan urged Merlin up the ridge. Macaijah and Silas fell in behind as he circled the long meadow, passing through the cover of trees on its western perimeter. They heard more sporadic gunfire, then there was quiet. They continued through the trees, bending low in their saddles to look for signs of the fighting to their right. Suddenly through the trees Jonathan sighted the flicker of low-burning flames. He slowed and steered a path nearer to the meadow. It was the cabin and it was burned nearly to the ground. No more than a jumble of charcoal timbers remained.

Near the ruins, he counted the bodies of four Hessians. This was bad. They had been taken by surprise. Two of them were slumped over a rough plank breakfast table that had been set up in front of the cabin. Gunfire crackled again from above the cabin and this time shouting and taunting was heard.

"To the barn," Jonathan urged. The others nodded and followed through the trees. Suddenly Jonathan stiffened and stopped. Immediately ahead he saw men at the ruins of Marvin's still. He dismounted, tied Merlin to a tree limb, and sneaked forward on foot. Macaijah and Silas did the same. Shielding themselves behind the foliage of a whortleberry patch, they crawled forward for a clearer look.

Sitting cross-legged on the overturned boiler was Jacques LeFevre. He calmly whittled at hickory nuts while he conferred with a dozen men gathered about him. Silas grabbed Jonathan by the arm, very tightly. He pointed. Jonathan looked where he pointed. Melody, tied and gagged, lay on the ground.

"My Lord," Jonathan whispered in agony, half rising and drawing his pistol before Silas could jerk him back down.

"She's alive!" Silas rasped. "Wait."

They crawled back to the horses.

"First let's find out who else is alive," Silas said.

They mounted up, keeping a grove of trees between them and the renegades at the still. This time they rode a deeper circle through the trees until they approached the meadow again on the latitude of the barn. Every step away from Melody, captive at the still, only increased Jonathan's determination to press the attack directly at that point as soon as plans could be made.

They came in view of the barn and dismounted again to assess the situation. The barn had been chosen as the most defensible structure on the Stalker property. It was a crude replica of much finer versions built in more settled country. It had a sloping shake roof which covered a haymow and corncrib loft. The loft had an opening on either end. On the ground floor were stalls running the length of either side. The walls were of hand-froed timbers with little or no chinking between. Rifle barrels protruded from these openings all around the structure. The defenders were using it to good effect, or so it appeared. Jonathan and Ethan had discussed this plan of defense thoroughly with Klaus and his Hessians.

Inside the open-ended breezeway of the barn they saw the silhouette of Ethan's wagon. The team of English shires had not been hitched yet. The horses were apparently still in their stalls. Jonathan wondered at this, because defense plans had called for the wagon to be prepared to run for the fort in case the attackers set fire to the barn.

From their new vantage point they saw a group of a half dozen renegades who had taken the Stalkers' belongings from the cabin. Furniture, kitchenware, and clothes were piled in the center of the meadow beyond effective rifle range. Some of the men were trying on dresses and aprons, pantomiming lewd poses while other members of the gang destroyed the household table, chairs, and beds with axes and tomahawks. They hooted and jeered at the defenders in the barn as they continued their destructive play. Others of the band roamed the meadow keeping a watch on the barn. Their activity seemed random and loosely organized. LeFevre had evidently broken off a full attack.

Silas signaled Jonathan and Macaijah. "LeFevre wants those horses, those shires, in the barn. He hasn't seen their like out here and he knows they'd be worth more than gold. That's why he hasn't set fire to it. He's got the girl," Silas went on, "but there is something he wants more than the horses or the girl. He would like to get me."

Jonathan nodded seriously. He recalled LeFevre's madman discourse at the spring.

"I will distract the group at the still," Silas said, "so that the two of you can get the girl free."

"How?" Jonathan asked.

"I will kill me one of them on my run to the barn. They'll give chase."

Jonathan thought about it for a moment, then nodded decisively. "Then ride my horse."

Silas' eyes glowed with appreciation. He shook his head with gratitude. Merlin would give him the best chance for survival.

Macaijah and Silas tied their horses to a tree. Then Silas mounted Merlin. He sat for a moment, checking the priming of his long rifle. "I will try for LeFevre but it's easier to say than do."

Jonathan looked up at him. "Just get them to chase you, lean low and head for the barn." He patted Merlin's sweating neck. "Merlin will do the rest."

"Jonathan!" Macaijah said. "They won't fire on me. They know I am with Tecumseh. When the others go after Silas, they will leave someone to guard the girl. I will come to them. You come from behind."

Jonathan acknowledged. He turned and reached out a hand to Silas, who caught it and hoisted him up behind the saddle. Jonathan drew his pistols as they backtracked toward the still. Macaijah loped in a straight line toward the still, keeping trees between him and the men gathered there. The muscles of his giant torso glistened with sweat in the late-summer sun. When Silas and Jonathan reached a point near the whortle-berry patch, Jonathan dismounted, lowered himself to all fours, and began to crawl forward. Silas continued toward the lower flank of the still. They would approach from three different directions. The surprise at least would give them an advantage. Their only advantage, as far as Jonathan could tell.

Branches slapped his spectacles twice from his face as he crawled through the thicket. At the end of the whortleberry patch he was no more than a hundred feet from the still. He heard the men talking and laughing. He raised his head to peer over the last sheltering foliage. The men were on their feet, holding their horses, except for one who sat in the saddle. One of the men passed a jug of whiskey to the man on the horse. They certainly did not seem to fear an imminent attack. Jonathan looked to his left for a sign of Macaijah. He saw nothing.

Then the men grew strangely quiet. Jonathan heard what they heard. The sound of drumming hoofbeats. The man on the horse sputtered and choked on his whiskey, pointing frantically toward the trees behind Le-Fevre. LeFevre leaped up and whirled in time to see the telltale red mane of his old enemy flying in the wind and the barrel of his long rifle bearing down with deadly intent on his chest. But the killer renegade was clever like a snake. He began to dance, dodging left and right to spoil Silas' aim.

Silas had used a point of trees to bring himself within two hundred feet of the still before flattening Merlin into a full charge. Now he was barely fifty feet away, bearing straight at LeFevre. The other men scattered. Some led their horses, others tried to swing into the saddle, some were dragged with one foot caught in the stirrup as their horses plunged and careened into one another. At twenty-five yards Silas fired. He held the long rifle in one hand like a pistol. It was a good shot under the circumstances but merely creased LeFevre across the chest as he dodged to the right. The shock of the hot lead spun him all the way around.

As he came around, however, he made a rush for Silas. With amazing agility he leaped as Silas passed him, stabbing his short-bladed knife into the exhorter's shoulder and snagging him by the hair with the other hand. He held to him like a demon, bending Silas backward in the saddle, nearly unseating him as the renegade prepared to slash his throat. Merlin slowed, having been thrown off balance by the sudden shift in weight on his back. He nearly went down in a series of wild lunges.

It took every ounce of Silas' strength to recover. He held to the front of the saddle and pulled himself forward with the renegade leader holding to him still. He spurred Merlin again. At the same time he swung his wounded arm, heavy with the long rifle, forward, then back. The stock of the rifle slammed into LeFevre's chest and knocked him backward from the horse and rider. He hit the ground on his feet, running to keep from falling on his face.

"Silas!" LeFevre screamed, hurling his knife futilely at the fleeing preacher. "Kill him! Kill him!"

Confusion reigned. The men were shouting and milling, some firing after Silas without aiming, in an attempt to prove to their leader that they were trying to do something. One of the men brought LeFevre a horse. He mounted it on the run and led the others after Silas in the open meadow. Two of the men held their horses back, remaining at the still as the others sped away.

Jonathan was already running in a crouch, both pistols drawn. He would not wait for Macaijah. He would kill the men and release Melody himself. He raised from his crouch and sprinted forward, aiming his pistols. But Macaijah was suddenly there, striding boldly toward the two men from their left. They saw him and glanced quickly at one another for explanation. It was then that one of the men spied Jonathan running toward them from behind. He swung his long rifle around at point-blank range—

"No!" Jonathan screamed.

One pistol spouted fire. The barrel flashed from only ten feet away, showering the man with spent wadding and scorched powder. The second pistol barked. Numb with terror and rage, Jonathan saw the ball enter the man's temple. His head flew back and he flipped clear of the saddle, landing behind the horse on his back. His mount squealed and pounded away, the saddle empty. There was a bone-crushing impact as Macaijah dispatched the other rider with a blow of his rifle barrel to the head. The man hit the ground moaning and Macaijah was immediately on top of him.

Jonathan did not watch Macaijah finish his kill. However, it seemed insanely comforting to notice, in the heat of battle, that his former slave killed another black man. Jonathan was sure now that Macaijah held no allegiance to LeFevre and his gang. Jonathan knelt quickly where Melody lay. Drawing a knife from his belt, he cut free her gag and the thongs that bound her arms and legs. He glanced to the meadow, panting heavily. Several of the riders had dropped out of the chase with Silas. He saw the legs of their horses beneath the branches of the trees. They were returning to the still, which meant Silas must have made it to the barn. Jonathan jerked Melody to her feet. She sank down again, her arms and legs barely responding.

"I can't move them," she whimpered in his ear.

Jonathan picked her up in his arms and ran harder than he had ever run in his life. His lungs began to scream, his side bore sharp pain, but still he ran.

Macaijah was running beside him. "Let me have her," he said, lifting her from Jonathan's arms on the run.

"Take her to the spring," Jonathan said, panting gulps of air. "We'll hide her in the cave until this is over."

"No," she demanded. "Put me down. I'll be all right."

They found a secluded spot, sheltered by underbrush, and stopped. Jonathan saw no pursuers anywhere in sight. He knelt beside her and began to frantically rub her legs. She moved them as he worked over her, moving the joints to restore circulation where the tight thongs had bound her.

"Get me back to the barn," she seethed between clenched teeth, "and get me a gun in my hand."

Jonathan looked at her sadly, then nodded. He could not argue. Her family was there in the barn. If she had never wanted to live in this wilderness land they had chosen, she would still fight beside them. He loved her for that.

"Macaijah," he said, still rubbing her legs, "ride for Logan's Fort. Joburn is there. Bring every man with a horse and gun. Tell them this is the come-down from their stupid raid on LeFevre's cave. I need them now to make amends!"

Macaijah was quiet, rubbing Melody's upper arm. Jonathan checked the sun. It was about three o'clock. "If you go now, you can be back before daylight."

"I want the fight here," Macaijah said.

"There isn't time, Macaijah. I need someone who can get through for us. Now, go for your horse before they find him and it is all over."

Macaijah nodded, and slowly stood, eyeing the woods around them for signs of pursuers. Then he was gone. Jonathan turned back to Melody.

"They need our help at the barn," Melody said, starting to rise.

Jonathan nodded, and gently pushed her back down with his hand.

"Poppa was trying to trade the shires to get me back. LeFevre was going to trick him to get the horses, then keep me. But thank God, you came."

"How did they capture you?"

Her eyes grew dark. "They attacked the table during breakfast. I was serving the men when they came out of the trees. It was terrible. The men were dead before I even knew what was going on. I thought it was just a dream. I didn't even hear a shot, the men just fell over the table dead all of a sudden, and I was screamin', and then the men on horses grabbed me and jerked me away. I didn't even try to run"—she began to sob—"I was so scared!"

Jonathan reached to hold her but she pulled away.

"I'm not scared now," she said, choking with rage. "The Hessians, Jonathan, they were so brave! They were quick and they fought back for the children . . . and Momma and Poppa, too. They made a wall and began firing their guns while Momma and Poppa got behind . . . and Uncle Ethan and the other men, they all ran for the barn. I saw two or three of them fall. I don't know who made it, but nobody would have without those men."

Jonathan nodded and touched his hand to her mouth. He rose to look around. Seeing no one, he squatted again and took her hand, stroking it.

She looked deeply into his eyes. "Jonathan," she sobbed, "I saw you kill that man. I can kill, too, I know I can. I can kill those men." She wailed aloud. "They won't touch me again—"

He pulled her to him, crushing her words against his chest. He could not bear to hear them, but he knew these were the words of survival. She clung to him now and, feeling the warmth and softness of her body against his, he suddenly knew it was wrong to hold her now. It weakened her resolve to fight and kill. His, too. He pushed her back, holding her at arm's length. Then he reached forward and quickly wiped the tears from under her eyes. She did the same for him.

"I'm ready to go," she said.

He rose to a crouch. Looking carefully beyond the thicket but seeing no danger, he took her by the hand and helped her to her feet. She tried her legs again, took several careful steps. She walked stiffly and painfully but she nodded that she was ready to go. They ran through a stand of pine in a semicircular path that took them to the ridge. Once there, they worked their way along it toward the upper end of the meadow, stopping, listening, looking frequently in all directions as they went. Jonathan had already decided that they would have a better chance of breaking through to the barn if they approached from the back side, opposite the still. But it took another hour before they could work themselves up, across, then down the ridge, under sparse cover. They took such precautions—crawling, lying flat as renegade searchers rode past, sneaking from cover to cover—that Jonathan's spectacles were cracked on one side, Melody's skirt was torn and her knees were bleeding.

At long last they slipped forward and lay on their stomachs in a patch of mountain laurel which grew among pine trees at the edge of the meadow. From that point they would still have to run through the open meadow for about seventy yards to reach the safety of the barn. Jonathan pointed to a familiar figure at the breezeway of the barn.

"There's Klaus," he whispered. "He made it."

Klaus and another of his men guarded the rear entrance to the barn. They stood at the corners of the breezeway and kept their eyes constantly alert. Above them in the loft of the barn the guns of two more soldiers could be seen.

Jonathan checked all around the meadow. He saw no renegades in the open. Several, however, sat covertly on horseback in the edge of the trees watching the meadow. They were sure to see Jonathan and Melody as soon as they began to run for the barn.

"You will have to run as fast as you can across there," Jonathan whispered. "Once you start, nothing must stop you. Keep going for the barn. Klaus will give you covering fire as soon as he sees what you're doing."

She nodded, pursing her lips with a determined look.

"Ready?"

But a sound so sinister, so clear, like a steel whisper behind them, arrested them before they could move. It was the mechanized click of a rifle hammer being locked for firing. Jonathan placed his hand over Melody's mouth. Her eyes were wide with terror. She had heard it, too. Slowly he pulled one of his pistols from its holster and turned. It was then that he felt the sting of his own stupidity. He had not reloaded.

Through the branches of the laurel Jonathan saw a leather-clad black man with long matted hair and a full beard. It was the same man he had seen at the Indian camp with Macaijah. His buckskins were filthy, he wore an ivory-toothed earring, and two fresh scalps hung from a leather thong about his neck. They dripped blood down the front of his shirt. He was barely twenty yards away and approaching stealthily. His eyes were red-rimmed and swimming from the effects of whiskey, giving Jonathan reason to hope that all was not yet lost, even with his unloaded gun. Perhaps at least he could save Melody.

"I ain't hurt her, boy," the man rasped. "Just give her me. C'mon now, give her over an' den ya go free." He laughed nervously, swinging his rifle left and right as he eased ever closer, searching the brush.

"I will give her to you," Jonathan said soothingly.

The man tensed, swung his rifle toward the sound, and Jonathan was sure that he would momentarily fire. Trying to calm the desperate pounding of his heart, Jonathan rose slowly from the laurel, holding his hands above his head. The renegade stood only ten paces away. Close enough for a single lunge.

"Please don't shoot," Jonathan said. "She is over there." He pointed to a place several feet on the other side of the man.

The man looked where Jonathan pointed, then quickly back. He laughed an evil laugh; his eyes grew hard and his hand tightened on the stock of his gun.

"Run, Melody!" Jonathan screamed, and lunged forward.

Instantly something slammed into Jonathan's chest, tumbling him backward to the ground. He heard Melody's horrified screech. He lay for a moment, breathless, stunned, then Melody's agonized face appeared above him. So this was death.

"Jonathan!" she cried.

His head slowly cleared and he struggled up on his elbows in time to see the renegade before him step haltingly forward. His chest cavity had been torn through. He pitched face downward at his feet. Incredulously Jonathan felt his own chest. His hand came away with a lead ball. It was misshapen and bloody but he suddenly knew it was not his own blood. The ball had passed through the man before it hit him in the chest, with not enough force to penetrate.

Jonathan looked about. One hundred paces deep in the forest, half concealed behind the trunk of a pine, crouched one of Macaijah's Powhatan companions. On his face, the pair of spectacles. He was quietly reloading a smoking long rifle.

Jonathan scrambled to his feet. He pulled the rifle from under the dead renegade and raised his arm in a salute of gratitude. He recalled the Indian's words on the Green River when Jonathan had given him the spectacles: "My eyes will watch always for your enemies."

He turned back to Melody. "Run for it!" Taking her hand, they sprinted for the barn.

"Klaus, cover us!" he shouted as he ran. But Klaus was already alert to their escape. He knelt outside the doorway with his rifle held at ready. Behind them they suddenly heard the drumming of horse hooves. Ahead Silas now ran from the doorway with Uncle Ethan and two more soldiers. A volley roared from their weapons simultaneously. Jonathan glanced back and saw a riderless horse galloping back toward the trees. Then they were in the barn. The soldiers pounded Jonathan's back, while Maggie grabbed Melody into her arms, wailing, "Baby, my baby, baby!"

"It's all right, Momma. I'm here now."

"No," sobbed Maggie. "It's not all right. We're gonna die, baby."

"Momma, stop that." Melody pushed her back and shook her, but Maggie continued to cry bitterly.

"Nobody says it," she wailed. "I'll say it. We're gonna die!"

"Shut up, Maggie!" Marvin bellowed from where he lay wounded in the straw.

"No!" she screamed back. "I'll say it, an' I'll say it's your doin', Silas Will. Your doin'!"

Melody slapped her mother's face, wheeled, and wrenched the renegade's rifle from Jonathan's hand.

"She don't mean it," she panted. "She just gits this way." She hurried to where Marvin lay and bent over him. "Poppa, how bad you hurt, hmm?"

"Fire got me a little. I went back. Thought you were in the cabin, darlin'." Marvin's rifle lay nearby, loaded and ready.

Jonathan turned to Klaus. "How many of us left?"

Klaus could not hide his grief. "I lost seven. They catch us good. Two more wounded, there." He pointed to the loft.

Jonathan looked next at Uncle Ethan.

"Tibbet is gone," he said, holding his grief back with effort. "The others are in the loft."

Silas moved to the breezeway and stared across the meadow. Jonathan walked over to stand next to him.

"Maggie is right," Silas said softly.

"We can hold out here," Jonathan insisted. "I've sent Macaijah to Logan's Fort. He should be back with help by morning."

Thunder rumbled below the meadow. The air in the barn had grown hot and sticky.

"We have four Hessians, Abercrombie, Ledbetter, Ethan, you, me . . ." Jonathan began.

". . . Maggie and the children," Silas said, finishing the list. He took a deep breath as he continued to stare out of the barn.

"Everyone stands with you, Silas. Maggie is just—"

"I know Maggie. This time, she's right. This *is* my doing."

26

The Just
and the Unjust

Afternoon passed into evening. The skies darkened early with heavy thunderclouds. Intermittent flashes of lightning illuminated the worried faces of the defenders in the barn.

Silas had assured everyone that LeFevre's plan was not to attack—that would prove too costly for him. Rather, he would burn them out. Burning the barn was the short road to revenge. As the defenders ran for their lives from the flames, LeFevre's men would shoot them down in the open, one by one. Silas counted on the laziness of evil men to the very last.

The shires were hitched to the Stillwell wagon. In the back of it, Maggie and the children huddled together. As a last resort, they would try to drive it to safety. But now a macabre twist had been added to the battle plan. The men gathered out of earshot and pledged solemnly to one another that if they had clearly lost the struggle, whoever remained alive would use their last loads to kill the women and children mercifully, rather than let them fall into torturing hands.

Silas ordered four holes torn through the roof of the barn large enough to accommodate a man. The men positioned in the loft could then climb through them to the roof during attack to retrieve any burning firebrands thrown there, hopefully before they could ignite the rough cedar shakes. The two wounded Hessians were brought down from the loft to defend positions on the ground floor. Silas placed two of Klaus' soldiers in the loft, along with Ledbetter and Abercrombie. He instructed them to shoot from there and protect the roof from fire. If the fighting entered the main floor of the barn, they were to abandon the loft and help implement the evacuation in the wagon.

Once this plan was agreed upon, the small band of defenders spent the rest of the time at their positions, discussing and rehearsing the various instructions with Silas, Klaus, and Jonathan. Rifles were reloaded, checked, and double-checked. When all was ready, Jonathan, Silas, and Ethan stood at the front entrance to the barn. Melody, Klaus, Andrew, and Marvin waited at the rear. The others stationed themselves along the barn stalls.

Darkness grew full without the stars. Occasionally the round September moon would peek through a passing hole in the clouds. The glow of a bonfire in the vicinity of the still was sighted from the loft. Then the light began to move through the trees. Two lines of riders emerged from the timber, each rider carrying a flaming torch. The lead rider of each column also carried a white flag. When the last renegade cleared the trees, Jonathan and Silas looked at each other and said, "Thirty-three." They had each counted the odds and they were not favorable. Thirty-three attackers to ten able-bodied men and Melody, plus three wounded men. It might be possible to hold them off in the barn. But if they torched the barn, there was little hope.

The two lines of riders came to a stop boldly in front of the barn, spread out in a V formation. From the center stepped Jacques LeFevre flanked by two of his band, a black runaway and a heavily bearded frontiersman. They walked forward on foot toward the door of the barn. Jonathan and Silas watched from opposite sides of the breezeway.

"We can kill LeFevre," Jonathan offered. "It would weaken the others. Then we could hold them off."

"I'd say shoot him down," Silas returned, "but this barn is dry as a tinderbox. The fire wins this one, with or without LeFevre. Look how he walks. He knows it."

LeFevre moved with a calm swagger. He was unarmed except for his ever-present whittling knife, which this time he used to peel a crab apple. When they were within a dozen yards of the door, he stopped and held up his hand. Four riders walked their mounts forward to stand behind him. Their torches illuminated the circle of ground around the doorway.

The renegade leader stressed the second syllable of Silas' name because of his French accent. "Silas! Silas Will, come talk with me," he called in a sinister singsong as he concentrated on peeling the apple in his hand. "My old friend, where are you?"

"Here." Silas spoke from the inner darkness of the barn.

LeFevre took several steps forward. "Let me see you, Silas. I want to see how I get you today." He chuckled as if it was a joke between them. "I get you good, huh?"

"Not good enough. You are dead men out there. Our guns are on you," Silas warned.

The men on the horses shifted uneasily.

"True. And you too are dead." LeFevre placidly took a bite of the apple from the blade of his knife.

Silas stepped from the darkened doorway into the firelight. He held a rifle leveled at LeFevre's chest, cradled across the arm that had been bandaged from the knife wound. "I have other guns on you. Why should I let you walk away? If I shoot, everybody in the barn will shoot, too, and you and your men, Jacques, will stand before the judgment seat of God."

"My men will see that you join us there," he replied, lifting his head. "All of you."

Jonathan taunted him from the other side of the opening. "Your men would do that for you? Or will they turn tail on your dead body like coyotes?"

LeFevre took another bite of apple.

"Your pup barks," he said to Silas, "shut him up." He steadied himself for a moment, then exploded. "My men kill for me!" he screamed at Jonathan, gesturing wildly and panting from the exertion of his sudden rage. "I say kill, they kill. These men are not wanted by you! No. You made them slaves, you hang them, you put them in chains and cages. Jacques LeFevre set them free! They kill for me. I gave them a home." His eyes blazed at Jonathan in the shadows and slowly the anger subsided. "You have seen mercy from Jacques LeFevre, pup. Did you tell Silas? No? You dog's butt, I put my life before your guns to offer mercy." He spit angrily into the dirt, then slowly turned his focus back to Silas. He took a flask from his pocket and drank liberally, defiantly, from it in Silas' face.

"Whiskey Warrior, do not make more death here. I give the others mercy. I want you, Silas, my old friend."

Silas was quiet.

Jonathan could see his exhorter-father actually pondering the lesser of two terrible costs. He couldn't allow it. He stepped from the doorway and cocked his pistol directly at LeFevre's heart.

LeFevre's eyes grew wide, then angry. "You dog's butt," he hissed.

"No, Jonathan!" Silas commanded.

Jonathan's finger was tight around the trigger. With one added ounce of pressure he could wipe LeFevre from the face of the earth—and rid God's garden of one evil weed. In one stroke, Silas would be saved from the hands of this butcher and LeFevre would be justifiably dead. But over LeFevre's shoulder, the torches of his outcast army watched Jonathan like glowing eyes in the meadow. Would they kill for the man who gave them sanctuary? Jonathan's finger hesitated on the trigger. He trembled, seeing in his memory the roots of the pennyroyal Silas had torn from the ground and the countless dying shoots of grass around it. Was this the time to pluck evil by its root? Or the time to wait, and pray?

The night had gone quiet. Everyone held their breath watching him, wondering what he would do. From within the barn, Maggie's infant began to cry aloud.

"Shhhh," Maggie soothed.

Slowly, trembling all the way, Jonathan lowered his pistol to his side. Jacques LeFevre began cackling, low and derisively. He counted on the decency of good men to the last. A lightning bolt stabbed the ground in the distance. Thunder sent shock waves rustling through the dry straw in the barn. The horses in the barn squealed and kicked against their stalls. LeFevre's laugh rose high. Then he calmed himself suddenly, looking again at Silas.

"We can make a fight," Silas warned. "And a good one."

LeFevre nodded. "A good one. A very short one."

"I will not say yes or no just now. Give me time to decide. I need time."

LeFevre shrugged. "I am sorry. I am here too long already." He made a hand motion.

One of the horsemen handed his torch to the black renegade, who gave it, in turn, to LeFevre. LeFevre took his knife and began to sharpen the bottom of the pine stock. When he had done it, he came forward another step, raised his hand, and brought the torch down hard, stabbing the sharpened end into the ground so that it stood erect on its own.

"Here is your time," he said, and began backing cautiously into the
night. His men began to shrink back as well. "When the flame is gone, I
will come for you, Silas."

He turned, and his men scattered like coyotes in the dark, afraid that
someone in the barn would break ranks and fire on them after all. Jonathan looked toward Silas, who slowly turned toward him. They both
walked from the flickering torchlight back into the shelter of the barn.
Melody, Klaus, Ethan, all stepped back, leaving them alone. They moved
to one side.

"You can't do this," Jonathan began.

Silas raised a finger, interrupting him with a low-voiced warning. "Be
strong for Maggie and the children. They will need that from you. Especially from you."

Jonathan swallowed and looked away. "There must be another way."

"I see just one. If the rain in those clouds comes down and wets this
barn until it will not burn, that would turn things quite around, I'd say."

Thunder rumbled through the sky above the barn. Jonathan examined
the clouds. They swirled in several directions at once, not yet massed for a
cloudburst.

"God could do this," Silas said.

"Then, you will pray for rain?" Jonathan was filled with doubt.

"Yes."

"But will . . . God . . . ?"

"He is God. We should ask what we will."

Jonathan began to feel wretched. "The way you asked for the sick child
at Logan's Fort?"

"Let's pray," Silas said, bowing his head. "Father in Heaven . . . who
made this world, yet Your enemy, the Prince of Darkness, roams it, seeking whom he may devour. We ask that You move the rain against him
. . . We know You will prevail in this world, and in the world to come.
So, Great God, in this hour . . . we pray in the name of Your son, Jesus
Christ, who taught us to pray . . . and who also prayed alone at his
appointed time, saying, 'Let this cup pass . . . nevertheless, not my will
but Thine be done.' Even so, pray I tonight, not my will but Thine be
done. But I add to my prayer . . . for this one who is my own son. I was
no father to him. But you are father of all, Lord. If by the bitter wages of
sin, we have come to my appointed time . . . If my son, Jonathan, is to
go on alone, I pray for his soul . . . that it will never be lost to the Evil

One. Keep him, Father. If all of my prayers must go unanswered, let this be granted. Amen."

Jonathan stared out at the sky, his mind swirling like the clouds. He felt small beside the faith of his father. He felt no faith at all. After a long pause he began to speak absently, as if he did not know what he was quoting: "The earth which drinketh in the rain which cometh oft upon it, and bringeth forth herbs meet for them by whom it is dressed, receiveth blessing from God. But that which beareth thorns and briers is rejected . . ."

". . . and is nigh unto cursing; whose end is to be burned." Silas finished the passage. "From the book of Hebrews," he said. "Do you speak it for LeFevre?"

"No. It was the scripture underlined in Emily's Bible on the very page where I found your letter."

Silas shook his head regretfully, and stepped nearer to Jonathan. They both stood now before the torch, fluttering low, blown this way and that by the breeze.

"Emily, your mother . . ." Silas seemed stuck for a long moment, unable to go on. "I loved her." He swallowed and averted his eyes.

Jonathan felt something release. Something dark and ugly that had tied itself in a knot within him since the day he first read the letter his mother wrote to this red-haired man. At the sound of the words "I loved her," the knot released.

"No one . . . no one ever filled my mind like she did," Silas went on. He turned again to Jonathan. "You made me remember. I thought it was all dead and buried in the sea, but you came along, alive, and . . . I'm glad you came, Jonathan. Except that"—his voice filled with agony—"in G___ name, I don't see why it's come down to *this*. I make no sense of it, Jonathan." Sweat stood on his forehead. "But I am proud . . . very proud to learn that you're my son."

Jonathan embraced him, clutching him unashamedly and tightly to his chest. Tears squeezed from the corners of his eyes. Silas' arms locked around him in like manner. He felt himself grow in that embrace, taking on something of his father's spirit, something he would need if indeed Silas' prayer was not answered.

The last flame of the torch winked out. A delicate plume of white smoke curled upward now.

Jonathan released Silas and stepped slowly back. He was amazed to suddenly notice that he was the taller of the two. It seemed a strange thing to notice at a time like this.

"I have bowed at the door, Silas. The night on the Bends of the Green, on my watch, I prayed the prayer: 'God, be merciful to me, a sinner.' "

The transformation on Silas' face at hearing this from Jonathan was truly remarkable. It glowed with an inner strength, a light. He straightened himself, the light remained in his eye. Facing his imminent death, this light spoke to Jonathan of the amazing quality of his faith. This simple prayer which signaled entry into the invisible Kingdom was as real to Silas as the moss on the bark of a tree or the singing of the cicadas.

Silas changed. Now he spoke more purposefully. "About the way Emily died . . . calling for me, saying she was rejected . . ."

Jonathan listened.

"We all see God through a darkened glass, son. There are times when I think I see Him clear and perfect, but none of us truly do. Not in this world. Emily, she saw what she saw, and she thought she was rejected, but that doesn't make it true. Some things are sure. I know this much, she stood alone before God. She did not bear my sins there, nor anyone else's. And when she was dying, she didn't see God clearly then, either, son." He drew a long breath. "Nor do I just now. But I believe this, as I stand before you—in the end, God wipes away the tears. That's from the Book. Face to face . . . God is mercy. God is just."

Across the meadow the twin lines of torches danced again from the cover of trees. This time the riders rode at a full gallop and thundered around the barn, hooting to one another as they circled the defenders.

Silas turned from Jonathan. He spoke quickly. "Going with them will buy time. Keep everyone on watch here. If the rain comes, they will likely leave when they are through with me and that's that. If not, fight until you lose the barn to fire, then run. By then you may have your help from the fort. You know what to do."

"Silas—"

But Silas stepped from the entrance. "Jacques LeFevre!"

After a moment, from the distant dark meadow they heard an answer: "Silas!"

"Come get me!"

"No! You come here to me!" LeFevre answered.

"Call your men first! Then I will come!"

Silas waited. The men continued to circle the barn. Then one or two or them peeled off in the direction of LeFevre. As they drew to a halt, the light of their torches illuminated his familiar features in the center of the meadow just beyond effective rifle range.

Jonathan stepped out of the barn to Silas' side.

Silas began removing his powder horn and cartridge pouch. He handed them to Jonathan. He reached into his vest and removed the letter from Emily. He patted it into Jonathan's hand to draw his attention to it.

"Silas!" LeFevre called. The renegades had all gathered again in the center of the meadow.

"Remember," Silas said, "we all stand before God. Do not sin the sin of vengeance." Then he turned away.

A wave of grief twisted at Jonathan's face, pursed his lips, and nostrils. It wanted to shake his entire body, but he clamped his jaw tightly shut and held it in check.

Silas continued steadily away from the barn. He did not hurry or delay.

Jonathan could not watch him. He turned away. Behind him, he traced the head beam of the barn doorway over to the post and down. He saw Ethan on one side, tears glistening on his rounded face. At the other doorpost stood Klaus, leaning on his rifle stock, his back forlornly to the meadow, his forehead resting on the barrel. Maggie and the children huddled in the straw in the back of the wagon. He saw Melody, kneeling next to the wheel of the wagon clutching her long rifle. Something hot sprang to his eye at the sight of her, but he quickly brushed it away.

Silas had reached the halfway point between the barn and LeFevre. He had not slackened his pace.

Suddenly Jonathan called to the defenders, loud enough to carry across the meadow, "All right! Look to your stations. Check your charges and stand ready. I want killing shots if they attack us!"

Jonathan turned again as Silas was ten paces from the renegades. One of them stepped forward and threw a rope around his neck. It settled, then he jerked him violently forward.

Jonathan spun around and planted his back against the inside of the barn doorpost, folding his arms tightly across his chest.

Ethan continued to watch. "We will be back, Jonathan," he promised. "We will finish this!"

A clap of thunder rolled above the meadow.

"What are they doing?" Jonathan asked.

"Taking him back where they came from. To the still."

Shouts and laughter echoed across the meadow.

"Have they gone?"

Pause. "Now they are gone."

"Everyone keep sharp!" Jonathan shouted through the barn. "If it rains, we may well have this thing won! If not, then we will have to hold out till morning when the men from the fort arrive!"

Jonathan turned around and hunkered down at the doorpost where he could watch the glow of the torches against the tree branches above the still. He looked down, examining the items Silas had given him. The rifle, the horn, and the letter. There was something strange about the letter. Silas had written all over the envelope. Jonathan stood up and walked to where a lantern burned in the barn.

There were names printed on the letter: Joshua Martin, Stewart Cartwright, Benjamin Adams . . . and a host of others. At the top of the sheet were two underlined words, "Gideon's Army."

"Sin not the sin of vengeance," Jonathan mumbled thoughtfully to himself.

For what seemed to be another two hours, angry shouts, war whoops, and laughter continued in the distance.

"Some are half-breed Injuns," Marvin said, his commentary leaping from the darkness unexpectedly.

There were more shouts; then everything settled into an ominous quiet.

Well past midnight, a large wet drop landed in the dust in front of Jonathan. He looked up numbly to the sky. The cool splash of another drop landed on his shoulder. "The rain falls on the just and the unjust," he mumbled to himself in the darkness. "So says the Book."

The roar of approaching rain drew his eyes to the lower meadow. It had already disappeared behind a gray curtain of rain. Soon the barn was creaking and groaning as its timbers first absorbed, then shed the weight of a thousand streams of water. He moved back several feet from the open door to find shelter and to watch for morning.

27

The End of One Thing

The rain stopped suddenly after several hours of downpour and a pre-autumn chill settled over the darkened meadow. Fog rose from the wet, cooling ground and hung in feathery columns as high as the trees. Jonathan sat in the doorway of the barn, staring into the night. Water dripped from the roof into puddles in front of him. A pale glow appeared in the east and coolly enveloped the entire meadow as the rising sunlight was diffused through the fog. Jonathan heard the sound of approaching hoofbeats. He bent his head toward the ground, cocking his ear to the side. A rider appeared through the fog.

Andrew called from his perch in the loft. "Macaijah! Come along! We're here!"

Macaijah's gray was lame, running head down and limping badly. Horse and rider were covered with mud. Jonathan rose and walked from the barn to meet him. The others scrambled from the loft.

"Return to your stations!" snapped Jonathan. "We're not out of this yet."

They made their way back, looking curiously over their shoulders. Macaijah slid to the ground in front of Jonathan.

"Where are the others?" Jonathan inquired.

"Coming."

"We've survived so far here," Jonathan asserted. He looked curiously at Macaijah. His face was painted. A charcoal zigzag ran beneath his right eye to his chin. Two parallel slashes marked the opposite cheek.

"What is this?" Jonathan said.

Macaijah looked away. He was silent for too long.

"What is it? Tell me."

After more silence, Macaijah finally spoke. "Tenskwatawa, brother of Tecumseh, is a prophet. Before we left the Ohio he had a dream and in his dream he saw me with my feet on two sides of a river. On one side was the Whiskey Warrior. On the other, a killing ground." He pointed to his cheek. "He saw my face painted. Tenskwatawa drew the signs for me here." He turned up his breechcloth and showed Jonathan a tattoo of the designs imprinted in the doeskin.

Macaijah continued speaking with his eyes cast downward. "Tenskwatawa said that in his dream I bent and washed my face in the river once, and the river turned to blood. The Whiskey Warrior waded the river to the other side. Then I washed my face again, and the river turned to clear water. I asked him what this meant. He said I would know the answer, and when I knew, I should say to the next person I meet, these words." Macaijah now raised his eyes to look straight at Jonathan. "The end of one thing is the beginning of another."

The sound of running horses grew in the distance.

"I have seen the answer to the dream. Go to the still and see for yourself."

"LeFevre is gone?"

"Their tracks lead to the four winds."

The army of horsemen from the fort pounded through the fog into view of the barn.

"See them on in," Jonathan said to Macaijah. "Everyone down from the loft," he ordered. "LeFevre has gone."

There were sober congratulations and silent embraces among the occupants of the barn. Little more. Jonathan greeted the men from Logan's Fort. The first to arrive was Logan.

"How do you fare?" Logan asked, dismounting hurriedly.

Fully fifty riders reined in about him, the hooves of the horses filling the air with particles of mud and flecks of lathered sweat as they pounded to a stop. Jonathan recognized several of the men from the earlier raid.

"Is there a doctor among you?" he asked.

"Aye, Mr. Dowd here."

"Some inside are wounded," he said, then turned back to Logan. "Logan, send half of your men to circle the meadow. Over the hill is a spring in a cave. Check it with care. I will return soon, and we can decide how to proceed from here."

Macaijah walked with him a short distance toward the still, then he stopped. Jonathan went on alone through the morning fog. He moved with a measured step. In his mind he saw Silas walking to meet LeFevre the night before. He tried to match those steps, not walking too fast or too slow. He passed the stiffened body of a Hessian soldier. Death-fixed eyes stared at the sky, his scalp was torn away. He had faced his enemy's fire. Children would laugh and play in this meadow, Jonathan mused as he passed on, lovers would stroll and collect its wildflowers, farmers would till it—all ignorant of the debt they owed this man from Hesse-Cassel.

He came to the smoldering remains of the cabin. Small pockets of coals survived the downpour, hidden beneath the fallen beams. A steamy smoke rose to mingle with the fog. The log bench where he and Melody had sat and talked so many evenings survived. Its backside only scorched. He passed the bodies of the other Hessians lying across the breakfast table. Their clothes had been stripped from them. Then he crossed the cleared field where Marvin had run in a drunken stupor from Silas the day Jonathan first came to the farm. He looked again where the cabin had stood, recalling his first sight of Melody in the doorway.

He moved through the trees to the still. At the ruined site, an oak had been stripped of limbs. At the base of the tree, burnt logs radiated out from the trunk in all directions. There had been a bonfire here. The ground was worn at the outer edge of the circle. A charred body slumped at the base of the tree. Jonathan understood the significance of what he saw. He understood that in this arrangement each of LeFevre's men participated in the slow killing of Silas by pushing a burning log closer to the oak tree in the center. Silas had been made to suffer, this much he understood.

There were many things he did not understand, however. He sat down on the upended boiler, his thoughts fragmented with questions. What good did it do to ride the long road of service to God if it brought no better passage to Heaven than this? What kind of God would allow Silas to die, and let Jacques LeFevre live? In his mind he heard Silas' voice answer, "God is just," and he wondered if he now saw God face to face.

"I will never get over you, Silas," he said huskily to the burned body at the pole.

Then he simply sat, for a long time, trying not to think at all.

As the sun began to dissipate the fog, those in the barn and the riders from the fort moved out and assembled in quiet groups near the cabin. Some walked on toward the still. Those who did saw someone else there with Jonathan. And seeing this, they turned back.

Jonathan sensed her moving behind him. He heard her soft footsteps on the wet grass. Melody's slender shadow had grown on the ground in front of him and he felt the warmth of her body through the shirt on his back. She reached forward and touched his cheek, and when she did, he began to shake. His restraint gave way and he cried. She took his hand and held it to her cheek as his cries grew.

In time his weeping subsided and he attempted to talk, words tumbling out quickly, mixed with still more tears. He spoke of things he had wanted to say and had never said—to Silas, to his mother, to God. The words were tangled and confused—except to his heart and, he felt, also to hers. In that moment, more than ever again in his life, he felt that he was completely and profoundly heard.

Epilogue

The Barratt caravan departed Kentucky on the first day of October 1784 from Logan's Fort. The first dust of frost lay on the ground, but the skies were blue and clear.

There were goodbyes but only with plans for a return. Marvin Stalker hobbled to the stockade gate on wooden crutches, his burns not yet healed. Maggie, her children, Melody, the Logans, Joburn, all came to see the travelers off. The plan had been agreed upon; the Stalkers would remain at Logan's Inn until spring planting, when Jonathan would return with the Barratt Enterprises' Green River Expedition. He would oversee the construction of a blockhouse at their ruined farm.

As they prepared to mount up Jonathan took Melody Stalker to one side. A tear trickled onto her cheek, but she continued to smile bravely, ignoring it. He had never wanted to stay with anyone as much as her. He kissed and held her until the group of onlookers began nervously clearing their throats and coughing.

"I'll be back for you."

"Get on your horse and go," she said, pushing him toward Merlin with a smile.

And so he went . . .

Every day, for a month of days, following their return to Bath, Jonathan, Ethan, Andrew, and Abercrombie could be found at evening time in the bathhouse. Chayta would sprinkle their steaming water with scented herbs, and then sit back and coax from them stories of their Kentucky adventure. Especially those about her son, Macaijah.

Macaijah had ridden with the Barratt caravan as far as the Cumberland crossing before returning to the Shawnee camp. Jonathan told him, just before they parted company, that upon his return to Bath he would immediately give certificates of freedom to Chayta and Andrew as a gesture of friendship to his Indian runaway. That had been done.

During the evening baths, Ethan became the most vivid storyteller of the group. Jonathan gloried in lighting a pipe, sitting back, and listening again to Ethan's tales of the Wilderness Road. He could almost see the scenes as Ethan described them, reflected on the fogged lenses of his spectacles. Occasionally, he found it necessary to correct a point of a story for the sake of modesty. But for the most part, honesty was set aside for the sake of a good story.

One particular evening Jonathan asked, "Ethan, do you think you would like to purchase this inn?"

"Not for any obvious purpose. Why do you ask?"

"I would like to own it. Part of me will always belong here in Bath."

In a matter of weeks Ethan and Abercrombie negotiated the purchase of the Bath House Inn from Orville Hudson. When they announced that it was done, Jonathan said, "I want you to put out the word that any riding preacher who passes through Bath is to be received at the Inn and housed free of charge, and a given time for them to preach shall be posted at the playhouse stage."

"Consider it done."

In November the first riding preacher passed through Bath. He had no intention of stopping, he said, but as he was quite weary, he consented to spend a night at the Inn. His name was Reverend Freeborn Garrettson and he was the first to preach from the playhouse stage.

Before he retired for the evening, he confided to Jonathan that he was riding to summon all of the riding preachers from their circuits to their first annual conference in Baltimore. Francis Asbury, their leader, had made an urgent request for all to attend.

In the bitter cold of December 20, 1784, a black landau drawn by a matched team of dappled grays set out on the Martinsburg road from Bath. It traveled four days before arriving in Baltimore.

The landau drove slowly through the city. Baltimore was shaking with a soul-saving thunder. On nearly every street corner, a long-coated lay preacher exhorted the pedestrians and mounted travelers who endured the sleet of Christmas Eve. Unless they stopped their ears against the words, they were challenged to brave the exposure of their cold hearts to the God of John Wesley, John the Baptist, Francis Asbury, and Silas Will.

"Repent! Bow at the door of Salvation!" preachers and exhorters cried from street to street as they entered the city from every point of the compass.

The landau stopped on Lovely Lane in front of a humble two-story meeting house. Jonathan Barratt, dressed against the cold in a beaver cape and top hat, stepped from the carriage. Inside the meeting house was a disparate assortment of sixty itinerant Wesleyan preachers. Jonathan had received special permission to accompany them upstairs to their first conference in America. He was given the chair reserved for the member of their fellowship who rode the wild Kentucky circuit.

Francis Asbury presided. Asbury had come to America from England in 1771 at the bidding of John Wesley. Through the years of the war with England, many of the Wesleyan ministers in the colonies remained loyal to the Crown and returned home. But not Asbury. He took to the back roads of the colonies, riding six thousand miles a year, meeting the poor and the dispossessed of the land where they lived. He converted and commissioned exhorters from among them to carry the gospel of the primitive church. Now John Wesley sent Thomas Coke to America to consecrate Asbury as the Superintendent of the Methodist revival in America by the laying on of hands.

On Christmas Eve, in the upper room of the Lovely Lane Meeting House in Baltimore, the following letter was read:

> To all to whom these Presents shall come,
>   John Wesley, late Fellow of Lincoln College in Oxford, Presbyter of the Church of England, sendeth greeting.
>   Whereas many of the People in the Southern Provinces of North America who desire to continue under my care, and still adhere to the Doctrine and Discipline of the Church of England, are greatly distressed for want of Ministers to administer the Sacraments of Baptism and the Lord's Supper according to the usage of the said Church: And whereas there does not appear to be any other way of supplying them with ministers,
>   Know all men, that I, John Wesley, think myself to be providentially called at this time to set apart some persons for the

work of the Ministry in America. And therefore under the Protection of Almighty God, and with a single eye to His Glory, I have this day set apart as a Superintendent, by the imposition of my hands and prayer (being assisted by other ordained Ministers), Thomas Coke, Doctor of Civil Law, a Presbyter of the Church of England, and a man whom I judge to be well qualified for that great work. And I do hereby recommend him to all whom it may concern as a fit person to preside over the Flock of Christ, in testimony whereof I have hereunto set my hand and seal this second day of September in the Year of our Lord One Thousand Seven hundred and Eighty-four. John Wesley.

Dr. Coke, as Superintendent ordained by John Wesley, in turn proposed the ordination of Francis Asbury as Superintendent of the American church. But Asbury refused to accept the ordination without the vote of his fellow American circuit riders.

So they voted. When the roll call sounded the name of Silas Will, Jonathan rose from his seat.

"I am Jonathan Will," he said, "son of Silas Will, an exhorter recently killed by renegades in Kentucky. He was a man of God who died faithful to his calling."

Asbury stood transfixed at the center of the room. Thousands of miles of road had been logged between them since their last meeting, but he instantly recognized Jonathan of the wealthy and sinful resort of Bath. He was Jonathan *Will?* Son of Silas Will? This had been his secret? Asbury marked the eloquent young man for serious conversation following the meeting.

"There is no doubt," Jonathan went on, returning Asbury's gaze, "that Silas Will would cast his vote today, were he here, in favor of the Superintendency of Mr. Asbury, the man who led him to God on a road in Carolina many years ago."

The vote proceeded to be a unanimous one.

Not only did the conference of circuit riders ordain its leaders according to John Wesley's wishes; it exceeded his wishes. Against Wesley's strong protest, the circuit riders called their General Superintendents "bishops," in disregard for ecclesiastical precedent of the Church of England. Anything "English" was no longer sacred in free America.

Thus, before America had a Constitution, and five years before another unanimous vote would give the new nation its first President, the Christmas conference at the Lovely Lane Meeting House in Baltimore gave birth to the first Methodist Episcopal Church known to exist in the world.

As the conference continued, the central theme of discussion was the question: "What may be reasonably expected to have been God's design in raising up the Methodist preachers?" The answer was written and agreed to by all present: "To reform the continent and spread scriptural holiness over these lands."

The conference adopted instructions to its riders: "Never be unemployed. Never be triflingly employed. Neither spend more time in any place than is strictly necessary." And it set the annual salary of all preachers, including Asbury, at "$64 and no more."

Yes, Jonathan mused, as he watched the proceedings, this group did truly embody the religion of that Kentucky ex-renegade, Silas Will.

May 22, 1785. The return to Kentucky had been difficult. The weather had warmed and cooled, then warmed again. The rivers swelled beyond their banks with the sudden snowmelt from the mountains.

The crossing of the Cumberland River took days and was not without its casualties. Several head of livestock had drowned and the party stopped to butcher what meat was salvageable before they continued onward. Other travelers had gathered on the banks of the Cumberland in order to cross Kentucky under the protection of the Barratt Expedition and its mounted Hessian guard. As they waited, they prevailed upon the young Mr. Will, who accompanied the expedition dressed in his black long coat, to exhort from scripture and pray with them.

The morning of their departure from the Cumberland, Jonathan Will awoke before daylight. With his Bible, he stole to the edge of the camp and knelt under a tree.

As the sun rose, a young father and his son approached the kneeling figure. Jonathan had finished his prayer long before. It had sounded inadequate in the shadow of other prayers he had heard. Now he merely watched the sunrise over the Kentucky plain and let his thoughts drift away to Logan's Fort, and to Melody Stalker, with hair like sunrise.

"Preacher Will?"

Jonathan started and rose to his feet. The man had stolen close to him unnoticed on the wet grass.

"Mr. Clark," Jonathan replied, recognizing him from an earlier meeting. "Mr. Clark, I ask that you remember, I am merely an exhorter. But how may I help you?"

He saw pain written on the man's face, and trouble in the boy's eyes. He already knew the grief they suffered. The man had buried his wife the evening before at the Cumberland River crossing, a victim of a consumptive ailment, aggravated by the inclement weather.

"It be my boy, Preacher. His momma, she . . . well, she was religious and all, an' he asks troublesome questions. Wal, I ain't never took too much to her religion, so I just brung him on here to you. Now ask, boy."

The boy backed away shyly. Unable to speak.

"Go on ahead," urged Mr. Clark.

Jonathan knelt in front of the boy. "Well, I'll wager you have a lot of questions, for sure," Jonathan said.

The boy did not look up.

"And how do I know about such things? Well, I do, because my mother died, too. When I was just about your age."

The boy looked up at him.

"What's your name?" Jonathan asked.

"Todd Clark."

"Well, Todd, my momma died, too," Jonathan went on, "and I'll wager I know what those questions are that you want to ask. I probably asked them myself. Oh, I still do, I suppose. Sometimes. But how about if you ask me the one that you want to ask the most. Hmm? What is that question, Todd?"

The boy's mouth puckered; he looked off across the meadow with angry eyes. "Why did God take her?"

"That's the one, all right," Jonathan said gently. "When my mother died, I asked that very same question."

The boy looked at him suspiciously.

"The answer is . . . God did *not* do it."

There was a long, stony silence.

"You see, God's enemy took your momma away from you. God made this world full of life and good things, but His enemy got into it and made death. And now everyone, and everything that lives, has to die sometime."

The boy took no comfort in this answer.

Jonathan sighed. "But there is a harder question than that one, Todd."

Todd looked at him again, still unsatisfied.

"The really hard question is: Why did your momma have to die now? Why did she have to die before she lived all of her life out with you? That's the hard one, isn't it?"

Todd thought a minute, then whispered reluctantly, his lip quivering, "Yeah."

"I'll wager your poppa would like to hear an answer to this same question. Do you think he would? I would like your father to sit down here on the grass with us for a moment. Mr. Clark, will you? Just sit here, anywhere."

Slowly, reluctantly, Mr. Clark eased himself down on one knee while Todd settled cross-legged before Jonathan.

Jonathan set his Bible aside and leaned forward between them, spreading his hands across the grass. For a while he just brushed the grasses, bending them back and forth.

"Do you see the grass that grows here?" he asked. "Do you see how many different blades there are? Well, down there under the soil, they all have roots that make them live and grow. You can't see them just now, but they are there, growing all tangled together. You know about roots, don't you?"

The boy nodded.

Jonathan's hands suddenly stopped and his fingers wrapped around the minty stalk of a pennyroyal. It grew tall above the tender blades of grass. He held it for a moment and looked up at Mr. Clark.

"I want you to watch very closely," he said. "What I show you now, you should never forget . . ."

Journal Entry, 1786

"Rode to the Springs called Bath; now under great improvement, I preached in the
Playhouse and lodged under the same roof
with the actors . . . I have spent twenty-
three days at this place of wickedness . . .
I am compelled to linger here another
week."

Francis Asbury.

Historical Background

In 1784 only obsessed men traveled far on the dangerous backroads of America. Among the men to travel those colonial byways, none outdistanced Francis Asbury, who logged a grueling six thousand miles per year on horseback. He rode shoulder to shoulder with the explorers, the exploiters, the soldiers, the highwaymen, the renegades, the drifters, the criers—but long after the others had settled, Asbury continued on, driven until the day of his death by an urgent sense of mission.

Asbury's commission came from the hand of England's great revivalist, John Wesley, but his sense of mission came from within himself. Arriving in America in 1771, he found the large colonial churches to be self-serving and ineffective in reaching the people who were most in need. In the manner of his English mentor, he forsook the comforts of the city pulpits and rode by horseback to reach the people who were unchurched. Thus he and a handful of recruited circuit-riding lay preachers introduced the scattered, illiterate, and largely Calvinist population of America to the Arminian gospel of Methodism.

The collision between the ideas of Calvinism and Arminianism was nowhere more evident than among common settlers of the frontier who incorrectly perceived the "elect" of Calvinism to be the blessed rich. It was nearly impossible for the struggling American settlers to feel "elected of God" when they daily suffered unrelenting tedium, backbreaking labor, and the harsh opposition of the wilderness. Under the prevailing influence of Calvinism, the rich seemed "elected" for both the pleasures of this life and for Heaven in the afterlife, while the poor seemed to be nothing more than God's chosen "vessels of wrath." In the eyes of these sufferers, Calvinism placed the approval of God upon the very unfairness of life. Who would not rebel against such a God? Among the poor, Calvinism often produced despair, which drove them away from religion, many to find solace in drunkenness. "Drunk for a penny, dead drunk for two" was the standard advertisement of an alehouse, where it was taken for granted that there would always be plenty of straw for sleeping off the effects of overindulgence. Drunkenness became the religion of the poor, and the hellish effect of it upon the fabric of civilization in young America is well documented.

Into this American wilderness came Asbury and his recruited army of lay preachers. With little regard for the distinction between cause and effect for the evils they scourged, especially liquor, they nevertheless applied a hopeful new remedy: "No man is predestined, every man is 'elected' by God. You can be born of God *of your own will*—choose today whether you will serve God or the Devil." As they dispensed their Arminian "good news," these zealous lay preachers also divided the people of the land into opposite spiritual kingdoms, with no middle ground. "Middle ground is the Devil's ground," they cried. "Choose the Savior or you're damned already." Asbury and his recruits uncompromisingly vowed not to leave America as they found it but to move it, by any means, toward the Kingdom of God.

The strength of the circuit rider's calling was greater than the desire for home and hearth. This was so, or Asbury considered the call invalid. "I fear the Devil and women will get all my preachers," he lamented. (Or perhaps he prophesied.) He set a nearly impossible example for his recruited riders to follow, covering from four to six thousand miles every year, collecting only a sixty-four-dollar annual salary. Many of the lay preachers could not endure the rigorous pace set by the one they respectfully dubbed "the Prophet of the Long Road." Marriage took some of them from service. Others simply endured too much and went insane. Many fell from the saddle with cruelly broken health. Others lost faith. Rewards were few for those who remained true in the saddle. One fourth of them were dead within five years, nearly half of them died before they were thirty years old, and two thirds of their number were dead before they had ridden twelve years. They died of persecution, disease, and sheer exhaustion. Their story is one of immeasurable sacrifice for the sake of spiritual warfare. Some would say Asbury's "spiritual-war mentality" was tragically unnecessary, but today nine and one half million American

Methodists build the superstructure of their faith upon the foundation laid by those itinerant laymen.

Asbury outlived and outrode all of his recruits, never failing to decry a nation he found to be full of dead, putrefying religion. Until his death on the road at the age of seventy-one, he stopped only to strengthen every sign of spiritual life and to lay a withering curse at the base of every religious tree that bore no fruit. He would no doubt find great fault, if he were alive today, with the state of the church he founded. His perspective is well documented. Every day he recorded the rich details of his unique view of America in a voluminous *Journal* of his travels. That *Journal* is now an American treasure, included in the National Archives in Washington, D.C., where also a horseback statue stands, bearing the inscription, "Francis Asbury, the Prophet of the Long Road."

Asbury and his earnest recruits placed their hands on the root of the nation with its far-flung rural class and forcefully demanded that it live above savagery in the name of God. Their religious zeal and often flamboyant methods produced a significant part of the interwoven value system of modern America. Looking back two hundred years to the 1784 Christmas Conference in Baltimore, the first annual conference of Asbury's circuit riders, and the meeting that founded the Methodist Episcopal Church in America, it can be said that Asbury and his circuit riders fulfilled their vow: they did *not* leave this land as they found it.

Riders of the Long Road is fiction set against the backdrop of post-Revolutionary history. It is a tale of three desperate horsemen in the time of Francis Asbury. Asbury encounters these three riders in his proper historical context. This novel owes much of its inspiration, perception, and flavor to the thousands of stories, chronicles, and descriptions recorded so purposefully in Asbury's *Journal.*

Historical figures appear or receive mention throughout the narrative: George Washington, Lord Fairfax, John Wesley, Thomas Coke, Tecumseh, Tenskwatawa, Daniel Boone, and Francis Asbury. The exchanges that take place in *Riders of the Long Road* between the historical characters and the fictional ones are invention but invention in keeping with what is known from history.

The same is true for the roads and settlements in Maryland, Virginia (including what is now West Virginia), North Carolina, and Kentucky. Where information was not available, invention was rooted in knowledge that was available about similar historical sites, so that the descriptions illuminate many of the realities of American life in 1784.

The author wishes to acknowledge his debt to the following sources: *The Journal and Letters of Francis Asbury*, Vol. I, II, and III (Epworth Press, London; and Abingdon Press, Nashville); *The Story of Methodism* and *An Album of Methodist History* (Abingdon-Cokesbury Press, New York and Nashville); *The Romance of American Methodism* (Piedmont Press, Greensboro, N.C.); and *Atlas of American History* (Charles Scribner's Sons, New York).

Personal gratitude is expressed to editor and friend, Dr. Miriam Herin, and to Kenneth A. Horn, James Bellamy, Russell Burson, Parker Duncan, Richard Howle, Larry Lambeth, and Willie Middlebrooks of the Council on Ministries of the Western North Carolina Conference of the United Methodist Church. A special thanks to the United Methodist Bicentennial Committee.

About the Author

STEPHEN BRANSFORD is a novelist, screenwriter and director. The son of a lumberjack preacher, he grew up in the remote communities of Oregon. A lifetime fascination with the unsung history of the circuit-riding preachers inspired him to write this story. He lives in Las Colinas, Texas.

CHRISTIAN HERALD ASSOCIATION AND ITS MINISTRIES

CHRISTIAN HERALD ASSOCIATION, founded in 1878, publishes The Christian Herald Magazine, one of the leading interdenominational religious monthlies in America. Through its wide circulation, it brings inspiring articles and the latest news of religious developments to many families. From the magazine's pages came the initiative for CHRISTIAN HERALD CHILDREN and THE BOWERY MISSION, two individually supported not-for-profit corporations.

CHRISTIAN HERALD CHILDREN, established in 1894, is the name for a unique and dynamic ministry to disadvantaged children, offering hope and opportunities which would not otherwise be available for reasons of poverty and neglect. The goal is to develop each child's potential and to demonstrate Christian compassion and understanding to children in need.

Mont Lawn is a permanent camp located in Bushkill, Pennsylvania. It is the focal point of a ministry which provides a healthful "vacation with a purpose" to children who without it would be confined to the streets of the city. Up to 1000 children between the age of 7 and 11 come to Mont Lawn each year.

Christian Herald Children maintains year-round contact with children by means of a *City Youth Ministry.* Central to its philosophy is the belief that only through sustained relationships and demonstrated concern can individual lives be truly enriched. Special emphasis is on individual guidance, spiritual and family counseling and tutoring. This follow-up ministry to inner-city children culminates for many in financial assistance toward higher education and career counseling.

THE BOWERY MISSION, located at 227 Bowery, New York City, has since 1879 been reaching out to the lost men on the Bowery, offering them what could be their last chance to rebuild their lives. Every man is fed, clothed and ministered to. Countless numbers have entered the 90-day residential rehabilitation program at the Bowery Mission. A concentrated ministry of counseling, medical care, nutrition therapy, Bible study and Gospel services awakens a man to spiritual renewal within himself.

These ministries are supported solely by the voluntary contributions of individuals and by legacies and bequests. Contributions are tax deductible. Checks should be made out either to CHRISTIAN HERALD CHILDREN or to THE BOWERY MISSION.

**Administrative Office: 40 Overlook Drive, Chappaqua, New York 10514
Telephone: (914) 769-9000**

From *Het Groote Tafereel der Dwaasheid*, a 1720 folio satirizing the Mississippi Bubble and other "get rich quick" schemes